C0-AMS-395

BY
THE KING'S
COMMAND

A NOVEL BY
SHIRLEY SEIFERT

J. B. LIPPINCOTT COMPANY
Philadelphia and New York

COPYRIGHT © 1962 BY SHIRLEY SEIFERT

SECOND IMPRESSION

PRINTED IN THE UNITED STATES OF AMERICA
LIBRARY OF CONGRESS CATALOG CARD NUMBER 62—18849

WITHDRAWN

BY THE KING'S COMMAND

Contents

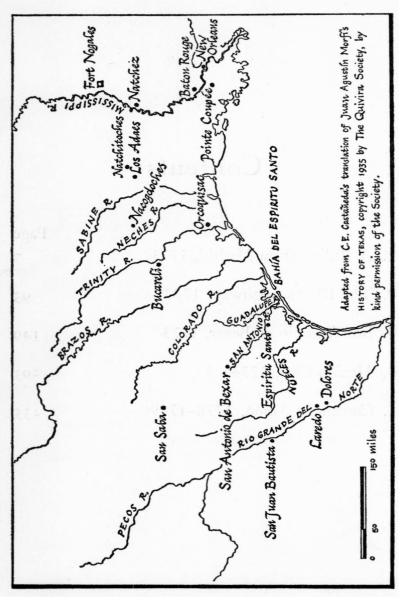

Texts in the time of *By the King's Command*.

Adapted from C.E. Castañeda's translation of Juan Agustín Morfi's HISTORY OF TEXAS, copyright 1935 by The Quivira Society, by kind permission of the Society.

1

A Ruling from Madrid, 1773

"In June, 1773, the inhabitants of Los Adaes, Spanish capital near the Sabine, were suddenly given five days in which to abandon their homes, the order having been issued by the governor of Texas in obedience to a command of the King of Spain."

from *Texas, a Guide to the Lone Star State*

CHAPTER 1

"Extinguish . . ."

The word still rattled in Antonio's head like a seed in a dry gourd. Surely he had been mistaken. That was not it. His ears had deceived him. He knew he was not mistaken. He could still hear—he would hear as long as he lived—the words as they fell: "It seems best to extinguish the town known as Los Adaes."

And he had sat there, dumb as the dead, listening. What else? Only a fool or a madman would openly oppose his will to that of imperial Spain. Even though his heart cried out in protest: You can't do this. A town is people. Good people, bad people, the high, the low, the rich, the poor, friends, enemies, strangers— but people.

The month was June, the year 1773. The morning was fair as only a June morning could be; and nowhere was June fairer than in these Sabine hills of east Texas. A light wind sang in the tops of the pine trees. The sun on the needles drew out a fragrance that was balm to everything breathing. A little river, tumbling down a hill and across the *Camino Real*, gurgled and chattered and shone. The only cloud in the picture was the scowl on the dark features of Antonio Gil Ibarbo.

A darkly handsome man, this Antonio Ibarbo. A *ranchero* by the looks of him, and a rich one. Silver braid down the outside seam of his black corduroy trousers, more on the short *charro* jacket and the flat, broad-brimmed hat. Silver spurs, which he never used, on his boots. A light jingle of silver on the trappings of his horse—a coal-black mare with the small head and pointed ears and delicate strength of the purest Spanish–Arabian stock. A rich man, used to soft living, but also knowing the other kind. A tough man to deal with if he was your enemy. That was in the hard line of his jaw, the set of his shoulders, the strength of his muscular legs, the firm hand on Fatima's rein. Gentle his hold might be on what he treasured; it was never slack.

To say that, because he frowned, he was unaware of the fairness of the day would have been a mistake. He was alive to the whole scene, to himself as part of it. That was why he frowned. This land of green hills and forests and silver rivers and lakes, unlike any other part of Texas—and he had seen most of the province—was native to him. He had been privileged to be born there. Suppose, then, someone had said to him, "Within days you must leave—forever?" How would he feel? What would he think? What would he do?

Abruptly his face cleared. Temporarily he was laughing. The mare, on reaching the ford of the little river, had stopped and was now arching her neck, pulling on the rein, asking to be allowed a small drink, please.

"Trifler!" Antonio chided, allowing the leather to slip through his fingers, and speaking as a man does who in a lonely time makes both pet and confidante of a favorite mount. "Cheat! You are not thirsty. A half-hour from your own well? What is this lately, that you must stop at every wayside pool? Is it to remind me that water was set beside the road to furnish drink for animals that might be thirsty? When were you ever one of those? It must be the desert in your blood. Don't twitch your ears at me now. Drink . . . oh, you've had enough? I thought so. Let us be off then about our unhappy business, which will not go away for wishing it had not happened. Up!"

Five minutes later, to the muted jingle of silver, he rode into Los Adaes.

It was a pretty town, as one might expect, knowing its location.

Trees shaded the central plaza. The little river flowed along one side and then on through the town. The river made possible a small fountain in the exact center of the square. A bird, its feathers blue and green with a touch of scarlet, perched this morning, since nobody came near to frighten it away, on the rim of the fountain. The square, except for the bird and now Antonio on his black mare, was empty.

In all his life Antonio had never seen the square like this. On any bright day, before the sun was up, those who had houses with shops on the two sides at right angles to the river would be out sweeping their doorsteps; then later in the day they would come out periodically to see who of their town acquaintance or what strangers had appeared, possibly on their way to the market—another open place leading off from the southwest corner of the plaza. At almost any hour, except siesta, knots of men would collect under the trees, engaged in deep discussion. It was their way of gathering news, local and general, of exchanging opinions, of obtaining information or advice—of passing an idle hour. Today there was no one.

One sweep of his eyes was enough. Antonio turned from the empty square to the *Casa Real* opposite the river. It was even emptier. It had been so for two years now, ever since the capital of the province had been moved from Los Adaes on the eastern border to San Antonio de Bexar, two hundred and fifty leagues to the southwest. After the departure of the Governor, and with him all his secretaries, bailiffs, military aides, and clerks, nobody had been considered of sufficient importance to occupy the house. Its walls looked back blankly at Antonio. In this region of abundant rains a vine growing up the side of the building had gone wild and had crept around to the front, covering a high window. Still, while it stood, this was the government house. There was no other. Fastened to one of the pillars before the door was a copy of a public notice. From where he sat Antonio could see the black letters at the top: *PROCLAMA.*

He did not bother to ride over for a closer look. He knew what was there. So, apparently, did everyone else in town; and the question that he had asked himself repeatedly, What would the people do when they heard? now was answered: they would go into hiding. In fear, in mutiny—the reason did not matter. They were all hiding. He knew that the little shops were not empty, although he saw no one. Across the way Natividad Acaro hid somewhere behind her display of mantillas, laces, and shell combs, though it was generally known that since her husband's death she did more business through her back door than the other way. Just today concealment seemed preferable to showing herself in her newest silk shawl on the doorstep. And behind him, Rosario Terrero, who dealt in herbs and general humanity, and whose carnal sins were also beyond reckoning, unless one counted her children, was also either at home or out dosing or poulticing someone stricken. If she was out, other bright eyes would be watching from her place. So Antonio could have accounted for all the occupants of the two rows of commercial dwellings, but did not. Quite sure that by now his presence was known; that, as soon as he turned his back, the news would travel, he touched his hat in salute to those who might be looking and turned off into the nearest side street.

It was one of the better streets fanning out from the square. Most of the houses, substantial, built of wood and plastered adobe, some on foundations of stone, were two stories high. Each had, besides a door, a barred gate leading to a concealed courtyard or garden area. Antonio pulled up before the third gate on the left. He vaguely had in mind a list of people to see, and might as well start at the top, unless this house, too, should be locked to visitors. No, the gate opened.

A servant in a fresh, white cotton shirt hanging down over short, loose cotton breeches, happily barefoot, bare generally except for the shirt and pants, stood in the opening. He seemed startled.

"Señor—Don Antonio," he stammered. "The *Señor Alcalde* did not say . . ."

"He did not know," Antonio said. "What is it, Juanito? Is he not here?"

"Don Antonio, no. He has gone to Nakatosh. Early this morning, very early. If he had known . . ."

To Natchitoches—in Louisiana. The *Alcalde Mayor* of the town. Here could be a situation.

"If he had business in Nakatosh," Antonio said to the servant, "he had to attend to it at once. The time is short."

"Señor, I do not know if it was just business. The Señora and the young Señoritas went with him."

He had decamped. It seemed impossible. Not for the *Alcalde Mayor* so much as for Gil Flores, who held that office. An anxious little man, but anxious usually only that he should do what was right. If he had a fault, this was it, and, naturally, it could not be held against him. Now . . .

"He will return tomorrow," Juan said. "He told me that."

"Good! I hope so. Five days will be only four tomorrow." Five days for preparation. Presumably a day or two of grace might be added. And nobody hurried.

"He will come tomorrow, Señor, I am sure. But not the Señora, I think, or the young Señoritas. They will remain in Nakatosh—for now. They will not go. . . ."

Suddenly, respectful politeness, with only a slight tremor under it, deserted the man at the gate. He clasped his hands. His face contorted into an expression Antonio had seen before—on a prisoner facing the whip—or death—with nobody present to save him. It was terror.

"Don Antonio, it cannot be true. Is it true that, when that day comes, everyone must go—even one like me, who is nothing and has nothing? Señor?"

Answer him, Ibarbo. Why else are you here? Answer him truly.

"Yes," Antonio said, but the word came hard. "When that day is here finally, everyone must go—you, the *Señor Alcalde* and the rest—taking with you what you can carry. If you have nothing, you are fortunate. You will leave nothing behind and will not be burdened on the way. I am not making jokes. I am sorry for everybody, believe me. You have less to fear than some others. The *Señor Alcalde* will look out for you. He will not let you come to harm. Juan?"

The anguished face cleared slowly. The eyes were now those of a dog that wants to put trust in a stranger, but is not sure.

"Señor, always I live here. I have not ever been away, even to Nakatosh. This, I think, is farther . . ."

"Much farther, Juan, and in the opposite direction. West, not east. West, where the evening sun goes down."

Useless to speak of leagues to one so simple. Juan turned in the direction indicated.

"Señor, how will it be there? What will I find to do? Here I raise the flowers in the *Señor Alcalde*'s garden. Will you come and see?"

"I have seen, Juan. I would take time again today; only there are others I must talk to, since the *Señor Alcalde* is away. Will you give him a message from me? Say I was here—on business, and disappointed not to find him at home."

"Business, Don Antonio?"

Assuredly business. Life went on, did it not? Here or there.

"Business," Antonio repeated. "He has not made me a price on sugar this year. If he has not sold this year's refining at Nakatosh . . ."

"Señor, nothing was said about sugar, just that he will be here tomorrow. Don Antonio, nothing can be done, then, about this going away? I thought you, maybe . . ."

"No, Juan. It is the King's command. Nobody can change that. Say to the *Señor Alcalde* that I shall be at the ranch every day this week. If he would be pleased to come there, I would like to talk to him about sugar—and other matters. Now go back to your flowers, and do not worry. All will come out right— somehow."

A clenched fist of a promise that he knew would not be kept. Why did he make it?"

"*Adiós*," he said then. "I will see you again, perhaps, before you leave. If not . . . *hola*, who are you?"

"You" was a boy, who seemed to come up out of the ground near Fatima's head.

"Señor, if you wish to make a call anywhere, I will hold your horse."

"You?" Antonio said. Here was a mere twig of a boy, with large, round eyes in a pointed face. "You . . . how much do you charge for your services?"

"A peseta, if I should be engaged. But for you, Don Antonio, it will be enough to be allowed to hold the horse."

14

A passionate declaration, if Antonio had ever heard one.

"You know me?" he said.

"*Sí*, Señor, because of the horse."

"I see. Well . . . what is your name, then? I do not seem to remember."

"Pedro," the boy said. "I am Pedro Coronal. My father . . ."

"But I know your father, I think," Antonio interrupted. "Tomás Coronal, the weaver. You are one of his?"

"I am his son, Señor."

Yes, surely; but the youngest, Antonio thought, and said so.

"I am the only son, Señor. The other two are girls."

"Now, that is how things happen," Antonio said. "Your father is one of those I most want to see in town this morning. I believe the house is some distance away. How is it that you are so far from home, young Pedro?"

Young Pedro hung his head.

"*Mamacita*'s head is bad today," he said in so low a tone that Antonio had to lean from the saddle to hear him. "Because she cried too much, *papacita* says. All last night she cried; so now her head is sore. If one knocks over a stool, she screams with the pain. *Papacita* said for me to go take a little walk and maybe she would become quiet and sleep. So I went out and I walked. There was nobody else in the street. I kept on walking. I thought maybe I would go to Tía Rosario and she might come and help *mamacita*. Then I heard the silver bells on Fatima, and it was you. So . . ."

"So here we meet," Antonio said, wishing only to soothe a child, touched by the sorrow of mankind. "Would you like to show me the way to your house? I am not sure I know just how it goes from here. And, since you have walked so far, perhaps now you had better ride."

Up came the bowed head, and the round eyes shone. "Ride?" they asked. "On Fatima with you?"

"Give me your hand," Antonio directed, reaching for it. "Climb the stirrup. Now, up—yes, of course, in front of me. How could you see anything behind my broad back? Up! There you are. Fatima, behave yourself. This is a friend, and his weight is nothing. Are you secure, Pedro? Good. Let us move on, if this is the right direction. When it is time to turn, put out one hand or the other. Forward, Fatima! Let us go."

"It is so high, Señor. I never rode so high before. It rocks— a little, but I like it. Turn here, Señor. Quick. I almost forgot."

There was much turning. The streets fanning out from the square went straight as sticks for a while. Then, as more came in, regularity was lost. Sometimes a house had been built before a street came that far, and it stood in the way, and the street had had to bend to go around it. The houses soon were not as fine as the *Señor Alcalde*'s; but they were tight little houses, with trees and bright flowers. In this country birds and wind planted flowers, if man did not.

"How old are you, Pedro?"

"I have almost ten years, Señor."

Ten. Was it possible that at ten he had been like this small wriggler, Antonio asked himself; but he knew he had not been like that. At ten he remembered himself as only a little short of manhood.

"What do you think to make of yourself, Pedro, being ten?"

"Señor, I have thought of many things. Today I know. I will be a ranchero—like you. Señor, is it true that Fatima is a King's horse?"

"No," Antonio said, with quick denial, "she is my horse. Only her blood is royal. I have a paper that says so. I will show it to you some day. Can you read such a paper?"

"*Sí*, Señor, if the letters do not have too many curly tails. Señor—we turn here. I go to school at the mission—to Fray Josef. Every day, but not now. Not any more, I think. We turn again, Señor."

So, Antonio thought, even this one knows. But naturally. How should one of such sharp ears and inquiring eyes not know?

"Señor, I think also maybe I won't see Fatima's paper. I will be gone from here soon. Again we turn, please. But it will make no difference about school. My father says there will be missions at San Antonio de Bexar, with priests to teach, and I will go on studying just the same. What do you think, Señor?"

"He is right," Antonio said, more harshly than he meant to speak. "There will be missions and priests to teach. That I can promise. And if your father wishes it, you will study. When I was ten, I thought I had had all the school I needed. I was a big boy. At least, I thought so. Fray Josef was a young man and new here. I had an argument with him over Latin." Pedro sighed. "You know? I said Latin was for priests or lawyers, maybe, but not for a businessman. So Fray Josef took me to my father and said, 'I can do nothing with this wild colt. What do you advise?' And my father said, 'Leave him with me now. I will teach him.' "

Pedro squirmed with delight and anticipation.

"So he did," Antonio continued. "One hour of every day I practiced penmanship, or worked on problems of numbers, or read from thick books on my father's bookshelf, until I had read them all with him."

"Latin?" Pedro asked.

"And Greek, for all I know. My father, praise God, had them in Spanish translation. That was hard enough. One hour every day, the best hour often; and that is how much good it did me to stop school."

"Your father was a man of learning, I think," Pedro observed. "My father has none, but he feels the same about school. Tell me some more about your father, Don Antonio. I like to hear."

"There is nothing more to tell, my friend. My father has been gone a long time now. I am sorry I caused him so much trouble."

They rode on, to the delicate chiming of Fatima's silver bells, the boy dreaming over heaven knew what, Antonio musing not so pleasantly. Four hundred families in this town, he thought, at least that many, all with children like Pedro, some older, some younger, and in almost every household someone who is old or otherwise infirm. How . . . An excited cry from Pedro stopped everything.

"Señor, I forgot to say turn. I forgot to watch. We have come too far."

They had reached the far edge of the town. A pond lay only a few feet ahead.

"Now, now!" Antonio said. "Do not be disturbed over a little thing like that. Fatima does not mind. I do not, and you have had a good ride. But we will turn now and go back and both of us will watch where we go. By this time your father must be wondering about you."

Tomás Coronal stood in the narrow street before his house, looking the image of anxiety as Antonio and Pedro rounded the corner. He was a man of Antonio's age—they had been boys together—but toil and many anxieties had made him look much older. He was a weaver by trade, an excellent one, a magician with threads of wool or silk or cotton; but excellence did not save him from having a stoop to his shoulders. His eyes had the look of one whose work was close and absorbing. Only his hands were not rough. That would not be good for handling silk spinning, for example. They were large, smooth, with the fingertips somewhat flattened. This Antonio knew well, also that Tomás was a mild-tempered man, but he was afraid that two anxieties at once might produce an outburst, so he called to him quickly.

"*Olé*, Tomás! Are you looking for a boy? I have one here."

"I see you have," Tomás said. "Where did you find him?"

"He found me, I think," Antonio said; "but I was the one who suggested that we take a little ride together. I am happy to have made the acquaintance of your son in this way and hope you will forgive us both, Tomás, for that reason."

He swung himself to the ground; but, when he moved to help Pedro dismount, he was waved aside. Making the same motions as nearly as he could for lack of inches, the boy lifted himself from the saddle and swung himself across Fatima's back and to the earth—as lightly as a butterfly.

"All right, enough!" his father said. "You have had your fun. Now, inside with you. But quietly. *Mamacita* is asleep."

"My father, first I must make my farewell to Fatima. Don Antonio, is it permitted that I touch?"

"Ask her," Antonio said, knowing Fatima. "She is the lady involved."

Sure enough, curious now about this human flea who had so freely perched on her royal shoulders and now stood on the ground beside her, Fatima stretched her neck and nosed him.

"*Ai-ee!*" Pedro squealed in ecstasy, put out his hand to stroke

18

her, then drew it back and kissed her quickly on her questing nose. "*Gracias*, my treasure," he sighed, then ducked and ran for the house.

His father, shaking his head, watched him go. When he turned again to Antonio, his eyes were misted over.

"What becomes of him now, Antonio?" he asked. "Tell me, if you can."

Between Antonio Ibarbo and Tomás Coronal were twenty years and more of friendship and respect. They had been boys in this town together, though living at different levels—Antonio's father a government clerk and notary, not well paid but steadily employed, and the father of Tomás a humble weaver. Means, however, had nothing to do with the boys' instant liking for each other. From the first they were partners in play and mischief, whenever Tomás was allowed to play.

Later, when their paths had separated—Antonio advancing to possessions and position at a rate that even he sometimes thought remarkable, and Tomás improving his circumstances more slowly, and only because he was a better weaver than his father had been—the friendship had remained. Antonio, a licensed trader as well as a rancher, had been able now and again to sell a piece of cloth from the loom of Tomás in Natchitoches or New Orleans at a price unobtainable in Les Adaes. The sale was never an act of charity. The cloth always merited what it brought in trade, and Antonio's standing was elevated by his having such goods to barter. All this was between them as they faced each other, and now this other thing, this black destruction, which was neither desired nor deserved, and yet there it was. What could Antonio say to such a friend?

"Tomás, I am sorry. I would like to be of help."

The weaver's lined face softened. He blinked his eyes.

"It is good that you are here, 'Tonio, though if you had not come, I could have named more than one reason. There was no need."

No need?

"Look at this town," Antonio protested. "It is half dead already."

"Mostly it is sleeping," Tomás said. "We rested little through

19

the night. Fray Josef talked to us after vespers. Many attended. He rang the bell extra loud—as if there were a war or fire—to call everybody to the mission."

"I heard the bell," Antonio said.

"At the ranch? Well. He read the order out to us. At first we did not believe it. So he read it again. In five days we must get together such belongings as we can carry, and on the sixth day, leaving the rest behind, we must close our doors and begin our march to San Antonio de Bexar, to make new homes and a new life. The town is to be abandoned."

Extinguished was the word, Antonio was sure.

"You know, Antonio?"

"I saw the order at the fort yesterday. The Governor's courier left it as witness to the King's command. I was there, also Flores and Fray Josef and, naturally, *Teniente* Gonzales. Garza said he would like to read the order to you and say a few words before the *proclama* was posted at the *Casa Real*."

"He read the order twice," Tomás said; "and, when we could not deny what our ears had been forced to hear, there was a terrible crying out. Women wailed and wept. Men stamped their feet and clenched their fists and swore black, brave oaths, where they did no harm—or good, either. Two women fainted. Fray Josef had trouble making himself heard over the uproar."

"What did he say?" Antonio asked.

"He said, 'Be still!' "

Tomás smiled wryly. Antonio laughed. He could hear how that had sounded. Fray Josef Francisco Mariano de la Garza, born, one fancied, on a bare rock in Spain's bare mountains, knowing hardship and privation through childhood and youth, then disciplined in a missionary order of the priesthood, had looked, even as a young man new to the provinces, like someone carved out of stone rather than like one having life through natural processes. Twenty years of serving the Mission of San Miguel in the pine forests of east Texas had made him look no softer. Partly that was because of the way he was built. He was a big man. His rough and craggy head emerged impressively from the cowl of his friar's robe, the forehead jutting out above the eyes, the nose and mouth big, the chin square. His hands were large, his feet enormous. He walked barefoot over any trail not set densely with thorns; and he would not mount a mule unless the journey was long and there was need of haste. He knew by name any Indian he had ever talked to and all his parishioners, most of whom he had by now either baptized, confirmed, or married—sometimes all three. And yet, in this time of stress, over his own anguish—for the King's command had dealt him a blow, too—his order to his frightened flock was just as Tomás had said: "Be still!"

"Then he said," Tomás continued, "it was only to be expected that we should grieve; but there was not time for too much of that. He said for us to go home and spend the night in prayer and thought, and perhaps in communicating with friends and neighbors, because a burden seems lighter when it is shared; but today we must begin to make ready. He said we had no choice but to obey the command given us, however hard it seemed. If we were strong and brave and kept our faith in God, it could turn out better than we thought—someday.

"So we did as he said. We went home and we thought and we talked together—most of the night. It helped a little—perhaps. At least we were tired and could sleep—some of us, at any rate. Now it is day. I was preparing to take down my loom when I thought I had best look at the street for a sign of Pedro."

"Must you take down the loom—just today?" Antonio asked; ". . . even if there is a piece of work on it to finish?"

"It will remain like that," Pedro said. "Unfinished—to mark this hour."

"Tomás, is there some place other than the street where we can talk?"

"I want that above everything right now," Tomás said, "but not here. The house is too small and Mama is asleep. Anyhow, there are others who should benefit by what you have to say. Pablo Rojas—last night he said, 'What we need is someone who knows—Ibarbo, for example. He has been over the road. He has seen San Antonio de Bexar. He has dealt with governors.' "

"Several," Antonio agreed. "The present one I liked very much until now. But I did not do so well with the one just before him."

"You were more than equal even to him," Tomás reminded him. "It is as Pablo says, you know. Flores the *Alcalde* is a good man, but . . ."

"The *Señor Alcalde*," Antonio said slowly, doubt hanging a weight on each word, "will do his best for you. At least, he will have only the town to think about. He is in Nakatosh today— with his lady and the children, who will remain there, I believe, until Flores has seen Bexar."

The weaver's face contorted in sudden anguish.

"That is what it is to be rich," he said in rare bitterness of complaint. "You will agree, Antonio, that Flores acted wisely there?"

"He acted," Antonio said, still slowly, "as one might expect him to do. Whether it was wise or not, time alone will show. It may be months before Señora Flores can hear how things are with her husband, or he can hear about her and the girls."

Anguish drained out of Coronal's seamed face—also slowly.

"I see what you mean," he said. "His family would be safe, but . . . my Rosa would not agree to such a separation, I am sure. Still, if I could arrange something. . . ."

"We will put our heads together on that presently," Antonio promised. "Shall we talk with Pablo first?"

CHAPTER 2

On foot, leading Fatima, Antonio and Tomás rounded one corner, then another, and came finally to the substantial house of Pablo Rojas, the stonemason; but at the door a dark-eyed girl with hair still tousled from bed said that her papa had just left, to consult with Señor Esteban Andorro about wood for chicken cages.

"Good!" Tomás said. "We will follow him there. Esteban," he confided to Antonio, "pretends that he can walk as far as anyone, but he is always lame afterwards. We can talk in his carpenter shop as well as anywhere."

The shop was an open shed behind the Andorro house, built as one would expect of anything built by a master carpenter, raised off the ground, with a board floor—to protect from the rain Esteban's tools and whatever small things he was making. Today the small thing was a table; but Esteban had already laid aside his tools to welcome Rojas; and the two of them were deep in earnest conversation when Antonio and Tomás arrived. The welcome was now for them.

"*Olé*, Antonio!" Rojas cried, his voice as strong and hearty as ever; but that was his way. He was a strong and hearty man, as one who works with stone must be.

Esteban Andorro came from behind the table, dusting off his carpenter's apron. He was slighter than Coronal or Rojas, a little older, and worn by illness and other trouble. His lameness was the result of a fall years before from the roof of a house he was building. His right hip had been injured at the joint; and it was thought at the time that he might never walk again. But he had thought otherwise. It was not like him in the first place to fall from a roof. There had been just one misstep.

It had happened on a day very much like this one. While Esteban was at work, his wife and his four children were enjoying an outing on Lake Adaes, a pleasant stretch of water not far from the town. A summer storm came up without warning. It caught them in a light skiff out on the lake, with the oldest boy, Cecilio, not quite twelve, at the oars. Before rescuers could reach them over the roughened waters, a sudden gust of wind picked up the skiff and turned it over, throwing everybody out. Only Cecilio was brought out alive, and he fighting to go back and find the others.

Of all this, except that he had seen the cloud and watched the wind pass through the trees, Esteban knew nothing until a friend came running down the street to tell him what had happened at the lake. It was then that he made the one unwary step of a lifetime and fell. Later, lying on his bed in agony, unable to march in the funeral procession of his loved ones, he might have accepted the fate promised him but for the one remaining son.

It was the sobbing of the brokenhearted boy that lifted Esteban from his bed to wooden crutches and finally made him able to walk, though haltingly.

It was Antonio's misfortune today to have deep regard for both the father and the son, the latter now a handsome young man, as skillful with tools as his father ever was, and a credit to all who had shared in his rearing. Affianced, Antonio recollected, to a girl in the town whom he also knew, pretty little Teresa García, able, in spite of strict upbringing, to flash a smile at a young man that was certain to set his blood racing. They were to be wed—but when?

"The table," Esteban explained, "is for Cecilio and Teresa's new house. Until yesterday there was plenty of time. Now there is none. Cecilio talked with Teresa and her family last night. This morning they went to the mission to consult the priest. I was just telling Pablo. With the priest's consent, they will marry today. With or without it, Cecilio says, the house being ready, but that is talk. Fray Josef will agree, I think. Have you seen the house, Antonio?"

His eyes were as searching as Tomás Coronal's had been earlier.

"No," Antonio said uncomfortably, "but I have heard it is very fine."

He was sorry not to see Cecilio. The young man was part of what he had to say to his three friends; but, before words of greeting and friendship had been exchanged, other men came. Antonio had been right in his surmise that the town would know at once of his presence. Then curiosity had pursued him to the weaver's house, to the stonemason's, and finally here. One or two at a time drifted into the carpenter's yard, until finally, besides the three he had come to see, at least twenty men were grouped under the trees, looking toward the shop expectantly.

Some of them he knew well, some only by name, some by sight but no name, and some not at all. They were men whose clothing made them out shopkeepers, farmers, artisans, traders—all kinds. One was a Negro—a freedman, from Louisiana, Antonio guessed, who had found life safer in Spanish Texas. Several were mestizos, mixed Spanish and Indian; but most, he thought, were of as pure a strain as his own—one or two generations removed from Spanish-

24

born parents. Some wore sullen faces, some were frightened, some were still half asleep, some were as mistrustful of him as of everyone else; but all wanted to hear what he might have to tell them. They were finally so many pairs of eyes watching, so many ears listening. For that reason Antonio became mistrustful of himself. He knew that every word he said would be carried away and repeated, incorrectly as often as correctly. He would be honest as far as possible, but he must also be careful—as he would not have needed to be careful in speaking to Tomás Coronal, honest, sensitive, generally submissive; to Pablo Rojas of the rough, work-scarred hands and the round face made more for jollity than its present look of care; to Esteban Andorro, gentled and lamed by life's cruelty and now waiting to see what this new threat might come to.

Then suddenly it was not to twenty pairs of ears that he spoke, but to Tomás Coronal, who, unschooled and with no knowledge of the world beyond the boundaries of this town, had said, "Tell us how this thing has come to be, Antonio, because you know." He leaned against the unfinished table, drew a deep breath, and began.

To make his explanation clear and complete, knowing there was no justification, he went back fifty years—to the beginning of everything. It was then that Spain had begun the establishment of settlements on this, the eastern border of Texas. A fort came first, to defend the border against encroachments by the French of Louisiana, though there had never been any serious threat of invasion. Trade between Texas and Louisiana was forbidden, and smuggling had been the result, which no fort could have prevented; but generally peace had prevailed on the border.

At this point Antonio glimpsed a man in the yard whom he seemed to remember from the Adaes market place, a dealer in small, miscellaneous merchandise, gathered from he alone knew what sources. Antonio chose to ignore him. Trade, lawful or unlawful, he was certain, was not the reason for the Madrid decree.

He returned to discussion of the fort. It was a strong fort. Nothing had been spared in the way of ramparts or armament. Cannon had been mounted above the gate and on the walls, especially those facing Louisiana. A garrison had been installed, commanded by an officer of the Royal Infantry, because at that time the fort was considered the most important boundary of the Texas province.

For the same reason a town was set up near by, to be the seat of provincial government: the city of Los Adaes. The fort was named the Presidio of Los Adaes, after a neighboring tribe of friendly Tejas. Settlers were brought from Spain to people the town. Since all the wealth of Spain was known to come from the Americas, many were glad to leave the old country for the new; and those who were settled in Los Adaes considered themselves especially fortunate. The land was beautiful, with hills and valleys and forests and abundant water. The climate was kind: neither too cold in winter nor too hot in summer. The soil was deep and rich and would grow anything. One hundred families came, then two hundred more. Antonio's parents had been among those settlers. Most of the people present could say the same. As the good years added up, more came, and the population increased.

Very soon there was a mission. With every fort and every settlement there was a mission to keep the settlers mindful of the true religion and also to convert the Indians. For Los Adaes there was the Mission of San Miguel. Later, for other Tejas Indians, there were two others—one on the east side of the Sabine River, one farther west among the Nacogdoches Tejas. That was how the picture was in the beginning and for more than forty years afterwards. Everybody was happy—contented and prosperous. Life was good. Madrid was pleased. The town, the fort, the missions were important. They were so no longer. And that was it, as Antonio understood it.

A murmur rose. Pablo Rojas, the stonemason, half got up from his bench.

"Antonio," he growled.

"Wait," Antonio begged. "I will explain further. Ten years ago France had bad luck in a war on both sides of the ocean. She lost all her lands in America east of the Mississippi River to the English; and, for fear that she would lose the rest, she quickly handed Louisiana, west of that river, to Spain. With one stroke of the pen, our border became only a boundary between two Spanish states—and that is how we lost importance."

He allowed time for that to digest, if it could be digested.

"Inspectors came, one after another. They wrote reports. They said the fort was useless. It should be dismantled. This would result in a saving of at least seven thousand pesos a year, and that is important to those who guard the King's treasury, which seems to have ten holes for emptying to every one for filling. That was the first command in the present *reglamento*. The Presidio of Los Adaes is now being dismantled. The guns are coming down, the ammunition is being packed. The garrison is under order to report to the Governor at San Antonio de Bexar."

Twenty men under an aging lieutenant. He could remember when there were a hundred men whom the Captain-Governor commanded; but he must keep to his explanations.

"The missions come next," he said. "They are also the King's property and an expense. The Franciscan Order provides the priests; but it is, as you know, an order dedicated to poverty. The buildings and any money needed come out of the royal treasury. Naturally such property must have soldiers at hand to guard it; so the missions, too, are being dismantled."

But not, he knew, because of the expense of maintaining them. The missions, the ruling said, had not shown the proper zeal in making Christians out of the Indians. The number of baptisms proved it.

"So," he said, "that leaves the town of Los Adaes without military protection or spiritual guidance, a condition which the Royal Council of War and Finance in Madrid considers intolerable—and so the ruling, destroying the town. You see, things fall apart faster than they are built."

"Faster?" the man whom Antonio did and did not remember objected. "Ten years—is that fast?"

Antonio frowned. He did not like the man's tone.

"The ocean is wide," he said, with forced patience. "It takes time to cross it both ways. Time to name an inspector. Time for him to make an inspection and write a report, which then must be studied by the Royal Council. If a second inspection is made—ten years is not too long."

"But we are allowed only five days," a farmer said from the yard.

"Once it is decided that a tree must come down," Rojas reminded him, "it does not take long to swing the axe."

"Still," the farmer said, "I think it is too little time for us. Enough, perhaps, for one who has nothing to carry away and nothing to leave behind—one sheep, one cow and a little corn. But for one who has a flock of sheep with lambs, and cows and two mules, and corn ripening in his field to feed his house until the next harvest, with some to spare for the market, I don't know how it can be done."

"Harvest the corn," Antonio said quickly. "If your mules are not enough to carry it all, talk to the *Alcalde*. He will be here tomorrow to advise about such things. It will be a long journey and corn will be needed. As for sheep and cows, they drive well. The first settlers in Bexar, I have been told, brought their herds with them all the way from Mexico. The *Alcalde* will surely arrange for an *arriero* to take charge of the extra animals."

He must remind Flores of that necessity.

"*Gracias*, Señor," the farmer said humbly; and a friend standing beside him put a comforting hand on his shoulder.

"Don Antonio," gentle Esteban Andorro said then, "some of us may wonder why, in leaving Los Adaes, we must travel so far."

"I could have told you that," Rojas said in the same half-laughing, half-angry tone he had used about the axe. "The farther we go from here, the harder it will be—if we don't like Bexar when we arrive there—to turn around and come back."

Antonio did not like the way he spoke. Rojas, that big, strong man, was as shaken as anyone.

"San Antonio de Bexar is the place," Antonio said, "only because it is the new capital. The movement of people is to complete the change of capitals."

It had probably—no, undoubtedly—been planned that way. The order was too specific not to have been planned. Five days to gather their portable belongings together, then the long, long march at the end of which, the newcomers would be given lands, the ruling said, to replace those they had abandoned. How could he tell them the nature of the new lands? A second farmer spoke.

"Señor, you spoke of first settlers. This, then, is not a new town?"

"No," Antonio said, "it is an old town; but until recently it was not blessed with the good fortune of Los Adaes."

"Why would the King's Council now name as capital a town that has not prospered?"

"Again," Antonio said, "it is a matter of importance. The western border of Texas is now the one that needs defending." Should he speak of the Plains Indians? No. How would that help? "The soldiers from Los Adaes will go to strengthen the fort at Bexar, the people to make the city look better and stronger, more as a capital should look."

The trader with the sullen mouth and the hard eyes spoke again.

"I think," he said, "that is not all of it. As for time, I think it is not just that it took ten years to make ready this order which we have now been given. Lately things go much too fast. The official who was here for a short while only, before the governor we have now—how do they call him? Do you know, Señor?"

"*Inspector Comandante*," Antonio said. "That is Don Hugo Oconor's present title, if you are referring to him"—Don Hugo Oconor, Interim Governor of Texas, now *Inspector Comandante* of the Interior Provinces. A man with a fierce red beard, a fiercer temper, ruthless in advancing himself.

"Inspector," the trader said. "He was the one who took the capital away from here. And now this. Señor Ibarbo, when Don Hugo Oconor was here Louisiana was already Spanish. Still he made arrests, charging people with dealing in contraband. You must know that."

Again Pablo Rojas rose from his bench, and again Antonio with a look told him to sit down. The whole town knew that Oconor had once arrested Antonio Ibarbo on a contraband charge. Later he had not been able to prove the charge and had had to let Antonio go. This had not engendered any affection between him and Antonio, but surely . . .

"Where there is trade in country like this," Antonio said carefully, "we hear continually of contraband. When contraband was goods smuggled across an enemy border, it was easy to define. In the present situation, it is not so easy. Contraband then is the buying and selling of forbidden goods; and you are right, Señor, in thinking that the interpretation of the law depends often on the official whose duty it is to look into such practice. For example, everyone knows that gold, silver, and precious stones that come from the mines are the King's treasure. Only he has the right to use them to his profit and to Spain's. This is true also of crops grown on royal property at the royal order and of industries which the King's Council promotes. Well, it can go on and on. A man owns land only by the King's grant. What profit he makes from it is his—if he satisfies the tax collector first." Did he hear groans of laughter? He had, he hoped, led the talk away from personal accusation. "More directly, the King owns the armament of forts—that is why he can take them away at will. Towns, established by him at royal expense, are also his property."

"And so are we," the trader interrupted. "Is that it, Señor Ibarbo?"

Pablo Rojas could sit still no longer.

"What else?" he demanded angrily. "When has it ever been otherwise? Our parents were the King's subjects. They were sent here on his order, on his ships. They were settled in this fine country. They were allowed ten years without tax collections, to establish homes; and all the years after that were never too bad. Now it is the King's will that we move again and repeat the process in another part of Texas. Whether for better or worse —and I am one of those who fear it will be worse before it is better—we have no choice but to obey the ruling and make what we can of the change. I begin to comprehend now, and I think we owe Don Antonio thanks, not rocks, for making things so clear. His one desire is to help us as much as he can. Am I right about that, my friend?"

"My thanks to you, Pablo," Antonio said, oppressed now because he had not told all of the truth, "for your trust; but I too see some things more clearly than before. The only help of consequence would be to destroy the King's command, to say it had ceased to be. Since I cannot do that, my friends, I can only agree with Pablo Rojas. You have no choice but to obey. Do not try to run away or hide. If you are troubled, talk to your *Alcalde* and Fray Josef de la Garza, your priest. If, after that, you still are troubled, come to Rancho Lobanillo . . . and we will see. For the rest, go with God and may this worst of misfortunes soon turn into something better."

The meeting in the yard dissolved then, as it had assembled. One by one and two by two, the men went away, some talking excitedly, some finding nothing to say. Antonio was alone with his three friends.

Esteban Andorro brought wine. The four sat around the unfinished table, sipping the wine slowly, thoughtfully.

"Well!" Antonio shook off his trance of thought. "Meaning to be of help, I think I have only made more confusion. May I say now what I wanted to say in the beginning? I came to town this morning, intending to offer a certain number of people a home in the Lobanillo pueblo. Naturally, you three were at the top of the list."

The three chosen ones looked at one another and at him. The offer was not unexpected, he thought, and yet . . .

"You have room?" Tomás Coronal asked, thus putting off a real answer.

"The pueblo has no walls," Antonio said. "There is room for half a dozen families, if they are the right kind. Esteban, I want you and Cecilio. Cecilio, because he is a fine young man, the close friend of Luis Ramón, now overseer at the ranch, and because he is your son and a good carpenter. Such are always useful, and I know you will not come without him or he without you. I am saying this all crisscross, I am afraid."

Esteban put out his hand and clasped Antonio's arm.

"You are the best of friends, Antonio," he said, "and we thank you for the offer, my son and I. You are right about a separation. Cecilio is about to begin his own man's life and we will live apart now; but I could not finish out my days happily if I could not count on seeing him in his house or in mine a little of everyday. I am sure he feels the same. So, I must go where Cecilio goes. That will not be to Rancho Lobanillo."

When Antonio protested, Esteban gently shook the arm he held.

"Cecilio," he said, "is marrying, Teresa García, who also has a family. A large one. Will you make room for the Garcías, too? No, surely you will not. And Cecilio at this tender moment is not one to wrench little Teresa entirely and forever away from her people. So, they will go to Bexar with the rest, and I will go where they go. But we thank you from our hearts for your offer."

"It will kill you," Antonio said, angry with apprehension. "It is a long road and a hard one. You will be on the way most of the summer."

"If I should die," Esteban said, with the disturbing calm of one who has lived through much trouble, "I will do so holding the hand of my son."

Then it was Coronal, and after him Rojas, who said no to the offer of asylum.

"Antonio," Tomás said, "I can see how a carpenter or a stone-mason can earn his right to live on your land, but a weaver? Forget what I said a while ago about safety. It would be pleasant. My son would be enchanted, but . . . no."

"What are we to do for cloth?" Antonio asked him. "You—any of you—can set up business of your own there as well as any-where. You would not need to work for me. I would not require it."

"Antonio," Pablo Rojas said more gruffly, "there is more than one reason why we cannot do what you suggest. You were sorry for those people here this morning, were you not?"

"Not so sorry as I am for you, whom I know."

"Still, you were sorry. It showed. You were so gentle—for you—so patient. I said to myself, Is this Ibarbo being kind to nobody of consequence? Fray Josef was rougher yesterday eve-ning, but there was a thing he said which we must not forget. It was not only that we must keep our faith in God to make things come out right finally, but we must be true to one another. One man alone, the strongest, would not be able to bear this cruel mis-fortune; but, if we cling together, the strong helping the weak and the weak lending something that takes the place of strength, we shall endure. We talked about that last night and we had to believe Garza was right. Even in Los Adaes, where anyone can have cotton or wool to wear and corn and meat and eggs and melons and cheese and fruit to eat for only a little work, still the strong always support the weak a little. You know. So, how would it look if three—no, four, counting Cecilio—if four strong men withdrew their support? We spoke of Rancho Lobanillo last night. Naturally the first thought one has is of escape; but no, we agreed we would stand by each other and the town."

"But you don't know what you are choosing," Antonio objected—angrily still, because Rojas always meant what he said.

"We can guess," Rojas told him. "Your face tells us this is a bad town—this new capital."

"As evil a town as I ever saw—when I last saw it," Antonio said.

"I thought so. How is it evil? No, don't tell us. Let us find out for ourselves. Because, whatever the evil is, we must go there. That is our duty and our will."

"You are a fool," Antonio told him.

"So much a fool, my friend, that I will not do this thing to you. Antonio, it was not right for that man, a stranger, to speak publicly just now of your difficulties with the Red Devil who was our governor for two years before this one; but we know it was a bad time for you."

A bad time certainly, while it lasted. The charge had involved horses and mules which Antonio had bought for the Los Adaes fort, paying for them with the King's silver. Oconor had declared that the Indians with whom Antonio dealt had stolen the animals from the royal garrison at San Antonio de Bexar, and that Antonio knew it.

Antonio could still see himself standing before the Red One, manacles on his wrists like a common thief. Anger was hot in his blood but a chill cramped his heart. He knew that his friendly Indians had not stolen the mules, but he was not at all sure about their source of supply.

"I have the right, I think," he said, refusing to show how badly he was shaken, "to know the evidence on which this accusation is made. Surely San Antonio de Bexar brands its animals."

This was a bold stab in the dark, but Oconor had agreed to a search for brands. None turned up. Reluctantly then, he had set Antonio free. All this had been three years ago. Buried now, surely.

"Have you forgotten?" the stonemason asked.

No. And he never would; but that Oconor's ill feeling toward

33

him should lead to the destruction of a town was still incredible.

"Don Hugo Oconor has other things to think about," Antonio said, "in his present high office. I learned from the courier who brought the *reglamento* that he is away fighting the Apaches. They have a terror of his red beard, it seems."

"He had nothing to do with this order, you think?" Rojas insisted. His name was signed to the paper. Antonio could still see it. "Nothing was said about you and the ranch?"

"Why would I urge you to come there to live in that case?" Antonio asked.

"Good! Then let things remain that way. If Oconor has forgotten you, we would not want to attract his attention by hiding on your land. That might create a situation. Well, I must get back to my chicken cages. Antonio, if you still want to help the house of Rojas, you might lend a mule or two, if you have some to spare after the *Teniente* takes what he wants for moving those old guns at the fort. Mama Rojas declares every chicken will be taken except those that go into the pot this week. Now, there is an inspiration. If there should be a wedding feast, Esteban, let me know. It will mean one or two crates less for me to build."

But, as he walked away, there was a new heaviness in his step; and he and Tomás found nothing to say to each other.

CHAPTER 3

"Will you look at Cecilio's house now?" Esteban Andorro asked Antonio, after Coronal and Rojas had taken their leave. "I will go with you. It is not far."

Around the elbow of one street, then another, and they were again at the edge of town, this time near the little river. Cecilio had had to clear away trees before he could build. So far he had cleared only enough land to make room for the house and a small yard. The rest, he had thought, could come later.

It was a small house, modest enough; but skill and care and a young man's fancies had gone into the building. The adobe walls, not whitewashed as yet, but dried to a pale tan, hard as if baked in a kiln, were well lined up and met exactly, making smooth corners. The roof of tile had a good slope, to carry off rain; and it reached out beyond the house so as to spill the water where it would do no harm. The door was the fancy part. The step before it was a slab of rock, dragged with labor from the river, then chiseled to size and smoothed, to wait for the polish that feet would give it over the years. Above the door was another small piece of roof, so that one could stand there and look out in any weather. The door itself was painted blue, the blue of the sky. It had at eye level a peephole, and its lock plate was of brass, which had been polished that morning and would require frequent polishing if it was to continue to shine as it did now. That was not likely to be its history.

"He did it all himself," Esteban said, "except the step. Rojas set that for him."

Antonio nodded. If he added words, he could not afterwards have said what they were. Because it was as he stood before this house, with no occupant as yet, that he knew how Los Adaes would look after it had died.

This evening, tomorrow at the latest, Cecilio would bring home his bride. They would not come alone. A long procession would accompany them—Teresa's sisters and brothers, the parents of both, cousins, uncles, aunts. Hardly anyone Cecilio's and Teresa's age now in the town would be related to fewer than a dozen families. Fray Josef would lead the procession, halting it at the door while he blessed the house. After that there would be feasting and jesting and laughter. Even now there would be that. The house would overflow with people. It would be hours—too long—before Cecilio pushed the last joker out and barred the door. He would turn then to Teresa, waiting. Would she be shy or eager, a little afraid but not unwilling? However she seemed, Cecilio would gather her to him. If there were candles burning, they would be doused. Darkness would enfold the house and the lovers.

"It will be only a few days for them here," Esteban said, "but they will remember them always."

A few days. While they lasted, these two would, like children, cover a lifetime in pretending, paying no heed to time as it was. Until the last morning dawned. Then, carrying whatever they could save—Cecilio would have taken care of his tool chest the day before—they would go to join a procession of another sort in the street. Many, leaving their homes so, would not bother to close the door behind them. Cecilio, Antonio thought, would close his and pocket the key.

Days would pass. Weeks, months. The empty house could not defend itself. Before a year had gone by, the paint on the door would fade and begin to flake off. Weeds would hide the stone step. Some would have climbed the walls. Vermin, reptiles would use the vines for ladders and enter by way of the high windows. A wind might loosen a roof tile or several. Older houses, not so sturdily built, would have begun to sink into a heap; but Cecilio's house, though slower to decay, would be just as dead. That was how a town could die, crumble, and rot.

Antonio turned to his friend.

"My felicitations to you, Esteban, on your son. He is a man."

The carpenter's face shone.

"Yes, I think so," he said. "Will you come to see him wed, Antonio?"

"Am I invited?"

"You and all your house. We have neglected this morning to express our regard for your gracious lady. Your mother also, and your son. How old is Anastacio now?"

"Twelve, almost thirteen."

"A fine boy, I am told. Bring them all. You will hear in time."

The carpenter walked away on uneven legs, and Antonio rode Fatima back toward the center of the town, because that was his best way to the *Camino Real* and home. He was more sure than ever that people were watching him pass, but he hoped none would come out into the street to stop him. He had seen enough. His heart was as heavy as Cecilio's doorstep. But, when a metal boot hanging from a bracket before the door of a shop dwelling creaked in the wind, he halted. Inside the shop he could hear muttering and scraping. He dismounted, threw Fatima's reins over her head, gave her a command, and went up to the door. Again he listened a minute, then knocked and entered.

A gnomelike man, his face like a piece of the leather he handled, freed bowed legs from a cobbler's bench and bent double.

"*Mi* Señor—Don Antonio," he said obsequiously, almost worshipfully, "I was not looking to see you here today. Is it boots? Before I leave? There is little time, but I will see what I can do."

"I have not come about boots today," Antonio told him. "I was in town and passed, and thought I would see how you were getting along with your preparations."

"Preparations, Don Antonio?" The cobbler made a despairing gesture.

"At least, you are at work."

"Work, Señor? It is nothing—slippers for Teresa García. I had them begun. I can finish them easily, even if the wedding is today. It is not really work, just something to busy my hands. I think better so. I must think . . . but here is so much. You see how it is?"

The shop was a litter of leather scraps and cuttings, bottles and jars of oil, stains and ointments. Bundles of hides filled the corners. Bundles of lacings hung from nails on the walls. Forms for boots and other patterns were everywhere, and, in the midst of the confusion, the little shoemaker, bowed, old—but then, Zapatero had looked the same for as far back as Antonio could remember.

"My friend," Antonio said, "this journey is not for you."

Zapatero would shrivel and blow away. He could not survive. But now he straightened his back and stared at Antonio in amazement.

"I mean it," Antonio said. "Look. I will go home. I will send a strong young man with a wagon. He will load everything here on the wagon—you, too. You will not need to go to San Antonio de Bexar. You will come to Lobanillo, instead. I will give you a house in the pueblo."

"Don Antonio, you know I cannot do that. Fray Josef said . . ."

"Ah, what does the priest know? Why can you not do as I say?"

The shoemaker turned away to look at a bit of parchment on one wall—a frayed old document, but with the brightness of gold

37

in one corner. His back straightened a little more.

"I have my license as bootmaker from the King," he said, "as my father had before me. I was brought here to make boots for the soldiers at the fort. I must go now where the King orders."

"The King," Antonio objected, "has forgotten that you exist, if he ever knew."

"Still," the cobbler insisted, "he is the King and I am a King's man. It is as Fray Josef said. We have no choice but to go where we are sent. My only trouble is in the thinking. Fray Josef said we must think what is most necessary of our possessions that can be carried. For me it is a little of this, a little of that, the license naturally . . ."

"Your bench?" Antonio prompted.

Pride crumbled some at that.

"I would want that most of all, Señor. It is old, but it fits me. Only it is too heavy."

"Too heavy for you," Antonio agreed, "but not for a mule. If you must attempt the journey, I will provide you with a mule; but I still think you would do better to settle at the ranch. Otherwise, what are we to do at Lobanillo for shoes? Must I come to Bexar when I need boots?"

Zapatero's wrinkled face brightened and softened.

"Now that is more like my Señor. Shall we see you, then, at Bexar?"

"I go there frequently on business," Antonio reminded him.

Not too frequently. He had been there once since the new governor had taken office, the one who had seemed, until now, all benevolence compared to Oconor. Zapatero, however, did not question the truth of "frequently." He clasped his hands, his smile widened, and suddenly he burst into speech.

"Don Antonio, go with us now. You know the way. You know the city. We lack a guide, a leader. We are all so afraid. . . ."

What was this?

"Come, come," Antonio said. "Surely you know that is not possible. I am not wanted and I am not needed. The road is clear. There is only one road. And the Governor's instructions named your leaders. *Teniente* Gonzales and the soldiers from the fort will head the march. They will give you protection if the necessity should arise. Flores, too, will be there."

"Don Antonio, you think the soldiers will keep good watch over us?"

Twenty soldiers to more than a thousand people? The garrison of a neglected fort? Gathered originally from the streets and the huts of the poor? No.

"The *Teniente*," Antonio said, "is a strict officer. He will keep the soldiers to their duties."

"The *Teniente* grows old, too, now," the cobbler said. "He was young when he came here, but that was a long time ago. I remember . . ."

So did Antonio remember—or he thought he remembered— José Gonzales as he had first seen him. Thirty years ago it must have been, and Antonio was a boy of five or even less; but the picture was still quite clear. It was of a young officer—Gonzales had the rank of ensign then—slender, erect, proud, on a dark horse, fine leather boots on his feet, silver buttons on his coat, silver lace on his dress hat, a sword with a silver hilt at his side. The sword flashed to emphasize a command, given in a high, ringing tone. There was a companion picture—a beautiful young Señora with snapping black eyes watching, and a baby in long, lacy robes, a nurse for the baby, a maid for the Señora.

Now the proud young officer was an old man, not as old as Zapatero, but older than Esteban Andorro, old enough to have been the father of a man like Antonio; and he was more certain of annihilation than anyone else on the march. That, too, had been made clear in the Governor's orders. After the soldiers from Los Adaes arrived at Bexar, those who were fit for further duty would be added to the garrison there, the rest would be discharged. José Gonzales would, without doubt, be the first to go.

"The *Teniente*," Antonio said now to Zapatero, "is, to be sure, no longer young, but he is also a King's man and very brave. All of Spain's soldiers are brave, no matter what else they may or may not be. I will give Gonzales a statement, saying that a certain mule is for you. It is to be loaded only with your supplies, including the bench; and you alone are to ride on it when you are tired. I will say the same to the *Alcalde*."

I will do this, I will do that, his conscience clamored as he

39

took his leave. I will do all in my power to make this journey of banishment easier for these poor unfortunates—all but what this one asks. That is an absurdity, not to be taken seriously. Through the door, as he closed it behind him, he could feel the eyes of the shoemaker following him. Inside the shop there was now no muttering, no scraping of leather. His hand left the latch reluctantly. He mounted Fatima slowly, stiffly, like an old man, but headed her with determination toward the square. He would see no one else now, talk to no one. What did it profit to talk?

He hurried Fatima forward. The hour was now close to noon, and the town was coming more and more to life. Not as briskly as on a happier day, but still a rhythmic sound hung on the air. It was the muted slap-slap of women in yards and courts making the day's tortillas. In any case, one ate. In the square, as he entered, there was even a man before the *Casa Real*, reading or rereading the *proclama*. *Dios!* If there was one more than any other on whom he wished to waste no time—he backed Fatima, meaning to ride around the square; but he was too late. The man had heard Fatima's jingle, and turned.

" 'Tonio!" he screeched, his voice high and thin, the magnified squeaking of a bat hunting. " 'Tonio, come here!"

There was no escaping the fellow. Had Antonio tried, he would have been pursued by the screeching, which would have called everybody out into the open, to see what the alarm was about. Scowling, he rode over to the *casa*.

" 'Tonio, have you read this document?"

"No," Antonio said shortly. "I know what it says without reading."

In his breast dislike coiled warily. He could not control the feeling. Most people disliked Hernando Calles. Poor Hernando, some would say, but all would avoid him as they might a piece of poisonous carrion. He was ugly in a blighting and blighted way—a scrawny man, with round shoulders and back above long, thin legs, and a vulture's head mounted on a long, thin neck. He had staring, protruding eyes and a sharp, inquisitive nose—and the curiosity of ten women.

He was a clerk, when he found work to do, which was not too often, though he was an excellent copyist. Don Mathieu Ibarbo,

Antonio's father, had employed him whenever he had more writing than he could do himself. That was how Antonio had come to know Hernando. The picture of him bent over a table, his sharp nose seeming not to follow but to direct his skinny hand as it set down words on paper, had been to the boy Antonio one more warning against too much literacy.

Even good, scholarly Don Mathieu Ibarbo, though he pitied the fellow, had not liked him or trusted him wholly. He had been careful in choosing the documents he gave Hernando to copy. That others shared this feeling was demonstrated when the capital was moved. All the other minor officials and clerks connected with the business of government had left Los Adaes at that time, but Hernando was not among the chosen. Things had gone badly for him after the death of Mathieu Ibarbo, and were now worse than ever. How he lived Antonio could not begin to guess. His coat today was torn in the rear above the tails and patched crudely in several other places. He was starvation-thin. But, in his misguided way, he was cheerful.

"Only consider how things happen," he said in his bat squeak. "I have been looking for a way to reach the capital. I should have gone long before this if I had been able."

"Why were you not able?" Antonio asked coldly.

"Alone?" Hernando said. "Without even a horse to ride? It would not have been safe. But now opportunity is here. You do agree with me, I hope, that I will find work in San Antonio de Bexar. Where there is government, there are always documents. And Bexar being so much nearer the capital city of Mexico, with people coming and going, also the government post . . ."

And six clerks to every one Hernando had known in Los Adaes, fighting among themselves for enough work to provide them with food and shelter. Governor Ripperdá might even have brought his own copyist from Spain. Seldom did a new appointee sail for the provinces without at least one or two relatives holding fast to his coat. That ruling which Antonio had studied in the presidio the day before had had beautiful writing on it. On the other hand, it might have been copied in the City of Mexico. There might not be that many clerks in Bexar. To be able to write intelligibly and handsomely was an accomplishment.

41

"I wish you good luck," he said finally, "but you will have to look sharp."

With a pressure of his knee, he suggested to a willing Fatima that they move on. But he was not to be rid of Calles so easily.

"Don Antonio!" the screeching cry, more obsequious now, pursued him. "Could you give me a letter of recommendation? You know . . ."

"Have you lost the one my father wrote for you?" Antonio asked, turning Fatima halfway around. "In San Antonio de Bexar, one Ibarbo will do as well as another."

Again he would have ridden on, but he could not. A few words on paper, chosen cautiously—what harm could that do? Poor Hernando . . .

"I will write you a letter," he said, unwillingly, "later—at Lobanillo. I will send it to town by Flores or the *Teniente*. Tomorrow or the day after. *Adiós!*"

He thought surely then that escape was in his hand. Fatima jingled merrily acros the square, only to be pulled up a few yards short of the opening of the little road that led to the *Camino Real*. Two women coming from yet another street off the plaza stood in the way. Rather, a woman and a girl. Antonio knew them at once and they him just as instantly. The woman was Rosario Terrero, the girl the ganddaughter of *Teniente* Gonzales.

Rosario, ample of bosom and wide of hip, could have blocked almost any path if she chose to do so. When Antonio stopped, she did the same and stood, arms akimbo, making her even wider than she was naturally. Her face, round, smooth as a girl's, in spite of her age and the many children she had borne, generally amiable, clouded over with mistrust. What are you up to, Ibarbo?

Rosario, alas, was one of those who remembered Antonio too well as a boy, no more mischievous, though perhaps more inventive, than any other, but one who, from breeding and training, might have been expected to do better. When finally, and mostly by his own will, he had done better, the feeling persisted that he would still bear watching.

The herb woman's attitude today, of course, was emphasized because of the girl, toward whom Antonio had no evil design.

His one thought when he saw her had been, "This thing has fallen on you, too, Niña?"

She was, naturally, everything that Rosario was not. They were dressed in the same style—white blouses, cut low, a wide ruffle around the neck falling over bare arms for all the sleeves there were, full skirts of gaily printed calico, and light *rebozos* ready to shelter their heads from sun or wind. They also wore thong sandals over bare feet; but there the similarity ended. Two of the girl's footprints could have been obliterated by one of Rosario's. Her blouse was of finer cotton, the ruffle exquisitely embroidered; her skirt was a blending of soft blue with green vines and white flowers, as opposed to Rosario's black, splashed with every color; and her *rebozo* was also blue, where Rosario's was a flaming red. She was as slender as the stem of a flower and equally graceful, her face as fair as a flower, her hair dark, smooth, still worn in two childish braids.

Out of respect, and only a little with a wish to torment Rosario further, Antonio dismounted, and removed his hat with a flourish.

"Angelita!" he said. "It has been a time . . . you do not know me? I . . ."

If the exquisite face had a fault, it was that it was too serious, too soberly thoughtful for one so young. That was not just because of the present. It was always so. She did not smile now, but she did brighten.

"Surely I remember you, Señor Ibarbo."

Surely; but her eyes, like Pedro Coronal's, were on Fatima.

"You know the horse," Antonio accused. "Next time I come to town I will ride a mule." Rosario snorted, and the girl again almost smiled. "Angelita, you have grown since I saw you last."

"Surely," she answered. "I am now fifteen."

Fifteen—had it been fifteen years since a Tejas Indian, one of Fray Josef's unrecorded converts, had summoned the priest to a village of his people, saying a Spanish woman was dying there and would give no name but that of Fray Josef? Could it possibly have been that long since Garza had returned from the journey to place a baby in the empty arms of Señora Gonzales, telling her that it was the child of her daughter, that the daughter was the woman he had found at the point of death when he reached the Indian village? There had been time only for him to know her and her to know him and receive his blessing and interceding prayers.

The Señora, hardly realizing what she had in her arms, had held the baby, but numbly. Dry-eyed, those who stood by reported, she having no more tears to shed.

One had to hope that Garza was mistaken, that the poor dead woman had not been Ángela Gonzales—pretty Ángela, who had lived only a small piece of a lifetime. Ángela, who had been the baby in the long, lacy robe of Antonio's remembering. Ángela of the soft, dark hair and shy, sweet smile, who sang like an angel even in the games of childhood. Ángela, the only girl in Los Adaes to whom Antonio in his youth had ever given a second look. She was very young at the time and he not much older; but he was old enough to place himself with a self-conscious swagger among other young men, who each evening gathered beside the little river at the hour of the *paseo*, to watch the girls parade in the square. If he waited for a shy glance from a particular one in return, and if she gave him that look, why, at the time that was all there was to it.

But *Teniente* Gonzales, risen in rank by then and already in command of the fort, though under the titular authority of the resident governor, and his Señora had taken fright. They were justifiably proud of their charming daughter and had other ideas of a future for her. They would not have considered any young man of the town a suitable match. Finally, to keep her from forming such an attachment, they had taken her to San Juan Bautista near the Rio Grande and placed her in a convent school. They took her themselves and came away with the shadow of loneliness already hanging over them. She had cried so, begging not to be left!

What happened afterwards was never too clear, but this was the story as the nuns told it—twice: once, when Ángela disappeared from the school, and again at the time of her death. There was a man, it seemed, a foreigner, *inglés*, they thought, though he spoke Spanish. The survivor of a shipwreck, he said.

He came to the convent as a peddler, his pack artfully stocked with treasures dear to young girls—combs, jeweled pins, strings of beads, bright ribbons. The mother superior at first had said no to his request for permission to enter the convent area; but he spoke fairly and respectfully, and two sisters, young enough to remember the world they had abandoned, had interceded. The girls, some at least, they pleaded, were homesick. The excitement of examining the peddler's wares, of buying some trifle, would give them something to chatter about for days. The mother superior, to her everlasting sorrow, had consented then to let the man in.

Not into the convent itself, naturally. He opened his pack in the garden. The girls were all there, much excited, and the guardian nuns equally so. Each girl selected an object to buy, nothing too valuable, except, possibly, the choice made by Ángela Gonzales—a bit of jade on a thin silver chain. The incident would hardly have been noticed except for what followed, and for the fact that at the time the mother superior had again objected. She said Ángela must choose something more nearly equal to what the other girls had bought. At this the peddler intervened. Respectfully, not boldly, he assured the mother that the jade was not valuable. Look! It was a scrap, broken accidentally, he thought, from its matrix. A pretty piece of stone, no more.

It was true, the edges were rough. Only the color, here translucent, here opaque, made it seem precious. Ángela had picked it out at once from the surrounding baubles. Now she spread the chain over her hands, so that the jade swung a little, and turned her pretty face to the mother superior with such appeal that a marble statue would have been softened.

"Reverend Mother," she begged, "may I have it?"

And the mother superior, knowing perhaps that if she were in error the real fault lay in her allowing the peddler into the grounds, yielded. The peddler, laughing, as if at a charming child, which Ángela was, took the chain from her and dropped it and the pendant over her head.

"And now," the mother superior said, "I think you had better go."

He left at once, making no objection, polite, respectful to the

45

last, not even turning back to look at the pretty girl to whom he had in effect given the piece of jade. If he had looked back he would not have seen Ángela. At a gesture of command from the mother superior, the sisters had led the girls away.

That was the last anyone at the convent saw of the peddler. In the weeks that followed his visit, nobody not a guardian or otherwise closely related was allowed to enter the place. At work or play the girls were never without a sister or two watching their movements. None could walk in the garden alone. They must go by twos and always with a sister in attendance. That was how it was on the day that Ángela disappeared. She had gone to walk in the garden with a close friend and a young nun, one who shared the girls' interest in flowers. Ángela in particular had a way with flowers. She had only to pat the earth about a plant to make it grow and bloom. Today, however, it was a strange butterfly that caught and held the girls' attention. They followed it in flight from bush to bush.

"If I only had a net," the sister fretted. "We could capture it and add it to the school's collection. We could name it. Wait! Wait here! Do not move—except, of course, to follow the butterfly."

They were at the end of the garden nearest the convent kitchen. The sister went to the door to send someone after a butterfly net. She wasn't away as long as five minutes; but when she turned back to the garden, only one girl kept vigil over the butterfly. Ángela Gonzales had vanished.

Even her friend and confidante was not aware that she had gone until the sister cried out to ask what had become of her. The girl, intent on watching the butterfly, had heard nothing, seen no one. No one? A man, perhaps, looking over the wall? Nobody, she declared, in storms of tears, as the questioning went on.

But there must have been someone. There must have been a plan. There must have been communication. No, no, no, Ángela's friend declared. At least, she had been told nothing. And that was all anybody really knew of how Ángela had left the garden. Poorly equipped to invent a scoundrel's plotting the mother superior had sought help from outside, but to no avail. The school was closed, the girls were sent home. The nuns were taken away to discipline at a mother house; but all that did not uncover the whereabouts of Ángela or her abductor.

"It was the *inglés*," the mother superior insisted. "It could have been no other."

But, when a search was made, nobody for miles around recalled having seen a man answering the description of the peddler, with or without a companion. It was too easy in the provinces to escape from settled country into wilderness. Poor, dear Ángela! It was hoped that somehow the two had taken ship and sailed away; but a year later, when Fray Josef was called to minister to the dying woman in the Indian village, that hope was denied. Garza did not think in advance to connect that woman with Ángela Gonzales. So he went alone. Nobody knew he was going until he came back with the baby.

"Ángela? You are sure it was Ángela?" Señora Gonzales said, wanting and yet not wanting to believe.

Garza was sure, or said so, though there were always those who wondered. He knew how the Gonzales' family had grieved and would grieve unto death if something did not come to fill their empty lives. So he had brought the child, saying it was theirs; but there was no proof. Where, for example, was that piece of jade, for which Ángela was said to have sold herself?

The Gonzaleses chose to believe the priest. They took the child without question into their desolate home. They idolized her, but so did everyone else in town. Angelita, the grandparents named her, little Ángela. Rosario Terrero was called in as a nurse—Rosario, of all people—because she had a mother's milk to give. Also a breast overflowing with compassion. From the first Rosario loved the child with that ferocity which Antonio today had observed in its mildest form, a possessiveness which could hardly have been the wish of the grandparents when they engaged her as a nurse. But Angelita lived, and for that they had to accept Rosario's share in her guardianship.

Angelita was five when Antonio first saw her. Life in the meantime had changed for him even more than for the Gonzaleses. Antonio no longer lived in the town. He had established himself on a ranch near the *Camino Real* farther west. He had a license to trade. He had married well and happily, and the prosperity which made him now the richest and most influential man of the surrounding area was already beginning to show. The latest stroke of good fortune had been a contract to purchase supplies for the Presidio of Los Adaes, offered him by the Governor then residing in the *Casa Real* in the town.

Offered? Antonio could not refuse and never had any intention of doing so. The contract opened avenues of trade that might otherwise have remained closed to him. As it happened, this very contract was the one that later almost ruined him. At the time, however, most significant was the fact that he would now be meeting *Teniente* Gonzales regularly and in an entirely new relationship.

Their first meeting was stiffly formal, the second less so. *Teniente* Gonzales showed in his face what he had endured in the year of his daughter's disappearance and death. He held himself as rigidly erect as ever, he performed his soldier's duties punctiliously; but his eyes were sunk deep in his head and his hair was frosted with gray. He was already an old man. Antonio, blessed with every good fortune, had to pity him. He and the aging officer had never been friends, but now with each encounter a mutual respect grew.

Señora Gonzales was another story.

The Presidio of Los Adaes stood on an eminence beside the same little river that flowed downhill, across the *Camino Real*, and on through the town. Opposite the fort, on the other side of the river, was the Mission of San Miguel. A narrow footbridge connected the two. Riding out of the fort one day after an accounting with the *Teniente*, and feeling in good spirits—supplying the fort was proving profitable—Antonio saw Señora Gonzales and the child, accompanied by a servant, coming from the mission toward the bridge. They were still far enough away for him to have ridden on down the hill, appearing not to have seen them; but, on impulse, he dismounted, threw the reins over his horse's head, and walked across the bridge to speak to them.

What he said to the Señora or what she replied was of no consequence. She, too, bore marks from her time of sorrow. Her eyes alone kept their fire. They blazed at Antonio. It made no difference to her how he had improved himself. She might even in some dark way have transferred to him the blame for the grief she had endured. She stood where she was, neither refusing nor accepting the amenities he tried to offer.

Antonio was not moved to pity the Señora. Nor did he feel disposed to retreat in disorder. He turned to the child. She raised her eyes shyly when he spoke to her—and stabbed him to the heart. It was not that she resembled Ángela. Her dark eyes and her dark hair could have come from the one said to be her mother, but that was all. Ángela had been a pretty girl; this one was exquisite, as fair and perfect as a piece of rare porcelain. Antonio could see now why some people in the town said she was not the child of any human woman, that the priest had found her under a bush and brought her to the Gonzaleses, making up a story to fit the situation.

Antonio, of course, believed no such thing. What, then, was the explanation? The Englishman? For the first time that part of the story seemed to Antonio halfway credible. An English father would account for that look of rarity. A difference in the shape of the small face, a delicacy, a near transparency in the complexion. She was not fair in the rose-and-white tradition of Northern people. Her skin was really pale ivory and would probably darken as she grew older—if she grew older in Texas; but there was that fineness of texture—well, *transparency* was his word for it.

Then another quality claimed Antonio's attention. He called it sadness. It was as if the sorrow of her story had marked the child, too. Well, naturally, if she must live with those two sad, older people, she would be like that. Ángela, the poor little mother, had been a merry girl, with laughter always ready. This child looked as if she had never laughed, and Antonio was seized with a desire to win a smile from her. With that in mind, he gave her a present. He had usually on his person some trinket calculated to please a child or an Indian squaw—anyone whose favor seemed worth having. On this occasion he produced a small mirror in a cheap frame. The child almost did smile, but not quite. Her eyes brightened and color warmed her cheeks. She showed the mirror to her grandmother.

"*Mi abuela*, see?"

"I see, little one. Would you like to give it to the altar in the church?"

Sure enough, the following Sunday, the mirror flashed prominently among other offerings of tinsel on the altar. Antonio, in a small huff, could laugh at himself presently, saying it was nothing to him, which was true; but no one could help being sorry for the child. Each year gave some fulfillment to the first promise of rare beauty and, at the same time, produced new evidence of a disposition so naturally gentle and virtuous that her guardians' one concern should have been to make her happy. But happiness, possibly, was the one thing they could not give her.

And now? If the girl's life had been shadowed before, it could hardly find new or brighter prospects in the immediate future. José Gonzales would march his garrison to Bexar and receive his discharge. What then? The Señora would not accompany him on the journey. She could not. Her health had failed lately. Dropsy, he had heard. And, if she did not go, the girl also must be left behind. But . . .

He yearned to ask Angelita what plans had been made, but naturally did not. Instead, he satisfied a lesser curiosity. Angelita had under one arm a round, deep, woven basket with handles. It looked purposeful.

"What are you planning to pack in that?" he asked. The answer might tell him what he wanted to know.

Rosario snorted again, and Angelita spoke quickly to cover the rudeness.

"We mean to dig up a rose," she said, "and plant it for Teresa García in her new home."

But the basket? Antonio turned back to Rosario. She lifted her shoulders in a magnificent shrug and said nothing.

"With the basket," Angelita explained, "she can, if she wishes, carry the rose with her to Bexar. Does that not seem possible to you?"

"For myself, I would not attempt it," Antonio said gravely. "For you, a rose should flourish under any and all circumstances. Little Teresa will be enchanted."

If his scowl had been dark when he rode toward the town, it was thunderous as he rode away. A town was now not just people. It included some who were very special.

CHAPTER 4

Lobanillo—that was to say, a small lump, meaning, in the sense of geography, a low, rounded hill. That was how Antonio Ibarbo spoke of his ranch when he first became a man of property. "It is on one of those little hills beside Lobanillo Creek." Rancho Lobanillo it had been called from that time; and from then on its rolling green acres had held all of his life's achievement and much of his heart.

In the beginning his holding had been small—only the one hill and a strip of land between it and the creek; but he had gotten it cheaply, there being always more land in the province than there were people to occupy it. All he had needed to secure a piece for himself was certain recommendations, such as character, place of birth, and, most important, good parentage.

His parentage, as it happened, was of the best. His father and his mother came from Andalusia. They were not of the nobility, even the small nobility, but neither were they peasants. His mother was convent-taught and his father all but a scholar. Antonio's tale to Pedro Coronal of his father's learning was no exaggeration. The hours could not be counted which he had spent, sitting quietly on a chair or lying on his stomach on the floor, stroking the cat, while Don Mathieu read endlessly from books about ancient heroes and one, more recent, whose story was the longest of all—a madman from La Mancha in Spain, named Don Quixote.

In Spain in Don Mathieu Ibarbo's day, however, a man could have all the learning there was in books and other accomplishments, besides, such as the ability to write exquisitely on parchment or paper, and still be very poor. Don Mathieu in Spain had been threadbare poor, so poor that he could not have won himself a wife had he not, through being able to read, learned of a bounty offered by the King to subjects willing to make their homes in Spanish America. With this promise of fortune he did win a wife, and together they took ship for Mexico.

Fortune continued to smile on them. From Mexico they were sent to the frontier capital of Texas and given a bit of land there and assistance in building a house. Don Mathieu found employment as a clerk and notary, and Doña Isabella's skill with the needle was still a legend in Los Adaes.

They must have prospered. Antonio could not remember ever being hungry. There was always a woman servant in the house, and a man outside to till the Ibarbo field and bring in the corn and the wood for fires. These servants, Esperanza and Tío Paco, now lived at Lobanillo. And yet, looking back, Antonio knew that his father had been homesick for Spain, poor as his life there had been. That, plus too much poring over books and papers, could have caused his early death.

At the time Antonio was what most people had thought him, a coltish youth, more interested in the talk and barter and gaming of the market place than in home or books. For learning, he could calculate swiftly in terms of pesos, he knew how to speak a little of three Indian dialects and some trading French, how to arrange a pack and fasten it to the back of a mule, and how to tell a good, young horse from one old and wind-broken. He could ride any animal he could catch—like an Apache, said the traders, who would toss him coins for an exhibition.

This haphazard living, however, ended when his father died. Grieved and shocked, he rode off that year with a caravan, going as far as El Paso del Norte. He went out as an *arriero*, hired to guard the *caballard* of extra mules and oxen and horses at the tail of the caravan. He came back riding just behind the leaders, mounted on a fine bay horse, followed by a boy leading three others, Antonio's to keep or to trade, as he chose. His mark was cut into the buffalo-hide wrappings on two bars of silver. For possessing that much of the King's treasure unlawfully, for delivering it later to the representative of a powerful merchant in

New Orleans, and for receiving in exchange money and credit that were a fair foundation for a fortune, he could have been thrown into prison if he had been apprehended; but arrest on a charge of dealing in contraband was reserved for a later day, when Antonio was rich enough and wise enough not to take such obvious risks.

But his greatest gain from that first long ride was a clear image of what he meant to make of himself in life. In the far west he had seen, wherever there was a town or trading post, that certain men lived apart on their own haciendas with their own flocks and herds, with pueblos for those who did work on the land. Go-betweens in trade and government, they lived richly and well. He would be one of those—in east Texas.

So, a few years later came Rancho Lobanillo. The King's grant in his hand was only the beginning. He bought stock—sheep, cows, horses—shrewdly. He peopled his pueblo just as carefully. He lived in a shed until he could build the kind of house he wanted, meaning then to go in search of a suitable wife. As it happened, the wife came before the house was built; but that was accidental. To make these gains, he kept his license as a trader. He traded with the Indians—Tejas—and, to the west, half-breed Comancheros. He established connections with Natchitoches and New Orleans through a shrewd agent on the lower Mississippi, an honest, reliable man, not the stealthy one who had taken the bars of silver. Westward, some of his ventures touched distant Baja California, though he never again rode the long, dusty trail with a caravan. For that he engaged others. By the time he was thirty, he had attained the eminence he had chosen for himself. Lord of his own domain, blessed with a superior wife and a promising young son, he was respected generally. Although not revered as his father had been, he was much more important.

Don Antonio Gil Ibarbo of Rancho Lobanillo never returned from a journey, long or short, to the small, rounded hill where his house stood, without experiencing anew the first thrill of possession. So it was today. The midday sun warmed the crimson roof tiles of his house and mellowed the walls of adobe and stone. Flowering vines threw masses of purple and scarlet bloom over the fretted ironwork topping the garden wall. In a fenced-in pasture not far from the house, silky-maned mares stood in deep green grass with their colts. On another, wilder slope, cattle grazed among trees. In a fold of land where Lobanillo Creek now wound through his acres, a cluster of small houses was his pueblo. Smoke rose from a dozen chimneys. Dinner was in preparation everywhere. Somewhere in the distance a dog barked, and a sheep's bell tinkled. It was all so beautiful, so serene—his house, his land. But . . . his property or the King's? Suppose . . .

He would not suppose. He was tired—not physically, but otherwise. Burdened with melancholy borrowed from the town. But he would not have it that way. He would not take that with him into his house. He shook off the mood to an extent and rode on to the courtyard gate.

A man, brown and wrinkled as a dried fig, opened for him. "*Ai-ee*, Don Antonio!"

There was affection, pleasure and a hint of ownership in the greeting. That came of keeping on as a servant one who had fished his young master more than once out of the Adaes River, and had dried him then at his own fireside, hiding him until Esperanza, his wife, came with dry clothing from the master's house.

"Tío Paco!" Antonio said in surprise. "You in charge again? Where is that big grandson of yours, Manuel Piedra?"

"He went with Magdalena to town this morning. You did not see them?"

Magdalena was Paco and Esperanza's daughter, one of several. Married, with a family of her own, she lived in the pueblo and regularly did the cooking for the main house. No, Antonio had not seen her or young Manuel.

"There were too many others," he explained. "Surely any son or daughter of yours, if in need of help, will come to me for it. Is that Esperanza in the kitchen?"

"Yes. Can you not hear? Mostly she is glad when Magdalena is away and she can rule the kitchen to suit herself. Today, excuse her, please. She is in great anxiety—about Magdalena, because of that tramp Juan Piedra. You know?"

Well enough. Not a tramp. Easygoing to excess, perhaps. Not a good provider, liking hunting and fishing better than steady work, Magdalena's husband much preferred life in town to the seclusion of the ranch, but was smart enough to know the advantage of having his family not dependent on his care. That was the worst one could say of him.

"When has Esperanza not been anxious about Juan?" Antonio said. "Well, will you take Fatima now, or shall I ride over to the stable?"

In the kitchen there was a loud clanging of iron against iron. With Esperanza that could lead to something.

"I will take Fatima," Tío Paco said, "and come back quickly." Then, with his hand on the rein as Antonio dismounted, his eyes were imploring. "How was it in the town, young master?"

"Not good," Antonio told him, "but not as bad as I expected. Very quiet. What lies under that it is hard to know." Mutiny? He thought not. The habit of acceptance was too strong. "This is a cruel thing that has befallen our friends, Tío Paco. Well! The ladies, I suppose, are at home."

"Yes, Don Antonio. Both the Señoras. The boy, too, since there are now no lessons. We wait only for you."

The gate of fretted iron swung to behind Antonio. A mighty *potpourri* of fragrance smote his senses—kitchen seasoning and the attar of every sort of flower—all roses to him, but beautiful, because they were the special delight of his beloved. Color smote his eyes—so much color that a hummingbird, hovering over a choice of nectar, added only a shimmer of light to the display. Melancholy, sadness withdrew on the breath of a sigh. Antonio took off his hat, smoothed his hair with his hand, and crossed the court to a flight of steps leading to the door of the house. As he approached, he heard voices inside—two women speaking gravely, one voice deeper than the other, or was it that the other was just lighter? Then came a boy's tumbling rush of speech—his son. Antonio drew another deep breath, stretched his back, and opened the door.

CHAPTER 5

"The *olla* is excellent, Esperanza. Everything is of the best. The *roscas*, all."

Doña María Ibarbo spoke soothingly, wishing to smooth with compliments the ruffled feathers of the best of all cooks. But who could soothe Esperanza when she was brewing a storm?

"The *roscas*," she said, "were hard. The crust baked too deep while we waited for this one to return. He was late—again. All his life he has been like that. Something occurs for which he must take a little more time. Then, home at last, he must wash and change his shirt."

Her hand, brown, wrinkled, and rough, plucked at the silk collar of the garment in question. Antonio looked across the laden table into the eyes of his lady. That, after fourteen years, this look should be still like a draught of rich, sweet wine, so quietly fond, so understanding! "See how she depends on you," Doña María's eyes said. "She is frightened, poor thing." "I know," Antonio answered with his eyes, "I know." On his right, Doña Isabella, his mother, also looked at him with love, but with anxiety as well, not too different from that of Esperanza; while on the left, the boy Anastacio watched and waited, divided between amusement and shock over Esperanza's disrespect for a man so justly an autocrat as his father.

"Esperanza," Doña María said, after a minute of this, "your *roscas* are our favorite bread. See how many we have eaten. Return to the kitchen now and give Tío Paco his dinner. You can clear away later."

Esperanza snatched her hand away and shuffled toward the door, then turned back, distress compelling her.

"Do you know what that fool Juan Piedra said early this morning?" she demanded. "He said, 'If my friends go to Bexar, so will I!' That's what he said."

"Let me answer this time," Antonio commanded his lady.

"What Juan Piedra says loudly," he reminded Esperanza, "is not always what he does. I will speak to him, however, when I see him."

Esperanza went away, muttering; but, when that had passed beyond hearing, the thing which Antonio had wished might not enter his house was there in the bright room.

"Antonio," Doña Isabella said, "how was it in the town?"

Doña Isabella, his gracious mother, shrunken a little from Antonio's young picture of her, sitting in some place of light with her stitching, bent a little now from continued activity with the needle, but wearing her widow's black with pride of person and the dignity of increasing years, sorrowed by her bereavement but thanking God every day for this man, her son. If only his father could have lived to see him as he was now! A mother's foolishness, to be pardoned—and treasured.

Her question was what three people were thinking.

"Quiet," Antonio said to her, as to Paco. "Too quiet, perhaps. Some give way to fear. Some stiffen themselves to endure what is to happen, but they don't know what that will be. And I can't make them know even if I try. 'Let us find out for ourselves,' Rojas said in effect; and that is how it will be. But that is the most terrible part of all—their finding out—worse, much worse than the going. Your pardon, *mamacita*. You asked."

Doña Isabella bowed her head, her lips moving without sound. Opposite him Doña María's eyes swam with pity. For the people of Los Adaes? No, for him, Antonio Gil Ibarbo, the most fortunate man alive at this moment.

María Ibarbo, born Padilla, but now for fourteen blessed years Ibarbo y Padilla, was perhaps not the most beautiful woman in the world, though to Antonio she seemed to take on new beauty the longer he knew her. As a girl, she had had only one beautiful feature—her eyes, dark and deep, and even then eloquent with feeling. Looking into her eyes, one forgot to consider the shape of her mouth, her nose, or whether her face was round or oval. As a matter of fact, it was long, the cheeks slightly hollow. It could have been a cold, haughty face; but the eyes saved it, gave it instead a charming reserve and gravity.

It was her eyes that had caught Antonio's attention at their first meeting. That was in the market of Santa Rosa on the Gulf, near the Rio Grande. There was a servant, old like Esperanza, with a basket, and, by contrast, this slender young lady, modestly dressed, half veiled by a mantilla, purchasing fruits and vegetables. A scuffle took place near them between a vendor and a thief; and in the chase the two rascals would have thrown the young lady down had not Antonio put himself in the way and knocked both men into the dust. Then others came, but first . . .

"*Gracias*, Señor!" He had never heard anyone speak with such cool sweetness and such dignity; but, more than that, there were her eyes, wide and dark and startled.

He could not forget them. He made inquiry and learned her name. From a mutual acquaintance he learned more. Her father was a man of means, highly thought of in that part of Texas and in Mexico. Excellent, Antonio thought, twenty-one at the time and now slightly mad. Again through mutual acquaintance he was able to present himself as a suitor. All went swiftly after that. Don Henrico Padilla had five daughters, of whom the incomparable María was the eldest. He had them all to settle in life, but María, naturally, came first. She was then eighteen, and that was old for a maiden. The trouble was, she had, heretofore, seemed indifferent to men's attentions. That did not dismay Antonio. A girl so refined—with such eyes—would not be satisfied with just anyone.

The courtship was brief. He had five conversations with his beloved, attended by a duenna, and was soon dizzily in love. He did most of the talking. He painted the Sabine hills in such colors that the city of Santa Rosa would have packed up and moved there if the inhabitants could have heard him. He described the ranch—the beautiful land, the little creek, his animals—and he forgot entirely to mention that his house was only a thing he had been arguing over with Rojas and Andorro when he had left the ranch to ride south on a bit of business, not dreaming of what he would find at the end of the ride. María's response to this deceiving eloquence was always the same: "How romantic! *Gracias*, Señor."

They were betrothed. They were wed. He found himself the husband of this exquisite, delicately bred, strange young woman

58

with the great, dark eyes. The day came when they must start for home. He had already spent more time away than was reasonable, and she could hardly wait to see his Paradise. So he had to tell her how it was—as lovely as he had painted it, but his part still a little new.

She was enchanted. There was no proper road, only a path from Santa Rosa to Los Adaes? They would ride horses all the way? How romantic! She had read of such marches. Now to share in one! They would camp? What an adventure! He said he would engage a maid to see to her comfort on the journey. She objected. No, please! She had been too much attended and watched all her life. Now that she was a Señora, she wished a little more independence. Please?

At Lobanillo, after a journey that had been exquisitely romantic and only a little rough, she begged to be allowed to live with him in his shed while their house was being built. There was no need to rent a place in the town for her. She would be too far away while everything exciting went on at the ranch.

"I can cook," she insisted—how would it look to live in a shed and be waited on by a servant?

Antonio studied her hands, smooth, with long, slender fingers; but presently he had to admit that never before had he eaten so well—or so much. He dared not leave anything she served to him.

"Only until the house is ready," he said repeatedly, liking and not liking to see her work before a fire. "When we have a proper *hacienda*, you will not do this kind of labor."

And she did not. She had then a new set of talents to display. She was as admirable in the new home as she had been in the shed, giving everything such grace that even Doña Isabella, who came to live with them then, accepted second place in the house with no complaint. This supremacy spread beyond the *hacienda*. In Los Adaes Antonio acquired new rank because of his lady. Rojas and Andorro, who had come to know her as they built the house, began this with their good reports. In the pueblo on the ranch Doña María was even more popular. She had, Antonio was told, a blessed, healing touch for anyone with illness or injury.

With all that, naturally Doña María was busy. Antonio was

even busier. He had now to work doubly hard to achieve the grandeur he had promised his bride and her people and—before them—himself. During the months when they had lived in the shed, he had refused to absent himself for more than a day at a time. Now he rode away on his trading ventures—sometimes for weeks. He was away when his son was born. It was a difficult birth. Doña María came near to dying. Only the fact that the boy was perfect, and the will that she should be the one to show him to his father, kept her alive. The crisis was past when Antonio returned, but she was still weak and ill. She cried like a child in Antonio's arms.

"*Querida*, beloved," he said, "I am sorry. I am sorry I was away. And that you had the pain and the suffering, but it is over now. Whatever the trouble was, it was not your fault. It happens sometimes like that."

"How do you know?" she asked.

He didn't know. He knew nothing about women, only animals. Sometimes a horse was too finely bred to endure strain. Fatima, for example, was the one foal of her dam; and now he was afraid to breed Fatima for fear that a foal might destroy her, too. Unwisely he groped for this thinking aloud. The tears stopped. Doña María freed herself from his embrace.

"I am not a horse," she said. "You will not shut me away. I will not be treated so."

Life had to teach her. There were two more births. The first child died before it came, the second lived two days. Again Doña María was disconsolate.

"*Querida*," Antonia rebuked, "you have a son. I have him, too. And I have you. If I had wanted a peasant wife, I would have taken one. I chose you. I am content. Then why do you grieve?"

He should have scolded sooner. She looked at him with those deep, expressive eyes as if she were seeing him for the first time; but she calmed.

"You are right," she said. "I will live now for you and Anastacio."

She had kept that promise. A more devoted wife and mother could not have been found. If she had a fault it was in the excess of her devotion. It was perhaps natural that, while the boy was very young, she should watch over his every breath or movement; but, as he grew older, the attachment became even closer. A similarity, a sympathy developed, to take the place of dependence. Not that the boy looked like his mother. He looked like Antonio. He was dark like Antonio. Not as swarthy, perhaps. "Black as a Moor," Doña Isabella had always said of her son, scolding him for his reckless exposure of himself to extremes of sun and wind. Anastacio was not quite that dark, but he had the same glow in his eyes that Antonio had and the same quick speech. His only outward resemblance to Doña María was in the indication that he would grow up to be more slender than his father. He had his mother's hands, with long, shapely fingers. Antonio was never fat—he was always too active—but he was sturdily muscular, and had always been so.

But the real similarity between mother and son—and this fretted Antonio—was the boy's inclination toward learning. He liked books. Moreover, in discovering that, Antonio learned what had escaped him before. His wife was richly educated. Since this had in no way detracted from her other good qualities, it need not have troubled him, but it did. He mentioned it one day to her—half in jest, but ruefully. She was astonished.

"But, my husband," she protested, "how strange that you do not see what is so plain to everyone else! Anastacio is so much more like you than like me. He has a liking for books, it is true, and a certain affection for me, his mother. We are much together, but . . . what is the objection?"

"There is no objection exactly," Antonio said, "just a feeling. I get to thinking. All I have to give him is property. This ranch will be his some day. What kind of ranchero will he make—with all that learning in his head?"

"A good one," Doña María said. "He is so proud to be your son. All he asks is to be a man like you."

Was that true? In that case, Antonio thought, he must take charge. He must give Anastacio a few lessons in operating a complex property. He began by choosing a horse for the boy. He taught him how to handle the horse, and there it ended. Antonio was called away on a bit of business. Luis Ramón finished the riding lessons. Antonio was sorry, but could do no differently.

Each year life seemed to move farther away from that ecstatic period when he and his love had lived in a shed while Rojas and Andorro built their house; and yet, how would it have helped if they had lived on in that shed?

Now there was this new complication, the damnable ruling from Madrid, which did not apply to him at all. How much he became involved in it was a matter for his own deciding. He could not put it out of his mind. Here at this pleasing table, three pairs of eyes watched him—two pairs, at least, with apprehension—and farther away, in the kitchen, a servant, who was also a mother and a grandmother, fretted and scolded.

"Did you see anyone in town to talk to?" Doña María asked.

Antonio said he had, and told of his meeting with Pedro Coronal.

"He says he too is taking instruction from Fray Josef. Do you know him, 'Stacio?"

"Yes, surely," the boy said, with animation. "He is good at his lessons, when he pays attention. Fray Josef says he is a dreamer."

"Is that bad?" Antonio asked.

"It is not good for the lessons," Anastacio said. "Otherwise," he laughed, "I like him."

"Good!" Antonio said. "So do I!"

And he went on to speak of Tomás Coronal, of Rojas, of Esteban Andorro.

"Cecilio Andorro," he said, "wishes to marry his sweetheart, Teresa García, at once, before they leave. Oh . . . you know?"

"We heard there was that possibility," Doña María explained.

"The wind," Antonio remarked, "must be from the east today."

Before he could go on, there were again sounds in the passageway leading from the kitchen—not a scuffle exactly, but some pushing and pulling. It ended with someone approaching the *sala* on tiptoe, awkwardly, suggesting boots with heels, possibly spurs. In a moment, Luis Ramón, the ranch foreman and Paco and Esperanza's youngest son, appeared in the doorway.

"Señor," he apologized, "I do not wish to interrupt, but my father and my mother are of the opinion that you will want to hear the news at once. The priest has consented to marry my friend Cecilio Andorro and Teresa García today at vespers."

Luis was a handsome young man, clear-eyed and strong, wearing with grace the loose trousers, the high boots, the wide belt with a sheathed knife, of a *vaquero*. His shirt was open at the throat, the opening filled with a gay handkerchief. Antonio's heart lifted at the sight of him. Luis had lived at Lobanillo from its beginning. He had been a little boy at first, younger even than Pedro Coronal. He had learned to ride before he could really hook his legs around a horse. Now Antonio could leave all the work of the ranch in his hands whenever business called him away. He loved Luis like a younger brother and trusted him wholly.

"Surely we want to hear," Antonio said. "Directly, for a change. And you, I suppose, would like to attend the wedding."

"Don Antonio, Cecilio wishes me to stand up with him."

This was said seriously. Luis was a serious young man. Antonio answered in the same tone.

"Oh? That is different. Your work here for the day is done?"

"I believe so. The horses for the fort are in the corral, waiting for the *Teniente* to examine them. If there is something else . . ."

Antonio stood up, took the young man by the shoulders, turned him around, and gave his back a hearty slap.

"Be off with you, then," he ordered. "Waste no more time on talk. We will see you at the church."

When he turned around, there sat his three—comfortable, well fed, secure . . . and still anxious.

"There will be a feast," Doña María said. "We should add something."

"No," Antonio told her. "A basket of oranges, if you have them, or a similar delicacy, but nothing more." He told about Rojas and the many chickens. "Let Cecilio's and Teresa's friends provide the feast, using their extra stores."

"My father," this was Anastacio, wriggling to match small Pedro, "may I go to the church with you? I have never attended a wedding."

"In that case you must go. Now . . ."

"Now," Doña María said, "it is siesta time. Away with you, 'Stacio. I will be along presently. We must all rest. A wedding fiesta is gay and sometimes lasts very long."

"Let this one be as gay as possible," Antonio said with unexpected violence as the boy went off. Both women were startled.

"Antonio," his mother said, "is there more that you should tell us?"

"There is much more, but no need to burden you with all of it. You will see for yourselves this evening." Then he had a thought. "The last person I saw as I left the town was Angelita Gonzales, with Rosario Terrero. They were making ready to plant a rose in Teresa's new garden. Have you heard, since you hear many thing before I do, what the *Teniente* means to do about his family?" Doña María's eyes were wide with question. "If the Señora is as ill as reported, it does not seem possible that she can make the journey."

"She is very ill," Doña Isabella said. "She can walk, with the help of her maid, Constanzia, from her bed to a chair and back again. So it is not possible that she make any journey. Just the same, she will go, if that is her will."

"How?" Antonio demanded.

"In a sling on a pack mule, if there is no other way. You know how she is."

"But, if she has no thought for herself, she should think of the girl."

"Who said she has no thought for herself?" Doña Isabella said. "She always thinks of herself. She did before. She does now. Señora Gonzales does not like Los Adaes, my son. Don't you know? It is inseparable in her mind from all her disappointments. In Los Adaes, her brave young soldier husband did not receive the recognition he deserved. Because of the town, she lost her daughter. Oh, yes, the town was to blame, not her foolish pride. Then La Niña. I am not sure she wanted the child when Garza brought her. But he did bring her, and even the Señora's hard heart seemed to melt for a while. Only for a while. Lately it has all come back. The girl is beautiful, much more so than poor little Ángela. She has a good mind and a noble character. She has the virtue of a religous, but all her devotion is toward her grandparents, I understand. So, now it is all to do over again, but how? Do I make myself clear?"

"Not exactly," Antonio said. "And I never . . ."

"Then I will continue. Señora Gonzales was bitterly disappointed when the capital was moved and José was left here in command of a fort likely more than ever to be forgotten. To her, therefore, the ruling from Madrid ordering the garrison and her husband to Bexar is the renewal of hope. She will go in spite of all."

Antonio thought of Hernando Calles, but the clerk's hope for a better future was glorious compared to the possibilities for José Gonzales.

"The Señora is wrong," he said.

"Surely," his mother agreed. "She is always wrong, but she will have her way at all costs. If, then, she is the one to pay, that is just; but one must feel sorry for her husband and the Little One."

"That sounds more like my mother," Antonio said, amazed at her hostility. "The Little One is now fifteen years old, she tells me, and, I think, as innocent of evil as when she was born."

"Poor child!" Doña Isabella said, and excused herself and left the room.

Poor child, indeed! Pity all the bright, young innocents. Pity the older folk. Pity them all.

"You have had a sad day," his María said with grave sympathy. "I hope you will take a good rest."

"It was sad," Antonio allowed, ignoring that about rest, "because I can give these people no hope. I would like to help them, but there is nothing I can do."

Pity young Pedro Coronal. Pity old Diego Zapatero. Pity . . .

Pity Teresa García and Cecilio Andorro, solemn in their bright wedding garments, kneeling before the priest that evening, taking his blessing—Cecilio so proud in his young strength that he could hardly bow his head in prayer, Teresa so small, so confiding, so devout beside him. Pity them as they came from the church, and the homeward procession formed. Except they asked for no pity. The future held no terror for them. Theirs was the bravery of youth and love. Now was all the time there was. To some remark made by Luis Ramón, Cecilio threw back his head and laughed without restraint. He then passed the remark on to his Teresa. She lowered her eyes demurely, blushed, and looked up at her husband; her face was as radiant as his. The declining sun spread a rosy glow over the lovers, over the faces of their laughing, shouting, singing friends, who placed themselves in line behind them and followed them away from the mission, over the bridge and down the hill. Everyone caught something of the moment's sweet madness.

"Bravo!" the older ones cried, watching the procession as it formed. "Bravo!" Who knew when or where they would have another such celebration? Nobody knew. So, if it was never to come again, they would make merry now.

"Bravo!" Antonio waved his hat and shouted with the rest. Anastacio, watching his father out of the corner of his eye, did the same.

The Ibarbos made their own group among the watchers. Antonio stood guard, not wanting any one of his three to be pressed too much; but that was never threatened. The townspeople had too much respect for the Ibarbo ladies to crowd them. Tomorrow they would say—the talk might already have begun—how gracious it was of the two Señoras to attend the wedding. The Señoras were like that always, proud, as was their right, but never putting themselves above other people.

"Bravo!" Antonio shouted, raised his arm to wave his hat again, and something stiffened it in the movement. He turned to Doña María beside him and spoke to her in as low a tone as he could and make himself heard.

"I have thought of something. I must go. I must act at once—while it is fresh in my mind."

By then the others had heard at least the urgency in his tone.

"It is nothing," he assured them. "I must leave you now. I have a matter to attend to at the ranch. Now—tonight. 'Stacio here will take good care of you—with the help of Olivaro. 'Stacio, you will ride . . ."

Another thought seized him. What a place for thinking!

"I must make explanation to Esteban Andorro, if I can catch him," he said to Doña María. "Perhaps he will consent to ride as far as the town, since we can make room for him. In that case, my son, I must ask you to ride in the carriage and leave the place up front beside Olivaro for our friend. You may ride there coming home. I will tell Olivaro."

Originally it had been his intention to drive the carriage to the wedding himself. It was a thing he liked to do, to handle the lines over a team of high-stepping horses or active mules. It would have been in keeping with the spirit of the evening; but at the last minute caution had told him to saddle Fatima and ride beside the carriage instead. It had been, perhaps, preparation for the later, stronger command.

"*Adiós!* I go now. Tomorrow you must tell me all that happened, eh, 'Stacio?"

And he went away through the crowd to where he knew his driver waited with the carriage and the horses—on a high perch, watching the wedding procession.

Antonio had no idea of the hour of the night which saw his family safely back at Lobanillo. He knew it was night, and dark. He had had to light candles in the room where he was working, and that had been some time before the carriage came. The room had been set aside for his use as a study, a counting room, really. Here he kept a record of all the transactions involving the ranch and his ventures in trade, using a method taught him by his father. Here also he did such other writing as the ranch and his complex business relations demanded. This was never too onerous, as only a few of those he dealt with could read. Still, he had writing to do and books to keep.

On arriving at home this evening, he had removed his coat, spread out on a table four sheets of good white paper, sharpened three pens, mixed himself some ink, and settled himself before these supplies, determined to make a quick job of what he had in mind. When the carriage bearing his family returned, several hours later, the picture had not changed materially. Candles had been lighted. A few lines of writing showed on one sheet of paper. The other three were scattered as his straining elbows had pushed them; and Antonio himself was doing what he had done most of the evening—pacing up and down the room, clenching and unclenching his hands, muttering aloud, occasionally pausing

67

to return to the table, seize a pen, think, and then lay the pen down again with a groan, and no word flowing from the point.

He did not hear the carriage arrive. His first notice of the return was a knock on the door to this room—a light, deliberate, resolute knock.

"Come in!" he said, knowing who was there; and Doña María entered.

What a relief to see her! So calm, so elegant, so cool! She had never looked more handsome. The black silk of her matron's dress brought out the clear pallor of her skin and the depth of her eyes. Or was it her silk-lace head shawl? When she would have removed it, he stopped her.

"You make a picture I want to keep in my mind," he said. "Well, how was the fiesta?"

"Very gay, very noisy," she said. "I was anxious to be here with you. Have you been hard at work all this time?"

"Labor, I would call it; and, for all I have accomplished, I could as well have remained where I was."

She considered this gravely.

"Am I permitted to know what it is you mean to do?"

"Assuredly. I am addressing a petition to the King in behalf of the people of Los Adaes. Any citizen has the right, if he feels himself unjustly treated or desires a favor, to address the King through his representatives in office, asking that the wrong be righted or that the favor be granted. The thought came to me suddenly this evening—though it may have been on the way longer—that this ruling from Madrid is an injustice, not because of any tyranny on the part of the King, but because he does not know the truth. In spite of many reports, he does not know how it is here. He does not know the country. He does not know the people."

"So, you will tell him," she said. "Is there time?"

"Time to reach the King or the Governor so that the ruling can be changed? No. All here must be done as commanded. However, if a strong petition could be sent to the Governor, if he could have it in hand before our friends arrive at the capital, they might obtain a hearing. I still feel, in spite of all that is taking place, that this new governor Ripperdá is a fair-minded man. My dealings with him tell me so. I do not blame him for this ruling. He had to issue the order. If I am right, if he will consider a petition with understanding and only a little sympathy, he can, if he dares, send it on with his recommendation to someone higher in authority who has the power to reverse the order. Meantime he can stay that part which applies to our friends at Bexar. He can give them temporary shelter while they wait to see what comes from higher up. It is a small hope, I know. But it is the only thing I can think of and it seemed worth trying. Well?"

"It is a beautiful idea," Doña María said. "May I read what you have written?"

He waved her to the table.

"But," she said in a second, "you have written almost nothing."

"I know. Will you read that much, please? The light is poor, but . . ."

"I can see well enough."

"Well?" he said again, when he knew that she had read all the lines and that what she had read disturbed her. "How does it strike you?"

"It is like a fanfare of trumpets," she said slowly. "Must you make all those high-sounding compliments?"

"Surely I must," he said, in deep relief. "That is how one opens always. We are, you see, in a sense in the presence of the King— His Most Holy and Worshipful Majesty, Charles the Third, King of Spain, Emperor of the Indies and the two Americas. The fanfare is for him. He expects it. So do his royal counselors, with another for themselves with only a little smaller flourish; and so on, until finally we come to the man we address directly, in this case Baron de Ripperdá, Governor of the Province of Texas. After that, when all have received proper obeisance, I appear and most humbly state the object of the petition: I, Antonio Gil Ibarbo . . . How did I say it there?"

" 'I, Antonio Gil Ibarbo,' " she read, " 'moved only by devotion to the King and to my Country, desiring to see it prosper in all ways, do beg and entreat a reconsideration of the royal decree ordering the abandonment of the town known as Los Adaes. . . .' "

"That's it," Antonio said. "If it were all that easy! But now we must state our arguments. I know, too, how that is done. Each argument is numbered: one, two, three, and so on. We begin with Paragraph One."

"You have written that," his María reminded him. " 'Paragraph One.' Then nothing. Why?"

"Not for lack of argument," he declared. "I have a dozen arguments. Twenty. Fifty, perhaps. That is my trouble. I have too many. I don't know which one to set down first. One needs practical, reasonable arguments, hard to deny. I have those. At the same time, my reason for writing the petition is that I want the King and his advisers to see this region as we see it before they destroy it, to see and feel the anguish of our friends over leaving it. But which should come first?"

"You are tired," Doña María said. "It has been a difficult day. Tomorrow you will know how to say everything."

"You think so? You would advise me to put up the papers? There may still be fire in the kitchen. I could burn them."

"No!" she said. "No!"

"Very well. Either way satisfies me—so long as I am relieved of this labor of composition." He went to the table and put the blank sheets in order. "Now am I to hear about the festivity in the town?"

There was no answer. When he turned to see why, Doña María had removed her veil. Her eyes in the light of the candles were lustrous—too much so.

"*Querida*," he said gently. "Tears?"

She nodded. He put his arms around her, drew her close.

"Now, tell me," he commanded.

"They are so happy, those two," she sobbed. "For them there is no King's command. Not now."

"I know," he said. "How could I not know?" It had been the saddest merrymaking he had ever witnessed. "Come, then. Let us mourn together."

CHAPTER 6

The week that followed was like weather breeding a storm, when dark clouds roll up at the horizon, then hang there, glowering, but drawing no nearer. The strain told on everyone.

José Gonzales came to Lobanillo to inspect the mules and horses that Luis had driven up and penned, to be delivered later to the presidio. The gray-haired Lieutenant's metal was as bright, his leather as well oiled as always, but the pallor that had settled on his face when the King's command had been delivered was now, Antonio thought, much deeper. His back had a forced erectness, as if an invisible rod under his coat kept it in line. His inspection was thorough, but in the way of duty. Heart was lacking. He asked about the strength of the mules and mentioned the cannon from the fort.

"The guns are a problem," Antonio agreed, then, thinking he had borrowed too much solemnity from the *Teniente*, forced heartiness into the rest of his reply. "I think I do not need to advise you to be reasonable with the loading. A mule will carry a great load without protest; but a wise man does not destroy a mule because he has a stout heart. Take the guns apart as much as possible."

"They are down from the walls now," Gonzales said, "and being dismantled. We will take only the best. I will report on the others. Would you consider buying the iron of those we leave behind?"

"You may mention the possibility to the Captain-Governor in Bexar," Antonio said with caution. "Let him name a price for the metal and inform me when the money is credited to me for the mules and the horses I am supplying."

They then went on to the horses—rough-coated, shaggy from being out on wild pasture. Antonio found himself explaining their appearance solicitously. They were, he assured Gonzales, all

71

sound, broken to saddle and bridle. Naturally they were not his best stock.

"They are acceptable," Gonzales said briefly, then broke his stiffness to release a little of what he felt. "You understand, I wish my command to look its best when I report to the Captain-Governor."

"Señor *Teniente*," Antonio said earnestly, wishing to express sympathy, "the plains are hot and dusty in midsummer. Your command will do well to stay alive. Keep both men and animals in good health. That is the most you can do. So, you will arrive in Bexar mounted at least. Another thing—picket the animals carefully at night, with a guard. They may not be Ibarbo's best, but Indians will think them good enough to steal."

"You have thought of everything, it seems," Gonzales said. "I give you my thanks."

Now, how, Antonio wondered, was he to speak of something more important than horses—Señora Gonzales and the girl? How did one break through the armor of such a man? The rod at his back was real, and permanent. He had it in place of a backbone. They were now riding away from the corral. In a moment Gonzales would take his leave.

"Señor *Teniente*," Antonio said at last, desperately, "I regret very much this harsh order."

"Why?" Gonzales asked. "It will mean a loss to you, perhaps, but not much and not for long, I think."

Before Antonio could feel either warm or cold at this thrust given by a man in pain, the Lieutenant's horse stumbled. It was a slight stumble and Gonzales kept control; but it kept Antonio from answering too hastily.

"If, on the other hand," Gonzales said then, "you are expressing concern for me, do not distress yourself. An order is an order. There would be no orders if those in command thought of each person involved."

"But I see only what happens in consequence," Antonio said, "and, when those involved are my friends . . . Señor *Teniente*, I regret to see you leave in this way. I extend my sympathy to you—also to your lady and La Niña. I am sorry to hear that the Señora is not well."

72

Did the backbone yield a little?

"She is very ill." This was a new tone—hollow.

"She will not be able to travel, then?"

Gonzales reined in his horse.

"She is not able," he said, in that same empty way, "but she—also Angelita—will go when I go."

"How?" Antonio demanded, forgetting to measure speech or tone.

"I don't know." The *Teniente* turned to look directly at Antonio. His face was haggard. His eyes burned. Plainly his nights now had no sleep. "I thank you, Don Antonio, for your sympathy, but . . ." Then came surrender, harder to face than resistance, "Have you a solution?"

"It is possible, if you think so."

Under a roof at the stables was a carriage, no longer in use. It had been Doña Isabella's, was hers still, though she preferred now to ride in the more comfortable carriage that Antonio had bought for Doña María.

"I give it freely to the *Teniente*," Doña Isabella had said that morning when Antonio had asked her permission to use the old carriage, "but, as for the Señora, why should you help her?"

"It is a way to help the *Teniente*," Antonio said, "and the girl, who will ride with her grandmother."

What he did not say was that the thought of his mother or Doña María in such a situation had haunted him.

"Will you look at the carriage, Señor *Teniente?*" he asked now.

Under the officer's regard, it seemed dustier and shabbier than it had looked to him earlier. It needed new cushions. It needed much.

"It will hasten the end," Doña Isabella had said in giving her consent.

"Is it strong?" Gonzales asked.

"I will go over it myself," Antonio promised, as if he were offering the vehicle for sale. "If any part needs strengthening, that will be done. Generally, the carriage should be sound. It was kept that way when in use. A bolt may be needed here or there, a new strap, but that is all, I think."

"If there is any expense . . ."

73

Antonio waved aside the suggestion.

"It sits here, rusting and rotting," he said. "The only cost will be the mules. You will need a team of young ones, broken to harness. I will charge you for those, but you need not pay now. When you arrive at Bexar, you can sell them. I will give you the name of a man who handles such credits for me. That is the arrangement I will make for all the pack mules I lend for this march. Well?"

"It is a godsend," José Gonzales said. "I have no words to express my gratitude."

"It will be on your conscience, not mine, if anything happens to the Señora because of the carriage," Doña Isabella said when Antonio reported that Gonzales had accepted the gift.

Doña María was more sympathetic.

"God will reward you for this kindness," she said; then she, too, shuddered. "Poor thing! That she should have to endure this. But what would become of her if she did not go with her husband?"

"I agree, *cara mía*," Antonio said. "Still, my wish was chiefly to help the *Teniente*."

The Lieutenant's back had been proud and stiff again when he rode away, and his face much less drawn.

As for other rewards, there were none. At least not for the present. When the old vehicle came out of hiding, a dozen defects showed. Finally Antonio ordered it dismembered and then carefully put together again, so that each part should be made secure. In the end, the carriage was perhaps stronger than ever; but skilled hands worked hard with iron and rawhide and oil to bring about the rejuvenation. It was not until the day before the march to Bexar began that Luis hitched the two young mules to the vehicle and drove it to the fort to deliver it to Gonzales, or take it on to the town if the *Teniente* so desired.

Luis . . .

The cloud hovered.

It was well to keep busy under the shadow. Two days of grace were finally added to the five permitted by the ruling, but nobody said now, "There is still time." Tension mounted. In the morn-

74

ings, after daylight came, Antonio found himself unable to sleep and was out at the stables or the corrals ahead of everybody else. The ranch had never been so active in midsummer. No, that was not true. It was a working ranch, and always active. Now there was just enough extra to make it seem to hum. There were the mules and horses for the fort and, in addition, extra ones for Antonio's friends in town, who increased in number remarkably before the week was over.

"Mules, mules, mules!" the *Alcalde* fumed on the day when he came to bargain about his sugar. He came in something more than his usual sweat of anxiety. "How many have you promised now? Do you know? I never knew you to give away mules before."

"I am not giving away any now," Antonio told him and explained as he had to Gonzales his terms in lending the mules.

The responsibility for the cost of the mules, to be collected in Bexar, caused the *Alcalde* to break out further in perspiration; and Antonio heard again Zapatero's plea: "Come with us, Señor! We lack a leader."

In addition to this business about mules and the Señora's carriage, Antonio discovered that the town needed help in organizing into a common herd its miscellaneous sheep and goats and cattle. He lent a man from the ranch to help with this and sent Luis to town every day to see what progress was being made.

Luis . . .

He was away from the ranch that week more than he was present. This was a thing, Antonio realized too late, that he should have noticed more particularly at the time it occurred. Whereas all he perceived then was how Luis's absence was felt.

Each day until noon Antonio was as active as any *vaquero*. The hum quieted then for the siesta, but he borrowed the last hour of the rest period to work on his petition in behalf of the people of Los Adaes. He was still determined to compose a forceful plea and forward it to the Governor. If his own belief in the petition had faltered, Doña María would have kept him at the task of writing, though, as it turned out, she had her own idea as to how the petition should be delivered.

Doña María was supremely confident that this document, if completed, would redeem Antonio's friends and win for him

75

their blessings forever, to say nothing of securing his own peace of mind. On the first afternoon of his work on it, unable to discipline her curiosity, she stole into the room while he wrote, with a book in her hand, meaning to read, she said afterwards, and make no noise to disturb him; but, when he looked up, there she sat, with the book closed tightly, her eyes on him, filled with her own brooding anxiety.

"How does it go?" she asked softly.

"Well . . . I have at last written something that I felt should be understood. About the beauty of this country which our friends must leave. Would you like to hear what I said?"

"If I may, please."

So he read what, at length, he had set down.

" 'To comprehend the beauty of this Sabine country, it is necessary to see it; but the land is not only beautiful to the eye. It is rich in every way. It abounds in timber—pine, oak, walnut, hickory, pecan. The soil is fruitful, suitable for many crops, such as corn, beans, melons, figs, even cotton and sugar cane. The water is of the purest, and there is plenty always. Little rivers flowing through the land everywhere, and there are many lakes, all abounding in fish. Geese and ducks settle on the water in the spring and the fall as they travel from south to north and back again. There is game of all kinds in the forests—deer, turkey, pheasant . . .' " He paused. " 'Also a few snakes, scorpions, ticks. What of it? Did not the king of serpents dwell in Eden?' "

"Don Antonio, my husband," Doña María cried out, "you did not say that on the paper?"

"No," he said, amused at her horror, but not enough so to escape from an emotion that had gripped him at this point in the writing. "Nor did I say another truth that should be said— that it is not to be supposed that the inhabitants of such a paradise will ever forget or find equal contentment in another part of the province. That, my dear one, is and will be the great anguish of these good people—life in a land that must seem to them harsh and unlovely in all its aspects. How can I tell the King the truth about the old capital and not add the truth about San Antonio de Bexar? That is what stops the composition today."

Doña María put aside the useless book and came over to him,

to lay the coolness of her white hands on his brow, his cheeks.

"So warm," she said, "so distressed, so tired, maybe. Tomorrow you will know how to go on."

"Perhaps," he agreed, catching a cool hand and kissing it. "Come, then. Let us go walk in the garden."

But the brooding cloud cast a shadow even over the bright garden. When Flores, the *Alcalde*, had come in a sweat over sugar, mules and everything else, the only gain from his visit had been a piece of news: the merchants of Natchitoches, it seemed, were in some agitation over a report that traders from the English colonies above Natchez were now sailing loaded barges boldly down the Mississippi to New Orleans. This gave Antonio his first "reasonable" argument to be embodied in the petition.

"It should be considered," he wrote, "that land as fair as the Sabine country will not be without inhabitants for long. I respectfully call to His Majesty's attention and that of His Noble Council the increased activity of the English in America and their proximity now to Spanish territory. They are a people whom a mere river will not halt in their forward march, if they see land beyond it to their liking."

"Do you believe that rumor?" Doña María asked, wide-eyed with emotion.

"A rumor sometimes should be weighed carefully, even when it is not entirely believed. It will do no harm to mention the English. They have always been archdemons in the eyes of Spain."

Meaning to lighten the conversation, he mentioned the legend of Angelita Gonzales.

"Does she know about her father?" Doña María asked.

Antonio could not say. He had never heard.

"Her grandparents are too old," Doña María said then. "If they should die, what will become of the girl, all alone?"

"Now," Antonio said, impatient with himself, "with all this going on, I had not thought of that. She will not be alone, actually. She has too many friends. La Niña, the whole town calls her. Her story is one reason for that affection. Besides, she is

77

most lovable. She is fifteen years old now. Some gallant—and fortunate—young man may woo and win her for his wife."

"Or, as Doña Isabella says," Doña María reminded him, "she may have a religious vocation."

"I could wish a more earthly happiness for her," Antonio said, "if it is possible."

His thoughts returned to the English. Theoretically, of course, Louisiana was a barrier between the English colonies and Spanish Texas. Vigilance in guarding that barrier was centered for the most part in the commandant of a fort, once French but now Spanish, at Natchitoches on the Red River. This commandant, Athanase de Mezières by name, now loyal to Spain under oath, had also begun by being a Frenchman. A turncoat, then, in Antonio's eyes, he was not wholly to be trusted. When the governments had changed, rather than deal with the turncoat, though he was reputed to be sharp in the ways of trade, Antonio had preferred to ally himself with an out-and-out Frenchman, one Nicolas de la Mathe of Pointe Coupée, Punta Cortada to the Spanish, on the lower Mississippi. He had never regretted the alliance.

Should he include a warning about De Mezières at this point in the petition, he asked himself. Or was he merely facing with anxiety his own business relations after Los Adaes had ceased to be? He must communicate with De la Mathe, he thought, at the earliest possible moment.

While he scratched on paper, Doña María watched, her face pale, her eyes still wide with unanswered questions. Presently, suppressing a shiver over some unnamed anxiety, she rose quietly and left the room. Turning at last with a question, Antonio missed her. His face paled slightly then.

"*Querida*," he thought, "I have frightened you. Why? What did I say?"

Every day Antonio held audience in some fashion. Although he was sure that his friends in town had not published his offer to them of asylum at the ranch, each day one or two people came, uninvited, asking for that privilege. Only he could say whether to admit them or not. Some were small traders, working on the fringe of enterprise. These he advised to try Natchitoches, saying they would find more opportunities there. Some were merely small, unimportant people, who eked out a living in Los Adaes by virtue of the productivity of small cornfields, a few goats or a cow, and the game and fish which Antonio had mentioned in his petition. To the best of these, if they seemed honest and had small children, he gave refuge. That created a problem of work and shelter. Some then, if the work seemed too obligatory, went away again; but a number stayed.

One whole day he gave to Sancho, the Great Chief of the Nacogdoches tribe of Tejas. Sancho was not the Chief's precise name, but was close enough to it to fasten itself to him after the first Spaniard had so addressed him. He was a power among his people, who in turn were as trustworthy as any Indians Antonio knew, and were also his most reliable source for Indian goods in the trading season. It was not surprising that, when Sancho heard of the abandonment of the missions and the fort and the town, he had taken alarm.

He brought with him to Lobanillo two lesser chiefs and his eldest son, whose name, translated, was Antelope. Antelope he was, when it came to running, everyone agreed who had ever seen him take a prize in a foot race. *Lope,* Antonio called him fondly, having taken a liking to the lean, brown youth whose eyes were as quick to see everything as his feet were to run. This, then, was a ceremonious visit. It took all day and much roasted meat and many speeches to get problems adjusted to everyone's greater comfort.

"What do you fear?" Antonio asked the Chief. "I am here. Rancho Lobanillo is here as always. Presents for you when you come to trade wait in its storerooms." And when Sancho brightened but waited for more reassurance, he added reluctantly, "If I should happen to be away when you come, there is always the Frenchman at Nakatosh, though I hope you will seek me first."

"The Spaniards are our first friends," Sancho replied solemnly. "That is why we are sad to see them depart, to see birds nest where once there were bells to ring in the churches. The people are our friends, and the priests in the brown blankets. Will you say to the King beyond the Big Water that it is not right to take our friends away from us?"

So it was that when the Indians finally departed, carrying gifts, the boy Lope riding a young horse, which had betrayed its Lobanillo progenitors by coming out in large spots of brown on white instead of in a solid color, Antonio hurried into the house as if hornets were pursuing him, to add a paragraph to his petition. He now had a second argument. Was it wise . . . ?

No, let it wait, while he walked the floor, up and down, shaping a more polite statement. He must beg the King and his Council to consider the effect upon the friendship of the Tejas tribes if all Spanish settlements were withdrawn from this territory. Here was an alliance that had grown over many years. The friendship was true and strong. It had been the great security of the Spanish settlements, placing a barrier of people between them and the more savage tribes to the north and west. It had, in turn, fortified the Indians. Knowing that the power of Spain was behind them, they could offer a bolder front to their enemies. He took one more turn up and down the room, then seated himself at the table and wrote.

CHAPTER 7

The day of evacuation arrived.

For the first time—he could not remember when such a thing had happened to him—Antonio slept late. He could have believed that loving hands had mixed medicine for sleeping in his wine at bedtime the night before, except that he awoke, when the time came, clear-headed, with every sense sharply alert. The heavy, prolonged slumber had been merely the result of weariness. He had ridden into Los Adaes the evening before to say good-bye to chosen friends with what cheer he could muster, and had come away more burdened than before with a sense of defeat and hopelessness. The papers of the petition, on which he had written earnest truths as they had come to him, sickened him when he read them over. He drank the wine and ate a little of the cake Doña María offered him, and went to bed.

He awoke at the height of the morning, not to a noise or other alarm, but to intense silence. The house, he knew at once, was empty. Pity—and curiosity—had drawn his family and the ranch people to the road, some, perhaps, to the town, to assist in the departure, to march a little way with the banished ones, to carry small gifts . . . God alone knew what each one would do to relieve his own sorrow. And he, too, except for the sleeping, would have been part of that.

In the kitchen, the fire on the hearth had burned down to embers and been covered. The food, under a flycloth on the table, was cold. He ate a little for strength, put the cloth back in place over what remained, washed in a convenient basin, and went on to the stable, where Fatima waited in her stall, saddled. She rolled her eyes at him as he backed her out: "At this hour we are going somewhere?"

"The last time for this," he said to her, brushing her forelock away from her eyes. "The last time, my dear one."

Since Rancho Lobanillo lay west of Los Adaes, and the *Camino Real* skirted one edge of it, a short run would have brought Antonio, even at this late hour, abreast of the main cavalcade, which would move, he knew, very slowly. Also, since this was the usual and swiftest way to town, he would soon have been among his ranch people. For that reason, he deliberately turned Fatima into a narrow, rougher trail and, after half an hour of picking his way over hill and hollow, pulled up on a crest from which he had a clear, unhampered view of the highway farther to the east. He was, in fact, almost directly above the spot where the road from Los Adaes crossed the *Camino Real*—the same road which, beyond the crossing, led up the hill beside the sparkling river to the Presidio and the Mission of San Miguel. He could see without being seen and he was alone. He wished to be alone. Since he had awakened to solitude, let it continue that way.

At that distance, he could not see the people in the road below distinctly enough to name individuals, but he saw enough. There was no form to the procession. People walked in bunches and at a gait which soon told him that he was looking at the last ones to join the march, the slow, the most reluctant. Presently in the road from the town he saw the animals—a double line of pack mules, then sheep, goats, cows, with an *arriero*, aided by half a dozen helpers, herding them.

It was the tail of the procession; and it moved too slowly to please those in command. Sunlight glinted on metal. A soldier guard rode down the uneven line of marchers until he came to the *arriero*. Sharp sounds of men in argument came up the hill to Antonio. The *arriero* did not move. The soldier rode past him to the helpers. The outcry now was sharper. Pain? Resistance? But the pace of the plodding animals quickened. Mother of God! Antonio thought, closing his eyes.

Anger consumed him. Intention, compassion, reflection, reason, purpose burned to ash. He could not move. When finally he left the hill, it was Fatima's will, not his, that turned them once more into the narrow trail. She turned softly, gently. Then her pace quickened. Swiftly and more swiftly she went, ignoring ditches, brush, declivities, and steep climbs. Let us go, my master. Home to our stable, where it is dark and cool and safe.

They arrived at the ranch buildings with Fatima in such a sweat as Antonio in his right mind would never have permitted. A *vaquero* came from a corral fence to take her.

"*Gracias*," Antonio said dully dismounting. "She is warm. Cool her . . . you know. *Gracias*."

And, without looking at the man to know who he was, he walked on to the house, his anger finding fresh fuel in a sudden unsteadiness afflicting his legs. Because of this he took the shortest way and entered by the kitchen. His mother opened the door for him. One look from her told him that other things were visibly wrong with him besides uncertain feet.

"My son!" she said in alarm. "You . . . are you sick?"

"No," he answered. "A little warm, perhaps."

"But, come in." Doña Isabella caught his arm. "Come in and sit down."

She pushed a stool toward him. And there behind her stood Doña María, looking more frightened than his mother. And Anastacio, also staring.

"What are you all doing here?" Antonio asked, not objecting, just wanting to know.

"Antonio," his mother said, "you saw the people on the road?"

"The last of them," he told her, glad of the stool now under him.

Anastacio spoke up excitedly:

"Some hid. The soldiers went to the houses with whips and drove them out."

Anger blazed up in Antonio. He remembered the soldier and those who drove the animals.

"Did you see?" he demanded.

"No. I heard . . ."

"However it was," Antonio admonished, "do not forget. Do not ever forget."

Doña Isabella now laid her hand on his shoulder.

"My son, this is a black day for all. María here has prepared a simple meal."

"She likes to cook," the boy said. He was as tense in every way as Antonio. "Don't you, *mamacita?*"

"Sometimes," Doña María said softly. "When there are only a few to eat." Antonio raised his head to look at her. Her eyes were at their blackest and deepest. Her face was very pale. "It is only tortillas and beans. If you will have some with us?"

She wore today the full skirt and blouse of a *paisano*. That much was like the time of the shed.

"They are very good," Anastacio said of the tortillas and beans.

"*Gracias.*" Antonio rose. "*Gracias, querida.* But I am not hungry. I had food not long ago."

"Sit down," his mother commanded. "Sit down and eat with us, my son."

Antonio resumed his place on the stool. He tasted the beans. They were, as the boy had said, very good. If he could have eaten . . . but nobody ate much.

"I suppose," Antonio said finally, pushing his plate away. "Esperanza is in one of her fits—because of Magdalena and the Piedras. I knew it was coming; but I thought, let it happen. Esperanza's pain is acute, but it will be briefer."

Anastacio would have added something then, but a look from his mother checked him.

"Let him speak," Antonio said.

"I meant only to tell about Cecilio Andorro, *mamacita*. He burned his house, my father."

"No!" Antonio said.

"Yes. It made a great smoke."

Antonio had not thought to look beyond the people in the road to the town.

"Did it spread?" he asked.

"No," Doña María said. "There was no wind. It was just the one house."

Ah! Bravo, Cecilio Andorro! Antonio rose.

"I thank you for the food," he said punctiliously. "It was excellent, but I have now had enough. I will excuse myself and retire to my study. Let nobody disturb me there, please. I have much to do."

Only Doña Isabella would have presumed to ignore that request. While Antonio was preparing pens and fresh ink, she knocked on the door.

"It is I," she said, and rustled into the room before he could stop her.

"Antonio, there is something we did not tell you at dinner. Anastacio wanted to, but we stopped him. It was not for him to say. I am the one who must tell you. My son, it is not only Magdalena and her family who have left Lobanillo. Luis Ramón also . . ."

She had to say it again before Antonio began to believe. Even then the truth remained outside, beating on his brain for admission. Luis had deserted Lobanillo? It was not possible. Luis? He was part of Lobanillo. Lobanillo was nothing without him. He knew every foot of the ranch from boundary to boundary. He knew every colt, every calf, almost every lamb that dropped. He had worked hard, devotedly. It was for Antonio, to be sure, but for himself, too. He had special privileges—his own horse, his own house, money to spend, his freedom when a day's work

84

was done. He could not have done this; and yet, it seemed he had. A dreadful hurt added itself to Antonio's bewilderment.

"The fool!" he stormed. "The ungrateful . . ."

"No, my son. He was all week making up his mind. In the end he could not tell you. Antonio, Luis took nothing with him from the ranch—only some plain clothes he wore and his gun and his hunting knife. His horse, the money he had from you, he left with Paco."

"Paco, then, remains here?"

"Paco and Esperanza. They are too old."

"Ah! Then I have not the comfort of calling even them faithful."

"My son, do not speak so. Sad as they are, Paco and Esperanza still will keep their faith. Esperanza will cook for us tomorrow. Antonio, what are you doing?"

He was pushing his papers into a heap.

"Do you think I can sit here now and write?" he asked. "No! I will saddle a horse for myself and the one that belongs to Luis. I will go and bring him back if I have to tie him on the horse and lead him home on a rope."

"Antonio, no!" Doña Isabella stamped her foot. His gentle mother. "You will not ride after Luis today." Then she lost her anger in tears. "Antonio, please! Listen to me. Today is full to the top for all of us with what has happened. Everyone is sad or tired or angry. Remain here today, my son. Busy yourself with the important paper or what you will; but let things go on today as they must. Tomorrow, if you wish, follow Luis. Maybe he can talk to you then and you can hear him more reasonably. Be fair to him as you have always been. These are his people, his sisters and brothers. He may even have a sweetheart in the town."

"No," Antonio said. "That I would have known."

"You think so? I am not so sure, with Luis. In any case, one day will not matter much. Poor lost ones, you can overtake them easily tomorrow. Antonio, I implore you!"

"My mother, I kiss your hands," he said, and did so. "My

heart, as you say, is already cooling—to a lump of lead. I will wait. But tomorrow early I will go in pursuit of Luis."

Alone once more, he sat idly at his table for the better part of an hour. He could think of nothing but the defection of Luis. Be reasonable, his mother had urged; try to understand. He could have understood this act in anyone else, but not Luis. He was so clear-headed, so sensible, so steady. Doña Isabella had suggested a sweetheart. Antonio still thought Luis would have let this slip in some moment of confidence. Luis would have wanted Antonio's support in case the girl's parents raised a question.

A question about Luis? Where would a father find a better husband for a daughter? True, Luis was of lowly parentage. Who would think of that, knowing Luis? With Antonio supporting his promise of a good future? Antonio had already wrestled with the thought that he should train someone to take over a foreman's duties. If he loved Luis, as he knew he did, he would not bar the young man's way to independence. He would help him—arrange that he should have acres for a ranch of his own, give him the first animals to stock it. Who, knowing Luis, would doubt that in that case he would prosper?

Antonio thought over the girls he knew in town. Actually he did not know many, but he did know a number of parents with daughters. He could not name any who would fail to recognize the worth of Luis Ramón. That would call for someone with the foolish pride of a Señora Gonzales. Señora Gonzales . . . Angelita? *I am fifteen years old, Señor.*

Why should he think of her? Why should he not? Luis was a young man of discernment. He had been encouraged by Antonio to select quality and reject what was inferior. But, Mother of God, had that led to this? Antonio's leaden heart came to life, expanding in a spasmodic urge to save and protect. How could Luis have entertained such a thought? Even were it not for the girl's guardians, there was the girl herself. The virtue of a religious, Doña Isabella had said, except for her devotion to her grandparents. What man in his senses would follow a girl like that?

But, if this were true, if Luis had thrown over every good thing in life to go where his love drew him, what did he hope to gain? He had left the ranch with nothing but the clothes he wore. What kind of clothes? And his gun and hunting knife. He went on foot. Antonio thought of the *arriero* facing the soldier, holding his ground. Luis? Surely not, but it could have been.

To get away from this whir of thinking, Antonio reached in desperation for his papers. He read once more the fanfare of his opening. His lips curled in scorn. He had no reverence today for the might of kings. No, but it was either pretend reverence or abandon the thought of a petition. His mouth straightened. In all conscience he must take some action.

". . . do beg and entreat a reconsideration of the royal decree, ordering the abandonment of the town known as Los Adaes." He reached for a pen.

"Paragraph One. With that in mind I beg leave to present an inhabitant's view of the land from which the unfortunate people of this town are on this very day, the 25th of June, 1773, withdrawing. It is . . ."

He copied his previously written description of the land.

In Paragraph Two he presented the threat of invasion by the English. Paragraph Three argued for the importance of keeping the friendship of the eastern tribes of the Tejas Indians. He wrote steadily, his anger, his outrage lending him vigor and a surprising clarity of thought. He arrived finally at a defense of the people. If the land, he demanded, cried out for occupants, who deserved to live there more than such loyal, obedient subjects as the original settlers?

"That they are such subjects," he wrote, "is proven by their instant obedience to the royal order."

This was, to be sure, the only test that had been made of their obedience. If they had known what trials lay ahead of them, would they have been obedient? Probably. That was simplest.

"They are a worthy people, descended, for the most part, from certain ones born in Spain, who were sent across the ocean to establish just such settlements as this town, now in ruin."

That about ruin would be true when the paper reached its destination.

"They are virtuous . . ."

Rosario Terrero, for example? And there were others whose

sins were less pardonable. But these were not many. On the whole, the people were virtuous.

"They are friendly with the Indians."

They were friendly with everybody. That, too, was easiest. It made life certainly more pleasant than strife. However . . .

"There is a solidity in this town, which comes from certain ones who settled it marrying among themselves, until now most of the people are related and feel themselves almost to be members of one family."

His pen stopped with a sputter. One family—that was why Rancho Lobanillo this afternoon was in such distress, and he without a foreman. He looked at his watch and pushed the papers aside. Siesta was over. If he was to be away tomorrow, he must leave someone in charge, give a few orders. As for the petition, it should be easy now to bring it to a close. He would finish it this evening, sign it, and tomorrow he would take it with him and give it to José Gonzales to deliver in San Antonio de Bexar. That was settled.

He had already removed his jacket. He changed now completely to working corduroys and a loose shirt, snatched up an old hat, and left the house once more for the stables. He hoped he would be so fortunate as to find Olivaro there—Domingo Olivaro, the man who had driven the carriage to the wedding the week before, the best man on the ranch after Luis, Antonio's choice if ever he had to replace Luis. Now, at least temporarily, the need was at hand.

Luck was with him. Olivaro sat on a bench beside the stable door. He had the look of someone waiting, his hands busy at the weaving of a light rope from long, tough blades of marsh grass.

"Olivaro!" Antonio said, with hearty relief. "Good! Was it you who took Fatima at noon? I didn't notice. I had much on my mind."

"*Sí*, Señor."

"You know that Luis went away with his friends today?"

"*Sí*, Señor."

Just that, spoken with neither joy nor sorrow. That was the Indian in Domingo Olivaro. He was mostly Indian, but not Tejas.

He was a Tlaxcaleño—and that told a great deal to one who knew about them.

The story of the Tlaxcaleños went back to the conquest of Mexico by Spain. Of the tribes conquered by Cortés, these people had chosen to live instead of to die, though living meant slavery. As slaves, however, they had lived proudly, learning the speech and the skills of their conquerors, but keeping still their tribal character. This in their thinking did not excuse them from the sterner duties of obedience and faithfulness; and so, finally, they had earned the trust of the Spaniard. Later they had been used as seed in the sowing of settlements over the provinces. When a mission or a new town was to be established, several families of Tlaxcaleños would be planted there. They were seed, in that once they had built their houses and cleared land for planting, the new settlement immediately began to grow. They were useful in other ways. Since from childhood each one must learn all the trades in his village—from blacksmithing to shearing sheep—a Tlaxcaleño had more than once saved a settler from despair and a town from ruin.

Tlaxcaleños had assisted in the founding of Los Adaes. Of these, one family, having lost its identity by mingling its Indian blood with Castilian, thus making all who followed mestizos, had continued to live on in the vicinity. Olivaro belonged to that family. When he had asked to join the pueblo at the ranch, Antonio had welcomed him without hesitation.

Mestizo Domingo Olivaro might be; but his copper-toned skin, his nearly beardless cheeks, his square-set jaw, his thick, stern neck, his jet eyes were all Tlaxcaleño. Touches of the Indian marked his *vaquero* dress—a hat, tied under the chin, a sheathed knife in the top of a boot, a *riata* interwoven with red and black symbols, and a whip with a thong-leather lash.

"I will see about Luis tomorrow," Antonio said. "Meantime, there are things to be done here. If you will saddle two work horses, we can ride over the ranch together."

They rode out the afternoon and part of the evening, Antonio giving an occasional direction, asking an occasional question. There was no other conversation. Dusk was thick when they returned the horses to the corral.

"I will leave at daybreak," Antonio said, taking from the stable his *morral*—a capacious woven sack for carrying small necessities for a journey. "Will you have my horse ready? Not Fatima, the gray one—El Turbelino. He is younger and stronger. Also Luis's horse, please."

Olivaro said he would have both horses ready; and Antonio, with his head clearer, but his heart still sore, went on to the house, again entering by way of the kitchen, where he could hear that Esperanza was now in charge.

"I will go after Luis tomorrow—first thing," he said to her, eating his supper there, to save labor and time.

"The Señora told me," Esperanza answered, not saying which Señora, as she busied herself in slaying a dragon of some sort on the hearth.

"I will take a little bread and meat with me, if it is not asking too much."

"I will be up early and will make the bundle," Esperanza said, giving the dragon a few more blows with the poker.

That was all until Antonio rose, ready to go on to the house.

"Do not remove the candle," he said. "Leave it burning when you are through. I have still some writing to do and will do it here. The warmth is pleasant as the night grows chilly."

"It will rain," Esperanza informed him.

"Do you think so?" he asked, and fled.

When he returned to the kitchen, Esperanza was gone, the candle still burned, and on the table lay a whip with a long lash, a braided *riata*, such as Olivaro made, and a new blanket rich with more symbols. Gifts, he understood at once. Gifts of gratitude for justice and good faith, and promising both in return. They held also a message: Good luck attend you, Master! His sore heart jumped and bled a little. He lifted the whip, the rope; he stroked the blanket. Then, with respect, he moved all three to the end of the table and, with a sigh that was more a groan, sat down, drew the candle closer, and spread his papers.

But he had no luck now with the writing. What he needed to say to close the petition eluded him. Finally he gave up trying, put the pages together once more, added extra sheets of blank paper to them, rolled all tightly, tied the roll with a string, and put it into his *morral*. As he rode tomorrow, he would shape the last few phrases. In the evening camp he would find time to set them down. He would give the petition then to José Gonzales—no, he had another thought. Fray Josef de la Garza, who had been here, there, and everywhere during the past week, though not at the ranch so far as Antonio knew, would be with his people of Los Adaes now. He would give the petition to Garza to deliver. The *Teniente* had too much else to do. Flores? No, not Flores.

Two sheets of unused paper still remained on the table. That was as he had meant it to be. Now—no later—he must write that letter to his agent on the Mississippi. If something should happen that delayed his return, Olivaro could keep the ranch going, but the business of trade and money must be given to someone else. He would address the letter to Nicolas de la Mathe, leave written instructions that if he, Antonio, did not return to Lobanillo within three days, Olivaro should give the letter to a certain merchant in Natchitoches, to be sent to Punta Cortada by the first downriver boat.

The door to the kitchen opened. Doña María, wrapped in a shawl, entered. Her eyes took in everything, then centered on Antonio.

"My husband," she said, "now you are going."

"Only after Luis," he protested.

"Luis," she said. "No. You are using him as an excuse. You are going to join your friends, to deliver yourself the petition you have written in their behalf."

"*Querida*, I swear I have no such intention." He mentioned Garza.

"Garza," she said. "Are you addressing a petition to the Father Provincial or to the King? It may not be in your thoughts but it is in your heart to take the petition to Bexar. And you should. You wrote your heart into the arguments. You should present them yourself."

"*Querida* . . ."

"I have seen it coming," she declared. "Every kindness you performed—and then the writing. You can't do otherwise than go, being you." She looked into his eyes, through them to his heart.

91

"But that you should go without bidding me good-bye, that is hard to accept."

"*Querida*, you are overwrought, without reason. It is late and I still have a letter to write. I am leaving early in the morning. I thought . . ."

"You thought to spare me the leave-taking? Why? Have I no part in this that you do? You think I am afraid? That my woman's heart won't bear me up? Yes. I am afraid. I have been in a state of tremble all week, and my heart is a woman's heart, made for suffering, I think; but I could not bear for you not to do, because of me, what you must do. Can't you see?"

"I see a dear, foolish child-woman. How can I do what you suggest? How could I forsake you—my son—all I hold dear, to save these others—if they can be saved? Go back to your bed and sleep. There is that troublesome letter—it is to Nicolas de la Mathe?"

"You see," she said.

"It is a letter I would have written in any case," he insisted. "So now, let us say good-bye—for a couple of days—no more. Then go. After I have done the letter, I will spread a blanket here on the floor."

"Tonight?" she pleaded.

"*Querida*, you will have your way? Then it is my way, too. After the letter I will come. I promise."

Again she searched his face, his thoughts, and at last opened the door again—to close it to the sound of water dripping on leaves.

"It is raining," she said, all the pity in the world in her voice. "Those poor people! Where will they take shelter?"

Antonio shook his head. Who knew?

2

The King's Highway, 1773

"The mournful cavalcade started toward San Antonio. . . . Graves of children marked the way."

CHAPTER 1

Doña María still slept—the whole house was like that when Antonio slipped away the following morning. In the freshness of a rain-washed dawn Esperanza waited for him in the kitchen. How long she had been there he could only guess. The smoke-stained room, separated from the main house by a long passage, was rich with the flavor of freshly made bread. *Roscas*—at this hour? But, when he would have protested, Esperanza's red-rimmed eyes hushed him. He ate two of the crusty little loaves and drank a large mug of chocolate, to stay him and to please her. After all, she knew where he was going and he knew why her eyes were red. Words were a waste. When he had eaten what he could, he thanked her and she gave him his bundle for the journey.

"*Dios!*" he exclaimed then, because of the size of the bundle; and to Esperanza now he insisted that he would be gone only a day or two at the most.

"With you, who knows?" she said hoarsely, wiped her eyes, shrugged her shoulders, and turned away.

It was not easy to leave Esperanza. In spite of repeated declaration that his absence would be brief, it was not easy to leave anything. Where the ranch road met the *Camino Real*, he could hardly make the turn into the highway. This was absurd, he knew. To make so much fuss over a simple errand, quickly done; and then he found himself riding, not westward after Luis, but eastward toward the town known as Los Adaes.

"Take a look," something urged. "The people have been gone a day and a night. See how it is now."

He wouldn't have believed it if he hadn't seen it. Desolation was as complete as it could be with the houses still standing. Some of the doors were closed neatly, but many hung open. Gates creaked on their hinges. After the rain in the night, a wind had risen. It had dried all but the deepest puddles, but had blown dust into heaps, which had settled on doorsteps and in corners, to remain there, since no one was on hand to sweep the litter away.

If the dust had been all—but it was not. As he rode into the square, he saw a bright but soiled handkerchief, half buried in a dust heap, and farther on, in the middle of the road, what looked to be a shoe. He dismounted, dropping the reins over the heads of the two horses, Turbelino, his young gray stallion, with light mane and tail, almost as dear to him as Fatima, and Luis Ramón's bay. Both stood quietly while he picked up the shoe. It was a slipper, a girl's slipper, some mother's pride, no doubt. The slipper had escaped from a bundle too loosely tied or from a careless hand. Its loss had probably not become known until evening. What a scolding that must have caused! He knocked the caked dust off against the heel of his hand, wiped off the remainder on his corduroys, and dropped the slipper into his *morral* beside his papers and the bundle Esperanza had given him.

The soldiers, he thought, looking around the desolate square, had done their work well in emptying the town. Los Adaes, abandoned for a day and a night, was well on its way to extinguishment. He could have wished that Cecilio's fire had spread. What was it he had said to Anastacio the day before with regard to the boy's tale of the soldiers and their whips? Never, never forget! That was what he felt riding through the empty town, and again when he stood before the ruin of Cecilio's house.

Everything of wood had burned to ash. Of the blue door

there remained only the brass lock, blackened by smoke, and the hinges. The roof, without supporting timbers, had fallen in. The four walls, cracked, only a little broken, still stood, but they would not stand long. With no roof over them, the rain would nibble at them and they would soon crumble.

Around the house, newly planted flowers were blackest of all. Leaves had shriveled and dropped from the rose bushes. One bush was missing. A round hole showed where it had been. Measuring the hole with his eyes, Antonio thought of Angelita Gonzales and her basket.

"We mean to plant a rose for Teresa García. With the basket she could even take it with her to Bexar."

Antonio's brows drew together in a brooding scowl. Teresa had apparently attempted to do exactly that. Teresa, Angelita, Rosario—how many others? From the habit acquired during a week of earnest composition, his thoughts shaped themselves into apology:

"You see, Majesty, these are simple folk—children. Abandoning their homes, what do they carry with them? Rose bushes, when it should be blankets."

The scowl cleared. Moving a rose might not be as foolish as it looked. It was like taking a flower from a grave, to keep for remembrance. All this around him was a grave, was it not? So still, so dead! Not a sign of life.

He was wrong about that.

"Miaow?"

It was a thin mewing, and weak, but persistent. It came again and again. A tame cat, not a wild one. Catamounts might come later, but not just yet.

"Kitty . . . Kitty?" And then he saw it.

A patch of fur on wobbling legs. It was old enough not to have to wobble, if only it had had the strength of a little nourishment. It was too young to endure long without that. When it made its plaintive cry, its sides caved in, almost meeting through emptiness. Antonio squatted on the ground and made soothing, inviting noises. The kitten wobbled toward him. It had to trust someone. Or had it been waiting just for him, knowing that he had a softness for the young of any animal and that he favored cats? Why? They were smart. They were shrewd. They knew what they wanted and knew ways of getting it. When they found what they sought, they pounced. This cat, to be sure, seemed an exception. Born foolish. Asleep when the migration began, its owner had been unable to find it.

"Miaow?" Pink nose quivered, pale eyes appealed to him.

But perhaps it was not a fool. Suppose its brothers and sisters had been drowned as an act of mercy before the departure. Then it would have been smart to hide. Still, to die of starvation was not good either. The kitten was very young. When Antonio's hands closed about it, its bones seemed like a bird's. He looked around for some source of comfort, and saw a puddle that the wind had not yet dried up. He carried the kitten there, dipped his finger in the water and held it to the kitten's mouth. The kitten tasted the moisture with docility, only then it looked up at Antonio and purred. For politeness. "*Gracias*, Señor, but no, thank you. There is no nourishment in brown rain water."

And then the miracle. Only it was not that. From three hundred to five hundred households, each family with one or more animals? It stood to reason that a number of animals would go astray at the last minute. A goat and her kid now coming out of a thicket, were no more remarkable than a cat.

Antonio, however, did not favor goats as he did cats. He had had painful encounters with them in his youth. They were willful animals. They could break through a fence and clean off a collard patch before the sin was discovered. Then try to catch the culprit and pen it! Only try! He did not like the eyes of a goat. They were like glass marbles. One looked one way, one another, neither looked at a person directly. This one had eyes of pale amber that stared at nothing. She was a fine goat, cream-colored, but had mated beneath her. Her kid was black as sin. Antonio thought he understood about her and about the kitten. Both had been wedding gifts to the Andorros. So, yesterday, when Cecilio had sent his bride away while he set fire to the house, he had overlooked a few things. Maybe he felt toward goats as Antonio did.

This one now, however, was a blessing. She was not hungry.

She was uncomfortable in another way. Her kid was too young to take all the milk in her udder. That was her only reason for coming out of the brush and tolerating the touch of a man.

From his past Antonio summoned certain necromantic words of command. They worked. The goat backed up and waited. What Antonio said then as he squatted was equally ritualistic, but more natural. Placing the kitten between his feet, he told the goat where she probably had come from and where she could go when he had finished with her. Off to one side the kid watched with interest, and at his feet the kitten purred. Scowling, he spread his hands, then gingerly went to work.

The milk came with a rush, covering both his hands. The cat, uncritical of blasphemy, licked them clean, and asked for more. So then Antonio must kick around through the ruins to find a cracked bowl, draw some more milk, and watch the kitten swell to roundness as it drank. That done, he drew a deep breath, emptied the bowl, wiped it with some grass, pulled more grass to line the bowl, dropped the overfull kitten into the nest, opened the *morral* beside his saddle, and set bowl with kitten down on the other things in the bag. The kitten would rest there, or fend for herself otherwise. She—he knew now with what sort of cat he dealt—fussed, but only a little, and went off to sleep.

That done, he made a loop in his fancy *riata* and dropped it over the goat's head. She could slip the noose if she chose; but plainly she was used to being led, and followed willingly. Naturally the kid followed her. Thus burdened—with a horse on a lead rope, with a shoe, a cat, a goat and her kid—Antonio Gil Ibarbo, *ranchero*, said good-bye at last to the dead town of Los Adaes, and a short while later looked up a slope from the *Camino Real* toward the buildings of Rancho Lobanillo and sent a second farewell, unspoken, that way. The morning was still new. No life stirred up yonder that he could see. It was as well. If anyone up there thought of him fondly as a hero, that one should see him now! *Dios*, he reminded himself more of that clown in armor who had been such a favorite of his father— Don Quixote of La Mancha. Well, what of it? Some child tonight might take comfort from a kitten under his blanket, if he had a blanket; and goat's milk was food. Even the misbegotten kid would be meat a month from now, if other meat were lacking.

At mid-afternoon he overtook the marchers. Once more he stood on an eminence, tree-covered, that overlooked the highway, and watched. The horses nosed over the turf, seeking grass to their liking. The kitten mewed complainingly, asking for another saucer of milk, but also turned aside to scratch around in the new herbage when she was sure no food would be offered in a dish. What did she think he was, Antonio demanded, a dairy hand for cats? The kid and the goat, naturally, made their own arrangements.

The three nuisances, one or all, could have run off and Antonio would not have noticed. He was too occupied with the line moving slowly over the road—a weary line, with merely the second day approaching its end. Only the legs of four-footed animals were accustomed to covering so much distance day after day; and even some of these were lagging. Later the marchers who survived this first weariness might be stronger. As for those who weakened—Antonio's throat filled.

First came soldiers, in a column of twos with a standard-bearer. They moved at a brisk walk. The carriage with Señora Gonzales and whoever rode beside her followed. The young mules had no trouble in keeping up with the soldiers. The pack animals and spare horses of the garrison did well enough. This part of the road, near settlements, was not too bad. Later it would be rougher. However, when that happened, loads of provisions would be lighter.

After the soldiers and the carriage came the first break, then men, women, and children walking. They made a ragged, uneven line. Children and dogs strayed and had to be recovered—a child, perhaps, to be carried a while in addition to other burdens. Everybody, so far as Antonio could see, bore a burden—in his hands, on his head, or on his back. Here and there, not too often, there was a cart on two wheels, with a handle that more than one man could lay hold of, to pull or to push. The cart would not last. Then those who owned it must take out what it held to carry on their already overburdened backs.

They walked in groups—bunches rather—related families, perhaps, or neighbors. Sometimes alongside there would be a few animals—sheep, goats, a cow or two, a loaded donkey—and a boy with a stick herding them. What was it those donkeys carried in the way of packs? One he saw looked as wide as the road.

Group after group passed that way, but slowly. People on foot could not keep pace with any animals except oxen; and those, far to the rear, were now not even in sight. Now and again some weary marcher would break free and sit down beside the road. Never mind me. I will rest now and catch up later. Outriders—soldiers again—prodded them to their feet, for their own good, naturally; and they walked on. The goat bleated unexpectedly and Antonio jumped. His whole face darkened with anger, which he turned on the innocent nanny.

"Ah!" he scolded. "You recognize someone down there, daughter of Satan? You want to be taken there now? More fool, you; but, if that is how you want it. . . ."

With his right hand he scooped up the cat, put her summarily back in her nest in the *morral;* with his left hand he caught up the trailing end of the *riata*, fastened it to his saddle and mounted; and, still dark with anger, he sighted a course that would take take him downhill obliquely to meet the procession at its head, and rode on.

CHAPTER 2

José Gonzales detached himself from the column of soldiers and rode out to meet Antonio as he came down the hill. In full regimentals, he gave an impression of authority, though his beard seemed to jerk when he faced Antonio. That could have been the goat and the kid following behind, which he could not help seeing.

"This is a surprise," he said, stiffly polite, but questioning.

"I am surprised myself," Antonio declared, but, naturally,

other explanation was called for. "I am looking for some of my property which is said to have attached itself to your command. Also, as you see, I have a few things to deliver to others." He opened his *morral* and took out the kitten and the shoe. "With your permission, *Comandante?*"

This was too much for the gravity of even a harassed lieutenant in the best tradition of Spain. Gonzales permitted himself a smile.

"Go with God," he said helplessly. "Will you report to me again—later?"

"Surely, *Teniente*," Antonio promised; and with that he slipped the shoe over the horn of his saddle and, carrying the cat, and leading Luis Ramón's horse and the goat, followed by the kid, he rode down along the column.

Antonio Ibarbo's arrival that day was reported by most who witnessed it as a miracle.

"We did not see him approach," they said. "We were very tired. It was not that we had marched so far—in two days; but, for the old ones and the bambinos who were too heavy to carry but, at the same time, could not walk so well, it was far. It was as if we carried them on our backs, along with everything else.

"So, maybe we did not look up too much to see what went on away from the road until somebody cried out, 'The horse! The horse!'

"There it was, sure enough. Even as we saw it, it lost itself in the trees, then came again, with no trees to hide it—the big gray horse with the white mane and tail. It was when the horse shook its head and brushed flies with its tail that we knew whose horse it was. 'Ibarbo—Ibarbo!' people kept saying. *Seguro*, it was his horse. *El Turbelino*, the wild one. But what mattered most was that if the horse was there, so was Don Antonio. And, if he cared enough to follow us, then God had not forsaken us. He, too, was watching. That was the miracle."

"My Cecilio, it is a sin for you to make small of the miracle," Teresa Andorro pouted in camp that evening. "That he should have found our Ba-ba and that he should take the trouble to bring her here is wonderful. I think you are jealous."

"Of the goat?" Cecilio asked. "It is possible. You have kissed her twenty times since she arrived."

"Not for herself, foolish one. It is because she is a sign that we should not despair. All will go well with us now. You will see. We have each other, and now Ba-ba. There will be more."

"Will there?" Cecilio said, so fondly that Teresa blushed all over.

"Cecilio, my husband," she begged, "do not look at me so. Everybody is watching."

"Not us, little one. They watch a goat eating the flowers you have put around her neck in place of the rope. Come away with me then, where others cannot see how I look at you. Come. We will make a nest of our own away from the camp. Are you afraid? No? Come, then. Yes. Ba-ba can come, too, since she is our good angel, and *babacita* as well. It seems we are a family."

The kitten, until someone with a better right should claim her, went to Pedro Coronal, who had got a thorn deep in his foot that afternoon. His father had drawn the thorn and poulticed the foot, but Pedro, in spite of a wish to seem manly in bearing the pain, had not been able to hold back tears. And here was a true miracle. With the first purr of the kitten, the pain stopped. The cat slept in a warm nest that night, her stomach again full.

"*Gracias, amigo,*" Tomás Coronal said with meaning to Antonio Ibarbo.

The shoe proved to be the property of tousle-headed Carmencita Rojas, who, approaching the age of twelve, and the eldest of six Rojas little ones, was supposed to be equal to carrying a bundle without spilling its contents, but was of a happy, never-fret nature to an extreme. Such a thing as a shoe falling she would never think to notice unless it struck her as it came down. She had not as yet opened her bundle to see what else she might have lost. Fortunately, when she did open it, there was the other shoe.

"See, *mamacita!*" she said triumphantly.

Mamacita made a motion to cuff her, but one knew that never happened.

"You are blessed beyond your deserving," she told her light-hearted, light-minded daughter. "Wouldn't you have looked a spectacle going to church on Sunday with only one shoe?"

Carmencita found that an amusing picture.

"What church, *mamacita?*" she asked happily.

What church, indeed? The eyes of Pablo Rojas, the strong one, were suddenly as red as Esperanza's had been at Lobanillo.

Shouts of welcome greeted Antonio as he rode down the line that afternoon; and that was to him the only miracle. Bubbling laughter flowed like a freshet. Tired heads lifted. Tired backs straightened. Who can laugh properly all bent over? Even those far off heard the laughing and, not knowing the cause, came forward to see.

Only Antonio, turning back toward the head of the column, did not laugh, though nothing could have been more amusing than the loads he saw on burros, mules, people. There was everything from sacks of corn to birds in cages. Chickens—black, white, spotted, and barred—nested together. Roosters, geese, turkeys stuck out their heads from makeshift coops. If the journey had been for one day only, they would have been tied by their legs and hung upside down on the mules; but for many days? No. Even a Spanish chicken could not have endured that.

Later Antonio found the heart to laugh at these absurdities; but at the time he hardly noticed. Among the marchers he had seen nothing of Luis—or of Angelita Gonzales, for that matter, though he could have explained the absence of the girl. She was, no doubt, in the carriage with her grandmother. As for Luis, in his heart Antonio hoped that, seeing his horse, Luis would come forward to claim the animal and make his apologies to Antonio. When, halfway back to the head of the line, Flores appeared instead, Antonio looked at the *Alcalde* sourly. You are too fat, he thought. So is your horse. A little hardship will not harm either of you, but for these others . . .

Flores assured him that Angelita was either with her grandmother or somewhere in the line, helping to care for children. She was fond of doing that.

"You overlooked her," he told Antonio. "That is easy among so many."

About Luis the *Alcalde's* information was more positive, and it justified the worst of Antonio's fears.

"In command of the *caballard*," Flores said cheerfully, "and I cannot express to you how strengthening it is to have him there. It was good of you to bring his horse, however. It will make his work easier among so many animals."

"I brought the horse," Antonio said, with more assurance than he felt, "to carry Luis back to his duties at Rancho Lobanillo. I will try this evening to persuade him that those are his first obligation."

"Oh?" Flores said. "I still hope he will want to remain where he is, though I know how you feel, Antonio. I, too, have lost one I thought a faithful servant. My boy Juan. He was with me night before last, but yesterday morning was not to be found. We could not delay the march to search more than my place. He hated so to leave his flowers . . . and he did not come to Lobanillo?"

"No," Antonio said. Juanito—who had been so afraid! "If he should come, we will, of course, keep him there, remembering that he is yours. But Luis is another matter. He is not a servant. I wish him only to do right for his own sake."

"Yes, yes, I know. Talk to him, by all means; but, if he should choose to go, let it be quietly. Do not say to these people what your reason is for being here. Their spirits have been lifted so much by your presence. This has been a bad day. Worse even than yesterday. We were late in starting yesterday and did not cover the distance that Gonzales had set for us. So today he has hurried us all the way. He says we must reach the Sabine before we camp. At noon I would have said that was not possible. Now, with better heart, we may make it."

"I will save my arguments for Luis until tonight," Antonio promised, not wishing to pursue the subject with this fussy official. "What did you do last night when it rained?"

"We were in the forest. Among pines. The younger ones roosted in the upper branches, the older ones took cover below.

One pine tree can shelter a whole family that way. It did not rain too hard."

"And the priest?" Antonio asked. "I thought surely he would be with you."

"Fray Josef? No. My understanding is that after he put things in order at San Miguel he went on to the Mission of the Nacogdoches, to help there with the burying of the bells."

So, the bells of the missions had been buried?

"Yes, as with the worst of the guns at the fort," Flores said. "There really was no way to carry so much weight. Later, if the bells or the guns are wanted elsewhere, it can be decided how to transport them."

Antonio brooded over this and other matters.

"I will camp with you tonight, the *Teniente* consenting," he said finally. "If Luis returns tomorrow to Rancho Lobanillo, I may ride on with you as far as the Mission of the Nacogdoches. Garza may join you there . . . Well, we will see."

Camp that evening was made, after all, along the east bank of the Sabine, if it was proper to give the name of camp to what was at first merely a sitting down of each section of the march as its members reached the area. Dropping their burdens, they sat down. Quite soon, however, cooking fires began to appear. Presently there could be heard the slap-slap of tortillas in the making; the braying of mules freed from their packs; the shouts of boys, set to the shaping of brush-walled enclosures where poultry could be permitted to scratch without too much danger of loss; and generally the sounds of people making preparations for a night that promised to be at least more comfortable than the preceding one.

While all this was going on, the driver of the carriage bearing Señora Gonzales found a place for it at the edge of the camp in a grove of trees. Antonio, who had ridden the last part of the march beside the *Teniente*, found himself a similar shelter between the carriage and the river, put his horses on short tether, and waited until the mules drawing the carriage had been freed and led away to forage, then waited some more. He expected each moment to see one door or the other of the carriage open and the girl Angelita step out. When she did not, when it began to look as if the Señora might pass the night there in stately isolation, he went over and respectfully announced himself.

"Enter!" a hoarse voice said from inside the carriage. "Enter, Ibarbo, since the vehicle is yours."

His it might be, but he had never seen it before with an armchair tied to the roof. Cautiously he opened the door nearest him, and there, in place of another passenger, rode two rose bushes. Weighted by dirt packed around their roots and fitted into baskets, they rested, one to either side of the Señora, as steadily as if they had sprouted and grown in such surroundings.

"It was the Little One's idea," the Señora said, yellow as the yolk of an egg with her illness, and tired besides. "Rosario, the fool, encouraged her. Well?"

"They seem content," Antonio said discreetly. "And you?"

"I am alive, as you see, but not from choice. It would be better to die, I am sure; but death, it seems, does not come even to the old and ill in answer to prayer. Not quickly, at any rate." Breath failed her briefly; when she went on, her voice was huskier than before. "Then you were good enough to supply this carriage—for which I thank you from my heart. With every rending jolt . . ." She sagged wearily against a nest of pillows, but roused herself again. "You object to the rose bushes, Señor Ibarbo?"

"I? No." For the first time Antonio felt respect for the Señora —and her wry humor. "I do not object to the roses. My thought was that you might prefer some person who would be company for you and who would do better riding than walking."

"Thank you, no," she said. "The roses at least do not occupy any of the seat, nor do they wear out my ears with senseless talk."

"I was thinking of the young lady your granddaughter," Antonio bargained.

"She is not a young lady," the grandmother said. "She is a child. Let her be with her friends. A sick old woman is no company for her. She is a good child. She comes now with help to take me from the carriage. There will be a tent somewhere. Constanzia, my servant, will have made a bed. I will do

107

my groaning there until morning, then start all over again in the carriage. If you will excuse me now. . . . No, there are too many to help as it is. Leave me to their ministrations and I will thank you for that favor."

Antonio saluted the Señora in his carriage and turned away, but not so fast or so far that he missed seeing Angelita, approaching with her volunteer helpers. As the Señora had said, there were too many. Six muscular young men, they could have lifted the carriage with the Señora inside and carried it to the tent she had mentioned. Surely they had duties elsewhere in the confusion of the camp, but they preferred to do what they were doing. Misfortune became good fortune if it allowed them to perform a service for Angelita Gonzales. In town, they would have had difficulty in approaching her. Now she needed them. They were, most of them, quite young. They punched and cuffed one another and grinned foolishly, since they were behind her and she could not see. Two were older and more serious. One was Cecilio Andorro. Then the other must be Luis, though he had done his best to make himself unrecognizable.

But, while Antonio saw all that, Angelita also saw him. The procession halted. For a charming moment he thought she would run to him, alarm and question overcoming shyness; but shyness triumphed and she hurried instead to the carriage and put her head inside. To see if the grandmother was safe? No. It was the rose bushes. When she saw that they were there, untouched, alarm turned to rapture. Again she looked his way and now she would surely have come, but the grandmother must have said something to stop her. As she turned once more to the carriage, Antonio had the good sense to lose himself among the trees.

It was not his intention, however, to remain invisible the entire evening. He was there with his horses, in plain view, when a little while later Angelita came with the servant Constanzia to thank him for permitting the roses to travel in his carriage.

"It was bold of us to put them there," she acknowledged, "but we could think of no better way. A burro could carry them, but the days are warm. If they become more so, the plants might die, exposed to the heat. We are very careful, Señor. Each evening we lift the bushes out, give them some water, and let them stand on the earth until morning. Then we put them back into the carriage, again being careful not to soil or dampen the floor. They seem to be doing very well, though to be sure it is only two days they have traveled so." What she said was of no great consequence, except that it was she who was saying it.

It was now nearly dark. Over the camp, wherever open ground showed among the trees, small fires burned. Around the fires sounded the cheerful gabble of the hungry about to be appeased, broken infrequently by someone scolding or a child crying. More persistent was the muted humming of guitar strings and the continued slap-slap of tortillas in preparation. Farther up the river, and apart, where Gonzales had ordered his soldiers into camp, there was more noise, the rude laughter of men making coarse jokes. Against all this, the girl's young, vibrant voice was the singing of a harp. The glow of the fires made a nimbus of light around her head. It was not strange that a young man should snatch at any excuse for following her. In the darkness she was a light, an essence, hardly real.

"It is understood," she finished, "that if anyone of our people falls ill or cannot for other reason walk the road, the roses must make way for him."

"That," Antonio said, "will be taken care of when the need arises. Meanwhile, the space in the carriage which your grandmother does not occupy is yours to fill as you choose . . . while the carriage lasts."

"You think the roses are too heavy?" she said anxiously.

"No, the roses are not heavy at all, unless . . . Who lifts them out and in again for you?"

"There is always somebody," she said artlessly. "Señor Luis . . ."

"Señor Luis," Antonio said with great control, "should be good at moving roses. He who can carry a calf."

"He is very strong, Señor," she agreed.

Luis Ramón had never looked more able than when he faced Antonio in the same spot an hour later. For that and other reasons,

Antonio's greeting was spoken with anger and disgust.

"Why are you wearing such clothes? What did you do with your others? Did you lose them when you lost your senses?"

Luis swallowed hard before he answered. When you have worked for a man many years, calling him friend as well as boss, when you have been proud to stand well in his sight, you do not all at once give him back anger for anger or rudeness to match his harsh judgment. He swallowed hard, but he stood firm. The clothes in question were the loose cotton breeches and coat shirt of a common peasant. He had not dressed like that since reaching manhood. He had been too vain of his *vaquero* trousers tucked into leather boots. He had still better clothes for fiestas and church. Well, he was still vain, it seemed. He had hair as thick and black as Antonio's but one lock gave him trouble. To keep it in place, he had worn, while he rode the ranch, a knotted handkerchief under his hat. The kerchief was still with him, and that softened Antonio's anger—a little. Moreover, Luis was as beautiful in his way, standing there, as Angelita was in hers. Only not so young or so innocent. With his shirt open at the throat, his arms bare, as were his feet and, his legs almost to his knees, his virile strength had never showed to better advantage.

"Luis," Antonio said, "why do you do this to yourself? Or to me?"

"I do not wish to be different from my brothers or my friends," Luis answered, still respectfully. "It does not seem right."

"No? I thought that was what you did want—to be different."

"That was before this happened, Don Antonio. All is changed now. I know you think it was wrong for me to leave the ranch the way I did. In a way it was wrong. At the same time it was right—for me. I had to do it."

"But you could have told me what was in your mind."

"Don Antonio, it was not in my mind. I did not know it until the end. Then there was no time to talk about it."

"There is time now," Antonio reminded him. "Can you tell me why you thought you must go?"

"Don Antonio, I will try." The young man knitted his brows. "These are my people. I am strong. So many here are weak—

women, babies, the young, the old. This is going to be very hard—on everybody."

"Very hard," Antonio agreed. "How far do you think you have come in two days?"

"Not far," Luis acknowledged. "Ten leagues, perhaps?"

"One twenty-fifth of the way," Antonio informed him, "and the easiest part."

The Sabine was the first of six major rivers to be crossed, to say nothing of smaller streams. The land between the rivers was wild, some of it unfriendly.

"Luis, I honor you for your bravery, but I cannot commend your wisdom. You have done a rash thing in leaving the ranch. How can you help in that way?"

"I will be here," Luis said simply.

"Nothing I can say will change your mind or intent?"

"I am sorry, Don Antonio. No."

From the soldiers' camp came suddenly a burst of loud laughter.

"Do you go armed?" Antonio asked, looking that way.

For answer, Luis opened his shirt. From a belt above the overlap of his peasant breeches hung a monstrous pistol and a knife about half the length of a machete.

"I watch by night and day," he assured Antonio. "I do not need much sleep."

"But that's no good," Antonio scolded. "One night like that is possible, maybe two. After that, you walk in your sleep when you think you are awake. How can you protect anyone in that state? Guards should be posted every night, with two or three to divide the time at each post. There are men enough. Call them together—now is a good time, while they are rested and full of food and courage. Will you do this or shall I . . . but I forget. Flores is the one to give the commands to this camp."

Luis's tension relaxed briefly. His dark eyes shone.

"It is all one," he said. "I will speak to the *Señor Alcalde*, but I still will post the guards. I should have thought of it myself."

"Tonight is soon enough," Antonio said. "Yesterday nobody might have listened. Have you weapons for all the guards? Knives or machetes are better than guns. All that is needed in case of an alarm is to awaken the camp. A loud shout will do that. If anyone fires a gun, let it be at the moon, not at an intruder. The intruder could be a friend. Or a child, or a dog."

What an uproar such an alarm would make! Again loud laughter came from the soldiers' station. Uproar, Antonio thought again, and hoped that nothing worse than noise would result from an alarm. All this talk of arms and guards was, to be sure, in indirect reference to the presence in camp of a particular someone needing protection. In Luis's case, Angelita? Antonio found himself unable to put the question directly. Such an attachment might be only a woman's interpretation of motives. Luis had spoken only of loyalty to his people. It was easier, finally, to talk about guns and all that, also now to mention Luis's horse. Luis wanted him, but did not want to take him. How could he ride, he asked, when others walked?

"Take him," Antonio commanded, forcing the rope into Luis's hands. "He is yours. Take him and go. The night will be half gone while you stand here with arguments and objections."

Very little argument, really, and, on his part, weak. Watching Luis walk away leading his horse, Antonio knew the reason. For the first time he saw Luis, not as a younger brother to whom he stood as guardian and patron, but as a man. A man in his own right, splendid in the vigor of first maturity, strong, fearless, armored against doubt or anxiety—or even sage counsel, whatever the distress of one who knew the young man walked straight toward the edge of an abyss.

Antonio thought of his unfinished petition. What he wanted most to present in the way of argument was a true picture of young men like Luis—or Cecilio Andorro—or any of a dozen others he knew. But it was dark now, and suddenly he too was weary. Also hungry. He would be welcome, he knew, at any of a number of campfires; but he chose to sup only with Antonio Ibarbo and his doubts and questions.

With hunger pushing him and, at the same time, sadness paralyzing his hands, he was clumsy about loosening Esperanza's bundle. Finally the outer wrapping, a coarse, serviceable towel, came away. Inside were spread two clean shirts, clean underdrawers, and two pairs of coarse socks. These surrounded two smaller packets, one of food, wrapped in a napkin, the other a bar of soap and a razor. It was not Esperanza who had made up the bundle. The scolding servant vanished. In her place stood a woman with eyes just as sad, but alight with understanding. No flowerlike, innocent girl. A woman, and his. What did a young man like Luis know of loving and desiring?

"You are going," she said. "That is right."

Right. Luis had done what he knew to be right. For Ibarbo the way was not so clear. All his heart, he thought, was back at Rancho Lobanillo. Then why did he not rise and return? Turbelino would make nothing of the distance, with home at the end.

The fact remained that he did not rise and return. Tomorrow, perhaps, he thought, as he spread the contents of his journey bundle on his folded blanket. Presently he selected the soap and the towel and went down to the river. Finding a secluded pool, he stripped and washed himself thoroughly—and thriftily put on again the garments he had worn through the day. He knew he would not return tomorrow. It might be a week before he saw Garza and gave him the petition to deliver. Olivaro could keep the ranch going that long. The letter to Nicolas de la Mathe would be on its way.

For a week, however, it would be better to reserve the fresh clothing. If he was away longer, he must secure the services of a laundress, also a barber, since he lacked a mirror for shaving himself.

When only partly dressed, he sought for and found clear water running over gravel and drank thirstily, but did not prolong his stay by the river. He was now hungrier than ever. Stepping lightly, he hurried back to the spot where Turbelino now grazed alone. Thinking only of bread and meat, he was half angry when brought to a halt by a new sound from the soldiers' quarters.

In a second he identified the sound. *Teniente* Gonzales was mounting guard. Good! Discipline still prevailed over there. The bark of command was audible, breaking a deep silence. Generally the sprawling camp slept. Fires had burned down to embers. The moon, rising above the trees, showed the sleeping groups only as shadows on the ground. At divergent posts around these shadows, presumably, young men watched tensely. So did Antonio Gil Ibarbo where he stood.

CHAPTER 3

In the light of later happenings, the crossing of the Sabine River could not be recorded as difficult or hazardous. Nobody drowned.

It was an old ruling from Madrid that every river crossed by a *Camino Real* should be provided with a bridge or a ford paved in stone. The King's stones under the Sabine were broad and smooth and clearly visible. The water was not too deep. Horses and mules walked across easily. Other animals, driven into the water, swam where they had to. Strong men, not mounted, also waded. They got themselves and the clothes they wore washed in the process but at this season that provoked only merriment. Big boys crossed in the same way—if they knew how to swim. But rafts had to be made to carry the packs and the older people, the women, and the children.

Rafts were not a problem in this forest country. Cecilio Andorro and the sergeant of the garrison, Juan Morales, had charge of cutting the logs and tying them together with wild grapevines. After that other cables were fastened to opposite ends of each raft, to be drawn tight or paid out by men on either shore.

It was Sunday. Without a priest, without a church, prayers were unceremonious and individual. But numerous. And fervent. Señora Gonzales, whose carriage, with the rose bushes, had gone ahead by way of the ford, sat enthroned in her chair on a raft, with chicken coops surrounding her and strong men walking or swimming alongside. She kept her eyes closed and told her beads the whole way over.

"So ill," her husband said, watching with Antonio on the far shore.

Antonio did not agree. He thought she did very well. This was the first good view he had had of her in full daylight, out in the open. Puffed cheeks obliterated her features, her swollen body was the image of discomfort; but, even as she prayed, her fortitude was remarkable.

"She does not eat," Gonzales said. "She will die."

The time was not yet, Antonio thought. She had that heart. She would not, for example, permit her granddaughter to cross on the same raft with her. If it should happen that the raft tipped with her weight and she went into the water, she wished to be the only one to drown.

But she did not drown. Antonio remembered afterwards most clearly the sick woman praying as she rode over the water, the look of age and despair on her husband's face, and the girl Angelita, care shadowing her, too, as she waited with Constanzia near the shelter to which her grandmother, still in her chair, was carried finally with safety. There was another to remember, who also watched—Juan Morales, a square-built man with hair on his chest like a gorilla's, and brute strength to match.

Six days later, in the middle of a Saturday, the cavalcade drew near to the abandoned mission, set up among the Nacogdoches Indians: Our Lady of Guadalupe of the Nacogdoches. There was no altar now in the church and the bell tower was empty, but the church itself and the adjoining cloister and the priest's house stood as they had been built. The distance covered beyond the Sabine in a week was not much more than double that traveled in the first two days, and that was not good. Every day the weaker ones had to be helped more. Antonio, Flores, and Luis walked more than they rode, to give their places in the saddle to the weariest; but still progress was slow.

However, with Saturday the week was over at last, and here they were. Friday, after having crossed another river, narrower than the Sabine, dark in the shade of tall cedars, but its water sparkling clear in a cup or one's hand, and cold like ice, they had come into the deep green of virgin forest. Birds sang in the trees. It was like Paradise, it was so beautiful. Advancing through the forest this morning, over a trail that was not too clear but soft to walk upon, one had to stop often, to look and hearken. The hoofs of the soldiers' horses made no sound. Except for birdsong and a light wind in the trees, all was deep quiet. Peace settled briefly on even the most anxious.

It was a peace of waiting and wonder, so that, when at the height of the morning the trees parted and the sun shone unobstructed on a meadow deep in grass and spread with flowers, watered by another sparkling little river, ecstasy came. The march halted. Only the soldiers still went forward. They were glad to be out of the thick woods, where spring rains and new growth had all but closed the path in places; and they viewed with misgiving another stretch of forest ahead. They knew nothing of what went on behind them until the *Teniente* rode to the front of the column, wheeled his horse, and put up his arm, commanding them to halt. Then they looked back to see the townspeople spilling out of the forest cover into the open glade and spreading out like flood water.

"Dismount," the *Teniente* ordered. "Unsaddle. We will rest here."

Afterwards Sergeant Morales said he thought at the time that the *Teniente* wanted rest for himself rather than for the others. He was the one who was most tired, who felt he could go no farther. He began to unfasten his coat before his feet really touched ground.

However, if the soldiers had a sign of what was to come, the people in the meadow did not know of it. They heard only that they were to make camp in this beautiful place. They laughed, they sang, they chattered. Mules, freed of their packs, rolled and brayed. Hens cackled, roosters crowed, and dogs barked. When someone shouted, "Look, look! Up there!" and pointed up the gentle slope of a hill to the mission, their joy seemed almost too much.

Saturday for rest and play, Sunday for church—there began at once a great cleansing of clothes and of people. Children, protesting, were called for a thorough scrubbing. Even the men, who with guns and fishing poles turned back into the woods and the undisturbed water behind them, were told to return in time if they wanted clean clothes for Sunday. That evening, divested of everything they wore and wrapped in blankets, they sat around, shouting rudely at the cooks busy over the fires. Afterwards a man could laugh and he could also weep, remembering. Everyone was so happy that, when Gonzales was seen riding from the soldiers' camp to pay a visit to his family, the hush that usually greeted his appearance did not smother sounds of other pleasure. Many, needing some person present whom they could blame for their misfortunes, had come to feel that way toward the commander of the garrison. Now they said merely, "Look, the *Teniente!*" and went on with what they were doing.

Who was the first to see him sway in the saddle was never clear. Many claimed the distinction.

"It was when he crossed the little river," they said. "We noticed, but we thought perhaps his horse had stumbled, shaking the *Teniente*. They came on, through the water, up the bank; and it was then the *Teniente* let go of the reins and fell forward, as if he had no bones to hold him upright."

Magdalena Piedra's oldest boy, Manuel, caught the horse. Juan Piedra and Luis Ramón, who had been visiting his sister, freed Gonzales from the stirrups and lifted him down from the saddle and laid him on the grass. Already someone had run to summon Rosario Terrero.

She arrived, breathless. Panting and heaving, she dropped to her knees beside Gonzales. She felt his wrist for a beat that was not there. She looked into his eyes. With a brush of her fingers she closed them. She straightened his arms and folded them on his breast and straightened one leg that was out of line.

"Dead," she said. "I will find La Niña, but who will tell the Señora?"

Late into the night Antonio and the *Alcalde* sat on stumps beside the little river, discussing the situation—a *junta* of two.

"One hesitates to criticize a ruling of the King," Flores observed with his usual profundity. "The trouble is, they do not know in Madrid how it goes with us here."

That was the whole trouble, as Antonio had known from the first. Who of the King's Council could see, or would notice if he did see, a sick woman sitting in a broad chair, staring at nothing;

117

a dark-haired girl at her knee, sobbing out fright and shock; and elsewhere a faithful servant saying her prayers, afraid to release one breath in order to draw another.

"I suppose," Flores continued, "the journey still goes on."

"Have you something else to suggest?" Antonio challenged.

"No," the *Alcalde* said in haste. "If we thought of returning now, we should only be ordered out again. But . . . who now will be our leader?"

"You," Antonio informed him. "You are still *Alcalde Mayor*. You will lead the people. Sergeant Morales already has taken command of the soldiers."

This indisputable statement of authority did not rest well with Flores.

"If Garza were only here!" he said. "Where do you suppose he has gone?"

"To some Indian village, to give counsel to his dark children," Antonio said. "If we knew which village, we could send word to him. He will come quickly, I think, when he hears what has happened."

"And you, Antonio?"

"That depends on Señora Gonzales. If she wishes now to return to what was her home, I will give her escort."

"Why should she do that?" Flores asked. "There is nothing for her in that direction now."

This was exactly how Señora Gonzales saw it after a night of emptiness. José Gonzales was buried in the mission churchyard on Sunday. Some thought it would have been more respectful to wait a day, in case Garza should appear. Indians came to the camp that morning and waited to watch the burial. One of them could have acted as messenger. But Sergeant Morales, big with sudden power, would hear of no delay. Sunday morning could be given to the burial. In the afternoon preparations must begin for resuming the journey on Monday.

Señora Gonzales, naturally, did not climb the hill for the funeral. She sat in her chair before her tent, hearing what she could of prayers and chants and, finally, the firing of a salute by the soldiers. Angelita and Constanzia, on their return, told her how things had gone; and others also stopped beside her to add a word or two. To everyone, her own and those she hardly knew, she gave the same response:

"It is well. He rests. Nothing can trouble him now."

It was not until preparations for the midday dinner drew other visitors away that Antonio found opportunity for a word with her. Angelita, at the insistence of one of her many guardians, was away. Only Constanzia rustled about the tent like an animated shadow. To Antonio the Señora said what she had said to the others; and, when he asked her about the future, she repeated almost word for word what Flores had said about her turning back. Prospects at Bexar might not be good, but there were no prospects at all behind her.

"José was a soldier of the King for forty years," she said. "That should be worth something. I wish to present my case to the Governor." Then came a flash of the bitter sarcasm which Antonio had come to expect from her. "You think I will not live to do that, perhaps? I will live, Ibarbo. I have a reason."

In the hour of the siesta Antonio sharpened a pen, prepared a saucer of ink, laid these articles and some paper on the smooth top of an aged stump, over which conveniently no ants paraded at the moment, then seated himself on his saddle before the rustic desk. From where he sat he could see the Señora, still in her chair, flanked by two vigorous rose plants. If she had in mind, he thought, to ask something for herself and her grandchild as a reward for the long and faithful service of her husband, it would do no harm for one who had known José Gonzales to add a word of commendation. Doing so might also ease some tension in the writer.

Before he had completed the salutation, a shadow fell across his paper. When he looked up, there stood Hernando Calles. Here, where everyone was generous who had a kettle to boil, the clerk seemed improved in health. Also he had participated in the great cleansing of the day before. His shirt was not as soiled as Antonio remembered it. But he was still Calles. There were the same grasping hands, the narrow head, the prying nose, the peering eyes.

"You are writing?" he said, ingratiatingly. "Could I be of assistance?"

"This," Antonio said, covering the paper with his hand, "is private and personal writing." Then it occurred to him that if he could find time to complete the petition, which now promised to run to several dozen paragraphs, the services of a scribe might be welcome. "Later," he said more gently, "if the need arises."

He did not mean then to look toward the Gonzales tent, but he did so; and the eyes of the clerk followed his.

"I hear," the vulture said, "that Señora Gonzales will go on to San Antonio de Bexar with the rest of us—she and the girl. Some think it is because of the girl. The Señora hopes in the capital to find a better husband than an ordinary villager for her grand-daughter. She is pretty, you know."

"The Señora?"

"Mother of God, no! The girl, Angelita."

"Señorita Angelita is unusually beautiful," Antonio agreed. "Now, if I could be alone, as before."

"I only stopped in passing," Calles told him, but he had one more question. "Is it permitted to ask what are your plans, Don Antonio?"

"Plans?" Antonio said. "At present I have none."

Except that he heard again, spoken imperatively, the old plea of Diego Zapatero: "Go with us, Señor. We lack a guide, a leader, and we are so afraid!"

CHAPTER 4

Two, Antonio counted, when they had crossed the Neches, the second of the major rivers across the road.

The aspects of the country now began to change a little each day. There were still trees—walnut trees, chestnuts, tougher, more gnarled varieties of oak adding themselves to the pines.

There was brush or small wood for fires in the evenings, but the forest did not wrap itself so closely about the camp. The ground was harder on the soles of one's feet; and the land went up and down in long swells, not in ridges with beautiful valleys between.

The course was to the south and west. Summer was advancing. The sun by day was too warm for comfort; and the nights, without the dense forest for cover, were chill by contrast. There was water always, but it did not taste right. The very air seemed different. Nothing was the same. Nothing would ever be the same again. They began to know that now.

Also there was the sickness. Whether it was the nights of exposure—there were not enough blankets to stretch over all— or whether the water did not sit well on their stomachs, or whether they had eaten poisoned meat, such as the poultry that drooped or was injured in the coops, or what the cause was, nobody knew. But it was in the stretch of country between the Neches and the Trinity rivers that the sickness struck.

A man then could not think of retreating from what was plainly his duty. There was work for all—Flores and Antonio with the rest. Water had to be carried, to bathe those who burned with the fever. Children and others who were weak were set upon horses as much as possible, which was more and more frequently as provisions dwindled. A man walking could relieve a mother fainting with weariness by carrying her child for part of a mile. If only Garza had been there to help and to advise! Why did he not come? Several times Antonio, feeling sure that to the right or left of them as they marched Indians followed watching, was tempted to ride out and find a second messenger to look for the padre in the brown blanket, to tell him his white people needed him and where they could be found; but he did not dare do this, for fear that he might meet hostile Indians in this strange land and be lost himself to those he wished only to help.

Rosario Terrero in these days won the respect of even those who at home in Los Adaes had viewed her general behavior with doubt. There were in the camp five beside Rosario, who called themselves herb women. She placed herself at the head of the five, and, in spite of the fact that each had her own idea of cures, persuaded them to put into a common store their supplies of simples. Also each day, when camp was made, two women went out with a guard to hunt more herbs and roots, to mark the places where they grew, and went back at midnight, when magic was more potent, for the harvesting. From each midnight sortie they returned with their aprons full.

Still, the fever raged. It showed no preference as to victims. It felled the strong as well as the weak, the young as well as the old. Pack animals, lightened of other loads, carried those who were able to ride—miserably—with a guard walking alongside, watching for the sick one to get dizzy and begin to fall. For the worst cases litters were swung between two donkeys, chosen for patience, docility, and sureness of foot. The old shoemaker, Diego Zapatero, rode in a litter. So did Carmencita Rojas, the sturdy young hoyden who could not be trusted to carry Sunday slippers in her bundle.

Carmencita was, for a time, more sick than anyone else. By day the sway of the litter lulled her into a stupor; but at night, when they laid her down on a bed on the ground, she would wake in a burning fever that drove her out of her head.

"She will die, my wild one," her mother wailed and Pablo Rojas, the strong one, went aside to pray.

Neither wailing nor prayer healed Carmencita. The potions of the herb women, tried one after another, failed to put out the fire that consumed her. One morning, however, she awoke, white-faced, wasted to a shadow of what she had been, but with the fever gone.

In the night, she declared, she had had a visitation. The Woman in Blue had knelt by her pallet and laid cool hands on her, commanding the fever to be gone. Saint Joseph had been there, too. She knew him by his rod—all flowers at the top. That was her story. She could tell no more, for weakness.

The visitation, at least in part, had been real enough. This was the night when Fray Josef Francisco Mariano de la Garza returned to his people. Even in the clear light of morning he could have been mistaken for his patron saint, since there he was, staff and all. Garza, rugged, tireless, could walk all day for weeks and show no sign except burrs in the hem of his robe.

"But I always carry a staff when I walk long distances over

unknown ground," he said to Antonio, who, wanting to be of the first to question him, had brought him a cup of coffee. "It helps in fording streams and is better than a machete for taking off the heads of reptiles, if one has the right twist in his forearm."

His rod, however, to his knowledge, had never bloomed. If faded flowers lay beside Carmencita's pallet that morning, someone else had dropped them there.

And the Woman in Blue?

"You know the story," Garza said, blowing to cool the coffee.

Antonio knew that the Indians had a superstition about a woman in blue who was said to visit people near to death and work miraculous cures.

"That is the legend," Garza said, "but who knows? A hundred years ago there was a woman in blue, with miraculous powers—a Spanish nun, Sister María de Agreda. After taking the veil, she never in the flesh went beyond the walls of her convent; but in a state of ecstasy she visited America not once but many times. I see you do not believe. Nevertheless, before she died, this Poor Clare sister made confession, declaring that she had been privileged to teach Christian beliefs to certain savages over here. She had written out most of the story, with descriptions of people and places exactly as they proved to be. After she was gone, missionaries in New Mexico came upon a tribe, the Xumana, who practiced some Christianity. They said they had the principles of faith from a woman in blue; and they described perfectly the habit of the Spanish nun. Those are recorded facts. As to the continuing legend of a woman in blue, I have no answer; but then, I do not profess to know everything."

No?

"Well, then," Antonio said, light-headed himself because a merry child seemed out of torment, "let us say Carmencita had a visitation. Not only flowers were there beside her this morning, but only a little farther away was a sack with small packets of medicines." The priest jumped as Antonio had never seen him jump before. "The labels were in Latin," Antonio continued. "So, Mama Rojas gave them to me as the most educated one present. Well, you know how I am with Latin. *Aconitum*—there I was halted."

He was now halted even more effectively. Garza standing, looked to Antonio where he sat, as tall as a tree.

"Give it to me," the priest thundered. "I have walked far enough as things are without going back a second time. So, that is where I dropped it." When Antonio looked mystified—for he was mystified—Garza shrugged his shoulders under his heavy cowl. "When I learned about the fever, I remembered these medicinal herbs and went back for them."

"How far back?" Antonio asked.

Garza did not answer directly, declaring merely that he walked in a day three times the distance covered by this ungainly multitude.

But how had he learned of the fever?

"The Indians," he said, more calmly.

It was Antonio's turn to jump. So the Indians had been close.

"Not too close," Garza said. "Especially since the fever. And now, if you please, the package labeled *Aconitum!*"

It was a powerful medicine. A little powder in a cup of water, from which a spoonful made a dose. Carmencita swallowed her spoonful, but with some difficulty, and pushed aside the hand that offered it, even though the hand was that of La Niña. Garza laid his big hand gently on the child's forehead.

"It is enough," he said to Angelita. "The fever seems not to be returning. Come, let us attend to the others."

Antonio, fastening the sack of medicines now into his string *morral* for safe transportation, studied the two as they moved about together, the girl in her blue *rebozo* and the priest in the brown habit of St. Francis. If the priest had been mistaken for St. Joseph, La Niña had been Carmencita's Woman in Blue. She had begged, when the sickness had first struck, to be allowed to help Rosario in her ministrations. It was soon evident she had a natural ability at relieving misery. No one could smooth puckers of pain on an older face so surely or quiet a fretting child so quickly with a lullaby. It was the beginning of a selfless devotion —or, perhaps, not the beginning, since from earliest consciousness her life had ben inclined that way. The new, more general devotion was a benefit in a measure. It took her mind from her own immediate sorrow, her grief for the loss of her grandfather. It added grace, but where grace was not needed. It did little, to supply what Antonio, and few others, thought was lacking—the healthy happiness of youth and laughter. Except for the priest and Rosario, La Niña walked through the time of sickness very much alone.

As for the packet of medicines—"*María mía, did you think I would not see your hand in this?*" He must question Garza—but not now.

If Carmencita's visitors in the night had been saints from heaven, they had not come to save the girl but to summon her. That morning on the road, every time Angelita or Mama Rojas looked at Carmencita, she was asleep, and thankfully they let her sleep on. However, when noon came and Angelita visited the litter again, Carmencita did not waken, because she could not. White-faced, Angelita looked about for help. The priest reached her side first. Again he laid his hand on Carmencita's forehead and kept it there.

"You are right," he said to Angelita while he still looked down into the litter. "The child is gone. Mary, Mother, receive her in pity. I will tell Señora Rojas. Do you," he asked Antonio, "know the father? I think it would be better if there is no outcry now. We can carry the blessed *muchacha* as she is until evening camp, when there will be more time—for everything."

Antonio was glad Garza had not asked him to be the one to hush Carmencita's mother. How did one tell a woman not to cry out and in the same breath give her a reason for doing so? Telling Pablo Rojas was hard enough.

"Carmencita?" Pablo asked. "That one? Why her?"

That evening Pablo Rojas dug the grave for his daughter beside the *Camino Real*. Though advised that the grave should be deep, he would take no help. This was his mourning for a child whose laughter would never ring through his house again. Mama Rojas allowed Rosario, aided by others, to wash the girl and smooth her hair, but with her own hands brought the clothes for her burial—Sunday best, even to shoes. It was a great waste, Rosario protested, thinking of several who might wear the things and be better off for having them, especially the shoes.

"Carmencita will wear gold slippers in heaven," she coaxed, but the mother would not be persuaded.

"She will wear her own, arriving," she insisted. "I will put them on her myself, to be sure."

That same evening under Antonio's tree at the edge of camp, Hernando Calles set down on paper at Antonio's direction the story of Carmencita Rojas, who was much too young and merry to die this way.

"I have a cramp in my fingers," he explained to Calles.

Then he made a path with his feet walking off his rage; and words poured from him like molten metal. Hernando's fingers flew, but again and again he had to beg for time. Finally, to get some rest, he put in a little conversation.

"If this is an official statement, so to speak," he suggested, "it should be on stamped paper. It will have no authority otherwise."

Antonio struck his head in fury. Assuredly the petition should be written on stamped paper, the stamps representing a tax paid to the royal treasury—also a small profit to the man who printed the paper and anyone else down the line who handled it.

"Do you have such paper with you?" he asked Calles.

"Yes, if you wish some. I can copy what I have written here and anything else you wish."

"You will copy what you have written," Antonio said, "and I will buy ten sheets for myself, provided the cost is no more than twice the value of the stamps. Agreed? Continue, then."

"If I continue," the clerk advised, "it will run to a second sheet."

"I will pay what it costs, fool; and you can count against me a favor, which I will repay in Bexar—when we arrive there."

They buried Carmencita Rojas beside the road. Cecilio Andorro made a cross for the grave. There was a cross on every grave that was made beside the road. Some were only small branches or sticks bound with a piece of string or a vine; these would not keep a hungry animal from digging, but might stop a thieving Indian, if he recognized the symbol.

The sickness killed Carmencita Rojas; but Diego Zapatero recovered. When he was able to ride a mule, Antonio felicitated him on his good fortune and the greater good fortune of his fellows.

"We have five herb women," Antonio said, "and three midwives, but only one shoemaker." And he, too, expressed regret over the good shoes that had been buried.

"You make talk," the old man told him. "Shoes, shoes, shoes. One man could not make shoes for so many if he had the leather. Two bundles of hides—how many thong sandals even will that make?"

"Cut sparingly," Antonio said. "I will send only patrons with small feet."

"It is to give the old man work," he explained to Garza. "That is the most I do, I believe—think of work for other people. So now I have another thought. If I could assemble from this one or that a few articles such as the Indians prize—knives, beads, ribbons, bright handkerchiefs—I might possibly trade them for moccasins, the Indians being near."

Garza regarded him gravely.

"Let the people keep their treasures," he said finally, his expression not changing. "I will talk to the Indians."

That night Garza disappeared again; but at dawn of the day on which the wanderers crossed the Trinity, there, on the other side of the tree that sheltered Antonio, lay the priest asleep, his arm over a pack of moccasins. They were a farewell gift from Tejas friends, he said on being awakened. Now the Tejas would follow no more, since to cross the Trinity would take them beyond their range.

"Will you give out the moccasins where they are needed?" he asked Antonio.

"But they were given to you," Antonio objected.

"I," the priest said, "am a dispenser of spiritual blessings. You are more like an earthly father to these unfortunates. At least, that is how they regard you."

"Really?" Antonio was so foolishly pleased that he could not talk other than foolishly. "In that case . . . look, here is an Apache moccasin."

As if it mattered who had worn the moccasins before this. When evening came, he took the Apache moccasins to Zapatero, pointing out the difference.

"Made by Plains Indians," he said, avoiding the dread name.

"Could you, perhaps, attach stiff soles like these to the softer moccasins?"

"Shoes, shoes!" Zapatero said again. "You look for trouble beyond this river?"

"What else?" Antonio asked. "*Querida, María mía, I am trapped now. I must go all the way with these unfortunate people. It may be a long time. . . .*"

CHAPTER 5

Three, Antonio counted, when they had crossed the river of the Holy Trinity. This again was an easy crossing. There had been no rain recently. The flat stones of the ford were plain to see. The day was warm, the water not very cold. Every walker but the smallest lifted skirts or breeches and waded. Nevertheless, strong men were stationed in the water above and below the stones, Sergeant Morales and Pablo Rojas on the downstream side, Cecilio Andorro and Luis Ramón opposite. Antonio and the friar watched from the near bank, Flores and the standard-bearer of the garrison from the other shore.

For this crossing the plan was different. Flores, with half the soldiers, went over first. Then, before the water became too roiled, obscuring the stones, came the people on foot. Thirty graves east of the Trinity did not make the number noticeably less, but it robbed the morning's adventure of most of its joy. For every grave, from two to twenty mourners would regard each river now as dividing the past, the known, the infinitely dear, from the never to be understood, only to be endured, and presently to be dreaded future. They took off their shoes, if they wore them, and stepped into the water, making no fuss, as docile and patient as before—what else was to be done? But tears filled their eyes, sometimes overflowing.

Only the young, the ever lighthearted, even the day after a grief, could laugh. From them came squeals, even shrieks, as a foot slipped or a playful push brought a complete ducking. Maidens, aware of admiring looks from the guards—bolder, hungrier, more intense than in the old days—dropped their eyes and turned away, but with some twitching. Teresa Andorro could still blush at her husband's too public show of proud possession; but these occurrences only made the sorrow more noticeable. Antonio moved Turbelino a few paces apart from the stony-faced padre and blasphemed in low tones, but continuously.

"Why do you move away?" Garza asked in an even more toneless chant. "Since what you say is not meant for my ears, naturally I do not hear it."

This part of the crossing over, it was time for the four-footed animals—first of all the mules with the carriage bearing Señora Gonzales. Young Manuel Piedra and a cousin rode the mules. To them Antonio gave no attention. On his mind was the Señora. Since the crossing was so smooth, it was thought safe for her to make it in the carriage. In fact, how else would she go? Also in fact, she was as safe in that vehicle as she had been any day recently. Antonio looked for the carriage to fall apart almost any time. He was tempted at each camp, after the Señora had been led to her tent, to make a test of his weight on the straps, but he never acted on the impulse. Such a test might have been the one thing needed to bring about their collapse.

The mules, urged on by the youths on their backs, entered the water with no more than the usual show of reluctance, and, once they found a footing on the rock slabs, moved on. The carriage, with ropes fastened to the rear wheels, slid down the gentle slope of the bank as intended. The front wheels entered the water. Then, just as the hands on the ropes were ready to let go, it happened. The right rear wheel came apart. With a soft plop, the carriage settled against the bank at a dangerous tilt. Whereupon, providentially, the left wheel also decided to go to pieces, so that balance was restored. A small gain, but it stayed disaster.

Shouts filled the air. Loudest was a cry of which Antonio could never be certain from whose throat it came—his own or Luis Ramón's:

"Free the mules!"

Whoever gave the order, Luis had the advantage of nearness. He was now at the front of the carriage, his hands on the mules' harness. When the buckles proved to be too difficult, his knife flashed in the sunlight, and the mules stepped away. The carriage remained where it was, against the bank. A great sigh went up, but not from inside the vehicle. From there came the next command:

"Take me out of this trap!"

"At once," Antonio agreed.

And the door he seized came off in his hand. Truly the hour of the carriage had struck. The other door came off and a front wheel was splintered before the removal of the Señora was accomplished. The rose bushes came out first. They got a wetting that day to last over several. Then the chair was somehow steadied alongside, and the Señora helped herself and was helped by others to a seat in it. Four young men, who by now were accustomed to serving as her porters, laid hold of the chair and carried her across the river.

Fortunately, the Señora's weight was now less. In the wretched time just past, that had been the real miracle. Either because of the forced simplicity, even at times scarcity, of eating, or because of the absolute need for her to move more actively, her dropsical condition had improved. The shrinkage of gross flesh had now reached a stage where many were fearful for that reason.

Nevertheless, it was no easy feat to carry a woman in a chair over slippery stones through moving water. The young men were panting before finally they could put the chair down; but they would have accomplished the feat had it been twice as difficult. Was not La Niña waiting on the far shore with clasped hands and parted lips to receive them—also the two who carried the roses in their sodden baskets? All made a solemn ceremony of delivering their burdens.

Antonio, watching, tossed the door he still held into the water and saw it float away. A few minutes later he reined Turbelino to a halt on the far side of the river beside the Señora, enthroned.

"Felicitations, *Madama Compadre!*" he said, sweeping off his hat.

"*Gracias!*" she answered drily, with a twist to her mouth and that unconquerable spark in her eyes. "I have to thank you once more for the use of your carriage, Antonio Ibarbo. If it is now destroyed—is it? Tell me."

"Completely," Antonio said. "What remains is either lost in mud or is floating to the Gulf. Anyone who finds a piece will wonder, but nobody will know."

Peace settled on the Señora. But she was still, perhaps more than ever, a very sick woman. Her color was bad. The loss of weight made her cheeks sag. Flesh drew into folds on her arms. Only that spark in her eyes and the sting near to malice in her way of speaking were reassuring.

"Then I can thank you with honesty for the carriage," she said. "Every day was torture, but still I thank you. I thank you and I thank God that so much is over. Do you understand?"

"Perfectly," Antonio said. "How will you travel now?"

The spark in her eyes exploded. She laughed. *Madre mía*, it was the laughter of one very young. Or very old.

"You think I don't know? In a sick litter. How else?"

"May you float as on a cloud," he said, knowing it would not be like that.

He went away to make the arrangement, also to provide for the roses. He would sooner have abandoned the old woman than those, he told himself. Miraculously almost as green as ever, the roses to many had become a symbol of hope. This was the day, then, when, in addition to distributing moccasins, he provided for the Señora's hammock, chose a pack mule for his personal use and invented for it a sling, which allowed two rose bushes to rest, securely tied, on pads against the beast's flanks. Leading the mule as he rode along the uneven line of marchers, he reminded himself more than ever of the crazed knight of La Mancha. Like that one, he too furnished amusement. At least, the tired and sorrowful had something to think about other than their own troubles. Moreover, at evening he won a sweet expression of gratitude for this new service.

"Señor Ibarbo"—it was La Niña, with the faithful Constanzia in attendance—"I give you thanks, many thanks, for carrying the roses."

Gracias, muchas gracias—a person would have to watch the words being shaped by such a young and tender mouth to know their full sweetness.

"It was not necessary to do this," she said further. "I thought we must abandon them. I am sorry people laughed at them on the mule. My grandmother says you do not mind the laughing, but I am not sure."

"The Señora, your grandmother," Antonio said, "is right. And you? Do you find my mule amusing?"

"A little," she said shyly, her eyes asking his pardon.

"Then laugh—for me," he commanded, "where I can hear you. *Dios*, there is too little laughing these days."

Her eyes smiled first, then her lips. Finally she did laugh, still shyly. To encourage her, Antonio laughed with abandon. Afterward he knew he had made the most noise, submerging even Constanzia's embarrassed cackling. Here in this wild place came what he had vainly tried to achieve before—a moment of near-normal merriment. Abandon the roses? Never!

"Good night. Sleep well," he said as Angelita and the maid turned away. Blessed child, no wonder everyone adored her!

But literally, everyone. Where she had been there now stood an angry young man, the more angry because he stoppered his wrath. Anger smoldered in his eyes, it swelled his throat to near bursting, because he could not, would not spill it in words.

"Señor," he said stiffly, "I am here to say that I regret having had to cut the harness on the mules. I could have waited for you to say so."

"There was no time for waiting," Antonio reminded him.

"But it was not my leather, Señor."

Now what, Antonio wondered, ails this young donkey?

"It is nobody's leather at present," he said. "The carriage is wrecked, but that is not your fault. We have to consider only how best to carry Señora Gonzales the rest of the way. She did not find the litter too comfortable this afternoon." It was like, she said, being in a small boat tied up in rough water. "She has expressed a wish to try riding a horse, if only part of the time, tomorrow. Something special will be needed for a saddle; and two must walk with her while she rides, one to lead the horse, the other to guard the Señora."

The look in Luis's eyes was less fiery. He was wary now.

"I will do what I can," he said.

"*Seguro!*" Antonio cheered. "Who could do better?"

The poor fool, he thought, to be so consumed with hopeless love. Could he not see that it was hopeless? Then he was a fool. Ah, but all young men were fools. He had been a rare one at Luis's age.

"Let there be no more nonsense about leather," he said, as carelessly as he could, and added, "That is a good knife you have. Do you still set guards at night?"

"Now more than ever," Luis said, in surprise at the question. "Is it—the soldiers?"

"One of them."

"Ah! But they, too, post guards. It would seem hard for them to pass their own sentinels."

"Not for someone with authority."

Juan Morales. The sergeant.

"Let us not speak his name," Antonio warned. "Promise me, Luis, that you will not be drawn into a fight with him. Promise."

"How can I promise?" Luis objected. "If he should find a way to enter our camp, if we should find him here among us some night . . ."

"You will only get yourself hurt," Antonio warned. "He is a bull without reason."

"You think I do not know? Still, I should have to try to stop him."

"No!" Antonio insisted. "Again I must remind you. Raise an alarm. Others, with the authority of numbers, will then deal with him."

Luis gave his promise at last, grudgingly; but at least he went away angry at an enemy and not at his best friend.

Three—they were now beyond the Trinity, and the land was stranger than ever. Trees were less frequent. Stands of cedar, with some oak and nut trees, grew along the water courses; but there were no more pine forests, no more pines. Between the stands of timber stretched the prairies, now deep in grass and bright with occasional flowers. Here was new peril. Serpents hid in the deep grass. A child, wanting only to gather flowers, was a threat to the snakes, and they struck.

Pedro Coronal was the first victim. The snake struck him in the fleshy part of his right leg. Pedro did not hear the warning of its whirring rattles, but he knew when the snake bit him. His cry of horror sent the other children flying to shelter and brought his mother, and, more potently, Rosario Terrero. She recognized the mark of the fangs. The flesh was already inflamed and beginning to swell.

She called for a knife. While Tomás Coronal held the boy, she cut across the wound two ways to let the poison run out with the blood and called for a live chicken, whole.

"Cut it open and give it to me," she commanded, without looking to see who had produced the chicken.

She folded the chicken, warm, hardly dead, around the leg.

"More," she said. "And have the knife ready."

All the time she was watching and counting. When she tossed the first chicken aside, its flesh was green with venom. Those who were closest swore to that; and it was true the chickens looked dark and poisonous when, at Flores' command, they were buried, to keep the dogs from trying to eat them. Six fowls were applied as living, pulsing poultices before Rosario was satisfied that the venom was gone. By then Pedro, who had cried out with terror when a small cut had been made in his flesh, was sitting up to watch the bloody treatment.

"He will be fine now," Rosario said to his parents. "The leg will be sore, but that is all, I think."

By evening the leg had swelled and the place of the bite was red and angry, the boy flushed with fever. A new doctor now offered help. It was Luis Ramón with a small earthen jar filled with a salve of his own compounding. It was, he said, good medicine for horses and mules, very healing. Rosario sniffed it and named a weed. He nodded, scowling. After all, this was his invention.

"Give it to me," Rosario said. "It can do no harm."

But Pedro, remembering her sudden way with a knife, drew himself into a ball and would not let her touch him.

"Let Luis," he said. "Only Luis."

So it was Luis who applied the salve, and a bandage—to keep the odorous mixture off the blanket which, as a privilege, Pedro was to have for cover that night.

"*Gracias*, Señor Luis," Pedro sighed, and slept.

"Now it is you, Señor Luis, who are a hero," Antonio mocked. "You see how easy it is. A pot of ill-smelling salve is all that is required."

The next day, he who had been bitten by a poisonous serpent and lived was a hero, able to walk short distances and, between times, to ride with Don Antonio on Turbelino and talk to Don Antonio about his cat, which someone else was carrying in a wooden cage that had been contrived for it.

"She is growing up to be a fine cat," Antonio complimented. "That bell she wears will not help her to catch mice, but she is easier to find, I suppose."

Pedro Coronal did not die of the snakebite. On the other hand, he never recovered his desire to gather flowers. Nobody gathered flowers now along the way. The soldiers at the head of the procession rode off four abreast and trampled a wide swath; and the exiles kept strictly to it. Evenings there was another general trampling and beating down of the campsite. Sometimes, if there was no wind, the grass was burned off. It did not make as comfortable a bed of the ground that way, but it was safer.

Still death struck. A hunter, one of Luis's friends, was alone, away from help, when a serpent with rattles stung him. He died in agony. Saddest of all was the death of Pedro's mother, Tomás Coronal's Rosa. She was of those who found the day-after-day marching especially tiring. Pedro's snakebite and his narrow escape were a shock from which she never recovered. One day, marching along, she stumbled and fell. When Tomás picked her up, she opened her eyes, sighed, and was gone.

"It is rest for her," Tomás agreed. "She was not strong. But what will the girls do now without their mama? And Pedro?"

"And Tomás?" Antonio thought.

Altogether, thirty crosses. . . .

Fear laid a hand of iron on the heart of now this one, now that. Then another, and another, and another.

CHAPTER 6

The Brazos was a strong river—of no great turbulence, but of pushing strength, and deep. However, where the water ran swiftest and deepest, it was not too wide. A good swimmer could cross there, though it was best to have hold of a horse or a rope. A raft was safer still; and that was how the packs and all the people—except the few who swam the river, to handle the rafts from the far side—and the smaller animals made the crossing. Mules and horses and such cattle as remained—there were not too many now—were driven into and through the water, with few losses; but goats and sheep had to be ferried.

Again, though there were fewer people and animals, and burdens were lighter, the crossing was slow and labored. There was now no merriment. Shouts of command or warning, hoarse bellowing at mules and cattle alone broke the solemnity of silence. Antonio, who had ridden El Turbelino across early, followed by his mule and the up to now imperishable rose bushes, stood this time on the far bank watching the crossing. In his right hand was his whip with the long lash. Why he had armed himself thus, only he knew; but his reason seemed to him sufficient.

The evening before, when camp was being made, as usual short of the river crossing, so that everyone's strength should be renewed by sleep and rest, that malignancy which could only be called fear had seemed to him more evident than ever. People looked at the river, flowing, flowing, flowing, and shuddered. Another river? How many more? dull eyes and quivering flesh demanded. Next came a thing too bitter to be hope, and yet, it was a sort of hope. Perhaps, without a bridge we shall not be able to cross this one. Here then the journey could end. Well?

At supper time Antonio had mentioned this sickness of the spirit to Flores and to Garza.

"It is a bad time to despair," he said. "Half the journey is now accomplished. After the Brazos, there are two other rivers of importance, but only one is bad. The other should give no difficulty."

"We are only halfway?" Flores said. "I thought . . . it is all much longer, much harder than anyone anticipated."

But the question was, Could anything be done to lift the hearts of the weary travelers? Prayers, Garza thought, no longer penetrated their dull ears or duller brains. Flores suggested wine then—a little, carefully rationed. But who had wine?

The soldiers. From their camp came the usual evening noises. The soldiers had wine, or possibly something stronger. Antonio took up his saddle and laid hold of El Turbelino's tether, speaking soothing words, as if it were the horse who had to be willing to go on the mission.

A short while later, mounted on the big gray, he had sat in the soldiers' compound, looking down on the bull-necked sergeant, and felt his courage amply bolstered by antipathy. Bluntly he stated his business. How many liters of wine or other liquor would the corporal sell to him and for how much?

"None," Morales said, just as bluntly. "I have none to sell."

Antonio let a moment pass before taking the second step in bargaining.

"*Aguardiente?*" he suggested. "Or a little *chinguirito* from Louisiana? Though what good soldiers of the King would be doing with contraband brandy is hard to see."

"None," Morales said again.

"Not at any price?"

The dark was not yet dense enough to hide the slow leer that spread over the sergeant's ugly face.

"Yes. I will make you a price. Remove some of the sentinels around your camp tonight, so that a visitor may enter."

"I have nothing to do with guards," Antonio said coldly. "I am interested only in your wine. Is it you who would like to visit the camp? Why?"

"You ask?" the leer was now in the rogue's voice. "You who have only to put out your hand and take the choicest morsel? Others are not so privileged. It is dull to be so far away every night from old friends—or new possibilities."

Antonio tightened rein on El Turbelino.

"Stand aside, Morales. Mind the horse. And keep away from the camp if you wish to live and reach Bexar and promotion. You who have given a reason for setting guards. I am sorry you have no wine to sell."

So now this morning he carried his whip ready and would do so, he thought, from now on.

Four—the Brazos was finally another rolling barrier behind them. Arid land, where mesquite flourished by way of trees, stretched ahead, except where water courses were still heavily wooded. In such a forested spot one afternoon two hunters startled a herd of wild cattle.

"Yahoo!" Luis shouted and ran for his horse and a rope. A dozen volunteer *vaqueros* followed him. In the resulting confusion only four cattle were caught and butchered; but never before had anyone tasted such beef. Cooked without seasoning, except for some peppery herbs that Rosario and another herb woman found on the banks of the little stream which accounted for the trees, it was still delicious. Eaten without tortillas—who remembered those?—the *sopa* was nectar. There was music with the supper that night. The volunteer *vaqueros* strutted and swaggered and talked of more hunts to follow. Who knew?

Luis came to Antonio, his eyes shining as of old, his face open and friendly.

"It could be good cattle country?" he inquired.

"It could be," Antonio agreed, his heart more squeezed by this nearly merry evening than it had been by many gloomy ones.

With all this, life went on in all the usual ways, and in some that were extraordinary. Between the Brazos and the Colorado rivers, Rosario Terrero acquired a husband. By lawful marriage.

138

This came about through circumstance, also the stubbornness of the man involved, and finally the firm dictum of Fray Josef.

In the first place there were the Coronal children, now without a mother. Nothing was more natural than for Rosario to take the poor things under her wing, which, it seemed, she could spread to cover any number. They came to her gladly, gratefully, all but young Pedro. To him Tía Rosario was not the one who had saved his life when the snake struck, but that woman who had cut his leg with a knife. He would have nothing to do with her and wept unashamedly over the desertion of his cat, which had no scruples about eating scraps from Rosario's kettle. In one way or another Rosario always managed food. She even brewed tea from the leaves of wild shrubs. It was not wine, but neither was it flat water. Taken with milk—goats' or cows' milk—it was warm and acceptable to hungry young stomachs. Even the cat lapped the beverage . . . but Pedro? No.

This was too bad. He needed food and a mother's care as much as his sisters did. His rejection of Rosario worried his father. Perhaps Tomás Coronal was also hungry, for kindness as well as food. However that was, one evening he took his whimsical son by the hand, and led him, by invitation naturally, over to the noisy, chattering, busy, squabbling circle about Rosario's steaming kettle. Pedro, by this time wanting very much to be part of the confusion, still pulled away, or tried to. But the more he pulled, the more firmly Tomás held him.

"I have come to ask forgiveness," Tomás said to Rosario, armed at present only with a ladle, "for this unhappy boy who thinks good women go around with knives, looking for children to cut to pieces."

Rosario put the ladle back into the pot and held out her arms. "*Pobrecito*," she crooned, "come!"

The warmth of the welcome, together with the smell of the *sopa*, was too much. Pedro came. This was the beginning of a new relationship, which flowered because of difficulties, not in spite of them. Long after the many children were disposed in heaps on the ground for a night of sleeping, gentle, tired Tomás Coronal sat beside Rosario's fire, talking softly to her—of his children and hers, no doubt. When this went on for three nights in succession, and people began to make sly jokes about it, Garza took Tomás to task.

"If," he said, in his unemotional way, "it is your desire to be father to fifteen children to whom Rosario Terrero will stand in the position of mother, a marriage should be celebrated. If for no other reason than that a good example be set before the children."

Tomás had his answer ready.

"I had that in mind from the first, Padre."

Rosario was trapped. She either had to give up three sweet new children; a charming cat, which cleaned up all the scraps of every meal; and a new friend of the opposite sex—or marry. Two mornings later, in place of matins, Garza celebrated a nuptial mass; and Rosario Terrero became Señora Coronal. All would have been perfect except that among those present was Natividad Acaro, who, in place of offering felicitations, stood off and jeered.

"*Ai-ya*, Rosario! You got caught this time, didn't you? It serves you right for being ready to steal any man who passes by. You . . ."

The names she called the bride were wholly unfit for decent ears to hear. Garza came out of stony rigidity to warn her.

"Silence!" he thundered, with such force that for half a minute Natividad did hush. But then her sense of justice and injustice inflamed her anew.

"Why do you tell me to be still?" she cried. "Who gave you the right?"

"God," the priest said, still thunderously.

"But what do you know—a priest?" Natividad countered. "How long is it since we began this abominable voyage? Where there is no fun ever. No sociability. Just march, march, march. It is enough for you, a priest, maybe, but not for me."

Unable to quell her by any sort of command, Garza resorted to Latin. Extending his big right arm, pointing a giant's forefinger like a pistol, shouting an incantation of which nobody understood a word, he advanced upon Natividad Acaro; and she, not knowing whether the incantation was the church's curse or what it might mean, began to shake. She stepped backward in fright, and finally turned and ran, to be out of the reach of the threatening finger and the awful sound. She ran until she was no longer pursued, then threw herself face down on the ground and beat her fists and sobbed out her anguish.

Spirits did not droop that day on the march. There was too much to talk about, too much to explain to the young, with their wide and wondering eyes. It was, Rosario Coronal told her fifteen, only that Señora Acaro wished that she too could have had a wedding; and most of the fifteen believed her. Only two or three of the older ones were not quite satisfied, but kept their dissatisfaction discreetly covered.

"Poor Natividad!" some women said, when they were where no young listened. "After all, why should Rosario have a wedding with the blessing of the church? In her day she has been as bad as the other."

"But it is not the same," others argued.

Both sides were right. If the sins of the two women had been set down in a book of accounting, they must have been listed under the same heading; but Natividad was more the professional sinner. In Los Adaes she had prospered, because, where Rosario gave, Natividad took. That was the difference.

For the venality of her sins, Natividad now lay in the dirt, howling; and for a long time nobody came to comfort her, until finally there was one. Hernando Calles, himself too often forgotten and always despised, came with a cup of water.

"You?" Natividad said, turning over to see who was there. Had it come to this now? Then she sat up and took the cup and drank, looked over the rim at Hernando, thanked him, and began to brush the dust and dry grass out of her hair.

"Come now," he said. "Everyone has gone. We must hurry to catch up with them."

"No need of haste," she sighed. "They crawl like caterpillars. Sit down. Talk to me."

Knowing all these things, Antonio could hardly wait that evening to unroll his petition for clemency to the people of Los Adaes. The paragraphs now numbered thirty-two, most of them devoted to the stories of various people. The three Gonzaleses, especially the granddaughter; Cecilio Andorro, who could build anything from a raft to a house; Luis Ramón, who had abandoned a good life on the Ibarbo ranch to lend his strength to family and friends; Zapatero the shoemaker; the Rojas family, minus one; and others.

Now he wished to set down the story of Rosario Coronal, the woman of many gifts, but none so remarkable as her gift for motherhood. As always, what he wrote seemed to him not to do justice to the subject. He could do more than write in blunt words the facts as he knew them: Rosario, who had a way with growing things, whether roses or cabbages, who knew the nature of herbs and simple medicines. Rosario, mother to fifteen, now the wife of a good man, her marriage blessed by a priest. A fine woman, all told, who would be even worthier now.

He did not write about Natividad Acaro. He cauld not mention all, and Natividad was most certainly high on the list of those who could be omitted. Anyhow, it was too soon. Not ready himself to say, "Poor Natividad," he thought, "Wait and see." The association of such a one with Hernando Calles was not likely to result in anything good. Nevertheless, as he rolled up his petition, the ink on Paragraph 33 being dry, Antonio Ibarbo had one of those periods of feeling good which blessed him at intervals on this pilgrimage.

It remains a town, he thought, looking over the camp, busy with preparations for the night. When he closed his eyes he could hear still that soft stirring which he had come to think of as a communal breathing. And yet . . .

"María mía, I know now less than ever how or when this will end."

CHAPTER 7

Of all the rivers crossed on the journey, the Colorado was the worst. Taking its rise high in the San Saba Mountains to the northwest, the range of the Lipan Apaches, it was joined between that point and the Gulf of Mexico by four rivers and fourteen creeks. Half of these surely had emptied their waters above the crossing of the *Camino Real*. Either that, or else there had been heavy rains that raised the river's height. The water as the weary marchers saw it that day was brown with sand and mud, and littered with drift. It frothed in angry eddies. A raft would have been only a few more logs tossed this way and that, and where could a raft be landed across the river? There seemed not to be enough ground to give a foothold to a swimmer, if one could have crossed through such water, as none could. A high, bare hill rose over there, like a wall. All the far bank was a wall, high and impassable.

And yet, here, of all places, there remained part of what had once been a bridge. It was now only the trunk of a giant tree, flung over the water, with cross timbers hanging from it. Originally there must have been a second tree, holding those timbers. A towering flood had wrecked the bridge and carried half of it away. Almost at the same time, however, a solution was offered to the problem of crossing. Here, on the near shore, grew the usual forest of cedar, with trees of exceptional height. If one could be cut and dropped across the channel . . . it seemed the only way.

It had to be a big tree, surely, and it must be dropped close to what remained of the old bridge. Most important, one must know what would catch and hold it on the far shore. Fifteen-year-old Manuel Piedra, Magdalena's oldest son and Luis Ramón's nephew, volunteered to cross the old bridge and see. Barefooted, he raced the length of it, so quickly that those who watched had no time to be afraid for him. Pedro Coronal's cat could not have done better. He reached the far bank, stepped off, and almost immediately turned, to flash a smile that said all was much better than anyone had supposed. There was cheering then: "*Hola, Manuel! Bravo, muchacho!*"

He waved in reply, then could be seen tramping about over the earth, testing its firmness. A few minutes of that, and, without warning, he flung himself across the tree and hung head down, studying what lay below. Luis cupped his hands about his mouth and shouted angrily.

"Come back! Come back now, witless one!"

Manuel waved a hand and went on looking. Only when he had seen all that was to be seen did he draw himself back over the log and stand once more, waving and smiling. Again Luis cupped his hands; but, before he could speak, Manuel was on his way back—still smiling, hardly looking at where he placed his feet, seeing only those who waited at the end of the run.

Again there was cheering.

"*Bravo, muchacho!*" his uncle mocked, as proud as anyone. "Well?"

There was ample ground at the far end of the bridge, Manuel reported, as pleased as if he had put it there. Flat, big enough for a house. His hands spread to show the flatness. A little soft, but then the tree would not splinter as it fell. Nor would it dig a hole because, under what remained of the old bridge, there was a cribbing of logs, with some stone taken from the bluffs. That was what he was looking at when he stood on his head. Now, if they could only have success in dropping the tree! Mocking, still proudly, Luis offered him axe and machete. And Manuel, still smiling, gave them back.

"That needs a man," he said.

It needed more than one man. One certainly who knew how to swing an axe and topple the tree, others to cut away the side limbs and top, while the tree still stood. The side limbs came off first, leaving spurs for climbing, also making it easier later to secure the cross timbers with rope. Next, while all held their breath as they watched, the unneeded length at the top was severed and sent crashing into the boiling river. Finally came the supremely delicate job of felling the tree. To weaken it in just the right place, enough but not too much. To persuade it to fall as near the remnant of the old bridge as possible, but not close enough to smash things further. There was another breathless moment when the tall pole swayed and then, with a fearful cracking and crashing, went over, its top digging into the soft mud on the far shore and holding—inches away from the cross timbers hanging there.

Time was expended in a short argument over where to begin the lashing of the cross timbers to the new tree. It was decided finally to take the far end. The head of the new tree was lighter, if it had to be moved. The base seemed lodged securely against its stump. Also, as they lay, the two trees were farther apart on the near shore. The boards remaining there would not span the gap, but that could be solved easily. The side limbs that had been taken off could be used until the gap grew narrower. Already some were being trimmed. Finally the bridge would be rough, but strong. It seemed still the only way across.

This was, assuredly, work for men. A squad of soldiers made ready to fit the first cross piece at the near end of the bridge. Cecilio Andorro and Luis Ramón, each with a coil of rope and a hatchet besides the knife in his belt, stepped out over the water.

They crossed safely. All that looked dangerous that morning went well. That was spoken of afterwards. Having arrived at the far bank, they put a double turn of rope around the head of the felled tree and moved it, but very little. Surely that did no harm. Then they went to work on the timbers, Cecilio testing them, notching them, helping to wrap the ropes, and Luis securing the knots. They worked fast. Soon Cecilio was standing in water. Once he shivered elaborately, and the two of them laughed and changed places briefly; but mostly it was Cecilio Andorro in the water and Luis squatting on boards already made fast. Then, as the water deepened, Cecilio straddled the tree and handled the rope from that position. They seemed to be enjoying the task, as young men would enjoy putting skill and strength to good use.

But now they paused for a discussion. The timber being handled seemed not to meet with their approval. Cecilio was still astride the tree, seated firmly, or so it seemed. He leaned forward a little and reached out with one arm to take the board from Luis, and then it happened. The tree moved first, then the whole bridge structure shook. The movement seemed not too violent; but in the act of reaching, Cecilio lost his balance and went into the water.

Still, that need not have been disastrous. The water was deep, but he, a swimmer, should have come up at once. Luis thought so. He did not wait longer than an instant. Before those on the other shore could cry out, he was into the river after his friend.

It was good he had not waited. Half a minute later he could not have caught Cecilio. As it was, when he broke surface he was his own length downstream, with one arm under the arm of Cecilio at the shoulder. With one free arm and all the muscle in his legs, he struck out for the land nearest him. If he made it, he would still be across the river, far from the friends who watched; but he knew he could not swim through to their reaching hands.

The river, however, did not mean to let him touch safety in any direction. Hampered as he was on the one side by Cecilio, whose bleeding head hung even then with a telltale limpness, he fought a losing battle with the current.

"Take the women and children away," Flores ordered. "Take them away."

Antonio was already on El Turbelino, riding for a point downstream where the river narrowed to make a turn. *Dios, now give me strength*, he entreated, and coolnes and clearness of sight and aim, as never before! Arrived at the point he had in mind, he checked El Turbelino, made a loop in his braided rope, whirled it and let it go. It seemed a long time before the noose settled, though it was only a flashing instant. By God's grace as well as because of the trained exactness of his arm, hand, and eye, it came down over Luis's head and shoulders. He, in despair of his own life by then, had wit and strength left to free his swimming arm, so that the loop tightened about both him and Cecilio. El Turbelino settled back on his hind legs and stiffened his forelegs; a great sigh went up on shore.

Minutes later many hands drew Luis, exhausted, up on land; but Cecilio was beyond saving. Falling into the water, he must have struck his head on some hard object below the surface, possibly that arrangement of logs and stone that Manuel had discovered. He had been dead when Luis found him.

Silence cut off the cheering meant to applaud a rescue. That silence told even those who could not see that all was not well.

"Stand back!" Flores fussed; and Sergeant Morales added his bull bellow to the order: "Back! Everybody back!"

But there was one whom no command could stop. Teresa Andorro, wife of less than two months, had left the river unwillingly in the first place. Now she broke away and ran back to the water's edge. Cries could not stop her, hands could not hold her. She pushed through rows of stupefied people, twisted past even the soldiers, until finally she saw Cecilio. A scream of madness broke from her, and she lunged toward the water.

Antonio was there. He dropped the rope he was coiling and caught her. His arms went around her; but, if each hand had not gripped the wrist of the other, even he could not have held her.

"Let me go!" she begged. "Let me go! I do not wish to live."

She fought with hands and feet, with claws and teeth. She writhed in Antonio's arms. He held her cruelly tight, he knew. But he also knew that if he loosened his grip she would be gone. Into the river. That was what she wanted—to die in the river like Cecilio. She screamed. She whimpered. She spent herself trying one thing after another. Bereft of sense, she would not listen to her mother or her sisters or her father or her friends.

"Dear Teresa, poor little Teresa, don't . . . "

Where was the priest, Antonio wondered, with his thundering *"Silencio!"* Maybe he knew he could not silence this stricken young thing. Finally there was only one to whom she did listen. That one was Cecilio's father, Esteban Andorro.

"Give her to me," he said to Antonio. "She is all I have left now of my son. Teresa, little daughter, come."

With a piteous sob, Teresa held out her arms then to him.

There was no more talk of finishing the bridge.

"Saddle your horse," Antonio said to Luis Ramón in the late afternoon, after a siesta in which few had slept or rested. "We will ride down the river a way. The water is falling, I think, and there must be an easier crossing somewhere."

Action, he reasoned, was what Luis needed. He, too, no doubt.

"Señor," Luis said ceremoniously when he reined up before Antonio, "once more I owe my life to you."

"So?" Antonio mocked. "Then once more make it worth the effort. *Vamos!*"

They rode slowly over the soft ground beside the wicked river, Antonio ahead, Luis following in the old way. It felt good.

"I cannot think," Luis said finally, "what jarred that tree."

"Do not think," Antonio advised.

"But a man must wonder. If I thought . . ."

"I said, do not think," Antonio repeated. "I was there. I saw nothing. In any case, it is now done and words won't change it."

However, to Luis's thinking, it was not finished.

"If it happened by intent," he said presently, "then I, too, should have drowned. It was meant so."

"But you did not drown," Antonio pointed out. "So it was not meant so." God, what misery it was to be young! "Now will you be still and give your attention to what we have at hand? We must find that crossing."

When they found it, it seemed too easy to be true. The river, weary of twisting around sharp bends, finding more level ground, had spread itself out here among a number of sandy islets. It looked almost as if one could jump from one bar to another. In truth, someone had done so recently. The print of large, bare feet showed on the wet sand.

"Garza!" Antonio said. "He went this way, and we should have looked for this place first—before we worked on that accursed bridge. He credited us with having that much sense. You had not noticed that Garza was absent? Neither did I notice until this morning. Now I recollect that I have not seen him since yesterday noon. He has left us again, to go on alone to Bexar."

Luis was already off his horse, testing the sand; but when he spoke again misery still held him.

"The sand will bear us," he said, "but to what end? There is a curse on this journey. Nothing will change that."

"It looks that way at times," Antonio agreed.

"Then, why are you here? Why do you go with us to Bexar?"

"Why," Antonio asked, "did you jump into the water after Cecilio?"

3

San Antonio de Bexar, 1773

"Captain Antonio Gil Ibarbo, Spanish rancher, petitioned the Governor for permission to return them to their homes."

CHAPTER 1

Two days after the crossing of the Colorado, a cloud of dust coming on from the west, which could have been a trader's caravan, a herd of buffalo, or even Indians attacking, turned out to be none of these, but rather a squad of soldiers with a pack train following. His Excellency, Governor Ripperdá, made anxious by the nonarrival of the expected travelers, had sent the soldiers out over the road to reconnoiter, so their leader said—a young lieutenant, handsome, even dapper, in spite of dust. Garza had met them on the way and hurried them forward.

Well! It was good to know that they had not been forgotten. On second thought, was it good? But there was no doubt about another benefit. The authority of Morales was now at an end. Those who stood guard over the camp at night could sleep with better conscience between this point and Bexar.

Finally, on a morning in late September, exactly three months after their departure from Los Adaes, the wanderers had their first view of the new capital.

Seen from a distance—and one could see a great distance on that arid plain—the city was as fair as an oasis. There were trees. They would be strange trees, naturally. One had ceased long ago to expect to see anything familiar. Still, there were trees; and so, there would be water. It might even be good water; and the thirst that had plagued them increasingly since they had crossed the Trinity might at last be relieved. Especially since, after today, there would be no more walking. They would have arrived.

A murmur, a repeated sighing, ran through the procession. There was even an attempt at spreading out, so that all could see the oasis. The sun, climbing fast, flashed on some bright object in the town, and the murmur became speech. That could be a cross. On a church. Some thought they could see walls among the trees, but they could not be sure. Two soldiers detached themselves from the column ahead, drew the people together again, and they moved on.

If they walked with better spirit now than they had in days past, it was only because the end was in sight. They wanted more than anything else to have the walking done with forever. They rested only for short intervals. Even at noon taking a siesta under that hot sun seemed worse than moving on. They did not talk much. They had learned that the less they talked, the less was the dryness of mouth and throat. There had been no fresh water the day before and so far there was none this day, except in occasional ditches along the route. Animals drank sometimes of that gritty, muddy water. A man would not, unless he was near to death from thirst.

They did not understand about the ditches, dug by the hand of man to lead water from a stream to moisten land where it was dry. When there was so much empty land where water flowed naturally, this seemed foolishness. Labor under this merciless sun must be unbearable—work for slaves or prison gangs, and cruel punishment for those. Why did not the people live closer to the rivers? Hot as it was here, land dried out very fast. A short way from a river the grass was brown or gone. Still, Don Antonio said, it was good grazing land. Buffalo and wild cattle found it so.

Buffalo? Only the hunters pricked up their ears, and they not too sharply. Nobody really cared about buffalo now; and, as for cattle, the picture everyone remembered was of fat, peaceable beasts in cool, deep grass with a pool of water to drink from whenever they felt like it, and the shade of trees over them at noon. Buffalo? Bah! This was ugly country. Bushes were cactus with thorns, or they were gray clumps of stems with little leaves that rattled in a high wind as they bent before it. The soil was mud or it was dust. Only let them arrive soon at that oasis called a town!

They were a sorry-looking lot. If the straggling line had stirred Antonio to angry pity when he had first seen it back in the Sabine bottoms, it tore him to shreds now. How many had died on the march? Nobody could say exactly. Too many, he knew. Too few, others would have said, unwillingly finding themselves on their feet and moving. They were not starving. The soldiers from Bexar had brought some food with them. There had always been a supply of meat or fish. They lacked milk, the cows and she-goats having gone dry. They lacked grain. The coats of the horses showed that, to say nothing of the people. But they had not starved.

They were parched and burned, like grass. A hat could keep one from sunstroke, but the light reflected from below was as hot as that which beat down from the sky. Women kept their shawls over their heads and their faces as much as possible; but their skins coarsened and darkened even so. Rosario, Señora Gonzales, and others wept to see the smooth skin of the children and young things like La Niña and Teresa Andorro lose its bloom. Bright colors faded. Dirt accumulated. At the crossing of the Guadalupe River, which was the last big one, there had been a washing and cleansing. Then it rained, and mud spattered the cleanliness. The same day, after the rain, the sun came out and pasted the mud fast; and the wind blew dust on the dampness, making every garment and every human body the same ugly, dusty drab. Not brown, not gray, but something of both.

Even Turbelino, better cared for than most people, needed now a stall and a groom with curry comb and brush; ointment on rubbed places here and there, especially where he had chewed at the sting of a poison fly; polish for his black hoofs. Equally Antonio Gil Ibarbo would be the better for the ministrations of a masseur and a clothier. His swarthy skin was now the color and texture of well-cured and weather-stained saddle leather. How deep the burn went, only time away from the sun's rays would establish. As to clothing, a white and whole shirt must be obtained at once. He had worn those from Lobanillo to rags. The rubbed jacket and equally worn trousers and boots might have to suffice until after his audience with the Governor. After all, he had been on the march, had he not?

That he would obtain a prompt hearing was fixed in his mind. The petition of grievances was now a document of many pages; but Ripperdá would read every word as he, Antonio, had written it down. The writing had been the one thing that could cool the burn in his heart, which had been kindled by and had fed on the patience of a submissive people—the wailings of bereft mothers and children and lovers, the pale faces of the dying, the hardening of good young men, the decay of virtue, the slow, unwilling abandonment of hope.

"See, Señor Ibarbo, the stems are still green!"

Every evening lately La Niña had come to examine the now not very verdant roses.

"The roses look good, *muchachita*," he would agree. "It will not be long now."

Not long. The city that had looked like an oasis in the early morning, appearing and disappearing through the long day, would give the answer.

The long and weary day. It was not until mid-afternoon that the walls of houses, in dun grays and browns, and the twin towers of the gray stone church behind a stone wall were near enough to be realities. Trees followed the course of a small river, which seemed just here to wind in a complete loop. The trees were palms—and several known and unknown varieties with leaves. The fan-shaped fronds of the palms and the leaves on the others made a dry rattling when the wind blew. However, the wind also parted the branches of the trees and allowed one to see, dimly and dustily, beyond the loop of the river, the rough stockade of a fort with a flag and the sun winking on what must have been a brass cannon mounted above the gate.

The looping river, the military establishment straight ahead, and the fortified church on the right offered a fairer prospect than the town, which began with a scattering of flat-roofed stone and adobe houses, and spread westward, following the southern arm of the river, and multiplied finally into a mass of buildings indescribably squalid. If there were streets, they could be only narrow alleyways. And yet, this squalid part, the villa of San Fernando, was a town in itself, with its own church, separate from the mission. Why a church? one might ask, knowing the character of the citizenry. The very sounds of life proceeding from the hovels—a dog howling, a woman scolding, a child crying, a parrot squawking—seemed villainous. A flight of crows passed over the low roofs and dropped out of sight in the dusty west, settling, no doubt, on a refuse heap.

People began to appear now among the houses. First came men in cotton shirts and trousers as soiled and stained as the tattered garments of the Adaeans, who had come two hundred and fifty leagues overland without a change of clothing. Some wore broad-brimmed straw hats. Others wrapped their heads in filthy head kerchiefs and had large gold rings in their ears. These were the infamous *Isleños*—renegades from the Canary Islands, freed of penal sentences to swell the count of Spaniards in the provinces. Hafts of knives, suggesting fangs, showed above ragged sashes. The women who followed were as bad. The gold hoops in their ears were even larger. Oiled black hair, dressed high with pomade, added neither nobility nor virtue to faces white with flour paste and daubed with paint. Bare legs showed boldly under full, wind-lifted skirts. Low-cut blouses left half of their bosoms exposed.

"*Jesu!*" Antonio said under his breath, placing himself on his horse between these banditti and his friends. The villa of San Fernando was even worse than he remembered it.

But, when he turned to see what effect all this might be having on his weary wanderers, their smudged faces were set stolidly, without hope or expectancy, in only one direction—toward the more distant fort, which now had opened its gates to release a fresh troop of mounted soldiers. The leaders were already crossing the first bridge, over the farther branch of the looping river, and advancing over a dusty road to a second bridge, which would bring them finally face to face with the dusty garrison from Los Adaes and its now equally dusty escort from San Antonio.

Dust swirled about the feet of the horses, but the sun flashed brightly on silver buckles and hat cockades, most brightly on similar ornaments on the leader of the advancing troop. Judged by the silver added to or substituted for the cold steel of his trappings and those of his horse, this could be no other than His Excellency himself, Juan María de Ripperdá.

In a minute a sharp command by the lieutenant commanding the soldiers accompanying the pilgrims certified the accuracy of this guess. Three-cornered hats, which had become intolerable because of the heat, came off saddle bows and were placed on heads still covered by head kerchiefs. Dog ears of red cotton showed under most of the hats, and the effect might have been comical, but nobody watching was moved to laughter. The young lieutenant, stiffly erect in his saddle, managing to hold up the head of his tired horse, became the impeccable, trained officer that he was; and his command looked to be what it was—a detail coming in from a long march to report to higher authority.

At the head of his dusty troop, the dusty lieutenant waited until the Governor came off the near bridge; then, leaving his men in position, he, followed by a standard-bearer, advanced to be recognized. Having arrived at the length of a horse before the Governor, who had now halted, he pulled up his horse and saluted. Words audible only to those close up passed between him and Ripperdá. Orders, equally unintelligible, were given to the Governor's guard, and others were relayed by a standard-bearer to those who waited in the road. The Governor's guard parted ranks. The Governor wheeled his horse and, now accompanied by the lieutenant, rode back the way he had come. The dusty soldiers off the road followed.

A new danger loomed. Would the exiles, dazed and weak from the labor of this day on top of all that had gone before, still clinging to a few pitiful belongings, be left with no protection against the inhabitants of the villa, who now made up a small but growing mob, ready to receive the new settlers after their own fashion? No, that too had been taken care of by the orders. The Governor's guard, instead of following the Governor back to the fort, formed in single file and rode between the sad-eyed strangers and the villainous *Isleños,* whose disappointment was made clear by jeers and even threats, but nothing worse. At the same time, where the meeting of Ripperdá and the lieutenant had taken place, there stood now a solitary tall, gaunt man in the brown robe of a Franciscan friar.

A sob of recognition was all the greeting that passed between Fray Josef and his lost sheep. With a motion of his big hands he indicated that they were to follow him and turned off in the direction of the gray stone church behind the fortified wall. Obediently those nearest him took fresh hold on their pitiful bundles, summoned what strength remained in their bodies, and began to move unsteadily where he led. Piecemeal, the whole ragged line stirred. Dust rose now about their shuffling feet, to become a fog over the whole column. Antonio, still on Turbelino, could see only those who passed immediately before him. He did not see the gate open in the wall or the people disappear behind the barrier. For what happened there, he had to be content with the story as the padre later gave it to him.

Having arrived days ahead of the exiles, Garza had had time to review the whole situation in Bexar, had talked things over with the brother in charge of the Mission of San Antonio de Valero, and then had been bold enough to approach the Governor with a request that the new citizens be given temporary refuge in the empty pueblo attached to the mission. Empty, because here, as at other missions, Indian converts did not take to living within walls.

It was to this pueblo then, behind the stone church and convent, or priest's residence, but still within the stone wall, that Fray Josef led the people that afternoon. If he had led them to the brink of a rock overlooking the deep sea, they might have followed just as stolidly. They were so tired! Only a few raised their eyes to note brass cannon in a penthouse over the gate in the wall. Guns to guard God's property? What heathendom was this?

Like sheep, however, they went through the gate and believed no more what their eyes beheld than they believed in the cannon. Houses? In rows? And a well? Dry tongues licked cracked lips.

"Move on," Garza said. "There is room for all; only move on."

They moved at the pace of land turtles, staring at the houses. They were small, but perfect—with a portico before each door. A portico? This was what it was to have the favor of the King. With a portico, who needed a house? Feet stumbled. Bodies swayed. Finally, with almost everyone now within the pueblo limits, the whole assemblage seemed to collapse, each one falling where he stood, some laughing idiotically, some asleep even before they had fallen.

How unfortunate, those who still remained awake thought, were the ones in charge of the animals, who had to remain outside to pen the livestock before they, too, could lie down and sleep! How unfortunate to be one of those—or even the servant of Señora Gonzales!

"Constanzia!" the Señora screamed over the murmur of people sinking into slumber. "Silly fool, what are you staring at? Don't you know a bed when you see one? Where then is my blanket? Where is the Little One? She will know."

What was this raving about a bed? Houses one must believe in now, with porticoes, and a well; but a bed? That was ridiculous. A few sleepers turned over. A child fretted.

"*Agua?*"

"Sh! Sleep now, little one. Sleep!"

CHAPTER 2

When the last of the weary ones had stumbled through the first gate of the convent, a friar, a stranger, closed the gate against Antonio. Also against Flores, who, lacking other guidance, had joined Antonio back in the road.

"Fray Josef will talk to you presently," the friar said, meaning when Garza had finished with the others.

"We will wait," Antonio said, the more calmly because of the anxiety popping out on the *Alcalde.*

Perversely he found the *Alcalde's* fearsomeness amusing. Never had the usually plump little man looked so pitiable. All his respectability was gone. He and his well-made clothes were equally worn and torn.

"This is a dreadful town—much worse than I supposed," Flores fumed. "What if Garza cannot accommodate us?"

"We will be no worse off than we have been all summer," Antonio said, then added, less heartlessly, "Garza at least knows we are here. He will be back."

He was back quite soon, with his report on the collapse of the wanderers, once they had found themselves safe in the pueblo. Rest was all they wanted now from God or man. Yes, there was room for Antonio and Flores—in the friars' convent, if that was satisfactory. Satisfactory? The harsh gray walls were sanctuary. But Garza's bulk still filled the now open gate.

"You will leave the horses outside," he said.

"We will do better than that," Antonio answered. "We will pen them with the others. Only—do not give away our rooms meanwhile."

"A bell rings for meals," was Garza's brief answer, as Antonio rode off, Flores still following.

The stock pen was ample, and fenced. Luis Ramón, his eyes like cinders, his cheeks darkened by a week's growth of beard, was in command. While Flores, still anxious, secured help for his poor beast, Antonio spoke with Luis.

"Is the fence tight?" he asked first of all.

"The fence," Luis said hoarsely, "is tight enough, but it can be broken or climbed. We can set guards, but will they stay awake, do you think?"

Antonio was sure they would not.

"Tie Turbelino in the stable," he suggested. "He is quick to suspect the presence of a stranger. He would give the alarm."

In the best of six stalls, he himself relieved the big gray of saddle and bit while Luis went for water.

"What is called a *madre* ditch," Luis said, returning with the pail, "is just outside the fence. So there is water for the present. And grass beside the ditch; but there is no grain. Just grazing— beside the ditch."

Fire smoldered under this information, but Antonio did not feed it.

"The beasts," he said, "will graze with contentment, having no work for a change. They can wait for other feeding, even this one of mine."

Turbelino raised his head and whickered gently.

"He wants to roll," Luis said, "like the others out there. And they will roll, in spite of all. If we do not take off their packs, they will roll on them."

"Name of God, take off the packs in that case," Antonio advised.

"Here?"

"Where else? In the pueblo, according to Garza, everyone is now too tired for anything but sleep. Tomorrow, no doubt, they will come seeking what belongs to them, but not sooner."

"We are to remain here?" Luis demanded.

"Where else?" Antonio said again, still not meaning to fuel the fire.

"The land is desert," Luis said hotly. "To have any water, one must dig a ditch—a great *madre* ditch, which in the land we left we would think was good only for a run-off after heavy rain. From the *madre* ditch smaller ones are dug. For the land to produce, there must be a network of ditches. Digging them is the work of slaves."

"Well, well!" Antonio chided, concealing sympathy. "All that need not happen tomorrow or the next day. Remove the packs from the mules this evening and put them where people can find what they want when they come. The rest can wait. Will you watch my horse now, or put someone else in charge?"

"Turbelino will be watched," Luis said, without heart.

"Good!" Antonio had already freed his *morral*. Now he removed his goad. "With your leave, then, I will return to my lodgings. If you have need of me, inquire at the convent of the mission. Good night. Sleep well, and let tomorrow keep what it holds for you and the others."

Walking away then, the woven sack slapping against his leg, he looked down to make sure that none of its valued contents had escaped, and saw the petition. Mother of God, in spite of careful wrapping, it was as frayed as the *morral*. Here he was, in Bexar, and still unprepared. Some of the pages must be copied on fresh paper. Who would be impressed by a document spattered with mud? For that he must have help and, he thought, immediately. He walked faster. He stopped only briefly to speak to Tomás Coronal, standing near the corral fence with the boy Pedro, who still carried his cat, now nearly grown. He ignored Flores altogether, who had not finished instructions about his horse. At the convent he handed the *morral* to a robed porter in charge, and hurried on to the pueblo.

An hour, perhaps, had passed. The people lay as they had fallen, scattered, or in heaps, like newly chopped firewood. Few had bothered to claim a portico. Constanzia was one who had. She slept now, her head in her lap, before the house which sheltered her mistress and, Antonio hoped, Angelita. Esteban Andorro slept against the door of another house, guarding his daughter-in-law—winsome Teresa Andorro, patient, and now not quite so sad, since she knew that a child was taking shape within her. That she should bear Cecilio's son safely was her prayer these days, and Esteban's was much the same, but went farther. He asked to live to see a second Cecilio on his way to manhood, able to handle adze and saw and hammer.

At first Antonio thought nobody in the place was awake, but then he saw a woman stepping around and over the sleepers, looking for someone; and he went up to her. It was Rosario. She had made a count of her children and it was not complete.

"*Buenas noches*, Señora Coronal," he called out, with the exaggeration of respect he used toward her these days. "Have you lost something? If it is Pedro, he is outside with the stock, wanting milk for his cat. The cat, he says, is hungry."

"You!" Rosario said, keeping still a suspicious attitude toward him and his benevolence. Then she added, "That boy! He will be the death of me or of himself one of these days."

"He will live," Antonio assured her, "to torment you and at least one other woman, but do not fret over him now. His father is with him. But, since you have been looking around, have you seen Hernando Calles? I need . . ."

"That vermin?" Rosario's mouth, dry as the desert with continued thirst and anxiety, made only the sound of spitting. "What use is he?"

"Little," Antonio granted, "but, until I am better acquainted here, he will have to serve. I have work for him to do. Do you know where I can look for him?"

"Only this," Rosario answered. "Natividad is also missing. I think he went in search of her."

Natividad? The manner of her going did not matter. Weeks of association with Calles would have sharpened her wits and her desire to seek other company. As to where she had gone— that would be the town. In a bold, excessive way she was a handsome woman still. On the long march she had taken better care of her appearance than most. Hernando Calles, during his possession, had abetted this by spending all he had—mostly credit with Antonio for writing and paper—to buy a seat for her on a mule part of each day. If, on reaching San Antonio, she had found an opportunity to escape into the mob from the villa, it would have been difficult, except for the lack of flour for her face, to distinguish her from others of her kind. So, if he wanted Calles, he must now pursue Natividad.

With no relish for the undertaking, but still with a need for the clerk, Antonio left the sanctuary and stepped once more into the dusty road. He wished now that he had not been so quick to stable Turbelino. He would be safer, he would look more impressive, mounted. On the other hand, Turbelino was also to be considered. For the first time, that day he had seemed to falter.

So it was that Antonio, kicking up a splendid dust in his exasperation, a driver's whip in his fist and a pistol in his belt, set off for the villa of San Fernando. It was a wearisome distance to walk, but it could have been longer. He did not have to go beyond the first *cantina*. Bull-throated shouts, drunken yells, and some shrill screaming advised him of its location when he was still many yards away. He quickened his pace. The brutish noises suggested a small riot. If Hernando Calles should be in the center of it, he had small chance of coming out alive.

Sure enough, when Antonio was merely near enough to judge which building in the narrow street was the *cantina*, two ruffians appeared in the door, bearing a burden between them. A minute later, as if it had been a dead dog they bore, they tossed the burden into the dusty street.

While they were still wiping their hands on their pants, before even a handful of followers could make their way through the door, Antonio, not knowing surely whether the man in the road was Calles, or whether he still lived, had the lash free on his whip. He had no time to study what to do, no time to address two words to his patron saint or any other. He must halt the attack while most of the mob remained inside the *cantina*. Faster than thought, his supple wrist and able hand sent the lash like something alive through the air and snapped it back with an explosion that momentarily stopped all movement.

Except his own. He had time to reach Hernando—surely, it was Hernando—bleeding from many cuts and God only knew how otherwise damaged—and to place himself astride the poor fool. Standing so, he found a bellow in his own throat to match that of a dozen rogues from the Canary Islands.

"Stand back," he roared. "Stand back—in the name of the King. Stand back! I swear I will wrap this lash around the neck of the first one who moves."

He could not conceivably have wrapped the lash around the necks of more than two or three, but who wished to have the honor of being one of those? The villainous roisterers stood where they were. From the dust, Hernando groaned.

"Now!" Antonio said. "Let two of you—you—" the whiplash hissed into the air and tapped the leader of the mob on his shoulder, "and your friend—you who are so strong that you can carry a man between you and throw him into the street to die, let you bring a board . . . name of God, the top of a bench, or that door hanging by one hinge only—just move. That is all. Move!"

By God's wonder, they obeyed. They tore the door loose from its hinge, brought it to the road and, still under the threat of the whip, lifted Calles and laid him on it. As their rough hands descended upon him, he let out a shriek.

"Be still, you!" Antonio said, as rough with him as with the others, to whom he now gave further direction. "To the convent of the mission. Get along!"

Afterwards he could laugh, telling others how he had rescued the clerk, who was certainly not worth the risk taken. At the time the affair was not amusing. By now other men and some pasty-faced women filled the gaping door of the *cantina*. They were a blur of peering eyes and open mouths. The appointed stretcher-bearers were nearer and clearer. One of them muttered something about pay.

"Pay?" Antonio roared back. "You will be paid, I promise you. All depends on whether you deliver this man alive or dead. Now will you please to stir a foot?"

The whiplash hissed again. Most unwillingly, again the men moved. Antonio followed, but at the side of the road. He walked the first half of the journey, stepping sideways. That way he could watch the stretcher and also the *cantina*. He dared not turn his back on the *cantina*, lest a rock or a knife, accurately thrown, take him in a vital area and lay him, too, in the dust. His flesh quivered with such anticipation until the wall of the mission rose up before him.

Now he could let the gristle that joined his bones stretch a little. He began even to fold the whiplash, then dropped it. In spite of his watchfulness, a light, barely audible sound to the rear warned him that he was still being followed. As he turned, a sob, part difficult breathing, part sorrow, indicated a woman. It was Natividad. But what a spectacle now! Her hair, of which she was so proud, robbed of comb and pins, fell around her like a squaw's. Her silk skirt, her lace-trimmed petticoats swept the dust. She walked all bent over. She shuffled. She stumbled. . . .

"You!" Antonio said in angry scorn. "You!"

She stopped. She straightened her back and lifted her arms imploringly.

"Mercy!" she begged. "Señor, I didn't know. I didn't think. Is he . . . ?"

"If he still breathes," Antonio answered, "no thanks are due you."

"Let me care for him now," Natividad begged. "I will atone . . ."

"Stay where you are," Antonio ordered. "Do you think to enter here, as you are? The good people will surely drive you out with sticks and stones. Stay . . ."

"Be still!" Garza's cold, flat voice tied the clapper of Antonio's tongue, Natividad's also. "Who are you, Ibarbo, to say who shall or shall not enter here? Let the man be carried inside, since you have gone to much labor to rescue him. Take him to your room and care for him as he needs. I will see to the woman. Her hurts are just as many and equally grievous."

Afterwards Antonio could laugh at that, too, but not at the time. To have risked everything to save this carrion on the door, who might not be of use to him for days even if he lived, and then to be rebuked publicly in this fashion! Everyone, he himself, Natividad, the two sullen porters, stood gaping at the priest, who was as unconcerned as part of the wall. It was bad enough to feel the fool without being made to look like one. Angry at the priest, more at himself, Antonio could only cover chagrin with more bluster. He strode to the head of the stretcher.

"Did you hear what the padre said?" he stormed. "Follow me."

The convent, as viewed from the walled yard of the mission, was a stark, forbidding structure, with windows set high up on two levels, allowing a small amount of light to enter the rooms indicated, but encouraging no sinful curiosity from within or without. However, about two-thirds of the way down this wall, an arched passage, with a barred gate, usually closed, but now open as Garza had left it, led to an unroofed inner court, planted with flowers and shrubs, and surrounded by arched galleries two stories high, from which all the rooms of the convent opened. Here, on the lower level, Antonio and Flores had been assigned chambers, clean as whitewash could make them, each furnished with a bed, a chair, and a prayer stool under a crucifix. Antonio's room was adjacent to the porter's lodge, that of Flores two doors beyond.

To these quarters, Antonio, still angry at being shown for the fool he was, taking directions from the staring porter, now led the men from the villa with their burden. He had a mind then, when he opened his door and saw how pure and clean the room was, being empty, to order the bearers to set the stretcher down on the floor of the arcade; and he would have done so except that he knew the porter, listening surely from his cell at the entrance, would return and object. So he stood aside and let the foul banditti enter. The next minute he was venting his anger once more in harsh command.

"Not on the bed, name of God. The floor, idiots. It will be a softer couch than he has known lately. Leave the piece of worn-out door under him, lest you damage him beyond repair rolling him off and we have our labor for nothing. That is, if he still lives. Does he?"

A groan from Calles once more settled that question. The leading bandit stood up, wiped his hands on his unspeakable breeches and grinned at Antonio. The evil of his face was compounded of every sort of cunning and sin that the world had known since Adam fell. You think you are safe from us here, don't you, the grimace said. Well, so are we from you. So, then . . .

"What about pay?" the monster said aloud. "It is warm and we have to walk the distance to the villa now."

"I will pay you what the job is worth," Antonio said, his fingers curling and uncurling on the whip handle, "and that will be too much, since you are probably at the bottom of all the trouble. Wait outside."

He must not, he knew, make any show of money before these brigands, unless he wanted to be marked for pillage wherever he went.

"How much?" the *Isleño* said.

"Enough. Now go."

"We will be charged for the door," the chief bandit still argued.

"That rubbish? But I will take it into account. Only wait outside until I see whether I can find a piece of money. Outside, I said. This room was not meant for so many."

Over the fresh whitewash it began to reek of blood and unwashed manhood. Every part would need to be scoured and whitened again to purify it. But for the moment Antonio was glad the room had only one window, and that high up, and a door that could be closed. He loosened the fastenings of a money pouch sewed under his belt and figured—a peseta each? Not a *real*—that smacked of riches. A peso?—the door opened a crack.

"For a day's work in the villa . . ."

"One hour," Antonio said over his shoulder, "and a waste hour otherwise."

It was a peso finally for each bearer and the same for the door, though he did not believe the owner would get the money. Nor did he care. If the man came to complain, he could recover his property. The brigands left grumbling, under the watchful eye of the porter. As they went away, a lay brother appeared with a basket containing cloth for bandages and sundry jars and bottles, followed by a bandy-legged Indian servant carrying a ewer of water and a basin.

Antonio apologized for the reek in the room, then went outside himself and waited until the servant came out with a full basin, emptied it at the roots of a tree in the patio, rinsed it and scattered that water over the planting generally, then took the basin back into the room and came outside empty-handed, to squat on his haunches in the gallery. Then Antonio went inside to inquire after Calles.

Cleansed, patched, bandaged, the clerk looked very different from the wreck of a short while before, but he suffered now from too much attention. He moved restlessly on his hard bed and muttered unintelligibly. The lay brother, an intensely serious young man, was rolling down his sleeves, preparatory to leaving.

"He is all right," he said of Calles—when Antonio asked, not before. "Mostly there are lacerations." He paused to seek a Latin word and found ten. "Only a few cuts are deep, none in a vital region." More Latin. "He has some fever. If it does not leave by morning we will try a febrifuge. Bloodletting in this case seems hardly advisable."

Por Dios, no! With Calles there was probably none to let.

The brother, however, was launched on an oral review of the case, and would not be diverted.

"He mentions a name over and over—a woman's name. Natividad? Would that be the poor creature Brother Garza rescued outside the wall?"

Antonio exploded.

"That is the one, and Fray Josef did not . . ."

"If she could be permitted to see her man," the brother said, "it would put his mind at rest, perhaps."

"His mind?" Antonio said. "Look. This blundering fool is a clerk, a scribe. I need his services. How soon will I have them?"

The brother looked at him in horror, but Antonio did not waver.

"How soon?" he repeated.

"Not for two days at the earliest."

"Make it tomorrow—at the latest," Antonio said. "A million thanks to you, brother, for patching him up. Is there now, perhaps, a little water left in that can? I could use a pond to better advantage, but will be thankful for a basin."

"I will leave water and basin and a towel," the brother said with dignity, "and I will now inquire about the woman Natividad."

"You insist upon that? Never mind. My thanks for the water."

I am in a strange place for me, he thought, as the lay brother knelt a minute before the crucifix on leaving. I would be more my own master in another lodging. When the bandy-legged Indian brought back the basin and filled it from the ewer, he had an impulse to part with another bit of silver, or a few coppers, but doused the impulse. A reputation for largesse could grow out of even such gifts. Gruffly, because of this denial—it was his firm belief at this point that all he did or had done in the past three months was contrary to his natural inclination—he directed the Indian to leave the ewer as well as the basin and dismissed him with a simple "*Gracias*," which astonished the man more than an offer of money. A very strange place, a priests' dwelling, Antonio thought again, opening his shirt.

It was just when he began to enjoy his ablutions, his shirt off, his head half submerged, his hands splashing water as freely as the supply permitted, that Natividad returned. A rustle of skirts, a low cry warned him.

"*Mi pobre!*"

Antonio sputtered, raised his head, groped for his shirt, wiped the loosened grit out of his eyes, and, still dripping, turned to witness a second miracle of purification. Somewhere in this abode of celibates a woman or women resided. A skirt of coarse cotton, indigo-dyed, and a bodice, bleached white, but equally coarse, had replaced Natividad's torn and soiled silks. Her hair had been brushed and gathered into a heavy knot at the nape of her neck. So transfigured, there was even a nobility in her profile as she knelt beside her battered and beaten lover. The transfiguration was, to be sure, mostly on the surface; but her cry of pity sounded genuine and her hands, touching plaster and bandage, were gentle.

"*Mi pobre,*" she insisted; and finally Hernando opened his eyes and knew her. The poor dupe could have thought he had died and gone to heaven and found his woman there. There was that look of wonder on his swollen features. He sighed and closed his eyes. Natividad gasped. Even Antonio thought Calles had fainted—or worse. But then he opened his eyes again and smiled. Like a child. Antonio put back his soiled, now dampened shirt, tucked in the tails, and left, muttering that he would wait outside.

The porter was in his lodge. A full cleric, not a layman, he was not as tall or as gaunt as Garza, but just as stalwart. His face was smooth, schooled in not betraying or, possibly, not even yielding to violent passion. He looked at Antonio calmly, but too directly for Antonio's comfort.

"You understand," Antonio said, "what goes on in there is not of my arranging."

The porter neither accepted nor denied the explanation.

"Two others," he said merely, "wait out there." He indicated the area beyond the passage. "A young woman from those who have taken the pueblo and an older woman, a servant, I believe. They cannot be admitted here, but you may talk with them in the outer court. They seemed anxious to have a few words with you. It is something about soup. I told them that Fray Josef had

arranged for you to have your meals with us in the refectory. . . .
Still, they wait."

La Niña. It could be no other. After Natividad and Hernando, after brutish assault and blood and sin, the mere suggestion of her presence was perfume. How could the friar speak of her as he had: "a young woman from those" and so forth? Now he was judging Antonio. Why should she ask for you? You are not fit for her to see.

Ah, but she had asked for him. Fit or not, he must go at once, before shyness turned her away disappointed. Sure enough, as he stepped through the passage into the outer court, her back was toward him and she was pleading with a discontented and disapproving Constanzia, who held a dish covered by a cloth.

Antonio indulged himself in a moment of contemplation. How wonderful to be young, he thought, with the power to recover so soon from wretchedness. That day and every day for weeks he had wondered how this journey might mark the pretty child; and there were no marks. There she stood—every line as he remembered it from Los Adaes, delicately molded, graceful as a flower, motionless for the instant but seeming to sway a little, her head up, her hair dressed still in girlish braids . . .

"*Muchachita?*" he said. "Is it you?"

She turned swiftly and he saw that he had been wrong about scars. Fatigue had stained her cheeks deep purple under her eyes. The pretty face was pinched. *Dios*—only fifteen! Then, in a flash all that changed. Her eyes sparkled. A flush of innocent rapture lightened every shadow.

"Señor," she said softly, "you are safe. I heard . . ."

What had she heard? Stone walls had never barred the invasion of rumor. The story of his sortie to the villa of San Fernando had probably come up the road faster than he had been able to do so with the bearers of Hernando Calles. He took no pride now in the adventure. He was not sure that he had acted wisely or well, and he knew he had showed no nobility of character. With those bright eyes on him, he was conscious of every bristle on his blackened face, and other roughness that might not be so apparent.

"I do not know what you heard, child," he said, "or how; but I am sure it would be best for you to forget all of it."

The flush faded from her cheeks. Her eyes showed hurt.

"But I must remember, Señor, how brave you were," she said with dignity, "to go alone among evil men to rescue poor Hernando Calles." That was the tale as her dainty ears had strained it. "Was he badly hurt?"

"Let us say 'painfully,' not 'badly.' He will live, to commit folly all over again at the first opportunity. And I was not brave to go after him. I needed him. I wish he were well enough to eat the soup, but I am afraid not just yet."

A puzzled frown now sat on the girl's brow.

"The soup is not for Hernando Calles, Señor. It is for you. Food came to the pueblo this afternoon. The Governor's lady sent a wagon with meat and vegetables to fill every cooking pot. When the soup was ready, you were not there and I wondered. I thought you must be as hungry as anyone . . . but now it seems you will have your supper with the priests. So, you were right, Constanzia. Shall we go?"

"Wait!" Antonio's cry astonished him, but Constanzia more. One more twitch and she would have dropped the bowl. "Supper with the priests," he said, "would be doubtful at the best, and certainly there would be no soup like this."

That was the truth. When the cover was off the bowl, one whiff proved it. Three months ago at Rancho Lobanillo he would have sent such stuff, if it had been served to him, to the pigs' trough. Now it was, "Excellent. I will take it to my cell."

"If you please, Señor, drink it now. We have only the one bowl."

One bowl? And had she said "drink?"

"Yes, please. We also have no spoons."

One bowl, no spoons. For manners' sake, he turned his back and took the soup in four deep gulps, chewing the meat desperately—flesh of a barracks mule or a cart ox. He finished by raising his arm and wiping his mouth on his sleeve. The shirt was done for, anyhow. Tomorrow he must visit a store.

"Now may I see you safely back to the pueblo?" he offered. "Before the cooking pots are emptied?"

But as they approached the compound, the gabble there was

something that suddenly—just this evening—he did not wish to hear.

"Good night, *muchachita*," he said at the gate. "Sleep well, and safely. Tomorrow I will call on the Señora, your grandmother."

Ah, tomorrow! Constanzia, well on her way with the one bowl, turned back.

"The Señora's bed is filled with rocks," she cackled, and hurried on.

Back at the convent, Antonio found the porter waiting. Supper was over in the refectory, the porter said. Señor Flores . . . Antonio waved porter and *Alcalde* aside, and would have liked so to dismiss Natividad, who, he discovered, had refused to leave until he returned. She waited now outside Antonio's room, listening. Not that listening was needed. Before Antonio came through the arch, he had heard the trumpeting of one gifted in the way of snoring.

"He is sleeping," Natividad said, and sighed.

"Yes," Antonio agreed. "He could have had the bed, if I had known."

He remained inside the room only long enough to pick up his blanket and his hat and dusty coat. Outside Natividad still lingered.

"Go in peace," he said to her. "Do not worry. I will know when he wakens."

The resulting quiet would sound an alarm. He folded his blanket for a pillow and stretched himself out at the edge of the arcade, coat and hat handy to cover exposed portions of his body if there should be mosquitoes. Natividad rustled away. The porter closed the gate and dropped the bar with thudding emphasis. Except for Hernando's bugling, peace settled on the patio.

But not on Antonio Gil Ibarbo. Tired as he was, he could not rest. Flat on his back, he was assailed on all sides by doubts and worries. Rancho Lobanillo—his wife, his son, his mother—did they know how far away he was? Garza was a master at not hearing questions he did not choose to answer. Nicolas de la Mathe—had he got the letter meant for him? Had he acted upon it? Antonio had never felt more adrift, with no mooring in sight.

Why had he insisted on finding Calles? Would the petition, in any state, ransom the people now penned in the pueblo? Would the brave, the strong—Luis, Rojas, and others—stay penned? Suppose the petition did not have a favorable hearing? What then?

Overhead, the sky softened from dazzling blue to pale gold, tinged with coral. Omnipotence, he prayed, inventing like an Indian a Great Spirit, I am, after all, only one man—a lonely man, Omnipotence, as lonely as any fugitive in the Indian compound. I have not even the comfort of communion, of being able to shape a prayer; but I can tell you, if no other, I have need of help. It is a monstrous thing I have undertaken to accomplish. I . . .

It was possible then that Hernando wakened, because the sound he made sleeping came to an end, at least for Antonio. So did Antonio's worries. He became aware of the green of the patio, of the bright gold of the sky, brightest just before the gray of twilight. He and one other creature. In some vine or other greenery, a bird stretched its throat in song.

"A linnet," the porter said from a shadow, as if Antonio had asked.

A linnet? A linnet was a small bird. The life of any bird even in a convent garden had its hazards. But perhaps the linnet did not know. A linnet—consider the linnet, Ibarbo. Consider . . .

·

CHAPTER 3

The *Casa Real* in San Antonio de Bexar was located on the north end of the main plaza, opposite the Church of San Fernando on the same square. With the military plaza and the fort only a gunshot away, it was, though new, still near enough to the squalor and savagery of the older villa to show traces of contamination. It was raw new. Rubble from the building lay on the ground all about. The front wall, facing the roughest of roadways and broken only by a single door with iron bars and by high, narrow windows, was almost as blank as the outer wall of the mission convent. All that kept it from being absolutely forbidding was a shaded gallery, running the full length of the wall, consisting of a roof extending over paving stones and supported at the outer edge by wooden posts.

Such shelters, called *portales*, Antonio informed Flores, as they drew rein before this palace on a morning in October, a full week and a day after their arrival in Bexar, were common in places where the sun was without mercy most of the year. That the shade was welcome was evidenced this morning by an Indian squaw with a papoose in the fold of her shawl, huddled at the base of one of the posts. Such Indians, solitary or in groups, were to be seen daily on the steps of the Church of San Fernando. They would sit motionless for hours, waiting for God knew what, just waiting. At the church they sought sanctuary. Here it must be the protection of their Great White Father, the King. Lacking the squaw's reliance, Antonio led the way to the opposite end of the *portal* and, with Flores, dismounted, then made a long business of tying Turbelino. While he was still at it, the barred door of the *casa* opened and a lieutenant of the Royal Infantry stepped out. *Dios*, the town sprouted lieutenants!

"The horses are safe," this one said. "Enter, Señores, if it please you."

The interior of the *casa*, then, was by contrast as splendid as the exterior was grim. Or, at least, the grimness was covered. Banners of silk—chiefly in the white and scarlet colors of Spain— with coronets or towers or other blazonry embroidered on them in gold thread, hung by gold cords against the whitewashed walls of the entrance hall. In the *sala*, where they were told to wait, there were portraits—His Excellency the Governor's ancestors, no doubt—men in velvet doublets and shining cuirasses, an occasional woman in a starched and fluted ruff. Proud people, amazed, startled, disdainful at finding themselves where they were, some too proud to notice. Below the portraits were chairs and tables of rich wood, shaped and carved by master craftsmen.

"You see," Antonio said, "why His Majesty must watch his treasury. He would not think of asking a noble governor to change his place of residence, carrying his possessions in a bundle."

Flores did not answer, horrified at such blasphemy. Then he took comfort in contemplating himself, restored to respectability by a new coat and small clothes of black cloth and a clean shirt. With finicking fingers he brushed a speck of lint from his coat sleeve. Was it not fortunate that he had insisted on their seeing a barber and a tailor before appearing here?

Antonio glowered. His face still smarted from the barber's ministrations; and he would have preferred on this critical occasion to appear in his worn and scuffed leather-reinforced corduroys.

"We look too respectable, too prosperous," he had argued, but in vain, and had let himself be persuaded finally, against his better judgment.

This had in no way improved his temper, which had been worsening in the past week under multiplying frustrations. A dispute over appropriate dress for petitioning beggars was the least of these. Delay was worse. The formal petition in behalf of the Adaeans had been delivered to the Governor's palace within two days of their arrival at Bexar. Since then there had been no acknowledgment, no word, until the summons came that had brought them to the *casa* this morning. Worst of all frustrations was Antonio's conviction that no good would come of that petition in the form it had finally assumed for the Governor's examination.

That final copy, except that it began and ended with the same plea, bore no resemblance to what Antonio had set down step by step on the journey, testifying in detail and with living examples, to the people's worth and the hardships they had endured in obeying the King's command. Everyone consulted had said Antonio's document was too long. Even Garza, his hand on Antonio's shoulder as he spoke, had said there were too many paragraphs. Who but themselves would read them all? They obscured what needed to be said.

What needed to be said had amounted finally to a mere double sheet of legal paper, signed—only at Garza's earnest behest—by the heads of most of the families still penned in the Indian pueblo, and saying in effect that, having without complaint, though with great suffering and loss of property, made the fearsome journey from their beloved city of Los Adaes to this vile one of San Antonio de Bexar, they wished to turn around and go back—with the King's permission, or that of his benevolent hireling governor—for reasons one, two, and three.

One. There was no place here suitable for homes as promised them.

Two. The land was entirely unfit for raising corn or squash or pumpkins—or even gourds—until, by great labor, water was made to flow through it. This labor, the digging of accursed water ditches, they would not and could not perform. If God had meant them to do that, he would have let them be born in such a place to begin with.

Three. It was an added cause for grief to think how the beautiful land which they had been compelled to abandon was now open to invasion by all sorts of enemies—Indians, who thought any property left unprotected was not valued by its owner; unscrupulous Frenchmen, who would steal anything; and the bolder, even more unprincipled *inglés,* now seeking to take possession of all North America, who were never known to let go of any land once they had seized it.

The actual petition, naturally, was not expressed in those terms. Antonio would have had more hope had it been so. Every comma was an obeisance to "His Most Gracious Catholic Majesty." Such deceptive phrases as, "if it pleases His Excellency the Governor," or "we humbly beg to state," sprinkled it with sugar. It ended by saying, "We remain as before, faithful and obedient." What would Doña María have thought? All was as dull and polite and ineffectual as . . . Gil Flores, *Alcalde* of a dead town, whom Antonio had more than once wished back in Natchitoches with his family, or farther, but never so much as he wished it now. No good would come of that eviscerated piece of writing, though a thousand names were signed to it.

Yet, it as this paper, this strip of dried pumpkin, that the Governor brought with him presently into the *sala.* Rather, a clerk, who could have been twin brother to Hernando Calles, except that he was better clothed and fed, carried the actual paper. He advanced with it to a table, laid it down with a flourish, and began a formal presentation: "His Excellency . . ." and the Governor halted him.

"There is no need, Uberto," he said. "Señores . . ."

At Los Adaes, Antonio had stood on occasion in the presence of three different governors of Texas, and was acquainted—from a safer distance—with the physical image of several more. In his mind they were all alike, in that they came to the provinces for similar reasons, usually from a command in the Royal Armies. Some were further embellished with titles of nobility. They bore themselves proudly; whether good or evil, they were brave; they trimmed their hair and their beards closely; and they gave commands with authority. With all that, however, they were men. Some sought or bought the appointment, hoping that greater opportunity would result in honor and promotion—also some gain in wealth—on their return to Spain. Some came only because they were ordered to an American command.

The Baron Juan María de Ripperdá, in most respects, was cast in the general mold. He was a soldier and patently of the nobility. He wore his braided coat with special elegance. His beard, trimmed to an uncommonly sharp point, and his hair, swept back and upward from temples and brow to another peak, emphasized a narrow, ascetic, wholly proud face. His mouth was firm and controlled, his nose a true eagle's beak; but then came a contradiction, which at their first meeting—brief, a mere matter of accounting, having to do with purchasing supplies for the fort at Los Adaes and payment therefor—had caused Antonio to label this governor benevolent. Baron de Ripperdá had eyes as gentle as those of Tomás Coronal, and as vulnerable. In the name of many angels, Antonio had thought at the first encounter, How had a man with such eyes come to be chosen Governor of Texas? Now, meeting those eyes again, he wondered how a man like that could have dictated that infamous order.

"Señores . . ."

There followed the usual politenesses, felicitations on a successful journey, however prolonged, on the accomplishment of leading so many people in safety to Bexar. That there had been delays and some hardship was easily understood; but he trusted that now, after a week of resting, all were in better spirits.

He waited for a response. Flores fidgeted. As for Antonio, all the frustration of a week of resting boiled up in him. He saw the mission pueblo as it had looked that morning—women sweeping with slack brooms, men standing about, their strong hands empty and idle. Speech burst forth in a flame.

"Excellency, no! They are hungry still—with a hunger that food will not appease. They are weary in heart and body and sick for home."

There! Before Flores could anticipate his intention, that much had been said. For an instant the enigmatic eyes of the Governor looked into Antonio's. Communication was intended; but, whether it was challenge or mere inquiry, Antonio could not tell. The next minute the Governor addressed his clerk.

"You may go now, Uberto. Wait, if you will, outside, where I can call you."

The clerk tiptoed away—a manner of walking habitual to him, perhaps; and yet, it seemed stealthy. Ripperdá drew a chair up to the table and seated himself, inviting Flores and Antonio also to sit. Briefly he seemed to study the petition on the table before him.

"Señor Ibarbo," he said finally, "if yours is a true report, and if you and the others who have signed this petition are in earnest in pleading that the people from Los Adaes be returned to the town they were ordered to abandon, I must believe that you do not know what happened there after you left. I thought somehow you would have heard. Nothing remains of Los Adaes now— nothing."

His hand came down on the petition in a gesture of final judgment. Antonio thought of the empty town. That must be what the Governor meant. Flores murmured something about three months of being deserted.

"It did not take that long, *Señor Alcalde*. I had the report in a letter from the *Comandante* at Natchitoches." He half turned to the door, as if to call his clerk, but changed his intention. "Never mind. I remember what he said. Not long after the people had gone, Indians came—to plunder. They took everything they could carry—door locks, tools, furnishings, clothing. Then they set fires."

Antonio stood up, seized with a cramp of anxiety. That was what it was—a cramp.

"Excellency," he said, "I own a ranch. . . ."

The Governor silenced him with a look. His face was colder. "Be reassured, Señor Ibarbo. Your ranch was not harmed. People from your pueblo saw the smoke and went to the town and drove the Indians off, recovering some of what had been stolen—the *Comandante* did not know how much—but they could not save the houses." He turned the petition over, to study the names signed to it. "Señor Ibarbo, how many citizens of Los Adaes took refuge at Rancho Lobanillo, to avoid obeying the King's command?"

So, Antonio thought, I am up for judgment again? Think fast, Ibarbo, and think true. Above all, speak the truth. There is less entanglement that way.

"Excellency, I do not know the number," he said. "Not as many as I expected."

Again Ripperdá scanned the signatures on the petition.

"Seventy-five names are here," he said. "I was told that five hundred families lived in Los Adaes."

"Some," Antonio suggested, "went to Louisiana. Small traders, mostly."

"Some," Flores added, "died on the way here." Good for Flores!

"Many died on the way," Antonio amended. "Others have died since. One whose name is on the petition we buried this morning."

"I am sorry to hear it," the Governor said gravely. "Still, seventy-five names seem too few. Señor Ibarbo, is it or is it not advantageous to you to have a flourishing town adjacent to your ranch?"

"It has advantages," Antonio allowed. "It is convenient. However, in the way of trade, I may do even better working through Nakatosh."

Again there was an instant of communication between him and the Governor—if only he could have read what His Excellency meant to reveal—or to conceal! Finally a shaken Flores had a suggestion.

"If, as you say, Excellency, the town is in ruins, it might be better to take land elsewhere. Another location, perhaps?"

"But in the same locality, I take it," His Excellency said sharply. "Some place equally convenient? Well, let us move on. The petition, amended, would express a desire to return either to the former town or some other site in the vicinity. We will pass that, also pass the episode of the Indians, though I understand they were your friends the Tejas." He opened the double sheet of paper—to the paragraphs. "You say there is no place in Bexar suitable for settlement by the Adaeans. They have been here only a week. Might they not in time feel differently about this?"

"They might," Antonio conceded. "Some will, no doubt. Those, for example, with trades—if they can be protected from rivals already established here. As for the rest, they know nothing but how to tend herds and raise corn. They do not find the land suitable—for the last especially."

"Have you looked?" Ripperdá demanded.

"Excellency, we have ridden from Bexar to your outpost on the Guadalupe. It is a question of water."

"Ah!" Ripperdá said. "The canals. They show a stubborn spirit there."

"Excellency," Flores again, "did we not make it clear that they are unable to face that condition? Being sick and exhausted from the long journey, they lack the strength to dig the ditches themselves; and since now they have lost all their possessions, there is no money to hire others to dig for them."

"No money?" Ripperdá questioned.

Antonio could have said, "Ah!" then. The gentle eyes were not dull. His Excellency knew that Antonio had both money and credit here in Bexar.

"Excellency," Antonio said—quickly, forestalling Flores, now in a typical sweat—"it is true that the *Alcalde* and I have still a little substance; but, if we should spend it in building an aqueduct, we, too, would then be destitute and everybody would be worse off than before."

"And yet," Ripperdá reasoned, "if your townspeople were

granted permission to return, there would be both labor and expense to that."

"But," Antonio answered, Flores still in a sweat, "there would be hope. With hope all things are possible."

"Granted. Señores, you have argued well." They had hardly begun argument. "I honor you for it." But then, when the prospect brightened, if only a little, he closed the petition once more and again weighted it down with his hand. His expression changed, becoming not so much cold as constrained. "I wish I could grant what you ask. Unfortunately, I cannot. I have no authority to act on the petition."

The interview was over. Only the sweating Flores continued it.

"Excellency, we understood that anybody has the right of petition."

"You have that right, *Señor Alcalde*. Your only error was in addressing the petition to me. If you had gone higher—gentlemen, I have nothing more to say. I give you leave to withdraw."

Outside, a spotted, rough-coated pony had been tied to a post of the *portal* not far from where the squaw still squatted with her child. Between that post and the door by which Antonio and Flores had just left the *casa*, an Indian, deeply bronzed and naked above the string that held his buckskin leggings in place, under the eyes of a sergeant was balancing a gun against the wall of the house. The squaw and the child might or might not belong to him. He showed no interest in them. He did brush a slit-eyed glance over the two Spaniards untying their horses, and a longer one over the horses, as, escorted by the sergeant, he went on into the house.

"He is a big one," Flores said.

"Comanche." Antonio rested a hand briefly on Turbelino's shoulder before he lifted himself into the saddle. "Our friend yonder has many problems."

They rode through the plaza toward the street of the bridge.

"You think he is our friend?" Flores asked.

"I don't know. I know the Baron de Ripperdá less now that I have seen him a second time than I did in the first place. He should be a success in matters of government."

Flores puzzled a few paces over that.

"The interview went badly, didn't it?" he asked then.

"No worse than I expected," Antonio answered, "except that I did not find a way to mention two personal petitions that might have fared better. Calles wants work as a clerk; and now that I've seen Uberto, I think the Governor might give him employment. And it would have done no harm to mention Señora Gonzales, but I did not."

The Señora had now revealed her plan for the future. Having seen Bexar, she was asking permission, and the means, to return to Spain, taking La Niña with her.

"La Niña," Flores said, "I understand, does not favor this move."

"She is young," Antonio explained, "and afraid. It is true that if the grandmother should die, she would be alone among strangers. However, it is most uncertain that the Señora's request will be granted. Still, I could have mentioned it."

They were now at the bridge.

"What did His Excellency mean by someone higher?" Flores asked there.

"I wish I did not know the answer to that," Antonio grumbled. "The next above him being Don Hugo Oconor. Beyond him there is only the Viceroy."

"Would you address a petition to either of those?"

"No."

"Then what shall we do? Return home? We have done what we can here and failed. Back there we have our families and business."

"It is a good thought," Antonio conceded. "I wonder that I did not have it myself." It was more surprising that the suggestion now had so little appeal. "The thing is, in spite of everything, I cannot persuade myself that all is lost. Let me see. How would it be if we turned here and rode out beyond the city in a new direction—south, for example? Perhaps, with a wider view, a nobler inspiration might come."

This was the effect on him of those dark men in velvet doublets back at the *casa?* Or even a lady in a starched ruff? The morning was now nearly gone. The sun beat down with its usual lack of mercy, baking the dry ground, leaching it of its last juices. Grass shriveled into a crackling straw and disappeared, showing gaping seams in the soil. Green along the watercourses, whether made by God or man, lost its brightness as the waters shrank. Fine dust made a thick haze. To protect themselves against it the two men tied handkerchiefs over their mouths and drew their hats down over their foreheads as far as possible. The protection was not enough.

They roasted in their warm clothing, but dared not remove even their coats, lest they be scorched. The land—brown, dry, hard . . . and empty—stretched out league upon league as far as burning eyes could follow. The King's domain. And, vast as it was, such a little part of that domain! But empty. Some day it might bloom, if people in numbers came to live upon it; but a few hundred weary and beaten exiles, in adobe huts like so many ovens, could occupy very little of the expanse. Most of them would shrivel like the grass. Inspiration did not come to Antonio. The reach for nobility passed, engulfed by a new wave of anger—and despair.

He turned Turbelino at last back toward the town and shelter; but, as he did so, he and Flores simultaneously saw another horseman out on the plain. He was a distance away, much nearer to a strip of green identifying the San Antonio River than he was to Antonio and Flores. Except for something familiar about the horse he rode and the set of the rider himself in the saddle, he would have been unrecognizable. As it was . . .

"Luis Ramón?" Flores said. "But what is he doing out here alone?"

"He is not alone," Antonio said. "With others helping, from time to time he takes our animals out for a taste of green grass and fresh water. It also gives the men something to do. But that is not the case today, I think."

Through the haze he thought he made out the greater density of smoke rising over the distant trees.

"They have gone for meat today," he said. "Deer or wild cattle. Tough meat when they kill it, and it will be even tougher because they must dry it in strips over a hot fire to keep it; but the teeth of the hungry are sharp, and those without teeth can drink the soup. Shall we ride that way? It might be well to mention the Comanches."

As he spoke, however, he changed his mind. The rider, as much aware of them as they were of him, had turned his horse and was riding back toward the trees.

"He knows us," Antonio said, "and goes back to his post for watching. We could still join him and ride back to town, following the river. It would be cooler but much longer. I for one should prefer the shorter road—as we came."

Flores agreed. Only let the return begin.

"Besides," he said, "if they are busy out there, and contented so, it would be too bad to tell them our petition had been rejected."

Antonio slapped his leg with sudden, new vigor.

"But it was not rejected," he shouted. "His Excellency said he could not do what we asked of him, but he kept the petition. He did not return it to us.

"You think . . . ?" Flores asked, but with doubt.

"I remember merely how he closed the paper, but kept it under his hand. Home, Turbelino, home to our stable and water and a little hay, then a good rest and a long afternoon of uninterrupted meditation. Who knows? We may yet find a way out of our difficulties."

The afternoon was and was not like that. Having stabled Turbelino and given the matter of hay and water into the hands of an almost too bright-eyed Pedro Coronal, Antonio arrived at the convent, thoroughly baked and very dusty, to find the porter waiting for him under the arch.

"You are late—again," the porter said. "You have yet another visitor, who has waited most of the morning. Our brother Garza said it would be all right to admit him. He is in your room."

At the door of the cell, a small, wiry man in the neat smallclothes and coat of a prosperous tradesman, who had heard, naturally, every word the porter had said, met Antonio with eyes brighter than young Pedro's.

Antonio stood in the gallery, not believing what he saw. This was the last place on earth in which he could have hoped to meet Nicolas de la Mathe, his indispensable agent and go-between on the lower Mississippi. But there he was. In another minute the two were embracing like brothers who had found each other after years of being apart.

"Nicolas, Nicolas!" Antonio still protested. "I have always thought of you as securely tied in your countinghouse."

"I wander occasionally, when you are not looking," the Frenchman said, his eyes snapping.

He had been on the road? He had visited Lobanillo? Name of God, was there to be news from home at last?

"I have been there," De la Mathe confessed. "Also to Nakatosh, and now I am here."

"Tell me of Lobanillo first," Antonio insisted. "The rest can wait."

For answer, De la Mathe handed him a letter. It was in Doña María's careful, neat writing. Considering Antonio's long absence, the letter was short; but each statement, when fully assimilated, lengthened into a chapter. All were well at the ranch. All? It was good to know that. Every morning Anastacio rode with Olivaro. He was happy to be free of lessons. So? He was brown and healthy and she fancied she could see him growing taller and older. Anastacio, his son. Well! And Olivaro plainly in command. Later in the day then, Doña María wrote, she and Anastacio studied the ranch accounts. That way they both had learned much that they did not know.

"I had in mind showing Anastacio about the accounts," Ibarbo said to Nicolas de la Mathe, "but the time never came."

The eyes of the little merchant shone like stars.

"Have you finished with the letter?" he asked.

No. There was a closing sentence. It was so little that they did, Doña María said, compared to his great service to his friends; but it was all they could do—that and pray for his continuing good health and success in his brave undertaking, and his safe return when the time was right. Nothing about money or any such need. No, Nicolas would take care of all that.

Antonio folded the letter and kept it in his hand.

"Nothing else you bring," he said to the merchant, "can have the value of this piece of paper. Just the same, my friend, you should not be here. It is not safe. You know how it was with me and that red-bearded scourge a few years back. That feeling about trading with the French still exists. This is a capital, with a strong calaboose, and an upright man for governor."

Nicolas de la Mathe chuckled.

"An upright governor," he said, "with a salary of only seven thousand pesos a year cannot conscientiously take enough from the provincial revenues to lay away anything for the future. It is only right and sensible then that he should investigate other sources of wealth. He . . ."

A bell, brassier, more commanding than the one in the church, cut off explanations.

"Dinner," Antonio said. "You will eat with us? Garza will have a bowl and cup set for you. The fare is not sumptuous, but nourishing. *Ai*, but I must shake off my dust and wash first."

"Give me the coat," the Frenchman said. "I will beat the dust out of it while you wash. No more talk now. That can come later."

It was good talk, lasting from the end of a shortened siesta until evening. From it Antonio Gil Ibarbo learned much. First of all, Nicolas de la Mathe acquired new proportions. A small man, tough enough, but no longer young, with a gnomelike head rising above stooped shoulders, with a small mouth that he pursed habitually while he listened to what others had to say, with a high, intelligent-seeming forehead, but small, bright eyes, a little strained, he had once seemed to Antonio one who spent all his waking hours studying accounts, appearing only occasionally on a wharf or at an animal pen. This businesss of travel was new to Antonio. But it seemed it was not so to the Frenchman.

"I began like that," he said to Antonio's repeated expression of surprise. "From New Orleans, with a pack on my back, I went out this way and that, as far as my legs would carry me. Later, when I established myself at Pointe Coupée on the Mississippi, it was not that I meant to stay there all the time. It was only a less hampered point of departure."

Now he traveled, no longer on foot, but on a horse strong enough to carry him, and still not one to tempt a thief; as before, a pack, or several, were carried on the backs of mules in charge of men of the woods.

"They do not go with me, understand," he said to Antonio. "They follow. I ride alone. It is better so. If I find myself in a difficult situation, surrounded by Indians, perhaps, who view me with hostility and suspicion, why, there I am, one little man, riding from this place to that, and I have lost my way. I make this known with signs, if other speech is not possible. Finally we come to an understanding, namely, that it will be more profitable to let me go, with a few directions or even a guide, than to destroy me. My men with goods? Ah, there is enough clamor at such encounters to warn them. They retreat to a hiding place and come on only when the road is clear. I have suffered a few losses, but in the end I usually gain. I become acquainted with new people, new places . . ."

"I am an apprentice trader only," Antonio said. "I should have sat at your feet before I started out on my own."

"You will never sit at anybody's feet," Nicolas told him. "You are a Spaniard. A Spaniard is a lord, or he is nothing. You are a lord in a sense, and always will be. So, now at the invitation and under the safeguard of another whose lordship is more extended, I am here. You see, it is only partly because of you, my friend, that I made the journey."

It had been a roundabout journey. As soon as he could, after receiving Antonio's letter from Rancho Lobanillo, the sharp little merchant had made his way to the ranch. That had been two months ago. He had found everything going as well as one could expect, he said, with the master away. The pueblo was enlarged, but Antonio knew about that. The families from Los Adaes who had taken asylum there were becoming used to their new home, though they could not be said to be happy. They grieved still over the separation from old friends and kin, and feared for them as they went farther away. Now that the town was gone, they had given up hope that any would ever return.

Yes, the destruction had been complete. The King's command had been carried out to the last word. The town of Los Adaes was now extinct.

"I am afraid not," Antonio said. "Most of it still lives—here, with me."

The little merchant's mouth pursed itself in thought. His bent shoulders drew up behind his ears, making him seem more the gnome than usual.

"Ah, my friend," he said, "that was a brave thing you did—to take those unfortunates in charge."

"It was not brave," Antonio objected. "Merely foolhardy. The devil, I sometimes think, hung them around my neck like a sack of stones, meaning to drown me."

"It was a venture," Nicolas said, "no matter what prompted it. A risk, but without risk there is never profit. I believe you will yet reap gain. Now, with that assurance, can you compose your-self to listen to the rest of my story?"

From Rancho Lobanillo he had gone to Natchitoches for a visit with Athanase de Mezières, the Lieutenant-Governor of Louisiana.

"That renegade!" Antonio said.

"So? Well, I suppose, when he offered his sword to Spain, part of the risk was to be called a renegade. I think of him as a citizen neither of France nor of Spain, but of America. He is a man of many abilities. He speaks Spanish as easily as French, and knows even a little English and some Indian. He can bandy Latin with the priests. . . . I must say that your governing coun-cils for once acted with wisdom in accepting his allegiance. Either that, or they lacked frontier agents. Did you ever see him?"

"No," Antonio said, puzzled to know where all this was lead-ing.

"No. He is off exploring. The French, you know, are great explorers. So are the Spanish; but gain, immediate gain, too often drives them. The French have more nearly the sense of adventure. Also they get on well with the Indians."

"They are sharp," Antonio said, "but I still do not see where that touches me and my unfortunate undertaking."

"You will see, Lord Impatience. Nobody was more shocked than De Mezières when the Spanish abandoned the presidio at Los Adaes. He would have strengthened it instead. He would have set others like it, as he could, at intervals along the line from Natchitoches to Bexar. And, with each fort, naturally, a church and a settlement. Not three missions in one spot and nothing for hundreds of leagues beyond. What good is it to increase the town and garrison here and leave the province undefended to the east and to the north?

"This, De Mezières feels, is to waste the support of Indians inclined to friendship along that line. Blood brothers of the Tejas tribes you know near the Sabine. Their range is wide, touching most of the rivers you crossed—with your sack of stones—and extending to the Red River on the north. Peaceful Indians they are called—well, no Indian tribe is safely peaceful; but they have been friendly to the Spaniard. He has been good to them. His soldiers ride fine horses, and the brown-robed priests are their doctors and teachers. All the Indian wants, besides, is evidence of friendship returned. For many years our Tejas have been a barrier against the savages of the plains. They are a better defense than walls and guns, but are impressed by those, too, knowing them to be the white man's way of protecting his property. Tell me, in your petition to the Governor, did you speak of the Indians?"

"Yes," Antonio said. "Also of the French and the English. The Governor had something to say about the Indians, nothing about the other two."

"Frenchmen, as French," the little merchant said, "no longer matter in North America, but no one should ignore the English. They are a thrusting people. They advance by settlements more than by force of arms. They have a genius for colonization. They already hold all of Canada and much of central North America east of the Mississippi. France could not stop them, so she gave Louisiana to Spain. Can we stop them? Who knows? Young men from settlements bordering the Mississippi, brave, strong, brazen in their defiance of man and nature, already come down the river in broad boats loaded with whiskey, which they make from corn; with tobacco, which they grow and cure; with glassware from a place called Pittsburgh; with furs from the north; and with knives and guns."

Here now, embroidered in detail, was the rumor that Flores had brought home from Natchitoches in June. "Clear to New Orleans they come with these things to trade. They trade sharply, even selling the boards of which their boats are made, and ride north again on Spanish horses with Spanish mules to carry Spanish-minted silver and gold, and silks and jewels and perfume for their women, and Spanish leather boots for themselves, and rum. . . . All this I have witnessed. I have heard, too, that boats from English colonies along the Atlantic have come into the Gulf of Mexico, though that is Spanish water, and forbidden.

"I have seen and heard these things where I live and move about. Athanase de Mezières has felt the thrust and push of these people to the north of our domain. Now what he has learned and what he fears and how he feels about this latest blunder in Madrid he has dared to communicate to the Governor here. With what result, do you suppose?"

The little hump-shouldered merchant had spread upon the packed earth of a narrow cloister most of North America, and Antonio Ibarbo had shrunk still more in his own esteem as he listened. It was by the ability to dream that men became great. Of Athanase de Mezières and his measure he was now sure. As to Ripperdá, no, he would not guess.

"Juan María de Ripperdá is a soldier," De la Mathe said. "He did not favor abandoning Los Adaes; but it was represented to him that, as a loyal subject appointed by the King to govern a province according to the King's will, he could do nothing but carry out the command. Now he knows his first instinct was right. He has assurance from others. He—you will see Ripperdá again, Antonio, my friend. In private, alone. You will hear what he has to say. You will go from that audience to the Viceroy in Mexico."

"Wait!" Antonio begged. "Dizzy as I am at mention of the Viceroy, I tremble more at the omission of one who stands between. What of Don Hugo Oconor?"

"That," Nicolas said slyly, "is what makes this time so opportune for you. The *Inspector Comandante* is at present far to the west, subduing the Apaches."

"I know, but how far west?" Antonio demanded.

"New Mexico—Sonora, perhaps. Many leagues of rough country lie between Bexar or Mexico and him. The whole matter can be settled before he returns."

Antonio was not so sure, but agreed that this point could be taken up with the Governor, if the promised second interview should take place.

"One thing more," Nicolas said, "would you like a guide on the projected journey? I had an excellent one coming here from Nakatosh. Lope, son of Sancho . . . "

Lope here? What sort of plot was this? No plot, Nicolas insisted, unless the youth's father in consenting to his departure had thought he might serve as a hostage insuring Antonio's return to the Sabine. At any rate, Lope was here. Garza had him in charge at the moment, exhibiting him—his convert from the land of the Nacogdoches. The Indian, to be sure, was impatiently waiting to see Antonio.

"Let us find the priest, then," De la Mathe said. "After that, write a few lines to your lady at home, which I will deliver when I can. Then I must go. The day is almost over. I should like to reach Cibolo on the Guadalupe before dark."

He would not stay for supper. After a glad reunion with Lope —shy on the part of the Indian, roughly kind on Antonio's part, to hide his pleasure—and the assurance that Lope had safe quarters from which he promised not to stray alone, Antonio, too, waved aside refreshment. His head buzzing, he had no hunger of the body.

His thoughts flew this way and that. Sometimes his spirit soared where the thoughts beckoned. Then they came home, wings drooping, to the immediacy of his situation. How easily and quickly he had undertaken to do a simple thing, and how deeply involved he was now in matters with which he, in his right mind, would never have chosen to meddle. The sack of stones—those poor people in the mission pueblo—still weighed heavily upon him; but now, out of nowhere, had come a stronger command, which he did not even comprehend.

While he sat on the low step of his room, looking at a green patio, but seeing the wide, dusty, empty plain of the morning; seeing a lone man of authority frowning at a paper in his palace; seeing two busy traders riding forest trails, cooking up nightmares or dreams, whichever they were—from an unseen

191

perch the linnet began its evensong. As always, the lilting warble pierced the fog of Antonio's thinking. That a creature so small, so defenseless . . . He rose and walked to the edge of the cloister, to hear better. The song continued.

"Thou bird!" he said, and laughed, when he should have groaned. "Thou . . . bird!"

CHAPTER 4

It was the man, Juan María de Ripperdá, rather than the governor harassed by a duty revolting to his inner nature, who received Antonio Gil Ibarbo alone on an afternoon three days later. An impassioned man, who knew his own doubts and frustrations and dreamed his own dreams. What had seemed coldness had been no more than repression. What a go-between Nicolas de la Mathe had proved himself, to release this flow of words, this unsuspected fervency of feeling!

Once more *ranchero* and governor faced each other in the *sala* of the dark portraits. Showing them on this occasion to Antonio, Ripperdá in reality seemed at first to address his eloquence to them. This one and that one had fought against the Moors. That had been brave fighting. Another had gone over the Inland Sea to the Holy Land with a Crusade. There was one, in cuirass and breastplate, whose hair and beard the Governor had copied exactly. Only the eyes were not the same. Those he had inherited from the Crusader.

"We are a family of traditions," he said solemnly.

It sounded like a vow, and it was. One could see plainly the battle between the courage and aspirations of the soldier and the heart betrayed by the gentle eyes. Juan María de Ripperdá had not sought an appointment to a command in America, but he had welcomed the King's summons. Not blindly. He knew that the list of those who had achieved glory in America was short—Cortés, De Soto, Pizarro, Balboa. More who had sailed from Cádiz had died in obscurity. Still, he thought, America could be his field of glory.

And then the reality. His first impressions had been at once inspiring and disheartening. The land was so big, so extensive, to one who had known the narrow limits of Spain. Vera Cruz, the port of entry, so busy, so turbulent. Wagons loaded with the King's treasure, waiting to transfer their cargo to the ship that had just come in, but, all around the treasure, raw violence.

After that, Mexico City, and a period of preparation, so called, for his duties as governor. How could one be prepared until he saw? During his first year he had traveled, when he could take the time away from his obligations at Bexar, to the diverse limits of the province. Realizing then the vastness of his domain, he had shaped a plan in his mind.

It was much more grandiose than anything De la Mathe had suggested. Ripperdá did not favor the abandonment of existing towns and forts, no matter how decayed or obsolete. In a land crying out for settlement, there should be more towns, not fewer. The impending evacuation of the settled area about Los Adaes—he had known almost at once about the ruling from Madrid—had sickened him, but more of that later.

He paced the floor of the *sala*, and ringing, sword-pointed words poured from him. He moved Indian tribes like regiments from one location to another. He settled towns where none had been thought of before. Defense? The towns and the Indian allies would supply that. He spoke of a citizen army, men defending their own homes, to be trained by soldiers. It would require only a few soldiers in each place to drill the militia and, afterwards, to visit the town regularly for inspection.

"Do you not think this is possible. Señor Ibarbo?"

Antonio could not answer at once. Towns? He thought only of the one that had been destroyed—the people with the burning eyes and starved, sick bodies, now vainly trying to establish or keep a weak hold on life in a borrowed mission pueblo. Tomás Coronal had discovered old looms in a storeroom and had begged leave to repair one. Rojas had risked exploring the capital for possibilities of hiring himself out as a laborer. Any toil, he said, would be better than stealing. Was there a prospect of that now?

"Come," Ripperdá said, impatiently, his eyes going deep into Antonio's thought, "not the town as it is now, but as it was. Could it have supplied such a force?"

"Excellency," Antonio said finally, "it would be possible even now, perhaps. Some would be good soldiers. Some would not care for the drilling, but would serve if they must. Some naturally, would be of no use."

"One could raise a full company surely?"

"Yes, Excellency; and, if the men could be held to their duty, it would be a good thing. Good for those who serve and for the town—better, perhaps, than hired soldiers in a fort."

"Ah!" the Governor said. "You see? Right now there is your ranch, with its flourishing pueblo."

Lobanillo had not been out of Antonio's thoughts since De la Mathe's visit. Doña María's letter and the merchant's report, comforting though they had been at the time, had aroused a dozen never wholly latent anxieties. Conditions at the ranch could not be as good as those two sympathetic ones had said. He knew. Two women, no matter how brave, one eager boy, and a *vaquero*, skilled, but without the habit of directing others— they would try, all of them, and they would do well, but it would not, it could not, be just the same.

"How large is your pueblo, Señor?" the Governor asked inexorably. "How many families?"

"Twenty," Antonio said—too quickly. "No, it was more than that before I came away. Thirty families, perhaps, counting those who took refuge there from Los Adaes. Pardon, Excellency, I must count again. Some turned back from Nacogdoches when the *Teniente* died. The number of families could be fifty now."

"Lobanillo," Ripperdá said, "could be our eastern outpost, with you resuming your proprietary rights. Then, if we could locate your unhappy charges from Los Adaes in a place satisfactory to them, not too far from their former home, but also not too near—you understand?"

To change the King's command, not to disregard it. The man was mad. He not only had these great ideas, he had written them down on paper. Now he had had them copied—by a clerk who was to be trusted, Antonio hoped—as the body of a letter addressed to the Viceroy of Mexico and the Internal Provinces.

"The procedure is so clear in my mind," he said, when Antonio could only stare in unwonted speechlessness, "that I talk too fast for easy comprehension. I can say to you now, in good faith and complete confidence, that to me the order for the abandonment of Los Adaes seemed a grievous blunder, but I, for the first time in my life—the only time, I hope—turned craven."

"You, Excellency?" Antonio could not help saying.

"I thank you for the doubt, my friend. It was represented to me by one with authority that as a soldier of the King I could do no other than obey his command. I was new to my rights and duties then, I had others to think of besides myself—well, I yielded and have been sorry ever since."

"The *Inspector Comandante*," Antonio said. The accursed, red-bearded devil!

"You know him?" Ripperdá commented.

"Excellency, only too well."

"But you will not turn craven as I did. You will deliver my letter to the Viceroy, along with your petition, on which we must make a few alterations."

Thirty-three paragraphs of alterations, if it came to that, but it would not.

"Excellency," Antonio said, "I would like to do as you say —for myself, for you and for my people, but I cannot."

"You would falter now?"

"Yes. I am afraid of Don Hugo Oconor as you could not be."

"You stood up to him bravely once."

"You know, Excellency?"

"I have heard something of the story." There was a new shine in the fine brown eyes. "But I would like your telling better, I am sure."

So, Antonio related the story of the questionable mules, and Ripperdá laughed.

"I wish I had been there to see, to hear," he said.

"You could have had my place, and welcome," Antonio said ruefully.

"No, I could not have handled the situation as you did. About the brands? Had they disappeared, or had the beasts really not been stolen?"

"Excellency, I do not know. If one trades with Indians, he must not ask where they have obtained the goods they wish to exchange. If one does ask, they pack up and take their business to one who does not question. As to the brands, it is possible sometimes to hide them, to cover them with other scars; but I did not know how it would be in this case. I hoped. And it was my good fortune . . ."

"It was more than good fortune, I think," the Governor said. "You showed great coolness and courage in a crisis. You will not, I repeat, turn craven now. Anyhow, as it happens, we have nothing to fear from the *Inspector Comandante*. He is very far away, fighting his favorite enemies, the Apaches. We cannot take the time to consult him. Time, I am sure you will agree, is most important. It seems as if this opportunity were designed for our needs."

"Excellency, I cannot feel that Oconor is far enough away."

"No? Let me show you."

Ripperdá stepped out into the patio. In a few minutes that dapper lieutenant who had twice ushered Antonio into the *Casa Real*, and only once showed him the way out, appeared with a rolled map. Ripperdá thanked him and dismissed him, then spread the map on the table.

"New Mexico is not far enough," Antonio said, studying the map. "Sonora would be better, Baja California better still; but only the Philippines would be really safe."

His Excellency laughed again.

"To me either New Mexico or Sonora seems safe enough," he said. "For a trained courier to find Oconor there would require an arduous journey through rough and hostile country. Not many would undertake it."

"Still," Antonio insisted, perspiring in good imitation of Flores, "I think how it would be if he should hear. I feel that he will hear."

"Surely he will hear," the Governor said, drawing himself erect. "I will tell him. I will not be craven again if I can help it. When you go to Mexico, you will deliver to the proper official in the Viceroy's Palace your petition, with my letter, and, at the same time, an exact copy of both documents addressed to the *Inspector Comandante*, to be forwarded to him by the next courier going that way. We have no such couriers here, you see. Everything farther west goes by way of Mexico. Well, what have I overlooked now?"

"If there should be a delay in my obtaining a hearing in Mexico," Antonio said.

"But," Ripperdá said, "the papers will show that they are from the Governor of the Province of Texas. Come, you will be rendering a service to Texas and to Spain, to say nothing of yourself and your friends. Will you take the risk, along with me?"

Only one answer was possible.

"I am yours to command!" Antonio said.

At that point the Governor's lady came with a servant, bearing cakes and wine for two men thirsty with much talking.

Of Doña Mariana Gómez de Parada Gallo y Villa, Antonio already had some information, of which possibly the most memorable facts had been supplied by the barber who had worked to heal his face of desert burn.

"A great lady," the barber said. "From Guadalajara—very rich. She, with His Excellency, lived at the presidio while the palace was being built. She did not appear to mind. She made a fine house of such quarters, a *sala* of state out of the guard room. It was there she bore her child, the first, observing all the ceremonies of rank—a doctor and a priest and certifying witnesses, and a fanfare on the trumpets to proclaim that the child was a son. But very kind and simple generally. Truly, a great lady."

Antonio believed the story wholly. His María would have conducted herself so. The Governor's lady and his had many traits in common. Doña Mariana de Ripperdá was not beautiful. She, unlike Doña María Ibarbo, had not one striking feature to give her beauty. With her it was a certain patent nobility of character, personal dignity, and unusual intelligence, which made

197

one overlook the almost plain features. Those qualities, and happiness. She was very happy in her marriage. She loved her husband deeply and admired him, if possible, even more. Confident happiness warmed her to a radiance more charming than physical perfection.

It was so pleasing, so warming to a lonely heart to talk with her that Antonio found himself thinking of ways to prolong the conversation. One was to mention the widow of José Gonzales and her wish to return to Spain with her granddaughter.

"I do not recall the Señora," Doña Mariana said compassionately, "but I think I know the girl. Pretty, graceful of movement, with a sweet, shy manner? She is somewhat apart from the others—am I right?"

"But entirely," Antonio said with a sigh. "I could tell you her story—" he wanted to tell it to her—"but you will hear it from others. La Niña, the people of the town call her, and she is very dear to them. Only Señora Gonzales wishes this passport. Nobody else. The Señora is now entirely alone but for the girl, and remembers family and others she knew in Spain. Her hope is that friends there can do something to insure a brighter future for the young lady."

Doña Mariana fixed her eyes on her husband in trusting inquiry, but he was slow to give the answer she expected.

"I will mention Señora Gonzales to the Viceroy," he said finally. "I hope that her request will be granted, but I cannot promise. There is a saying, you know, that anyone can obtain passage *to* America, but few to return."

"It is only a saying," Doña Mariana said quickly. "I do not believe it."

But she did believe it. So did her husband. The eyes of both, meeting, said so. They had talked of this before.

"Some," the Governor reminded his lady now, "are content to remain. So, we will do what we can for the widow of Lieutenant Gonzales. Are there others of your friends, Señor Ibarbo, for whom you would like to ask favors? Please speak freely."

Antonio mentioned Hernando Calles and his one ability; and, because this restored the cheerfulness of the evening, went on to talk of the rest—Luis Ramón, Andorro the carpenter, Pablo

Rojas the stonemason, Tomás Coronal, Zapatero . . .

"All this you should have written on the petition," Doña Mariana said.

"I did," Antonio confessed. "It was too much finally for anyone to read."

"I should like to read it," she insisted. "May I?"

"Some day, if you wish," Antonio promised. "Excellency, I speak of these few, because, if they can find work to do with pay, they will help the others; but that will be in the hands of their *Alcalde*. Flores, I suppose, remains here."

"You suppose wrong," Ripperdá said, that twinkle again in his eyes. "The good Flores will accompany you to Mexico. It will look better, in the first place; and you should not make the journey alone."

Antonio had not thought of going alone. There was Lope.

"The Indian, by all means," Ripperdá said, with enthusiasm. "Let them see a sample of our Tejas. And any guard you need . . ."

"Thank you, no," Antonio said. "Three are now almost too many."

Had he spoken of delay? In Mexico? In San Antonio de Bexar it was December before preparations were completed and Antonio said good-bye—again in prospect of a short absence—to his friends in the mission pueblo. As for preparations, his had consisted chiefly of exchanging papers of accounting, approved by the Governor, for gold and silver paid out to him by an official guarding the provincial treasury, then, for safety, leaving half of what was due him in exchange for a note on which he could make collection in Mexico—or in Bexar after he returned from his journey. Next, he gave half of the remaining coin to Garza to use for supplying needs in the pueblo. Cotton or wool for Tomás and his weaving, and whatever other enterprises might demand.

The whole population had assembled to bid him farewell. Hope—for what it was worth—had descended like a blessing on the enclosure: "Ibarbo is going to Mexico. He will present our case to the Viceroy. The Governor is sending him. All is not lost. He will tell the Viceroy—*olé*, Don Antonio, *olé*. Go with God!"

The weakest clung most tightly to hope. The strong were not so sure. Rojas, for one, raised no cheers. He had fresh scars on his hands. He had found work—the building of a good road from the *Casa Real* through the main plaza.

"Do you believe," Rojas asked Antonio bluntly, "that the Viceroy will care what becomes of us, when the Governor here will not listen to our plea?"

"He has the power to help us, as the Governor has not," Antonio answered, "but he cannot act if nobody brings the matter to his attention. That I will do, I promise."

"At all costs?" Rojas questioned.

"At all costs," Antonio declared, with a boldness he did not feel. "Meanwhile do not break your back with too heavy labor. That will not help those who depend on your strength to fortify them."

Tomás Coronal, also showing fatigue, was more quiet.

"I am sorry," Antonio said to him, "that the weaving brings no money, only gratitude. Profit may come later."

Tomás was now engaged in a desperate effort to provide cloth for new garments for everyone. He declared the money was not essential if he could trade the cloth for food to feed his family. He stood this day with a pretty, shy girl under each arm, one his, the other Rosario's.

"Go with God," he said, too, in farewell, "and do not fret about us. We will be here when you return, waiting and watching."

Luis Ramón had ridden again to the Guadalupe River, where he thought the water was better and, with it, the grass. He kept his face clean now, but his eyes were still hot and angry.

"Luis," Antonio said, "do nothing in haste now, please."

"Haste?" Luis asked. "it is six months."

"I know. Half of a year. The other half may be better. Do not try to settle anything for yourself until I return. Ride. Seek grazing land. Drive the animals to it, if you can find men to guard them—as many as possible, for their good health. For those who cannot ride"—here came a thrust such as he had not ventured to give before—"somebody should replace the baskets in which La Niña's roses traveled. I hear they went to pieces and had to be planted with the bushes."

Luis's eyes met his and wavered.

"If I could see light in any direction!" he said. "I am not sorry I came, you understand. If I had known how it would be, I still would have come; but now, all this talk of Spain . . ."

"Spain," Antonio said, "is farther away than Mexico. You have done well, Luis. Continue, please. Look. You brought no money with you from Lobanillo. I owe you some. Put this *real* in your pocket for luck. Or buy cloth for a shirt, if you can find a seamstress."

Luis held the coin in his hand for a moment, then gave it back.

"I will buy the cloth with meat," he said. "Take this to buy something more precious in Mexico—a ribbon, a piece of silk, a stone with fire . . ."

"I will do that," Antonio promised, "with another *real* of those I owe you. Keep this one, meanwhile, to dream on."

Finally he stopped at the small house which sheltered Señora Gonzales, her granddaughter, and the servant Constanzia.

"What," he asked Angelita, "shall I bring you from Mexico, Señorita? I know what your grandmother wants. For Constanzia I have only to close my eyes and reach blindly into any shopkeeper's tray; but you, Señorita, have named nothing."

The girl's eyes searched his face, not for the meaning of his words, which was clear enough, but for what they concealed with their rattle.

"It is the first time," she said, "that you have called me that, Señor."

"It is the first time that you appear so to me, Señorita. In a few months you have come to be altogether a young lady." This, alas, was sadly true. "Do not, I beg of you, while I am away, grow to be as old as Constanzia, for example."

A shadow touched her face.

"You are leaving tomorrow," she said wistfully. "Will you be gone so long?"

"Not too long, let us hope. While I am away, take good care, *muchachita*—oh, not of the grandmother, of yourself, please. Do not roughen your pretty hands with too much toil. Leave that to others, who will be better for having work to do. Do not prick your fingers sewing for the Governor's lady. . . ."

"It is a frock for the precious baby, Señor."

"Yes? He should be of the cherubim to wear a garment sewed by you. There are others nearer." Did a flush of color chase the shadow, or was it just a trick of the light? "Name of heaven, child, is there nothing you want from the capital?"

"I have only one true wish, Señor. It is the wish of everyone here—that you come back safely and soon. I will pray for you, Don Antonio, in Mexico and for your return to us."

It was at the end of the first day of the journey south that Antonio, opening his pack, found there a small, worn missal, with a rose pressed between the pages, which the porter at the convent must have been persuaded to place among his belongings. Persuaded? La Niña had only to ask that gruff one for a favor to have it granted.

The prayer book, a spicy fragrance from the scarcely dried flower, brought the pueblo sharply before him—the faces, old and young, with their common look of strain—but two in particular, young, with hope dimmed by trouble, but asking only for a little aid, a little good fortune from somewhere, to come brightly, eagerly alive again.

The blessed child! Quickly, before Flores or the Indian should see it, he put the missal safely out of sight again.

4

Mexico City,

1774

"At last he succeeded in obtaining authority to remove them to the Trinity. . . ."

CHAPTER 1

Incredibly the month was January, with February less than a week away. Antonio Gil Ibarbo, having arrived at the great capital of Mexico three weeks before this, having presented his credentials, documents, and the reason for his presence to as high an officer as would open a door of the viceregal palace a small crack for him, and, having received nothing but disregard since, was now trying a different approach.

He had not been idle those three weeks. There was not a square yard of the capital and the surrounding country that he had not inspected. He began each morning by purchasing his breakfast piecemeal in the market place. He had sat with beggars on the steps of the shining cathedral, as was the right of anyone, paying for the tolerance of his fellow mendicants with a few coppers when he thought it was time to leave. He had crossed the great square then, and with the jingling of more money had entered the shops of the merchants opposite, to handle opals and emeralds and pearls and silverware and silks and tapestries, and condole with the dealers in these luxuries on the difficulty of making a profit when so much had to be paid out in tribute. He had ridden Turbelino, proud in new leather and silver, over the *paseo* in the hour of the evening parade, drawing at least glances of curiosity from bright-eyed beauties in the carriages. He had traveled a piece of the way with the King's treasure wagons down the road to Vera Cruz, using his knowledge of animals to engage the drivers of oxen and mules in conversation.

Through this he had kept ears and eyes open and had gathered from all sources much-needed information. He had learned that, as a stranger without powerful connections on the scene, he was nothing but a courier bearing dispatches. The business of the Governor of Texas would be taken up in due course; and he, Ibarbo, might even be summoned finally to hear the decision of the Viceroy and his *audiencia;* but by then all would have been settled behind the walls of the palace without his having any part in the deliberations. This was in every way contrary to Antonio's intentions. So, he had made another tour among the high and the low and had learned that there were two ways out of his predicament. The one more suited to his character now engaged him.

He began selling horses, transacting his business in a small stock pen provided for drovers outside one of the six gates to the city. Purely as business, the venture had succeeded beyond his expectations. This was Saturday, the fourth day of selling; and his chief worry was lest his supply of animals be gone before noon or that the fence about the pen, not very strong to begin with, should collapse under the weight of interested onlookers, and a stampede of animals should bring him more notice than he wished. However, since he had not yet accomplished the real purpose of the venture, he had no choice but to continue a performance which by now surely had become well advertised.

Dressed suitably in a jacket of leather and full breeches of rough wool, tucked into stout boots with magnificent spurs, he held the center of the show ring, and played now to this portion, now to that, of his audience.

"My friends, the supply of animals grows smaller by the hour; but be sure that those which remain are as good as any that have been led away by satisfied purchasers. They are good stock, some from Coahuila, some from Texas. Sound. Broken to the halter, but not in spirit. Young. None less than four years old or more than ten. A little rough, you think? They are off the open range. With only a little attention—Lope, bring out the little . . ."

"You see," a stranger said, leaning against the fence at one corner, and speaking to a friend on the top rail, "that is how he does. Everything he says sounds questionable, but all turns out to be true. He is a wizard with horses."

"Bring out the little roan," Antonio continued, appearing not to hear. What he would have done without Lope, he could not imagine; and he was equally thankful that Flores had fallen by the wayside across the Rio Grande del Norte, the victim of too much good living at a ranch there. "My friends, here is a nice little mare, gentle—a little shy, but really gentle. See, a piece of sugar quiets her. She wants only kindness and care to make a riding horse that even a lady can handle. Lope, comb a few burrs from a piece of the mane so that our friends may see. Behold the difference! Naturally, we cannot comb out all of the mane or the tail. We are here to sell horses. Well, what am I offered? Ten pesos for such a beauty? Lope, take her back. We will show mules now while those interested in the roan take time to consider her worth. Lope—no, wait. Someone approaches."

Someone did indeed approach. It was a man in a long coat, belted over considerable girth, with a hat like a half-moon across the dome of his head and a staff in his hand, accompanied by two men in leather jerkins and high boots, with stouter staffs and wearing helmets. Antonio waved Lope away and took two steps forward. What had been promised was now about to happen, just when he was ready to abandon hope. He bowed ceremoniously to the pudgy stranger.

"Señor, you have heard of my small *caballard*, and have come to see for yourself? What can I show you in particular?"

The man scowled ferociously. At least that was his intent, but his face, as fat as the rest of him, was not made for ferocity. For emphasis he beat with his staff on the fence rail, from which temporarily most of the spectators had fled.

"What are you doing here?" he wheezed. "What is your name?"

"I am selling horses and mules," Antonio told him. "For that does my name matter? It is the animals that are for sale. I am not. I am perhaps the only person in this part of Mexico of whom that can be said, but it is true, nonetheless."

"Be still!" The staff again rapped the fence rail. "How dare you engage in selling in the City of Mexico without . . . ?"

"But I am not in the City of Mexico, Señor."

"Land that touches the walls is part of the city. Have you a license?"

"License?" Antonio exclaimed. But now he was not addressing this fussy man of small authority. Somewhat behind that one, obscured before this by the people who contended for room on the fence, stood two men who looked more important. "Now I will tell you my name. I am Don Antonio Gil Ibarbo. I come from the northeastern border of the Province of Texas. I have a ranch there, with the King's permission. I have a license to operate the ranch, also a license to trade."

"Have you," the pudgy one demanded, "a license to sell horses here?"

"Hold!"

It was the less imposing of the two strangers in the background who spoke; and yet, now that he had spoken, the eyes of all, Antonio included, turned to him. The long cape that covered him from shoulder to boots was a disguise surely. The wind, blowing off the snow thatch of the mountains ranged about the valley and its waters, was on this January day only pleasantly cool. A disguise then, but far from perfect. The cut of the cape, the bearing of the man under it suggested the military. So did the broad three-cornered hat, though it bore no insignia of rank. Compared to this one, his companion, though fully as well dressed, even more dignified, and a graybeard besides, if he had rank was only a civil servant of consequence.

While these speculations raced through Antonio's mind, the pudgy creature with the rattling staff had passed through every stage of surprise to abject servility. He seemed about to throw himself on his face in the dirt.

"*Excelentísimo!*" he gurgled.

Excelentísimo—it had been told to Antonio that this particular most excellent representative of the King in New Spain visited

frequently and incognito this place or that in his capital city—
a jail, a hospital, a market—and Antonio had chosen the sort of
market where he could best stir up interest. Now here stood the
Viceroy—it could be no other—and he, Antonio Gil Ibarbo, was
in almost as much consternation as the groveling underling outside the fence.

"*Excelentísimo*," that one faltered, "I did not know."

"No," the Viceroy said quietly. "How could you know? With
so much noise going on? Tell me now what the uproar is about.
Stand up, please, and speak clearly. You have nothing to fear."

But only when he looked at Antonio did the fool show any
coherence.

"*Excelentísimo*," his face again turned purple, "this man—for
most of a week he has been here, selling horses and mules without
a license."

"Señor, is this true?" Deep-set eyes, in a clear, clean, noble face
that could have been cut in marble, made their own inquiry.

"*Excelentísimo*, not exactly," Antonio answered. "I would not
think of doing such a thing." Especially not after inspecting the
jails in this place, which had seemed stronger than most. Actually
he had obtained a license a week ago by petitioning the *Court
of Strangers*—a tribunal that issued such privileges to merchants
from outside the city.

"Why did you not show the license on demand to the constable
inspector?" the Viceroy asked.

Antonio suppressed a shiver. The title of inspector, even when
applied to a fussy under-constable, chilled him. But it was now
or never.

"I was about to produce it when you appeared, *Excelentísimo*.
Before that there was no demand, only accusation. My name . . ."

"I know your name." The steady eyes brightened. "I heard
it as we came over the path just now. Señor Ibarbo, do you find
it necessary to engage in this sport?"

Antonio stood his ground.

"*Excelentísimo*, yes. I have been in Mexico now the greater
part of a month. On the day after my arrival I presented myself
with papers of official import at the Secretariat in the *Casa Real*.
A secretary of the Secretariat took the papers and my name

and that of the place where I had found lodging. He assured me that the proper persons would examine the papers and I would be informed as to any action taken. When time passed and I did not hear, it was made clear to me, by people who know better than I how things are done here, that if I wanted attention to come more quickly, I should have given the secretary who took my papers a sum of money, that it would produce even more speed to do the same with the secretary above him, and so on until I arrived at the top of the ladder. *Excelentísimo*, I cannot spend money like that. In my case it would be taking it from those who are starving while I remain here, idly waiting for notice."

Suddenly he had run out of words. At that moment the stock pen; the animals; the bright eyes of the Indian Lope, waiting only for a sign to run as he had never run before, to be safely away from the storm that threatened; his own rough clothing—all became clear in Antonio's eyes as sordid things that he would always remember with shame of his visit to the city of glory. He looked away vainly to the snow roof and smoking chimney of old Popocatepetl and the other mountains, entreating help to make his situation comprehensible and just; but no more words came.

He need not have been so despairing. The noble Viceroy had turned his attention to the graybeard at his side.

"My Lord Fiscal," he said—and, as with old Popo, there was smoke and ice both in his speaking, "is there truth in what this man says?"

"My Lord, a perversion of the truth, perhaps."

"But there is truth?" Fire showed through the smoke.

"Most noble Viceroy, surely you know how these things are."

"Not as I see them now."

"And the stranger has not yet explained this auctioning of horses."

"Señor Ibarbo, you hear what My Lord Fiscal says? Will it please you now to tell us why you are here, appearing to defy an officer of the law, if not the law itself?"

The Viceroy now neither laughed nor flamed with anger. His noble face was more downcast than anything else, because he knew that Antonio had spoken the truth. It was common practice in New Spain for the holders of office to buy their positions in the manner of concessions. They then faced the necessity of re-covering the sum paid, and enough besides, through fees, taxes, and payment for favors, to reward them for their speculation. It was not outright villainy. Some were reasonable in their demands. It was merely custom, which permitted villainy. But it saddened the Viceroy and, through sympathy, Antonio.

"*Excelentísimo*," he said, "it was only a device meant to obtain the attention of someone who could assure me of a report on the petition I deposited with your Secretariat."

"You wish a hearing before the *audiencia?*"

The Viceroy's high court—would it come now?

"*Excelentísimo*, that is my reason for being here."

"Very well. You will present yourself Monday morning at eleven at the *Casa Real*. That, My Lord Fiscal, I believe, is the day for public hearings?"

"Yes, my Lord," the other man said, "but that is soon. . . ."

"Not too soon for this petitioner," the Viceroy said, "who has been here most of a month. Señor Ibarbo, can you prepare your-self on such short notice?"

"*Excelentísimo*, I am ready now." Except for this wretched stock pen, the horses, the jackasses remaining. "I will close this business at once. If the constable inspector is still present, I will surrender my license."

"No," the Viceroy said. "Sell your animals as planned. We should like to watch, if we may. My Lord Fiscal especially is interested. Please proceed."

Amid a subdued rustling, which was the sound of the spectators of the early morning creeping back to the fence, Antonio called to the Indian.

"Bring out the mule, Lope. You know—the big, black one."

"Why the mule?" It was the Lord Fiscal who spoke. "Why not the cream-colored stallion at the far corner of the corral? I'd like a look at him."

"Lope," Antonio said, "never mind the mule. Bring out the golden one for his Lordship."

In the Street of the Leatherworkers, in the small house with a saddle tree and stirrups hanging over the door, where Antonio had his lodging, he took counsel that night of his host—a brown wizard of a man, reminding him of the shoemaker of Los Adaes, now in faraway San Antonio de Bexar—if he was anywhere. Except that the saddler was a shrewder man, having fought his way to a certain supremacy in his craft.

"Who and what is a Fiscal?" Antonio asked this wise one.

"Fiscal?" the saddler repeated. "My Lord Fiscal of the Viceroy's household? He is very important. The most important, after the Viceroy. He keeps watch on everything that goes on. He makes the final count of money or raw gold and silver—what goes to the King in Madrid and what remains here. He controls the royal mint. But chiefly he knows all there is to know about law and the courts. Why do you ask?"

"The present Fiscal," Antonio answered, "is also a judge of horses. He bought my best one today."

"*Ai?*" the saddler cried. "I hope the horse is sound."

"The gold stallion," Antonio said, "is in every way as represented. I have given over trickery for the present."

CHAPTER 2

The viceregal palace, occupying all the north side of the main plaza, had as many doors as the city had gates; and to one facing them from the street, there was nothing to indicate which led to the Viceroy's residence, which to the Department of the Treasury, which to the Hall of Deputies and the rest. All were the same, set apart at equal distances in a wall with the usual high, narrow windows, three rows in this case, going up and up to the parapet of the roof. Fortunately for Antonio Ibarbo, on the morning of his appointment, one, the third from the east corner, stood open, with a guard stationed at each side to bar entrance to anyone until he gave his name and his business, then letting everyone in.

But . . . everyone! The open door was at once an advantage and a cause for dismay. The promise which Antonio had hoarded ever since an appointment had been given him lost value when he saw so many being admitted, and more when the guards barred the door with muskets to him as to the rest, then dropped the barrier and hurried him into a corridor, down which other guards drove him on to a court filled with those who had come in before him.

Filled. There were at least fifty people there, all with grievances and all airing them simultaneously. Fists waved. Men shouted. Nobody listened, because who could hear? A parrot tethered to a stone post roused himself every few minutes and squawked, then subsided, fussing and glaring and ruffling his feathers. Noise and gesticulation suggested imminent mortal combat, though it never came to that. Orators were merely practicing harangues which they meant to deliver later in the audience chamber. At intervals, one of them, having shouted himself hoarse, stopped to consult an exceptional bystander, waiting in nervous silence. One of these finally had the kindness or curiosity to address Antonio.

"Which one," he asked, indicating the shouting chorus, "is your attorney?"

"Attorney?" Antonio said. "I have none. Is one required?"

"Naturally. If you have no attorney, who will speak for you up there?"

He indicated a door in the second story, opening on a railed gallery, reached from the patio by a flight of stone steps.

"I don't know," Antonio said. It had been his intention, as always before this, to speak for himself. "I am a stranger here, and unfamiliar with the customs." More unfamiliar, it seemed, with each day that passed, though a week ago he had thought himself steeped in knowledge. "Those who shout are all attorneys?" he asked; and when the stranger nodded, "It costs to hire one?"

"Surely," the stranger said. "The best are very costly, but it is better to have a poor one than none at all." He thought a minute, and a look came to his face that Antonio understood only too well. "Since nobody has been summoned up there," he nodded

213

again toward the door on the gallery, "and all these here are before you, there is yet time. I will tell you where you can secure an attorney."

"Thank you," Antonio said, knowing enough at least not to fall into this trap. "I am afraid it is too late for that."

It was too late. At that moment the bells of the cathedral rang in full chorus to mark the hour—eleven o'clock. Their clamor obliterated that of the patio and brought through the door above a bailiff with his rod of office and a paper of summons. With the last echo of the bells he made his cry:

"Hear ye! Hear all ye present! Don Antonio Gil Ibarbo, if he is here, will please show himself. . . ."

Suppressing a desire to leap, Antonio mounted the stairs. Behind him the harangues of the lawyers hushed. Only the parrot squawked.

With the same abruptness then, Antonio found himself in the center of a room as impressive as the patio had been rude. Narrow windows were draped in silk and velvet. Chairs, richly carved, inlaid with silver and gold, and cushioned with more velvet, were ranged in a three-tiered half-circle that filled one end of the chamber. Here, in long black robes, sat the judges of the *audiencia*, the Viceroy in lonely eminence at the top. To Antonio his majesty was celestial.

In the tier of chairs just below, then, he discovered the Fiscal. Now if only the stallion had not shown himself vicious or lame since the sale! Antonio had never felt more alone. Los Adaes— the presidio, the mission, the town—Rancho Lobanillo, even San Antonio de Bexar, were the width of the world away. If the Viceroy and the Fiscal were not in some small measure his friends, he had none here. Before his hearing got under way, the bailiff began to bring up the others from the courtyard, placing the lawyers in plain chairs near the door and the people they represented behind a wooden barrier at the rear of the room. Certainly none of these was a friend to Ibarbo.

There was no need for the bailiff to instruct anyone, though he did. One must keep his head bare and speak only when called upon and then in low tones. If the others were as awed as Antonio, if they shook as he did, it was a wonder that the chandelier in

214

the ceiling didn't rattle its crystal pendants loose. This, Antonio knew to be cowardice and frowned it down. Not for that had he risked his freedom to be here, or spent most of his profit from the sale of horses for new clothing—keeping to the short jacket and tight trousers of the prosperous *charro*, but choosing the richest material, with real silver trim. Tailors in the city of Mexico were superior to those at Bexar, but also more expensive. He stiffened bone and sinew and held his uncovered head high. Let nobody see how he trembled!

And now one of the judges, who called himself the Minister of Dispatches, brought out from the concealment of his robe the petition and Ripperdá's letter.

"Señor Ibarbo, you are familiar with what is written on these papers?"

"Your Honor, I helped compose the petition. Naturally I do not know what His Excellency the Governor has written in his own name."

It would not do to say here that he did know. The judge coughed, frowned and ruffled the papers. Then, out of all the questions he might have put, he chose the one that seemed least important, most unrelated to the trouble in hand.

"On this petition, Señor, mention is made of the danger of invasion of our borders by the English. On what information do you base this alarm?"

Antonio could only tell what he had heard of British colonials on the Mississippi and of English ships landing on the coast of Texas.

"What are your sources for this information?" the judge demanded.

Unhesitatingly Antonio named the Lieutenant-Governor of Louisiana and Nicolas de la Mathe. The black-robed judges stirred visibly on their cushions.

"You have seen no signs yourself, Señor?"

"A piece of cloth occasionally," Antonio said, "of English weave. A gun now and then in the hands of an Indian." And the smooth, transparent skin of a girl, which, naturally, he could not include.

"You know such articles when you see them?"

"Señor *Ministro*, having lived all my life on the disputed border of Louisiana, I know when a thing is neither of Spanish nor French origin."

"Thank you, Señor. We have a second question, but it concerns the people of the town Los Adaes, and can be stated better by the noble Attorney for the Poor."

Only one more question? But Los Adaes, it seemed, had an attorney if he, Ibarbo, had not.

"Señor Ibarbo," this one asked, "are these people truly as destitute as the petition states?"

"Señor *Ministro*, they have nothing. When I saw them last, they were near starvation. They may have passed beyond that now."

"You champion their cause with even more feeling than appears on the petition, Señor. With what authority, please?"

"None, Your Honor. It seemed to me at the time that there was need of someone to speak for them, and I was there. That is all."

And was this to be all of the hearing? The Attorney for the Poor still stood facing Antonio, but he showed no increase of compassion or any other readable emotion. The two rows of judges were equally unmoved. But this must not end so. He must do something. In his hand was the lengthy petition he had written on the road from Los Adaes to Bexar. When the Attorney for the Poor with a bow thanked him for his testimony and indicated that the hearing was over, he stepped forward in desperation and addressed the Viceroy on his eminence.

"Señor *Presidente, Excelentísimo*," he said, "I have here in writing the full story of those unfortunates who have petitioned the King. It is told on paper better than I could ever tell it again in such time as would be given me. I am going contrary to custom, I know; but, since you have acted with understanding and indulgence before in my behalf, I am presuming to ask you to read what is written here before final judgment is rendered."

He held out the roll of paper. He expected any moment to be seized by the bailiff and hustled out of the room. The stirring of the judges was now not only visible but audible. He could feel behind him the quickened breathing of those beyond the wooden barrier. In that instant the Viceroy rose. His robe trailing behind him, he came down from his chair of state with hand outstretched.

216

"Señor Ibarbo, it will be my pleasure to read what you have written. I will do so today—before the sun goes down."

Outside, in the main plaza, the sun was intolerably bright. The gold and silver and bronze ornamentation on the white stone of the cathedral repelled rather than invited, though Antonio, his hand covering a worn missal in an inside pocket of his new coat, had been tempted to enter and purchase a votive candle and say a prayer. Instead, without changing the position of his hand, he turned toward the Street of the Leatherworkers, meaning to ride Turbelino at a charging gait down the nearest road into the countryside.

Muchachita, he thought, you had best do the praying still. For me, for yourself, for Luis, for all. He remembered how she had looked, standing before her little house in the pueblo. "I will pray for you, Señor," she had said, her shadowed face at once fearful and trusting, but no more so than all the other faces, younger and older, watching him that same evening, except that many had much more fear than they had trust.

"All right, all right!" he said to the faces. "Only remember, it is my head that is now fairly in the jaws of the crocodile, not yours. You may keep yours, no matter what happens; but, as for me, who knows?"

CHAPTER 3

The morning of the first day of February in the City of Mexico began before dawn with a heaving of the earth. Since the motion was vertical instead of horizontal, it was unlike any quake that Antonio had ever experienced. The saddler, bending low, crept to the door of Antonio's room.

"Are you all right, Señor?"

"No," Antonio said, holding fast to his bed. "The devil! The whole house went up, then down—like a ship at sea."

"Yes, Señor. It is often like that. But . . ."

"Often?" Antonio interrupted. "This happens often?"

"Once or twice a year, perhaps, but it is never welcome. However, since nothing has fallen on you . . ."

"The roof could have." Antonio looked up through the lessening dark at a ceiling still whole.

"Señor, the roof will not come down unless the whole house falls; but sometimes a picture is shaken off the wall, or an image, even the crucifix."

"The devil!" Antonio said again, releasing the frame of his bed and sitting up in the exact middle of it. "In that case I would never hang anything on a wall."

Then he remembered. Once there had been a loud cracking. What was that?

"A wall," the saddler said. "But—no damage."

He seemed to Antonio extraordinarily calm.

"You understand," he said, in apology for his own trepidation, "this is my first experience. Do you think it is over now?"

"No, Señor. Old Popo is breathing fire today. That is a bad sign."

"And you are not afraid?"

"Señor, everyone is afraid, but there is nothing one can do but pray."

Pray? *Muchachita* . . . but you are not awake at this hour, and you cannot know what happens here.

"Everyone runs to the cathedral?" Antonio inquired.

"Many do," the saddler agreed, "but the walls of the cathedral crack like others. Once it was the dome. Some say this shaking is the ghosts of the people of Montezuma, whom Cortés murdered, rising up to destroy the palaces Cortés built on the ruin he made of everything. Do you believe that, Señor?"

"No," Antonio said. "It is more of a mystery than that."

"I think so, too, Señor. I think it is that fire which old Popo and the other mountains breathe. It is a big fire deep in the belly of the earth. It burns hotter sometimes than others. If it ever becomes so fierce that the chimneys of the mountains are not enough, it may explode, split the ground above it, to be free.

That will be the time to tremble."

"I think," Antonio said, getting to his feet, "I will put on some clothes now and go see how my horse is."

"Yes, Señor. Animals are always unquiet when the earth shakes."

Turbelino in his stall trembled and snorted softly, complainingly, when Antonio threw his arm over his neck; but the Indian Lope rolled his eyes wildly and went right on tying knots in a large bright handkerchief, filled with Antonio knew not what belongings, new or old. Flight was in the Indian's mind.

"What are you afraid of?" Antonio chided. "The man who lives here says there is no danger. It is a thing that happens where the mountains smoke."

"Then I will go fast to where they do not smoke," Lope insisted.

"Assuredly; and Turbelino and I will go with you, when this passes and after I have talked once more with the King's Great Chief."

The devil! That was today. Only yesterday a courier had ridden to the house with the summons. Three in the afternoon at the Viceroy's residence.

Then, as dawn broke, came a second shock, as violent as the first and longer. Turbelino reared, and Lope threw himself face down on the floor.

"Well, that is better than running," Antonio told him. "Sit there on the ground now, but keep an eye on this hysterical one. There is a house in the main square—I wish to see if it still stands."

"Welcome, Don Antonio," the Viceroy said that afternoon from the green of his private garden. "I hope you do not share the anxieties of my servants and guards. They think it folly for me to take my tea as usual out here on a day like this; but for myself I prefer the garden to imprisoning walls. The shaking seems more in the way of nature. That will be all, *Teniente*, I think. A boy has beaten the bushes to make sure there are no reptiles. We shall be quite comfortable here. Return to your duties, one of which will be to inquire whether a fire may be risked indoors to heat water. Go, please."

The palace aide saluted—stiffly, anxiously—and turned away into the house. The Viceroy watched him, only to make sure that he did leave, then turned back to Antonio.

"Be pleased to seat yourself, my friend. That chair, if you will. We can talk while they fuss inside over the tea, which will appear, if at all, much later. Tea is still a mystery to my household, though the preparation is quite simple. Everyone finds my taste for it strange, and nobody approves. That, naturally, forbids understanding."

Tea, Antonio thought. All this about tea. But . . . tea?

"I came to like it," the Viceroy said calmly, "while serving in the Indies. The English drink it morning, noon, and night. But they add so much to it that the delicate flavor is lost. I prefer it plain in the way of the Chinese. This will be China tea. But there is no reason why it cannot grow here."

"Tea is known here," Antonio ventured to say. "It is made from many kinds of leaves. Even roots."

"Medicine!" the Viceroy said. "Calling it tea should be forbidden. Real tea is different. Light, delicious, stimulating, restful . . ."

Tea, Antonio thought again. All this about tea. But, of course, it was the light, easy talk of a great person politely making himself known to a stranger, about whom he knew perhaps too much. Again a nobleman born, this King's first representative in Mexico. A gentleman, knowing and practicing all the courtesies. And brave. The earth, as he said, still shook, not violently as in the early morning, but in long, uneasy tremors. None of these through the sunny afternoon seemed to disturb the Viceroy.

Brave—but that could be said of any King's man. Don Hugo Oconor, in his smashing, ruthless way, was brave enough. Nobody who hunted the Apaches to their caves could be called a coward. The Baron de Ripperdá, Governor of Texas, in the tense, eager way of ambition was also brave. But His Superlative Excellency, Juan María de Bucareli, Captain-General, who was in person the King of Spain in Mexico and the Internal Provinces, was brave with a difference.

The chatter about tea having now exhausted itself, the Viceroy turned his chair and sat looking out over the green of his garden and its walls to the slopes of mountains beyond the valley.

In that direction these were not snow-capped or smoking, but all a deep green. Not so high, but high enough. Antonio's eyes, also traveling up the slopes, looked finally over the tops into the sky.

"Beautiful land, Mexico," Juan María de Bucareli said. "Do you have mountains like these in Texas?"

"In the western part," Antonio told him, "there are mountains. High mountains toward El Paso del Norte, but not like these. They are green only a short way up the slopes, then bare and rocky. The valleys, where there is water, are beautiful; but the mountains? I have not the word for them."

"Savage?" the Viceroy suggested.

"Savage," Antonio agreed. "At least, they seemed so to me. I saw them only the one time—long ago. I was still quite young. It is a hard journey of many days from the eastern border of Texas to the western line."

The Viceroy studied this statement.

"I wish I could make that journey," he said then. "I must instead remain indebted to you for making the picture clear. You have that power, Don Antonio. But now—your people. Don Antonio, I have read your petition—with such emotion that I took the liberty of giving it to my friend and indispensable adviser, Señor Areche, my Fiscal, who has also read it now."

"But it is so long," Antonio protested. "I wrote it in short bits as it came to me. Each time when I began writing I had an argument to present, but always I ended only with talking about this one or that one."

"Finally," the Viceroy said, "you made your argument. Again I am indebted to you for clearing my vision. So, now, if you do not object, I should like to hear you say once more why you, who had the most to lose by championing these people, chose to do so."

Antonio watched a banana tree shiver through another tremor.

"*Excelentísimo*," he said then, "only now, here in the City of Mexico, I have come to know the answer. This is a charge that has been put upon me. Do you understand?"

"Who could understand better?" the Viceroy answered. "I serve under a similar compulsion."

Out there in that green garden, all aquiver as the earth shook, he explained to Antonio what it meant to represent the King in Mexico. He had a double charge. First came his oath of fealty to King and country. He must keep that before him in every act, private or official. But with that was his duty to the people he ruled in the name of the King. At least, it seemed so to him. He wished the provinces under his rule to prosper, but equally he wished the people to prosper. He wished them to feel at the end of his time in office that they were better off in every way for his having taken charge.

"Well," he said finally, "that is a long speech I have made. I will keep you in suspense no longer. Don Antonio, My Lord Fiscal and I are agreed that your people were cruelly mistreated in being robbed of their property and having their town destroyed."

"Then, why . . . ?" Antonio could not help saying.

"Reports," the Viceroy answered, as if Antonio did not know. "Most of them military. Reports are all the King in Madrid and his Royal Junta have to go by." He smiled, a rare sweetness illuminating his features. "They lack my better information. Now it is for me to act upon that information. I have the power, I am sure you have been told, to countermand a royal order when it seems wise to do so. I shall not exercise that right often; but, with the support of Señor Areche, My Lord Fiscal, I am about to do so now in your favor."

Before Antonio could credit his ears, before another word could be said, a procession entered the garden bearing tea. One carried a jug full of hot water. A second bore a tray containing delicate cups with gold dragons on them, a matching porcelain pot, and a glittering small canister, which held the tea leaves. A third brought a flat dish, which he uncovered to show the Viceroy small, crisp wafers. A fourth came empty-handed.

"*Chocolate?*" this one inquired of Antonio.

"Thank you, no," the Viceroy answered for him. "The Señor will venture to taste the tea. Leave everything, please, and return in an hour. Do not show anyone out here meantime. I do not wish to be interrupted."

The servants set down their burdens and left. Afterwards, when he could think more clearly, Antonio realized that they shared his feeling toward the Viceroy. He was not what one would expect in that office, he was a man of whims; but they hoped he would live a long time and they be privileged to wait on him.

"*Excelentísimo*," Antonio said as the last one left the garden; but the Viceroy held up his hand.

"If you please, a minute," he said. "While I make the tea."

He poured water from the jug into the teapot to warm it, then emptied the pot off the edge of the paving provided for the chairs and table. Then he refilled it and ceremoniously sprinkled tea leaves from the canister on the hot water. He replaced the cover on the water jug, but did not cover the teapot until a new, delicate spice mingled with other fragrance in the garden. The taste, then, of the tea was disappointing, too faint to a mouth and throat accustomed to chili pepper and dry dust and distilled liquor. There was no fire in this flavored hot water.

"The English," the Viceroy said, "add milk and sugar. Rum is better, if one must add something; but it destroys the essence of the tea leaf."

Antonio drank from his cup again.

"It is not unpleasant," he said. "A man might come to like it."

Laughter flashed across the Viceroy's noble features.

"He might, indeed, Don Antonio. I will give you the canister to take back with you—to astonish your friends in Texas."

His friends in Texas. Of them the one who most probably would enjoy the tea was Señora Gonzales, but only on one condition. He mentioned her and her plea. The Viceroy said kindly that he would do for her what he could, but it might be best to let that request wait upon the larger decision.

"*Excelentísimo*," Antonio said, "I hardly comprehend your report from the council. Is it certain? Have I now permission to make my preparations for departure?"

"I think so," the Viceroy said. "We wait now only on final word from the *audiencia*. The Fiscal and I meet with them tomorrow. Please, do not look so apprehensive. I foresee no difficulty. You made a good impression Monday. The final word, I am sure, will be good."

Coming away from the viceregal palace, Antonio was surprised to see everything placidly the same in the main plaza. The evening sun gilded the cathedral, also the snow on the high mountains. Lope slid off the back of Turbelino and gave the rein to Antonio.

"The shaking is nothing much now," he announced. "It is said by those who know that it will not come again soon. Popo will sleep a long sleep. All the same, will we be leaving now?"

"Very soon," Antonio promised, warm inside with tea and gratification. "A few days at the most. What else have you heard, besides that about earthquakes? I was in the palace a long time, I know."

"A long time," Lope agreed. "Señor Flores is here, at the house of the saddle maker. He says he is cured of the sickness, he has no more pains in the belly, but he is very thin and the color of an unripe lemon in the market."

"He will be well," Antonio said, "when he hears what I have to tell him."

"Also," Lope added, "while I waited here for you, a soldier came to the great house of the Spanish chieftain with more papers. He carried them in a sack. I think he came from far away. His horse was very tired. Other soldiers came to lead the horse away. It did not want to go. It wanted to fall down where it was. To die, maybe. It was very tired."

From far away . . . papers . . . a tired horse . . . The courier, Antonio did not doubt, came from Oconor. That had been his fear all along, as one delay followed another. The copy of Ripperdá's letter to the Viceroy and his recommendations favoring Antonio and his petition had reached the Red One, however far to the west he might be; and he, at least, had wasted no time in dispatching his opposing arguments. That they would be opposing, even ruinous, went without saying.

All this flashed through Antonio's mind while Lope spoke. Meanwhile, the sun had sunk behind the mountains to the southwest, rimming the summits with a band of gold, but stealing light from the valley and the City of Mexico. Why, Antonio wondered, did all the mountains not breathe fire now? Why did the earth not shake, and everything, not just a tired horse, fall down?

CHAPTER 4

"Honorable Judges of the Court here assembled, I thank you from my heart that you have permitted me to appear before you a second time to plead my case, which is really not mine, but that of more than three hundred exiles living in near starvation and despair in San Antonio de Bexar while they wait on your final judgment. You said I might give my pleading to a lawyer, who would know better how to state these things. I know that is the custom, but no hired lawyer could know or speak the truth as I can."

Antonio did not shake this April morning. He was too angry. Like Old Popo, he, too, burned with a fire deep down, until some days it seemed that the top of his head must blow off and smoke and flames pour forth. Let it happen now, if that was to be the way of it. He had eight fingers and two thumbs counted off, each one for a thing he had to say. That was all his preparation. One thumb was already gone and he had said only the ceremonial *gracias*—and not quite all of those.

"Señores, I thank you that for a month of judging you have kept before you my petition for succor to my unfortunate compatriots of the Sabine country. Also that you have not thrown away so far the resolution you were about to endorse when opposition from outside stayed your hands. Your pardon, Señores, I am not here to make accusations. I am here to defend myself and my people. You said that I might do so.

"Señores, that was a beautiful resolution you made up for me and my friends—that we might return to the Sabine, that a new town could be settled in some likely spot in that wonderful country, that it should have all the privileges given to new settlements, freedom from taxation for ten years, for example, giving everyone time to recover from his losses. You promised even a priest and a church.

"All these things, Señores, you were ready to give my people. I was light-headed at the prospect of telling them the news. The effect would have been a resurrection of the dead, truly. Weak, sick, starved, they would have gathered their rags about them and hurried back over the long road without feeling the pain of any effort. Then came the dispatches from Sonora. Señores, I say again, I do not come here to make accusations. But you have permitted me to read what was said in the letters from Sonora, which make certain accusations against me. I wish, first of all, to prove their injustice.

" 'That mulatto!' Señores, a man's color is no fault of his own, though some attach a stigma to it. A man can, if he is strong and brave and patient and wills it so, rise above that stigma. But to call me a mulatto is an insult to my mother, who still lives, with honor, at my home in east Texas. As virtuous a woman as ever lived, she was born in Spain, of pure Andalusian blood. The same is true of my father, respected by all who knew him. As to my birth and baptism, they must be recorded somewhere, since my mother has a certificate signed by the priest."

At this, the Attorney for the Poor addressed the Viceroy, presiding.

"Señor *Presidente*, the record of baptism is now in possession of the President of Missions. That has been ascertained by this court."

"So much," Antonio looked down at his left hand, "for 'that mulatto.' 'Ignorance,' the letter says next. The plea to have the King's command set aside is made through 'ignorance.' I think the *Inspector Comandante* does not refer to lack of schooling, though I broke away from that when I was too young and I have regretted it since. He refers to knowledge of conditions on the Sabine–Red River frontier. Señores, I was born there. Surely I know something about conditions—more than one could possibly learn from visiting among us a short while, viewing us from his high office and the back of a horse, and always with suspicion, since he came with his mind made up beforehand. Señores, I am not ignorant of what goes on where I have lived more than thirty years.

" 'Greed,' the denunciation adds. Through greed the petitioners ask to have their town, their property restored. Señores, these, too, are respectable citizens, now destitute. Are they greedy when they ask for their own homes again, and fields of tillable earth which they understand?

"Or is it Señor Flores and I who are greedy? We have, it is true, not come to beggary as have those less fortunate, only because we had more to lose before we arrived at that. Look at Señor Flores, where he sits, the *Alcalde Mayor* of a town that is dead. He is not only poorer but he has been sick in the bargain. As for me, I have not seen my ranch or done a real stroke of business since last summer. I have already spent a considerable sum of money and I will spend more, no matter how this thing is decided. It will take years for those whom I defend to recover what they have lost, and I have sworn to aid them with all I have until that happens. Where do you find greed in that?"

He had finished the left hand now and could begin with the right. Heavy silence prevailed in the room of audience while he studied the second thumb.

"Señores, we come to the town. Los Adaes, that was. The presidio, the *Inspector Comandante* says, is useless. A fort does seem so when there is peace; but let us dispense with the presidio, though even that may be a mistake. The missions are a useless expense. They make no new converts among the Indians, and baptisms are cited to prove that. But I was to speak of the town.

" 'Carry out the King's command as it is written,' the *Inspector Comandante* says. 'By no means return the people of Los Adaes to their town—that den of thieves, that nest of smugglers. They wish only to renew their contraband trade, in which all of them engage at every opportunity.' Señores, what is this talk of contraband? When two sets of people live side by side, and each one has what the other lacks or desires, there is always an exchange of goods. Unless the two are at war, why not? It would seem to me a good way to have peace between neighboring peoples. It gives us peace with the Indians surely. So it is permitted, even encouraged, that we trade with the Indians—but not with the French.

"Señores, there has never been a time when there was not some trading between French Louisiana and Spanish Texas. It was smuggling, it was contraband, because it was forbidden; but it existed. Why should it be stopped now when there is no barrier? For ten years Louisiana has also been Spanish. A Frenchman crosses no frontier when he enters Texas from there. The nearest alien people now are on the far side of Louisiana. If the Spanish governor at New Orleans allows those aliens to bring peltries and other goods down there, why may we not have the advantage of the same port, much nearer to us than any in Mexico?

"But the *Inspector Comandante* says, 'Let there be no communication between the French and the Spaniard. The people of Los Adaes want to return to their former home purely for the purpose of renewing their illegal trade of selling guns and gunpowder to our enemies at Natchitoches.' Señores, if you please, that is ignorance. The French do not need powder from us, and they make better guns than we do. I know, for I have seen them. I have heard that the hostile English make even better ones; but so long as the Indians do not know that, they will be content with what the French make. But those they will have in spite of all. If we do not have them to exchange, our neighbors will. That is how trade goes. So, it would surprise the impoverished exiles to learn that they are to be forced to live in Bexar in order not to be able to sell guns to the French at Nakatosh.

"Señores, I am not making jokes. Neither is the *Inspector Comandante.* He says that this was the character of the town which he in the name of the King ordered extinguished, and he names me as the leader of unlawful enterprise. I buy and I sell there, it is true; or I did while the town stood. I am a rancher and a trader, both by royal license. I have enjoyed some success in both occupations and keep at the same time on good terms with all who do business with me. For years I alone purchased all the supplies for the fort at Los Adaes, to the satisfaction of every Texas governor but one. Don Hugo Oconor is the only one in all my life who has ever called me a thief and a—well, you have his letter. A person might believe from his attacks on me that it is not the town he wishes destroyed so much as Antonio Gil Ibarbo. Señores, he could spare himself the trouble. Ibarbo can destroy himself better than anyone. He now knows how."

He was down to the fourth finger of the second hand.

"One thing more I must mention. The *Inspector Comandante* complains about an Indian boy in my company here. How could the Governor of Texas, he asks, allow an Indian to make this journey, to discover the way into Mexico and the weakness of the capital's defenses? Señores, with an Indian, if he wishes to go some place, he will find the way, even if he has never seen the trail before. This Indian was our guide from Bexar. As for the defenses, I will tell you now what my young friend, the son of a great chief of the Tejas, will say to his people when he sees them again. He will say, stay away from the capital city of Mexico. It is built in the middle of great waters and is surrounded by high mountains that breathe fire. When the gods who live inside those mountains are angry, the fire roars and the earth shakes. Señores, have no fear for what Lope will reveal to his people about this city and its defenses."

One finger was left. His throat and his mouth were dry. His heart, which before he began his address had swollen big with all he had to say, shriveled now like forgotten fruit on a high branch.

"Señores, I will not tire your patience more. If this disagreement, this little war, this fire in the brush, is between Don Hugo Oconor and Antonio Gil Ibarbo, it can end only in one way. The *Inspector Comandante* is a man of power, of influence, with many friends. Ibarbo stands alone. That ranchero, that dealer in contraband. Destroy Ibarbo then, if that is how it must be; but do not forget to have mercy on these poor people singed by that fire. Send them home, that they may recover lost health and prosperity. I do not say where. It does not need to be near where I live. There is much empty land. Remember what His Excellency the Governor has said. More than two hundred and fifty leagues of a poor road extend between Bexar and Natchitoches on the Red River. In all that distance there is now no Spanish settlement. A new town to replace the one that has been destroyed will not be enough, but it may be better than no settlement at all. Grant our petition, I implore you, not only in the name of mercy, but for the preservation of Spanish rule in Texas. Señores, I thank you for hearing me."

"Do you think they will act in our favor?" Flores asked over his midday meal of goat's milk and wheat bread, which a doctor said might heal his stomach. "It was a fine speech you made, but . . ."

"But," Antonio mocked. "No, they will not grant the petition, at least not without more argument. Very probably not then."

"What will you do in that case?"

"What will I do? What will you do? Why must I . . . Excuse me, my friend. I have puzzled so much over this, controlled my temper out of respect for those in authority who are halfway on my side, that I have no patience left. What will I do? What can I do? I will return to Rancho Lobanillo, which I would have done well not to leave in the first place. I will make stronger my relations with the renegade at Natchitoches and with New Orleans. I will be welcome in both places, I think. Louisiana has long contended that the Sabine country belongs to that province. I . . ."

It was not the horror on the pale green face of Flores that halted his outburst. It was not the sourish savor of the milk into which Flores dipped his bread. Then, what was it?

"I must think some more," he said, rising and pushing back his beans with chili and his wine. "We do not need to make a start this afternoon."

He was in his room, the door closed as firmly as it would close behind him, before he spoke again.

"*Jesu!*" was all he said then.

Return to Lobanillo, he had said to Flores. Seek the protection of the French renegade at Natchitoches. How could he do either? Return—a failure? How could he face his mother, his son—before all, his lady?

"You are going," she had said to him, her eyes bright with tears she wished not to show. "That is right."

In spite of tears, in spite of trembling, she had wanted him to go. She thought he could do nothing else. She knew he could help the defenseless ones. She knew he would not fail. How could he fail—the strong, the unconquerable? And now . . .

Would he go directly to Lobanillo from Mexico? Would he not report to the Governor at Bexar? Or to the people waiting in the mission pueblo? To tired Tomás, patiently weaving coarse cloth on an old loom from a storehouse? To Pablo Rojas, slaving to build a road when he had hoped by now to be erecting a new house for himself and *mamacita* and their five remaining children? To the burning denunciation of Señora Gonzales? To Luis, wrestling with the problem of ranching where there was no water? *Dios*, he was not that much of a coward, he hoped. But what would he say to these? To *muchachita* of the utter faith?

"I have done all I could. I have forced my way into a governor's palace and then a viceroy's. Now there is nothing else, and I have failed."

He knew he had failed. The decision of the *audiencia* would not be favorable. It could not be. He had to admit failure, but—did he need to accept defeat? There must be some action that he still could take. He would dare anything, defy anyone now, if he only knew what it was that he must do. He walked the floor like a captive bear. He dropped down in a chair before the table, rested his aching head on the old missal, fragrant with the attar of a dead rose, and prayed. But nothing came.

CHAPTER 5

Before the *audiencia* had finished its deliberations, to make the denial of Antonio's petition more certain, new dispatches arrived from the Sonora–New Mexico border.

"Do not," the Red Devil of the Apaches warned, as if he knew that something not to his taste was almost accomplished, "be deceived into making a bargain with Ibarbo. Do not let that man, with or without followers, return to within one hundred leagues of Natchitoches."

Only two men in the City of Mexico did not accept this demolition of hope. They, however, were the two highest. On an afternoon in early May, Antonio sat once more in the Viceroy's garden. Also present, besides the Viceroy, was Mexico's Fiscal, Señor Areche. The air was heavy with the scent of tropical bloom. On the tea table was spread a map of Texas. It had been expertly drawn, each river in its proper place in the succession of rivers, each emptying through a characteristic delta into the sea. Bold circles marked the city of Natchitoches on the Red River and San Antonio, two hundred fifty leagues to the southwest. On a line connecting the two, but at a point nearer the former city, was a small dot, which had so far no name; but it held great importance in the opinion of the two high officials. The sweat of hard-won triumph decorated the nose of the Fiscal. The Viceroy's finer features, his paler countenance showed also a mild exultation. Both had fought nobly for a concession from the *audiencia*.

"You see!" the Fiscal said. "One hundred leagues exactly from Natchitoches. And the location could not be better. On the Trinity River only a short distance above the crossing of the *Camino Real*. The land is good; the Indians are friendly. They are strong tribes who have never had trouble with the Comanches."

It was a very small dot, this town site, with no other mark near it. Antonio's friends measured the distance with hinged instruments and gave them in days' marches: three days to Bahía on the Gulf, three to Bexar; but they reckoned on a man riding a good horse, not a procession of men, women, and children afoot.

"Trading should be good," the Viceroy suggested, "at the crossing of two roads."

Roads, *Excelentísimo?* And with whom do we trade?

"If the land is as fertile as reported, farms and ranches should flourish. In a few years you will be supplying horses and cattle to Bahía and Bexar, too."

You think it will come so soon, *Excelentísimo?*

"My friend," the Viceroy said now, "you have objections?"

"I, *Excelentísimo?*" Antonio said, a hundred objections clamoring to be heard. "How could I be so ungrateful? You and the Honorable Señor Areche have done all that is possible for my people. You will forgive me, I hope, for not being able to take it all in at once?"

"Well," the Viceroy insisted, "you do agree that the location is good?"

"*Excelentísimo*, it is remarkable." One hundred leagues exactly from Natchitoches. Almost as far from Lobanillo. "I will do all in my power to build this town. Only let us have a little good fortune now."

"You do not need to build the town yourself," the Viceroy said, his face clearing. "The order goes to Governor Ripperdá. He will send a detail of soldiers with the first settlers. He will provide wagons and mules to carry the people and some food. Naturally, you will direct those who lay out the plaza and locate the first houses. After that your duties will be merely those of captain of militia, *justicia civil*—such duties as you would assume in any case."

"That I shall be present is one certainty, at least," Antonio said. "That has been arranged for me. Will it be forever, may I ask?"

The Viceroy, who was really quite happy at having arranged for this new town, laughed. Even the Fiscal released a smile such as he kept usually for his new stallion.

"Nothing," he reminded Antonio, "lasts that long."

Not even Don Hugo Oconor, perhaps. Antonio wondered.

5

Comanche Moon,
1778–1779

"But the people, threatened by hostile Indians, grieved
for their old homes among the friendly Tejas; and in
1779 Ibarbo took matters into his own hands. . . ."

CHAPTER 1

"It is a bad thing, Padre," Antonio said on a September morning in 1778 to Fray Josef de la Garza, the two of them having met outside the town of Bucareli on the river of the Holy Trinity, "to have a mind that simmers continually."

Garza, who had been poking at the parched ground with his staff, stopped long enough to study Antonio or what he had said—or both. He was the same Garza, as strong and unconquerable as ever, his brown robe perhaps a little dustier—it had been a dry summer—his hair now gray and thinner, but his face keeping its changeless resemblance to stone.

"Yours is simmering again, Antonio?" he inquired.

"I think it has never stopped altogether," Antonio said, "since that day at the Presidio of Los Adaes when I heard for the first time the King's command. Even when I sleep something goes on, so that in the morning I waken in a state of mind about what was of no concern to me when I went to bed, and which often should not be of concern when I wake up."

Garza put his staff under his arm and turned more directly to face Antonio, placing his large feet in such a way as to brace his great frame and give him the effect of having grown where he stood.

"Is this," he demanded, "a confession you wish to make, my friend?"

"You know I do not make confession," Antonio said with vigor. "I wish only to relieve myself of certain thoughts and anxieties where I can with safety."

Garza's lack of expression did not change.

"You put such trust in me?" he questioned.

"So far," Antonio countered, "it has not been betrayed. This is it now—a thing Nicolas de la Mathe told me on his last visit, when he came to see how his church looked when it was completed."

"It is understood," Garza said gravely, "that Monsieur de la Mathe visits the town of Bucareli only out of his deep interest in the church he presented."

"Naturally," Antonio agreed, just as gravely. "When a man sends skilled workmen and pays for the labor of cutting down trees and building a church for a community, he has that interest. But this is not connected with the church. This concerns those *inglés*, of whom we hear more and more, it seems to me, as time goes on, ever since their provinces and ours touch each other in North America. De la Mathe tells me that the English colonies, southward from a place called Canada, are in a state of revolt."

In spite of planting himself carefully, Garza was caught off balance. He recovered quickly, but the start had occurred.

"That," he said heavily, "is not possible."

"Certainly it is not possible," Antonio conceded, "but it has taken place."

The little Frenchman of Punta Cortada on the Mississippi had been much excited in his report. The English colonials, he said, had good prospects of winning their freedom—so good that the King of Spain had ordered his governor at New Orleans and his lieutenant-governor up the Mississippi River at a post named St. Louis to aid the leaders of the rebellion with money and gunpowder.

"Now that," Garza said, "you surely cannot believe—that Spain would give encouragement to people in rebellion against their born sovereign."

"Not to encourage rebellion," Antonio allowed. "Only out of

spite against England. The thinking in Madrid is that if the power of England should be diminished in America, Spain will face much weaker opposition in extending her empire."

"The empire," Garza objected, "is larger now than can be ruled properly."

"Moreover," Antonio added, "people brave enough to free themselves from one king will not quickly submit to the rule of another. These English colonials are very brave people."

According to De la Mathe, one leader of the revolt with only a small command of militia had taken all the forts in the Illinois country, across the river from St. Louis. It was this one that the lieutenant-governor there was helping.

"You admire this rebel leader?" Garza inquired.

"*Dios!* How can one fail to admire him? I find only one fault in him. He is said to have red hair."

"Which does not at all reduce his fighting spirit," Garza mentioned. "But it is not admiration for this hero that rouses your sympathy. Being yourself in a state of revolt . . ."

"I?" Antonio protested; then opposition went out of him. "You may be right. Ever since that day at Los Adaes five years ago . . ."

"It is longer than that, I think. You were born in a state of revolt."

As Antonio looked back over his life, there was truth in that reflection.

"The difference is," he said, scowling, "when I was young, before that day, I had some success in my rebellion; and, after that, what? Defeat."

"Ah!" Garza said. "Now we come to the core of everything. Antonio, when will you learn that man's measure of success is not God's?"

Success? Angrily Antonio slipped from his horse to the hard ground.

The horse was a son of Turbelino named Valiant—stout-hearted, strong-muscled, his brown coat marred by a white blaze on his forehead and two white stockings, heritage from his Plains dam. He was a good horse, but was no Turbelino. Antonio still rode the gray when he went to Bexar to confer with Ripperdá, or down the river to the fortified outpost of Orcoquisac on the lower Trinity; but between such rides Turbelino now must have rest.

Dismounting, Antonio stood a minute, viewing with distaste his immediate surroundings. He and Garza had met in the middle of what could only with exaggeration be termed a field of corn. Some green remained in the stronger stalks, but the blades were as dry as straw. Their rattling in the wind, combined with the whir of preying insects, was a chant of misery. On the ground, vines, both wild and those that had been planted with the hope of harvesting beans, squash, and pumpkins, could not rattle, being prostrate. There was no problem of weeds. Those, too, had died. Patches of ground among the cornstalks were entirely bare, the earth splitting in great cracks. Antonio stamped his foot and left no visible mark.

"Does this look like success to you?" he demanded.

"Who," Garza returned calmly, "after the heavy rains of early summer, could have foreseen a drought such as this?"

"Anybody who had lived here, Padre. Four years ago I said, only let us have a little good fortune. So the first year there was a flood."

Corn had been planted that year in the lowland on the east bank of the river, where the ground was rich and well watered. In the flood all that corn had been lost, as well as a few houses too near the water on the opposite shore. A calamity, but it had been accepted as a warning. Henceforth everything must be kept to higher ground. So the second year was a dry one. The third year brought a pestilence. It had carried off poor Flores and others.

"This year," Antonio finished bitterly, "we have had both a flood and a drought. That is the measure of our good fortune."

"Antonio," Garza remonstrated, "the town still stands."

"The town?" Antonio raged. "Do you know why corn was planted here—again?"

"Yes. Because after the rains, the ground was dark and moist and rich."

"Also soft, Padre. By resting his weight on a stick, a man could make holes into which he could drop the seeds. That is a way of planting, you understand, that does not call for all this nonsense of plowing. Those who believe in it will not listen to contrary advice."

The first time the bottom lands had baked to a crust, Antonio had inquired of those who knew; and those, including Garza's Brothers of St. Francis, had said it was best to break up the land before planting, and afterwards keep it free of weeds. With difficulty and at great expense, Antonio had obtained two plows. All a man had to do was to harness a mule or an ox to the plow, then walk behind to guide the blade. The plows were free to all; but only a few—Rojas, Coronal, men like them—had tried them on the fields higher up. Their crop, because of the dry weather, was still not good, but they had corn. Not enough, but some.

"There are some ears here, too," Garza said.

"Without milk in them. Who can make tortillas out of corn without milk in the grain?"

"Then let those who planted here live on parched corn," Garza advised. "It is not good, but men have been known to subsist on it."

"You tell the miscreants so, Padre. Chew parched corn? Like a horse? They would rather starve."

"No. Men do not starve if any food, however poor, is at hand."

"Even so, Padre, taking the good corn and the bad, there will not be enough to carry over winter. And there is very little meat. Only a few have taken land outside for grazing, and the grazing this summer has been poor."

"The Indians?" Garza suggested. "They gave help that other hard winter."

"Indians," Antonio said with unusual scorn for him, "always plant corn like this. They will have no corn and just as little meat, since the dryness has driven the game away. They will have to dig wild roots this winter from the river banks and so will we. Anyhow, it is not good that the Indians should feed us. Not after a town is established. They expect then to receive favors, not . . . Ah, Padre, I do not wish to speak heartlessly of my friends; but they begin to take on a resemblance to those idle villains the *Isleños* at Bexar."

"Could this," Garza asked, "be their way of revolt?"

"If so," Antonio said, "it is against me."

"Not against you," Garza said, "or any other one person. Against circumstance and misfortune, perhaps. Why do you not go to your friend the Governor with your difficulties? He has never failed to help you."

Almost Antonio could have smiled. Wily Fray Josef! He knew, then, that a dispatch rider had come the day before with letters and instructions, and, in spite of outward calm, was curious to know what the papers had to say.

"Ripperdá will not be of help this time," Antonio said. "He is leaving his post at Bexar."

"No!" Plainly it was possible to bore through stone. "Someone has informed against him?"

"Beyond a doubt," Antonio said. "I could even give you the color of the informant's hair, though Ripperdá is not leaving in disgrace. The new appointment is said to be a promotion. He goes from Texas to Honduras. Well, is it a promotion or merely a lighter sentence of banishment than the Philippines?"

"I don't know. Honduras—jungle and mountains, forests of rich woods, an important coastline to defend. Will his lady go with him—and the two boys?"

"I think they expect to go," Antonio said. "His Excellency says they will leave Bexar as soon as they can make ready, in order to have time for a visit and rest in Mexico before going on to Honduras. But . . . who knows?"

Garza's large right hand fingered the knotted cord that belted his robe.

"In Mexico," he said, "Ripperdá will surely report to the Viceroy."

"Padre, here is more bad news. The most excellent Viceroy is dangerously ill—with pleurisy."

This had been another year of earthquakes. In the City of Mexico the shaking had continued for twenty days. The waters of the lakes rose and threatened the embankments. The cathedral began to sink. The people were in terror. So the Viceroy had opened his garden and placed himself there, ordering that all who came should be admitted. Through the twenty days he had sat in the garden, listening to everyone's story. All day into the night, people came. He had taken a chill. . . .

The knotted cord moved through Garza's hand.

"Texas," he rumbled, "without a governor. Mexico without a viceroy."

"As to that," Antonio said, "there will be replacements."

"Not . . ." Garza said, so prayerfully that Antonio had to laugh.

"Not Oconor," he said. "I have come to the end of bad news, I hope. The Red One has made himself too valuable fighting the Apaches to be removed from that command. Besides—ah, see what I have learned about government these evil years. Spain sends to America men of rank and quality, gives them authority in the name of the King, and trusts none of them entirely, often with good reason. That is why each must report the entire conduct of his office to the last sneeze. *Dios*, these reports must finally fill many storerooms. And yet, they are read, because every so often a special officer is sent whose duty is to observe on the spot what goes on. Such a one is in Mexico now, with the title of Inspector General, which places him above Oconor and even the Viceroy. If our friend should die of pleurisy, we can expect the Inspector General to represent the King in that office until a new viceroy is named. All of this, however, is apart from the reason for sending a courier here. You did not suppose that was merely to keep me informed?"

"No. I have been waiting for the true explanation."

"Compose yourself then." An absurdity, to Garza. "From this Inspector General I, too, have a promotion. He has named me deputy inspector, which is not a lofty title, but well above that of *justicia mayor* of an ailing town. I am ordered on a tour of inspection of the coast, where again a rumor has arisen of an invasion by the *inglés*."

"You will leave Bucareli?" Garza asked.

"Have I a choice, Padre?"

"Yes."

The priest's steady regard was not to be met comfortably. Antonio turned from it to the rattling cornfield, to the brown trickle of the treacherous river, to the rising slope of the opposite shore, where an intervening grove of cedars had been cut down to stumps. Visible beyond was a stockade, behind and above which showed the roofs of houses and finally a church, with an empty bell tower and a cross.

"The order," he said, "might have been intended to release me from all this."

"You asked to be released?" Garza demanded.

"No. I may have thought of it, but I swear . . ."

Before he could say more, from the opposite rise and beyond the town came a faint shouting. Instantly Antonio was back in the saddle.

"You will excuse me," he said hastily. "I must see what that means now."

As he rode on to the ford and crossed the river, he did not need to turn his head to know that Garza stood just where he had left him, watching. He could feel the priest's eyes stabbing him in the back. It seemed to him there had been another occasion when eyes had stabbed him so. A shoemaker back in Los Adaes . . . but the shouting was louder now and nearer.

"Up, sleepy one!" he said to his horse. "Let us go."

CHAPTER 2

A few minutes later Antonio was ordering two railbirds of confused ancestry to open the gates of a large stock pen outside the stockade and, after brief further study, also of a smaller horse corral. The shouting was now identified with two men riding the fringes of a broad fog of dust. They were, he could see, the former overseer of Rancho Lobanillo, Luis Ramón, and Manuel Piedra, his nephew, also a man now and insisting on being recognized as such. As he watched them approach, Antonio felt, as always, a pride of ownership; and his spirits lifted measurably. Again it came over him that no *vaquero* he had ever seen sat a horse so well as Luis. The younger Manuel had some of the same grace, but he was of a different temperament. Luis wasted no movement in anything he did. Manuel must add flourishes and a few capers.

Capers were, perhaps, out of place just now. The two were driving in the stock from land which Luis had, with Antonio's encouragement, occupied several miles west of the town, hoping to develop a ranch of his own. He had developed a ranch. He was now abandoning it, at least temporarily. There could be only one reason. When he had left the town, with a small bunch of cattle and a few horses, it had been understood that he could, if danger ever threatened him or his stock, return there, where he was still counted as a citizen. Now, either the creek through his land had gone completely dry or other disasters threatened. The cattle were here. The horses would surely follow.

Gravely, his elation undermined, Antonio rode wide of the dust cloud and waited.

The herd was penned. The cattle heaved and pushed and broke into smaller bunches. The gate was closed. Through a continuing haze of dust, Luis rode back to make his explanations to Antonio, whose pride was then lost in flaming anger.

"Mother of God!" he said. "I've seen Indians in a heathen dance wearing a buffalo's horns and hair, and they looked no worse. Luis, what the devil?"

Fire flashed in the brown eyes facing him, and went out, leaving the eyes as they had been, which was not good. Clear, fine, honest eyes, dulled by a sickness of denial.

"The thought of a beard amused me," Luis said, covering the offense with his hat. "I didn't know it looked so frightening."

"And now," a voice with an echo of the other, but mocking in tone, put in, "he can't sleep outside, for fear a bird will nest in the thicket."

"You!" Luis whirled on the speaker; but, fortunately, Manuel was still two lengths of a horse away and Antonio was able to place himself between the two.

"Here, here!" he said. "What is this now with you?"

"Not with me, Don Antonio," Manuel said. "This is the bad temper of my mother's brother. It comes, maybe, from living too much in the brush."

245

"Never mind," Antonio said. These two who had loved each other always! "I am glad you are here today, Luis; and welcome, Manuel. Your mother will be pleased."

"*Gracias*, Don Antonio. If I could wash a little first? I would not have her think that I, too, had taken the vows of a hermit."

"The river has still some water," Antonio said. "I will see you again."

"Did you," Luis growled, "fasten that gate securely?"

"No," Manuel answered. "I thought it would please you to find I had not."

And he went off, whistling like a bird in the chaparral.

"He has an insolence," Luis said.

"He is that age," Antonio said, "and you are not very much older; but we will come back to that later. Tell me now why you are here. You have lost some cattle?"

"Twice this week."

"Indians?"

"Comanches."

"How do you know?"

"By the way they destroy. They killed, took the meat, and left the offal—to draw the wolves."

The Comanches, too, were hungry, Antonio reasoned, and Luis's cattle were nearer than the wild game that had fled before the drought. Now, however, the same cattle were penned at Bucareli. Would that draw the Comanches to the town?

"If they come here, it will not be for meat," Luis said.

Antonio knew what he meant, or thought he did. It was not always cattle for meat or horses to ride that emboldened the Comanches to raid a settlement. They would butcher the cattle and steal the horses in any case; but increasingly of late tales were told of the savages descending upon isolated haciendas, killing the men and carrying off the women and children, especially young women and girls. Of those in Bucareli who had been young girls on the terrible journey five years ago from Los Adaes and had survived, most had taken husbands now and had little ones of their own. Even so, they were still young and fair enough to tempt a dark-skinned savage. Teresa Andorro, for one, was prettier than ever, after she had mended her heartbreak with devotion to her son and her husband's father. And there was Angelita Gonzales, still unwed, and with a grace now that made the charm of the girl she had been seem as shadowy as a promise lightly given.

Was it La Niña still for Luis? Antonio in truth did not know. He had been too burdened with other difficulties since the beginning of Bucareli to study his young friend that closely. There was someone, he felt sure. Luis had a reason for being angry always—not just at his nephew, Manuel. A man did not take up difficult, wild land and herd cattle and horses on it purely for his own satisfaction. Now he was back at the gates of the town with his livestock; and not to protect the cattle.

Was it La Niña still? Antonio thought it was, but he could have been wrong. Youth was youth, and manhood made its demands. After all this time, Luis could have made a second choice —the pretty widow of his dead friend or some younger girl in the town. The girl children who had lived through the dreadful journey and the hard time that followed were now of the age that Teresa Andorro or La Niña had been then. Pablo Rojas had a daughter as merry as Carmencita, and not nearly as wayward. Tomás and Rosario Coronal between them had half a dozen. All through the town were pretty girls. Pretty as a bouquet on a Sunday morning or in the evening parade. Food might be a problem and clothing another; but for the girls, also, youth was youth while life and love went on.

The Comanches knew. They knew too much. The town of Bucareli was now not so far from the Comanches range as it had seemed on a map in the Viceroy's garden four years ago. This very year, in the early summer—the season when the tribes, both hostile and friendly, were the most restless—Comanches had raided two villages of a neighboring Tejas tribe. This was too close for security. Antonio had the word from an Indian runner. Without a moment's hesitation he called out his militia, and divided the company into two parts, leaving one as a guard for the town, mounting the other to set out on a Comanche hunt.

"Indians," he said, "do not go to war to fight. They kill, they steal, and then they run. We will give them a reason for running."

The chase was more successful than anyone could have anticipated. The Indians were not expecting pursuit, certainly not from Bucareli, which they had not harmed. The militia came upon them, spread out in camp, feasting on their plunder. Again Antonio's decision was instant. Meaning only to drive home a lesson in fear, he ordered an attack.

He was right on one point: an Indian did not go to war to fight. The Comanches made no stand against the surprise attack. They ran for their horses. They ran for their lives—men, women, children, and dogs.

Some did not get away. They were killed in the first onslaught. "Do not stop to count them," Antonio had commanded, calling the men back from further pursuit. "The Comanches will do that when they return to bury their friends."

The militia rode back to Bucareli, busy the whole trip with the composition of great tales of conquest. Only Antonio and one or two others wished that the tally of the slain had been less. He did not regret the attack. He knew as well as anybody else that the fewer the Comanches the better. Bucareli was safe for this year, at least. But he also knew that the Indians were not likely to forget the number of their dead.

Antonio's uneasiness had deepened two days later when he saw riding up to the stockade gate an aging Comanche chief, accompanied by a much younger squaw leading a pony with a travois attached, on which was bound a youth, babbling with pain and fever. The chief asked to speak to the white man's priest, mentioning something about the Woman in Blue. That old legend, as Garza had related it, was, Antonio had discovered, more widespread among the Indians of Texas than one would have believed, and in Bucareli it had now attached itself firmly to Angelita Gonzales. The neighboring Tonkawa and Bidai Tejas never spoke of her in any other way. However, that the Comanches also knew her by that name was news—and unwelcome.

Nevertheless, Garza was summoned; and, since he knew a few words and more signs intelligible to the old Chief, he was able to get more of the story. The youth on the travois was the Chief's son. The squaw was the boy's mother. Going back to retrieve their dead at the camp which Antonio had destroyed, they had found the youth alive, but so near death that they were afraid only a miracle could save him. This miracle both the Chief and the squaw in anguish sought from Garza, and spoke again of the Woman in Blue.

"No!" Antonio said loudly and immediately; but Garza, breaking into such voluble protest as one would never have supposed he could command, had erased the denial before it could be heard. He had opposed Antonio's raid on the Indian camp in the first place; and now he said that to turn the sick Indian away, to refuse the plea of the old chieftain and the mother, would not be killing in combat, it would be butchery and would deserve to be remembered forever. On the other hand, to show mercy, as the Lord commanded, would bring a different reward.

"If he should die here?" Antonio argued.

"He will not die," Garza declared.

"You are sure? You had better be sure."

"I am sure."

The pony with the travois and the wounded Indian, also the squaw, had then gone in through the gate. The old Chief Antonio would not permit to enter. A small victory. Too small, when he remembered how the old warrior had looked, riding away alone down whatever path he had followed in coming. Who knew whether he had lived to rejoin his people? Who knew what had happened to him then? Nobody.

But that was how it had to be. To have the others inside was bad enough. The Indian youth had hovered between life and death for days. He was, on closer examination, younger than he had seemed when strapped to the travois. Not a day over sixteen, Garza said. He was badly hurt. A bone was broken in one leg. A horse, Garza thought, had fallen on him, though this seemed a strange thing to happen to a Comanche. As for the injury to his head, that, finally, could have been what saved his life. A fever brew brought on a sleep, which, with the stupor that followed and the weakness due to fasting, allowed the leg, set during his sleep, to heal. By midsummer, when Antonio had last seen him, the Indian, with the help of two sticks, was able to hobble.

Dios! He must be well by now. Antonio met the somber challenge in Luis's eyes with understanding, but he wondered. Was

Luis's anxiety due only to the presence of two Comanches in the town, or was it aggravated because Angelita Gonzales was involved? Involved? She had had most to do with the presence and, later, the healing of the Indian.

That she could heal, that, as the Woman in Blue she had become too widely known, perhaps, among the savage tribes, was another contrary result of the establishment of the town of Bucareli. Returning from Mexico in the early summer of 1774, Antonio had not brought to Señora Gonzales a passport to Spain. He brought only a sum of money still owed to her dead husband and the promise of a small pension while she lived. This did not appease the Señora. With screaming passion she reviled the King, the Viceroy, and, most of all, Antonio. The girl ran from the house in shame and terror.

If only she could have stayed away! The bright-eyed, ambitious, courageous Señora was mad. Or she would be if this kept on. But La Niña, alas, returned. This was her grandmother, ill, lonely, disappointed. Her good, loving grandmother—that is, when she was well.

It was the end of youth for La Niña. The grandmother grew worse instead of better.

"But there is no one else to care for her," La Niña said. "Only I—with Constanzia—understand. I do not blame you, Don Antonio. You did what you could. But do not talk to me of living apart from her. Not now."

Not now would soon be never. Antonio, who like all who loved the girl was beside himself trying to find a way to save her. In those days, while the preparations for moving to the Trinity went on, he found himself repeatedly surrounded by people begging him to tell again of his visit to Mexico. He obliged, but found himself really eloquent only when La Niña, pale, quiet, thoughtful, was briefly part of his audience. He watched to see which of the wonders of the capital interested her most. Finally, there seemd to be two.

One was the glittering cathedral, and, particularly, the Madonna with the three robes, one embroidered with pearls, one with diamonds, and one with emeralds. La Niña's eyes brightened, her lips parted. He could almost hear her wistful sigh. And he thought of the gift he had bought with Luis's *real*. "Something with fire" had been finally three colorful but imperfect opals. Luis had never presented them and would not now. He returned them to Antonio.

"She won't take them from me," he insisted, "but she might from you. You know what she will do with them?"

Antonio knew. Unhappily he gave the bright stones to Angelita, saying they were from a friend, too shy to approach her with a gift.

"A friend?" she questioned, but at once her thought took another turn. "A Madonna," she said softly. "We could have a jeweled Madonna in the new church."

Esteban Andorro had then made a small wooden image and painted worshipfully a face on the head. Angelita dressed the image in silk given her by the Governor's lady and lace of her own. A silversmith in Bexar shaped a crown and set the fiery opals in it. The statue stood now beside the altar of the church of Bucareli. When it was set there, Luis took land outside the town and built his hermit's hut.

But another tale Antonio had brought home had even a more absorbing interest for Angelita. He had been deeply interested himself in a hospital in Mexico dedicated to the service of the diseased and crippled poor of the city. Again and again La Niña asked him to tell about the hospital, the sisters who were nurses. Finally she expressed a wish. In the new town could there be such a hospital and might she have charge? She had medicine. Tía Rosario and the other herb women would provide more. As a result, when the town was being built, a small house was set up adjacent to the site of the then nonexistent church for La Niña. It was there that the Comanche princeling had been healed of his injuries. This, La Niña counted a grace to her from heaven surpassing any of her other cures. To have shared in saving a life! To have restored the youth to his father, to have made a friend of a dreaded enemy! Useless to tell her that nothing tamed a Comanche. Antonio on his midsummer visit had limited expostulation to a brief order.

"Keep him hobbled."

Today he would be sterner.

"I will send the wild ones away now," he promised Luis. "I should have done so sooner. So, in return for the favor, will you now remove that growth from your face? I should like to see you again as I once knew you."

The hard, younger eyes facing him softened, but not too much.

"I may show as many colors as a spotted pony," Luis warned.

"I prefer spotted ponies to angora goats. Ride now with me to my house. So many will be waiting for me there that I will go in from the rear. Magdalena will be watching. She will give you shears."

"Later, if you please," Luis said, his eyes still soft.

His horses were still to come, he explained. And there was his house at the ranch. It was, to be sure, not much of a house, but he had left most of his belongings there and naturally wished to retrieve them.

"Tomorrow," Antonio said, of the house. "Today I have work for you here."

CHAPTER 3

When, in the autumn of 1774, the settlement on the Trinity, overburdened from the first by its resounding name—Nuestra Señora del Pilar de Bucareli—had been laid out with a plaza, principal streets, a site for a church, and a trench all around, later to be filled by a stockade, it had seemed best to all for Antonio to have a residence of consequence. When the house was built—of peeled cedar timber—it was in everything but size a *Casa Real*. Though only two rooms in width, it had, nonetheless, a *portal* across the entire front, which sheltered any day in the year from two to twenty loafers, with a complement of horses hitched to the pillars.

Opening from the *portal* were two public *salas*. The first was a court of justice, in which disputes were heard and sometimes settled. Licenses were also issued there to traders, and punishments were meted out to offenders against the ordinances. Here also taxes were collected. Not royal taxes. Any new settlement was free of those for ten years; but it had seemed best to Antonio and had been agreed upon by the first town council that the King's fifth would be paid over that period into the town treasury, to be used for general needs. Collections, as things had gone, had been small, entirely insufficient. Major outlays, above what the Governor supplied from Bexar, Antonio had made from his own purse. Nevertheless, a show of collecting had been made.

This room also, when it was not a court of justice, was the place from which Antonio conducted what he had been able to organize in the way of private business. The table at which he presided as *justicia mayor* became then a counter over which he bought and sold, trading with lesser itinerant merchants, with the townspeople, with Comancheros from the west, and Indians, who came each year in greater numbers. That there were itinerant merchants demonstrated that Antonio's patrons in Mexico had been correct in saying that a crossroads was a good trading location, even when the roads were no more than trails. From these traders Antonio obtained the trinkets and cutlery and bright ribbons and occasional lengths of calico that he could use in buying furs and deerskins and buffalo hides from the Comancheros, and rough-coated, half-wild horses from the Indians—or food if they had a store and the town had not. The animals Luis took over at once and kept them until Antonio had an order from Bexar or one of the lesser garrisons. At least once a year Antonio went to Bexar himself, with pack mules carrying furs; also cloth from the Coronal looms, Tomás having now set up, besides his own loom, two simpler ones manned by assorted Coronals and Terreros; and, if a soldier guard was provided, a string of horses.

At this rate his purse would have been well filled against any need, for Ripperdá took all that Antonio brought and either sold it in Bexar at once, or, if it was needed by the garrisons, charged it against the treasury; or he might send it on to Mexico. Payment to Antonio in any case was sure—money or notes of credit. However, on the other side of the ledger, what Antonio obtained for Coronal weaving he gave to Tomás in full, keeping no profit. With other town products he followed the same system. If he bought food from the Indians, he gave it away to those who needed it. And, against his major sales, always some town expenditure waited. One good year without losses would have re-established a favorable balance for him. As it was, each year his purse looked leaner. Every time that Nicolas de la Mathe came with a report from Lobanillo and a letter from Doña María, Antonio yearned to write in reply that he was making arrangements for her to come to Bucareli, if only for a visit. She wanted to come and he wanted her always; but four times now he had said instead, "Not yet. Next year, perhaps."

Had he asked for his release, Garza had wanted to know. No, but now that the opportunity for relief had come, he must take it. He must get away where he could think more clearly how he could redeem what looked to him, if not to Garza, to be an impossible situation. Once more he saw the work—the sacrifice of—five years it was now—crumbling. Something different had to be tried.

So much for the first public *sala*. The second was reserved for more personal meetings between Antonio and the townspeople. From the beginning it had been in as much use as the other, nobody in Bucareli being without personal difficulties. To the rear of these two rooms, then, was an open patio, with Antonio's private quarters to one side and the kitchen opposite.

Over the *cocina*, over the house in general, presided as housekeeper Magdalena Piedra, sister to Luis Ramón and mother to Manuel, who had formerly cooked for the Ibarbo house at Lobanillo. This was, to Antonio, the one entirely satisfactory arrangement in the history of Bucareli to date. Magdalena, a strong, hearty girl—Antonio still thought of her so—lacked her mother, Esperanza's, tendency toward fits of hysteria, but had all of Esperanza's ability as a cook. She was, in addition, as hard and devoted a worker as Tío Paco had ever been. In this house each morning began with a thorough sweeping of the public rooms, also the *portal*, clear out into the street. This, usually while Antonio still slept. Later the patio and the rear of the house received the same attention.

This September morning, as Antonio rode up to the courtyard gate, Magdalena was still busy there with a broom. She had been delayed, she explained, with the cleaning, having had to stop to give Manuelito a little something to eat. He was still eating, she said, with a deprecatory sigh and an upward, beseeching glance of apology. How to control the hunger of such a one?

Antonio shrugged and opened his hands, indicating that Manuel was welcome to eat until he was satisfied. His house, at least the kitchen, was Magdalena's; and her children, one at a time, were naturally welcome. Magdalena smiled back, but with a slight quiver of the lower lip, which he understood as ardent gratitude. There was now no member of the Ramón family more devoted to him than Magdalena. Returning to work for her Don Antonio in his house, though it was by no means the old hacienda, had restored hope in her, if in no other. When the fulfillment of that hope seemed farther and farther away, she still was grateful. Without this work how would she have survived? To say nothing of her family. Juan Piedra, her amiable but not industrious husband, had, alas, with the establishment of a new home, reverted to early habits. He—well, he was of those who had planted corn in the river bottom. Since the drought had struck, Antonio had not seen him. Magdalena visited her own house when she could by day, returning to it always in the evening to spend the night there, but left it otherwise to the care of her oldest daughter.

All these facts, deep in Antonio's consciousness, made him glad to see the neat, aproned woman at his gate. Her son was indeed welcome to eat his fill in Antonio's kitchen. On second thought, perhaps Manuel should stop short of complete satisfaction.

"Luis will be coming later," Antonio said. "He, too, may be hungry."

"Will it be soon?" Magdalena asked.

"Not too soon. He has promised me to remove his beard. For that, he may need help from a barber."

"Manuel will be gone then," Magdalena said in evident relief.

I must ask about this now, Antonio thought, as he tied his horse.

"Magdalena," he said, entering the patio, "what is it between those two? They who have always been friends are now like two spurred cocks in a pit."

Magdalena set her broom against the wall. She looked up

255

beseechingly, then down. One hand picked up a corner of her apron.

"Woman business," she said—to the apron.

"Luis?" Antonio asked. "Manuel?"

"Luis should have married long ago. I know he thought he could not; but now Manuel is that age." Manuel? He was barely twenty. "He thinks of nothing else," Magdalena said. "He thinks, too, he will succeed where Luis failed." Desperately her eyes left the apron hem and sought understanding from Antonio. "Why," she cried, "must it be the same one for both of them?"

No! That wasn't possible. But how was it impossible?

"I do not speak against La Niña," Magdalena said, her two hands worrying the apron now. "So patient with that old witch—excuse, please—her grandmother. So devoted to her hospital and the sick. Also to the church. Helping the little ones with their catechism. She has no thoughts for Luis or Manuel or any other man."

That poor apron! It would be a rope soon.

"Luis knows she will always be like that. He should look elsewhere while he can. His manhood goes to waste. He turns sour and ugly—Luis, my brother. He needs a wife, a family. He could have them even now. There are plenty."

Plenty, as Antonio himself had observed. But, if Luis did not care to look elsewhere . . .

"It is a sickness," Magdalena said. "I ask myself will Manuel, too, come to be like that finally? Now he is only young and a little mad. He will not take no from anybody. Listen. He is tuning his guitar. He will sit outside the hospital if La Niña is there, and make little songs. Once he placed himself near the Gonzales house and sang until the old one screeched and drove him away. He went laughing, but still singing. But Luis does not laugh. He says bitter things to Manuel, whom he used to love. It is a sickness. I stand between the two—my brother and my son. If one of them in anger should hurt the other . . ."

"That will not happen," Antonio promised. "Any difference between them will stop short of that; but I will try to talk to each of them alone. If Luis could make up his mind not to pay any attention to Manuel, whose attachment is probably fleeting—

a young man's first fancy . . . Well, we shall see."

At that, Magdalena with a final sniff dropped her apron and returned to the kitchen. She had spoken truly, Antonio knew. There was a sickness, a malignant fever, not only in Magdalena's family, but all through the town. The stockade of cedar posts, which had looked so good, so strong, when it was first built, was now, not rotting, but falling down where rains—when there had been rain—had washed the ground away. The houses in the town were the same. Only a few had been built, like his, of timber. Most had been set up in a hurry—made of adobe and plaster and not too well supported. Rain had also melted down a corner here, a corner there. Brush huts in an Indian village, which were not expected to endure, looked better.

There was filth in the town—the filth of abuse, of helplessness, of "What does it matter?" Gullies that carried off human and animal and vegetable refuse when it rained were now dry and choked with weeds. For a while mosquitoes and green flies had bred in the ditches; then even they could not survive. Only filth remained, which no amount of dust could entirely bury. The fountain in the plaza, fed by a deep spring, gave less water with each week that passed. He must tell Luis to water his stock at the river, not to use the trough at the well. All that water—while it lasted—must be for people.

It was a sickness. There were those in the town who said now it would have been better had they never left Bexar. Things had been hard there, but they had had protection and some assistance. They forgot how many had died that one winter, how the rest had survived only by virtue of what they begged in the way of food and clothing—or stole. Now again they were begging and stealing when they could. Some cheated in trading with the Indians. When Antonio learned of such cases, he took everything away that the cheaters had gained, sought out the Indian victims and gave them goods of worth to replace rotten cloth and tin knives; and the Indians held him in esteem for that, but the town acquired a bad name.

That anyone should talk of returning to Bexar! There was no help in Bexar now, with Ripperdá leaving. He had been a good governor, too good, perhaps. Ambitious for himself, and even more for Texas. Bexar had prospered. He, too, had prospered; but what he had gained in wealth by dealing with such men as Antonio Ibarbo, Nicolas de la Mathe, and Athanase de Mezières was a small percentage of profit compared to what he had learned about his province and provincials.

There were those, however, who viewed his success only in the light of old corruption. "See," they said, "everything he does is only to make himself rich. All governors are like that." But Ripperdá was not like other governors. Above his sharp beard, his eagle nose, were those gentle, honest eyes. So, now he was being promoted to the jungles of Honduras. Perhaps, if the town of Bucareli had thrived . . .

Bitterness filled Antonio's throat. He had tasted it before—the deepest draught in his defeat in Mexico—but no bitterness had been like this of now. One valued friend was being banished. Another was ill, in danger of dying. He would have liked to report a success to the Viceroy in Mexico. He had never had strong hope for the settlement which the Viceroy and that strange, shrewd man, My Lord Fiscal, had promoted; but he had tried, wanting to prove himself wrong and them right. Now it only added to his grief to know that none of his highly placed friends blamed him for the failure. It was evidence of trust to be named a deputy inspector. He was to proceed as soon as possible to the coast. Could he go? Would he?

Shaking his head, almost as baffled as Magdalena, he went on into his house.

In the *sala* of the people waited, first, Esteban Andorro, the lame carpenter. The church roof leaked, he reported. He had known that during the last rain; but the drip had been only a little and the exact hole hard to locate. Then the rains had stopped and the timbers shrunk. Now from below he could see the sky through a gap the size of his hand. A new board was needed up there.

"Good," Antonio said, "only you will not place it. You must get some younger man to climb to the roof for you, Esteban."

"Who would that be?" the lame man asked.

"Come, there must be someone who can set a board, nail it fast and daub the crack. I see idle men wherever I go. They know how to build hen coops. They roof their own houses."

"Such roofs, most of them!" Esteban protested. "This is God's house, Señor."

"Nevertheless," Antonio said firmly, as firmly as he could speak to this worthy man, "if a hen-coop carpenter is the best you can do, you must engage one of those to help you. You must not risk a fall. We cannot spare you, Esteban. Your family cannot spare you. How is Teresa these days?"

The carpenter clasped his hands. His weathered face shone.

"Teresa!" he said. "My own daughter could not wait on me more lovingly, more patiently. She never complains. But it is not right. She should not wait on an old man like me. I do not speak disrespect of my son when I say Teresa should take a new husband now, if there is one deserving of her. There is the boy, besides. He should have a father to follow. A young man, able in body, whom he can admire."

"Well," Antonio said, "we can hope a young man can be found, smart enough to discern Teresa's worth, and deserving of so much good fortune. Meantime it is you who must stay on the ground and give instruction to a builder of hen coops about the church roof. If there is any cost, payment will be made."

"God's house?" Andorro said. "There will be no cost. *Gracias*, Antonio."

Bitterness in the throat. Anger, a helpless storm of anger. If he should let it go, someone would be hurt. Not, he hoped, anyone so blameless as Esteban Andorro.

And not Constanzia, the servant of Señora Gonzales, who stood before him next. Poor Constanzia! In four years she had aged twenty. Part of this was her worn clothing. Her white apron was whole and spotless. Somehow she managed that. But her black skirt and her shawl were rusty and had been patched and darned in so many places that it was a wonder the webbing held at all. However, the aging in the woman herself was harder to contemplate. She was really no older than Magdalena, but she walked now with a stoop. Antonio had seen Indian squaws bent like that under bundles of firewood. Constanzia's burden was heavier, because she could never drop it.

She did not come to Antonio often with her difficulties; so he knew, when she did, that she needed help. He placed a chair for her and, to persuade her to take it, seated himself quickly on another.

"Now tell me," he invited.

Constanzia brushed her hand across her eyes.

"It is the money again, Señor," she said in low, shamed tones.

But he knew about the money. He himself had delivered the first payment of pension to Señora Gonzales. She had snatched it from him with no expression of gratitude. Later, as soon as she was alone, she had hidden the money. This she had then continued to do with all she received. The payments were not large, amounting to a hundred pesos over the year; but that much in minted coin would have supplied every need of the household—food, clothing, and shelter. The Señora, however, would not release one peseta from her hoard. The house she lived in was built by friends. Daily necessities came the same way. "She is crazed," the givers said compassionately, "by all that has happened. At her age, who can wonder?"

This charity the Señora accepted without shame. After all, she ate very little. A few crusts soaked in broth, now that most of her teeth were gone, a sip of diluted wine, were sufficient. That her grandchild and her servant were humiliated by her behavior did not move her. She screeched at Constanzia if she remonstrated; and, if accidentally the poor servant discovered one of the hiding places for the money, she threatened to beat her with any weapon at hand. La Niña's entreaties she turned off with a cooing gentleness that was even more terrible.

"Some day, my pet," she said, "you will thank your grandmother for saving this money. When I have enough to buy you a husband. None of this rubbish around here. A man of position, who can appreciate a wife with virtue—and a dowry."

"My grandmother, please," Angelita would beg. "I do not wish . . ."

"There, there!" the evil one cooed. "Of course, you wish. You are a woman, are you not? I will take care of you that way, too. You will see."

Antonio had no better luck, nor did Garza, with remonstrance.

"Thou deceiver of trusting women!" she screamed at Antonio.

To the priest she said: "Ah, you have come to exorcise my demon, Fray Josef? Well, do not think to frighten it or me with incantations. We have an understanding, that demon and I. I will pay him off presently and be rid of him, with no help from you."

So, now, what could he, Antonio, do for Constanzia about that money?

"This morning," she said, "La Niña had a peseta. A trader paid it to her for medicine for his child. She asked the Old One if she would not like to give it to the priest for special prayers for the grandfather. The Old One smiled and said she was a good girl to remember the brave grandfather, and took the money. Later when La Niña, happy to have found a way at last to soften the Señora, had gone to the hospital, the Old One hid that peseta with the rest."

"She is worse than I knew," Antonio said, "but it is useless to try to reason with one who has no reason left. I will tell Angelita that she must not give money ever again to her grandmother. Good? I will speak to her right away. Now will you stop for a little visit with Magdalena in the kitchen? She is so occupied with feeding men that it will be a pleasure to her to entertain a woman. Come with me. I must go that way, anyhow, in order to escape to the hospital."

He knew that Magdalena would coax Constanzia to eat a little. After all, if she were to outlive her mistress, she must eat occasionally.

At the hospital, a low, one-room structure with thick adobe walls for coolness in summer and warmth in winter, in the shadow of the church, he found Manuel Piedra in a small yard to the rear, not playing a guitar, but whittling on a wooden shoulder yoke, designed to enable a man to carry two buckets of water at one time from the well in the plaza. The need for water was plain. As far away as the area allowed, the Indian squaw was doing washing in a wooden tub, spreading torn pieces of cloth and assorted garments on bushes so dusty that the benefit of washing was questionable. Near her, in the shade cast by the dusty bushes, her son, wearing only a breechcloth, lay stretched out asleep, his face pillowed on his folded arms.

The whittling went on outside the rear door, assistance of a sort being given by Pedro Coronal, now an overgrown fifteen, mostly bones and joints. Pedro, having begun and abandoned apprenticeship at various trades, was at present helping at the hospital and learning about medicine—or so he said, words blowing off his lips as lightly as plumed seeds carried by the wind, forgotten as soon as he had spoken them. His assistance to the whittling was in the way of advice and criticism. He begged Manuel to shape that yoke to his own shoulders and not to his, Pedro's. He would prefer to make two trips to the well for water, carrying lighter pails in his hands, to one journey under that backbreaker. Manuel was not being influenced by these opinions.

"Using a yoke," he said, "you can walk erect. When you carry water at the end of your arms, you must bend your back. That way you could grow a hump."

"I grow a hump just looking at that yoke," Pedro retorted.

Well, here were two, light enough of heart, Antonio thought, coming through the neat coolness of the empty house. Angelita, idle herself for once, stood in the door, also watching. She turned with a start at Antonio's good morning, then flushed in her delicate way when she saw who was there.

"Don Antonio! It is a long time!"

Just as quickly the flush faded and question awoke in her soft brown eyes. She knew that he had come about the Indians. It grieved Antonio to have to cross her in this, as it did to oppose her in any way. She would be quick to sense a rebuke—and so defenseless. This defenselessness made him think of her still as a child, though little of the child remained now. She was a woman these days, too solemn, too quiet, but fairer than ever. Probably the fairness was all younger men saw, but perhaps not. Luis or even dizzy Manuel might regard her in her mended blouse and faded blue skirt as light amid the general darkness.

To the typical *rebozo* she had added a gauzy scarf, also blue, drawn low across her forehead and fastened in a knot at the nape of her neck. In his man's way Antonio had told her how those who helped in the hospitals in the City of Mexico, and who were not veiled nuns, covered their heads so; and she had invented a style of her own to give a similar effect.

The blue of the scarf, alas, was reflected in the shadows under her eyes. Shadows, which had never faded after Bexar. That one so pure, so tender-hearted, should live in such never-ending darkness!

"Señorita, I kiss your hand. You are, as always, balm to my eyes. I did not mean to stay away. Just today I had a moment . . ."

Then, hearing the banter in the yard, he went on outside and spoke to the young men beside the step.

"I am glad to see you making yourself useful, also that you have such skill with a piece of wood, Manuel. Only this morning Esteban Andorro was asking me if I knew a couple of young men who could help him set a new board in the church roof. I will tell him about you two."

"Don Antonio, if you please," Pedro said with a sly smile, "it is Manuel who has the skill, not I."

"Perhaps," Antonio conceded, "but you will make a good team just the same. The two of you will climb to the roof for Andorro. There Manuel can study the shape of the hole to be mended and you, Pedro, can let down a rope and bring up to him the board he needs and nails and tools, which Andorro will fasten to the rope where he stands on the ground. I will recommend you to the carpenter this afternoon."

Further protest was then rendered impossible by Angelita. With what was a sharp outcry for her, she left the door and ran to the rear of the yard, where the squaw was in the act of tipping her washtub to empty it. At Angelita's approach, which was like the attack of a bird on some preying animal, she let the tub settle back on the ground, and settled herself at the same time on her heels in what looked to be defiance.

"I've told you," Angelita rebuked, with complete disregard for problems of communication, "that you are not to pour out the water. It is a waste. Pedro!"

"Pedro," Manuel said, "fetch the water pail. I am sorry the yoke is not ready, but let us see what you do with just your long arms. It is," he explained to Antonio as Pedro with a grimace carried a pail to the tub, "time to water the flowers."

It was a scene as amusing and merry as anyone could have

263

conjured up in these circumstances, or it would have been so except for the Indians. The squaw sat in the dust, watching with scorn the young white man demean himself by carrying water. The youth, her son, had not stirred.

"Do they," Antonio asked Angelita, "understand what you say to them?"

"They have a few words, Don Antonio, I think."

"Is he," he indicated the young Indian, "healed of his wounds?"

"Yes. Oh, yes! He limps only a little at times."

"Good! Then, with your permission . . ."

Without it, he walked over to the Comanche and brushed one bare leg lightly with the toe of his boot. On the instant, with the recoil of a serpent, the lad was on his feet, his eyes also as deadly as a snake's, his whole body tense, ready to run or to strike. If he had had a weapon in his hand, he would have struck. Antonio squirmed inwardly, realizing the threat, but held his outward calm.

"Good!" he said firmly and loudly, wanting all to hear. "Very good. I congratulate you, also the Chief, your father, who has recovered a son. Can you ride a horse now?"

Whatever else the Comanche understood or did not understand, he recognized the word *caballo*. The cold deadliness of his slant eyes was shot with fire. Then the fire went out, and he was tense and watchful and ready, as before.

"Good!" Antonio said, again loudly, and turned halfway to speak to Manuel, noting that Manuel, too, stood ready. "Manuel, do you know where the pony is kept that brought these visitors? Catch it, then; and, if it is able to walk and carry a rider, fasten a piece of blanket to its back and fit it with a rope halter, Indian style. Go at once. I will wait here until you return."

Feeling then some indefinable change in the attitude of the Indians, son and mother, he turned to the house, where Angelita stood, watching all that went on, fearfully. The fingers of one hand were pressed against her mouth, as if to stifle another outcry. Her face was white, the shadows under her eyes too plain. Abandoning caution, Antonio went to her.

"*Muchachita*, what is it?" he asked, taking her hands one at a time into his and holding them warmly, alarmed himself to

264

feel how they trembled. "Everything is all right now. What are you afraid of?"

"I was afraid for you," she said in a low voice, as if talking to herself. "Oh, Don Antonio, have I done something wrong, meaning only to do good?"

"You have done nothing wrong," he assured her. "You can do nothing wrong in my sight. You are not accountable for the evil in others. The Indians must go. That is all. The wonder is that they have not stolen away before. Except for the lack of a horse, they would have done so, taking as much as the old woman could carry. Come now. Go back to her without fear. She is only waiting to see what will happen. The same is true of her son. I think they would not harm you in any case, you who gave the young man back his life; but I will watch. Say to the squaw that the time has come to prepare for the journey away from here. Then help her collect a bundle that she can carry. Not too large, because she will carry it, you know. Even on a horse, the young brave will not help her. The son of a great chief? Never!"

Ah! That was better. Color returned to the fair face. Her breath still fluttered; but she would not faint now. Then, just as he was about to release her hands and let her go, another question came.

"Where will they go—alone?"

He risked a laugh, and she pulled away her hands herself.

"Back where they came from," he told her. "To their people. To the Chief, the young brave's father. It won't be far."

He wished it could be much farther.

"If someone attacks them, they are not armed."

"Who will attack?" he argued. "The Tonkawas, the Bidais? Our Indians? They will give the Comanches free passage and a wide, empty trail. Unarmed, did you say? The young man did not have a knife?"

From the corner of the house came a whistle, and Pedro Coronal put down an empty pail to measure with his hands the length of that knife.

"I thought so," Antonio said. "You will give me the knife, Niña, please. I will keep it until the Indian is on his horse and riding through the gate, then restore it to him. Unarmed? With the knife and a bit of string, they can even feed themselves on the journey; so do not be too generous with provisions in their bundle. Now, will you speak to the squaw? Manuel will be returning. When he comes, when the Comanches are ready to ride, the two of them, mother and son, will go. Without delay."

Angelita lifted her shoulders in a shrug of surrender, then went to speak to the squaw, who, weary of palaver or her labors or in anticipation of more to come, sat now on the upturned tub. Similarly at the house Pedro Coronal rested on his empty pail. Antonio was swept briefly into laughter.

"Carrying water is not easy," Pedro assured him.

"I am sure it is not," Antonio agreed. "When Manuel returns with the horse and we have seen the Indians on their way, I have other work for you—without carrying. I will hold a review of the militia this evening. In full force. All now of age to be enrolled in the company, and all who have served, even those who have been dismissed because they have taken land, all those who live here only part of the time—every man of military age. You may count yourself as one. At four o'clock this afternoon, following the siesta, in the plaza. You will go first to those who hold rank and then to all the other houses. All must be notified. I as Captain have not held a review in a long time."

Pedro Coronal shaped his mouth for a whistle that this time did not come out. Instead, he stood up, stretched, set his ragged hat back on his head, raised his right arm as if intending a military salute, hesitated, looked over the dusty yard to where Angelita stood talking to the Indians, let his arm fall, sagged briefly toward the pail, but again changed his mind and picked it up, setting it down beside the doorstep, now with the open side up.

"Always so," he explained, "in case it should happen to rain. I will do as you say, Señor *Capitán*. Up one street and down the other. The *cantinas*, too?"

"Those especially," Antonio directed. "Do not pass by the church even without looking to see who might be in there."

CHAPTER 4

Of the more than two hundred men now counted as residing in the town of Bucareli, less than half assembled on parade that evening in the plaza. Some, like Diego Zapatero, were too old to march. Some were ailing. Some were away on valid pursuits. More had absented themselves in haste when Pedro had delivered the summons. There were, Antonio thought, too many hiding places conveniently nearby. A search of Indian *rancherías* in the neighborhood might have added a number to the ragged double line. But there was no time for such a search, and those who might have been uncovered could not properly be considered good defenders.

"Do you wish a roll call?" Pablo Rojas asked. After the death of Flores he had assumed the rank and duties of lieutenant of militia. The same Rojas, earnest, reliable, not gifted, but something better—a good man.

"Is there a roll?" Antonio asked.

"But, of course, *Capitán* Antonio. I will order the standard-bearer . . ."

"I do not see our *alférez*. Do you?"

Rojas was forced to admit that the standard-bearer was absent. He expressed amazement. Antonio did not indulge in such minor emotions.

"We will dispense with the roll call," he said. "Have the Sergeant make a count by tens."

But now there was no sergeant. Drill had not been held over the hot months, Rojas reminded Antonio. Vacancies might have come because of that.

"Luis is here," Antonio said. "Tell him it is my wish that he resume the title and duties of sergeant, at least for now. He is in the front line, the first on the left. He has taken off his beard. That is why you didn't know him."

Luis, in truth, was almost unrecognizable. He was not only

spotted. Some of the spots in the rigors of barbering had swelled like bee stings. Otherwise, however, his general appearance atoned for the painfully swollen face. Somewhere—from Magdalena, no doubt—he had obtained a clean shirt and clean duck breeches. The breeches were too short, but whole. His gun was clean and freshly oiled.

The count was made. Luis gave the number, three less than eighty, to Rojas, who reported it to Antonio, who, after brief study, gave his next order.

"Let a leader be chosen for each ten men, and for the odd seven. Preferably let the leader be a man with a gun, not a stick. We will look into this matter of weapons later."

He knew, without examination, why the guns were short. The missing ones had been traded for food. That must be stopped. Roughly he finished his commands.

"By tens, fifteen minutes of drill. Marching, countermarching, the turns and so on. Finally forming in line. The Sergeant will endeavor, with the help of the group officers, to dress a straight line. I will review the company then and have a few things to say in explanation of this sudden muster."

He finished to an emptiness of silence. Rojas failed to acknowledge the order. Both he and Luis were briefly at a loss, then each found relief in movement, Rojas ordering Luis to carry out the Captain's command, Luis walking back to the line to repeat it to the others.

The drill was bad. Some had never gone through the movements before. The rest seemed to have forgotten all they knew. Some were, like Pedro Coronal, all hands and feet and elbows. The squad corporals had to learn from Luis how to command a group. The heat was heavy, the air still with the passing of day, the sky like dull brass. Soon everyone was panting and sweating, and the dust began to rise.

Antonio's heart swelled until he thought it must break through the bars of his ribs. He turned away from the parade. But the other half of the picture gave him no comfort. The families of the militiamen had come out to watch the marching. Children and hungry, scavenging dogs, and women—and this mock soldiery was all their protection.

The Andorros were there—the lame carpenter with his four-year-old grandson, who seemed to be making some urgent request of his mother, which she refused. A timorous mother, perhaps, unable to forget her great loss. What was it Andorro had said about Teresa's marrying another? Or, had that been Magdalena, speaking of Luis?

In another block of shade Rosario Coronal stood talking to a woman he did not know by name. Rosario was well represented in the militia, with a husband, a stepson, and two of her own brood marching and sweating in the dust. Rosario, the redeemed, doing her duty each day as it was laid upon her, strong, outspoken as ever, making her choice between right and wrong. Generous Mother Earth in a fruitful season, she deserved a turn in fortune; but how would it come now?

He saw no sign of Angelita Gonzales. He had not seen her since the departure of the Indians. She would not go with them to the gate when they left. She was troubled about them. She was troubled about many things, and who could look into that pure mind and heart and give her solace? While they had waited at the hospital for Manuel to come with the Comanche's pony, Antonio had found a minute in which to speak to her about the peseta she had given her grandmother that morning. Color had bathed her face, but it was the color of shame, and her eyes had filled with tears.

"Don't cry," he had said foolishly and helplessly. "It is not your fault, nor is it the Señora's, that she is as she is now. Only, if you have a piece of money in the future, use it for food or some other need. You will not be deceiving your grandmother, only acting with better wisdom. Will you promise?"

She had nodded consent, but her tears had run all the faster.

"*Muchachita*, dear one," he had said then, "if I could, I would put you on the back of Turbelino and carry you away from all this—if I could."

For the least bit of time, the tears stopped, while she searched his face.

"No," she said then. "No, that could not be."

"Of course not," he agreed, and the tears had sparkled again. "It was just a manner of speaking."

Then Manuel had appeared with the pony, and she had wiped her eyes and gone back to the Indians; but later she would not see them away. Where was she now? Cleaning some spotless corner in her hospital, perhaps. Still weeping and wiping the tears away? Praying in the church? All alone somewhere, he could be sure. Would tears and prayers be, like Luis's bad temper, her sorrow over happiness denied her? What happiness in particular? Ah, who could read a woman?

His heart swelled and swelled as he turned back to the parade area, where the weary squads were now once more being dressed into a double line. The line was slightly better than at first. When, at a word from him to Rojas, the leaders of each squad stepped forward two paces, it looked still better; but the men, covered with sweat and dust, looked worse. Protest, weariness, question, some sullen defiance faced Antonio as he walked the length of the line, then back to the center and stopped, raising his hand to command attention. Good! He could say what must be said with better spirit.

"Rest where you are," he began, though he had no intention of being lengthy. "You may ask why I called for a drill today." Overhead the sky was clear, but seen through a haze of heat and dust. Antonio did not sweat; he only burned. "Surely you know why we have a militia—or have you forgotten? Some of you did not see, perhaps, the departure of our Comanche visitors. They have gone and that is good. But it is not good to think that the Comanches are near enough to send one of their people to us for healing.

"Four years ago most of you did not know what a Comanche looked like. It was hoped that a strong town, surrounded by friendly tribes, would cause them to stay away forever. That, alas, has not happened. Every year, for one reason or another, they come closer. To trade, or it may be to see what we have worth stealing. That two should have lived all summer among us is, perhaps, no cause for alarm. There is no danger of attack at present. This is the time of year when all the tribes, friendly or hostile, go to their home camping grounds, to make sure their existence over the winter.

"But time goes by. The need for defense always comes suddenly. We have no defense here except our militia, a few guns, and the stockade. We are a long day's march from the nearest garrison—Orcoquisac on the lower Trinity. Much farther than that is Bexar, or its Cibolo outposts. Beginning now, the militia will drill once a week without fail. The missing men will be found and will take their places in the line. There should be half again as many as I see today. Ten squads of twelve, each with its own leader, is not too much to ask. There will be special drill for the leaders. You will take orders from them, and they, in my absence, from Pablo Rojas, your *Teniente*."

A tremor ran over the line. He had thought some were not listening; but all had heard that about "absence."

"I am compelled to be away for a while," he said.

Why not, he asked himself? What more could a man do than he had done? He had led these unfortunates to Bexar. He had pleaded their cause before those in authority. He had suffered when they suffered. He had begged food for them when they were starving. Finally he had led them out of Bexar to this place and helped them to build new homes. That had been four years ago. Surely now their welfare no longer depended on him. It must not depend on him.

"This is an order," he said, "that takes me away. It may be a good thing. You can now show your true worth. I think you will do that. Well, that is how it is. What remains to be said, I will say to Lieutenant Rojas. *Adiós*, my friends."

To Rojas, to Tomás Coronal, to Esteban Andorro, to Luis Ramón—and that was enough, though one was absent who should have been there—Fray Josef Francisco Mariano de la Garza. The priest had been at the stockade gate when the Comanches left. He had muttered a prayer as they passed through the gate, though the Indians had seemed not to notice. After that, nobody had seen Garza. But that was not unheard of. He had, no doubt, been sent for outside. When summoned, he always went. Antonio was not anxious about Garza. Still, he would have liked the priest to hear what he found to say to this small council.

"I go to Bexar first," he told them, "for further instructions. From there I will make my way directly to the coast. If trouble should come here that you think I should know about, you can send word to Orcoquisac or the Mission of Bahía del Espiritu Santo. Garza will give you the name of the priest. However, as I said, I do not think you will need me, or I would find a way not to have to go."

"Then stay," Tomás Coronal said. "We may not live out the winter if you abandon us now."

"Who said abandon?" Antonio challenged. "Look. The stockade needs repair. You know as well as I how it can be done. Let it be done then—and quickly. There is another matter—the cannon which Gonzales left at Los Adaes and De Mezières sent to us here. Let them be cleaned and loaded, ready for firing."

"The one at the gate is cracked," Rojas reminded him. "If fired, it will explode."

"Let one who is a fleet runner apply the match," Antonio said. "Indians fear cannon. If one explodes they will run all the faster. In case of attack, fire the cannon, even if one explodes and breaches the stockade. Luis, you will take charge of the drills. I will ask at Bexar that a corporal or a sergeant and a few soldiers be sent again as at first, to help bring order. It is important that everyone should know how to act on a command, where to place himself in defending the stockade or to meet a rush. I will also ask for muskets. *Teniente*, you will keep the arms. Give them out for hunting or practice only to someone who can be trusted not to trade them for profit or food."

Rojas looked back at him solemnly.

"When people face starvation," he said, "they will get food as they can."

Anger blazed in Antonio.

"Let nobody starve," he commanded. "If one has food, all must share it. There is meat and some corn. I cannot by being present make any more. If I ever thought I could work miracles, I know better now. I can do nothing that you cannot do; and, before God, you must do what is necessary. This winter will tell the story. This winter you can prove . . ."

What? It was as though Garza had returned to put the question. Antonio cut off his words where he had halted. Words were not saying, anyhow, what he wanted them to say. He had had coherent, reasonable things to communicate. Now it was only, do this or do that . . . if you do such and so. He was pleading with these friends as if they were helpless fools they represented. He was pleading . . . with somebody. Why should he plead? He got up from his chair and walked the floor stormily. The light was dim. It was now that time of evening. Out of the dimness he felt four pairs of eyes watching him, waiting, listening for profound wisdom from him, who had never had any.

No, they were not listening for that. It was another sound—a light, beating sound on the roof of the *portal*. Antonio went to the door and opened it wide. The beating was also on the hard-packed earth before the *portal*. There was a freshness to the air, a smell . . .

"It rains," Tomás Coronal said, close behind him. "It rains."

There had been in the western sky, everyone remembered now, as they had left the parade, a bank of what could have been clouds; but those had appeared before and had come no closer.

"That leak in the church roof," Andorro lamented. "We did not mend it in time."

"Now you can see better the extent of the leak," Antonio told him.

"But, if this should mean a flood now," Coronal added.

"Now, why," Antonio demanded, "must there be a flood? It is not the season for floods. It is raining and that is all."

"It is raining," Pablo Rojas agreed, "and, since for that reason things do not look as bad as before, perhaps you will not leave after all, Antonio."

"Why will I not?" Antonio roared at his good friend. "Did I not make it clear that this is a command? From the Inspector General at Mexico. There is a threat of invasion on the coast. Foreign ships have been seen. The Inspector General names me a deputy to see what it comes to. I leave tomorrow at daybreak. I must."

Four pairs of eyes stared at him through the dark. What did he mean by "must"? That he could not explain. He had been foolish to try.

CHAPTER 5

It was in itself, Antonio thought, strictly speaking, not an ocean-going vessel, this hull of a boat that lay half in, half out of the water against the bank of a little forest river, which could be an arm of the Neches, making its way independently to the sea. He had worked his way along the coast that far, he and Turbelino. According to the best advice—how far must one go to escape that?—it was exceedingly dangerous for him to be where he was, surrounded by hostile coast Indians and practically alone.

Practically, but not quite alone. From Nicolas de la Mathe he had borrowed the idea of protection that kept its distance. Only a league or two behind him, he hoped, every day rode two soldiers and a corporal from the garrison posted at the Bay of the Holy Spirit, where the Colorado River spread out and lost itself in the Gulf of Mexico. The soldiers had orders to follow him just that closely. He knew they were there, and so did the Indians. Even these coastal savages, known to be thieves and murderers, kept a certain respect for soldiers of Spain. Retribution followed too swiftly and certainly to permit any forgetting. Moreover, the Señor who rode the proud gray horse with the white mane and tail, who talked to that horse in language the stallion understood, who even sang to him at times to soothe his unrest, carried on his person a paper from which shone a gold seal, bright as the sun, over two pieces of rich, scarlet ribbon. The paper was magic.

All this was, under close analysis, flimsy protection perhaps, but so far it had served. Anyhow, fear was not among the ghosts that haunted Antonio Gil Ibarbo at this point in time.

There was this boat. It was a boat propelled by oars, such as larger vessels, merchant ships or ships of war, carried on their decks—for safety in case of wreck or for landing purposes. This one had four oarlocks on each side, but the oars were missing.

They had, no doubt, been carried away. But of what use were they to people who lived on land and had no boats except rafts and dugout canoes? An oar that pushed through ocean waters was too long and heavy for such paddling. The benches, too, the seats for the oarsmen, were gone. Of seasoned hardwood, they would have made hot fires or could have served as thrones for Great Chiefs to sit upon. Heavy to carry about, however, if a village moved. Well, they had been part of the boat, and they had been taken.

There had been, he thought, eight oarsmen, two at each of four benches for rowing. Shorter benches at bow and stern would have accommodated three more men possibly—one, no doubt, an officer commanding.

It was a new, compelling rumor, added to the general talk about English landings, that had brought Antonio to this remote spot. It had come after months of looking and listening and trading, when his performance as deputy inspector was practically at an end. He had been working on his report, which displeased him because it contained nothing sensational, only small facts and they not new. He himself had seen no English ships recognizable as such on the waters of the Gulf. It was his opinion, respectfully offered, that there were too few ships of any sort out there, especially ships of Spain.

Nevertheless, there was evidence that the English had visited this part of Texas, their open purpose being trade. To prove this, he had collected a number of articles of strictly English manufacture. He had three pieces of cloth, expertly woven—one a mixture of linen and wool, he believed, stout enough to make good outer garments; one of cotton, equally strong, dyed a rich red, which the Indians prized especially; and a third—this had cost him the most in trade—as smooth and lustrous as silk, but still of cotton, dyed black, with bright flowers printed all over it. He had half a dozen hunting knives with short handles and long, sharp blades, possibly of English steel, but fashioned, he felt—it was only a feeling—in America by someone who knew the needs of a woodsman. The same was true of the fowling piece. Its stock was of American walnut. The barrel and firelock could have been of English manufacture, though by now surely European skills must have been brought by their colonials to this continent. The gun was long, too heavy to be handled by a mounted man; but, when loaded properly and carefully aimed, it had a deadly accuracy, effective at a great range.

Those who had possession of these articles, which it had taken him the winter to trace, would in no case say that they had got them from an English trader. It was always some Spaniard or Frenchman or a mestizo, whom most of the time they could not name. If English traders were involved, it seemed probable that they delivered their goods by land or over water to some secret meeting place, where native traders, licensed or unlicensed, waited to receive them. The quantity of goods was not important, except that it was a beginning. The English were crafty. Many of their acquisitions of territory had followed an invasion by merchants.

It was at this point, while he was setting down his assembled facts, that Antonio had heard of an English ship that had been wrecked on the coast not far from the border of Louisiana. The wrecked ship could still be seen if a man cared to take the risk of going to that place. It was on a part of the coast occupied by Alibama Indians, unregenerate savages, who knew no humanity. An older story said it was they who many years before had murdered that brave Frenchman the Chevalier de la Salle, when he set foot by mistake on their land. In the case of the English ship, it had been driven ashore by a storm; and the Alibamas had overwhelmed the crew, killed them all, and stolen what cargo had not been destroyed by the high water.

Here was a thing, risks disregarded, Antonio thought, that could give him a rare reputation as a deputy inspector. With no delay, he had given his unfinished report and his merchandise into the keeping of the missionary at Bahía and set out for the land of the Alibamas.

So now, here he was, alive by his own boldness, and by the awe the forest people had for the power of Spain, especially when mounted on a horse of superhuman intelligence, which would scream and roar at the approach of an enemy and could kill with its sharp hoofs. And here was the fabled ship; except that it was not a wreck and it was not a schooner or frigate. It was a boat for landing. Its mission has been peaceful. Contraband trade, smuggling surely, but not hostile. If there were secret landing places for trade goods, this could have been one, but was not so now. Not after this boat had made land, to be seen no more by those on the mother ship, riding well out at sea. One could imagine that ship keeping watch for a certain number of days, then sailing away. Smugglers counted on such losses occurring. When they did, it was better to set a new course and try again. But elsewhere.

Antonio, the reins of Turbelino over his arm, paced the trampled shore of the little river, re-examining the boat. When he added this to his report, he must be exact. It was a long boat of its kind, built of stout timber—oak, hard, northern oak. Two winters and the summer between had not made a wreck of it. The Indians has possessed no tools that could break it up. The water in the stern had washed there in bad weather. The boat had gathered fungus scales and some mold, but it did not leak. Mentally he composed a paragraph. A long boat, well built of oak. It carried nine men, or more.

He led Turbelino away from the shore, stepping as lightly as he could. The boldest man would do that, walking over a grave. Eight men and . . . awe departed. He looked now at the Alibama Chief who, for a promised reward, had guided him to this spot. The Indian had really never been out of his sight. If he, Antonio Ibarbo, was to be killed like that noble Frenchman, it would not be from the rear. But now the ugly picture of the savage had a new aspect. As ugly an aborigine as Antonio had ever seen, with his broad face, his flattened nose, his long slit of a mouth, his cold eyes, his lank, unkempt black hair—and below all that, the faded grandeur of a white man's coat. In itself, the possession of such a coat was not unusual. A soldier's coat gave a chieftain added authority. But this coat . . . Antonio continued his paragraph.

A crew of eight, and at least one officer. He had worn a blue coat, with brass buttons and light yellow lining. On the Indian some of the buttons now were missing, the blue had faded, the yellow lining was stained. Antonio laid Turbelino's reins back over his head and, with a single quick motion, mounted.

"Beloved," he whispered, "let us go!"

Riding up to the Chief, he repeated the word, "*Vamos*," and pointed to the path that had brought them to this place. In two days of closer association than his nose was likely soon to forget, he had not improved communication between himself and his guide. Either the Alibamas had no Spanish or the Chief was concealing what he knew. Always signs had to make meanings clear. That was true now. The Indian knew Antonio wished to leave, but he stood stubbornly in the path. His hideous features contorted. He stamped his foot. He beat his breast.

Antonio nodded. He understood. The Indian wanted his reward and he would have it, but not now. Antonio had it in his pocket— a bright, silver medal, with a crown on one face and the image of Charles V of Spain on the other—but, without the return journey made, it would be folly to pay the Indian at this point. He beat his own breast. He beat his pockets and turned his hands palm up, empty. Again he pointed to the path.

The Indian spat. He stamped his foot more emphatically. And now he tore open his coat. To beat his bare breast, Antonio expected; but the Indian's breast was not bare. He already had a treasure there. It was a piece of jade—a fragment, but shaped by someone who knew how to work with stones, shaped and carved. It hung on a fine gold chain.

"*Ángela!*" Dizzily Antonio's thoughts leaped back over the years. Then, that much of another story was true. To be sure, this need not be that same piece of jade. Many a similar stone must have been strung on a golden chain; but, if it was that piece, and it went with the blue coat—*Dios*, the abductor of Ángela Gonzales had paid for his sin in a wretched death. Antonio leaned forward, reaching for the pendant. It was a foolish and unwary movement. The Indian closed his coat, clutched it to him, and hissed in fright and threat.

Then, with a snort, Turbelino took command. The Indian drew back, cowering; and, still clutching his coat, turned and went at a trot down the path.

It was night. Antonio was alone. At least, he hoped that he was alone. He lay on his blanket well up on a wide, sandy beach, his saddle and other belongings close to his left hand, a loop in the rope that held Turbelino on a long tether over his right arm. A rising crescent moon made the beach white as stretched canvas. Every object on it was sharply black against the white, and he was acutely conscious of all—himself on the blanket; Turbelino nosing herbage at the fringe of trees, eking out a supper ration of corn topped by sugar from Antonio's hand; beside the water a litter of driftwood, and near this fuel a fire, where he had boiled for himself some crawfish taken from a muddy slough, along with a handful of Turbelino's corn. Helped along by wine, it had been better subsistence than Garza's parched corn, but not much better.

The fire served another purpose now. Westward, where a similar beach of sand ran out into the water, another fire glowed. There his soldier guard would be encamped. Since he could see their fire, they might be expected to see his. Riding westward in the morning, he would meet the soldiers, speak to them in passing, and continue on to Bahía del Espiritu Santo, with them following as before. With no further hindrance, he should reach the fort in . . . not too many days.

At the mission he would complete his report. Because of this day's adventure it would be a more interesting paper to read and more worth writing. He could even add, with justification, a thing he had wanted to say all along. "It is my belief," he could write, "that, if the *inglés* should ever venture to invade the Province of Texas, it will not be by sea, where there are too many hazards, but from the north, over land, where hardly any barrier now exists."

That would reopen the old-new controversy about forts and settlements. Still, even with that possibly unwelcome statement of opinion, it would be a good report. It would make secure for him his present position of deputy inspector. It might even win him promotion. Ah, but he did not desire to be secure in his present office. Still less did he desire promotion. That was as clear in his mind now as it had been when, as a young man, he had chosen to stay away from office seeking.

It was no experience of his inspection that had reaffirmed that determination. It was a memory that had ridden with him out of Bexar the previous October. On his arrival there from Bucareli, he had found the capital in a turmoil of excitement. Don Hugo Oconor was expected. The *Inspector Comandante* was coming.

The Red Devil of the Apaches would be there today—tomorrow—soon!

"I think," the Governor had said, "you will have to see him, my friend. To leave without speaking with him, when he is expected, would be an affront."

It was Ripperdá, gray, tired, but as brave and kind as ever, whom Antonio could not offend. He had waited two days and had spoken with the *Inspector Comandante*.

It was a chill day, dismal with rain; but the *sala* in which the meeting took place had needed no fire of coals or of piñon branches. Heat in plenty came out from the Red One. His face was burned by sun and wind a deeper red than his beard. He was thin. Driving the Apaches to their dens, perhaps he had subsisted on parched corn. But the whiskers, the whole man, gave off fire, as always. His blue eyes stabbed Antonio—or they would have, had Antonio showed fear or anxiety. But this time he was neither afraid nor anxious.

"We meet again, Señor Ibarbo," Oconor said in greeting.

Antonio nodded. Bend his neck he would not, if he died for it.

"I hear you have been busy in many ways in my absence. Not too successful, it seems; and yet, you have found favor."

"If you refer, Señor *Comandante*, to my office of deputy inspector, I have been given work to do for which I am thought to be fitted."

"Exactly. In that, I, your superior in command, wish you good fortune."

That was dismissal. Antonio had bowed to the Governor, and begged leave to depart. But the heat of the Apache Terror went with him. All the way to Bahía, he had felt it. Good fortune, indeed. Oconor hoped a savage would cut his throat. If the savage did not and Ibarbo had success and thought of rising higher, Oconor would do the throat-slitting. This was not mere hostility. By the time he reached the coast, Antonio understood the real danger in the threat. It was Oconor who was afraid now. That was how it was when a man attained a high position. He then had to work and fight harder to hold his eminence than he had done in reaching it. The worst made the most of opportunity while it was in their hands. Others conscientiously tried to make a brave record. Almost all were haunted in some measure by the fear of failure, of losing favor, of being passed in the race. That it should be so now with Oconor!

Well, then let him rest easy as to Antonio Ibarbo, who had tasted the wine of favor and found it sour. He would write his report and beg leave to withdraw. Where? When? To what place and what destiny? Many other nights he had camped alone as on this one, watched the stars pale as the moon rose, and sought an answer to that question. On occasion a solution had appeared, but he had never got a firm hold on it. Today he had been nearest to doing that.

It was the boat, he thought—so strong, so firmly shaped, so well constructed. Of English make, he was sure, but still thought, not made in England itself, but rather in the colonies on another coast of this same America. The people there, too, were seamen and traders and boat builders. It was the boat, then, and a stained uniform coat that could have belonged to anybody, that had made a wish, only half real before this, now lay overpowering hold of him. What brave men those English colonials were, to rise up and fight against the rule of a king! If they won their fight, what a life lay ahead of them, masters of themselves and their fortunes!

Why not go to those colonies? A road was open—by way of New Orleans and the Mississippi River. Surely he could make a place for himself in that expanse of free land. But how free would he himself be in that place? That was how it went. That was how it went always. Let the wish be clear, the reasoning good; then, from this side and that, difficulties arose.

Would he leave behind everything that he now possessed in Texas? How much did he possess? Surely? The ban—not within a hundred leagues of Natchitoches—had never been revoked. If now, since he seemed to have found favor in the eyes of the new Inspector General, it should be lifted, there would be, first of all, Rancho Lobanillo. Lobanillo . . . five years, almost six, had passed since he had ridden away. He would not have thought it could happen, but the ranch was now not nearly as real to him as it once had been. He studied Doña María's letters, as De la Mathe delivered them, trying to see the things she wrote about, and himself as part of them. Each year realization had become more difficult.

He was so hopelessly entangled in immediate needs and problems. Ah, when his house was finished in Bucareli, he should have sent for Doña María. And for his son and his mother, if Doña María would not come without them. A way could have been provided. If De Mezières could arrange to haul the old cannon from Los Adaes, he could also provide an escort for Ibarbo's family. Garza had urged the move.

However, most foolishly, Antonio had said each time, "No. Wait!" Now he could wait no longer. He had seen today, he thought, the ultimate proof of life's cruelties. Well, then, he would go to Rancho Lobanillo, collect his dear ones, and flee, by the rivers still, to the nearest English colony. He saw no insurmountable obstacle. For sustenance, until a new life was established, he would remain in secret communication with De la Mathe. He had a feeling that De la Mathe would favor the move, would even enjoy the intrigue.

And he would break all other ties? Forsake his followers and friends who waited in Bucareli for his return? The brave, loyal older ones—Tomás Coronal, Pablo Rojas, Esteban Andorro, even Zapatero, truly a shriveled leaf now, but still alive and active? And the angry, hurt younger ones—Luis, Magdalena, La Niña? Over his meager supper Antonio had decided that it was as well that he had not succeeded in obtaining the amulet of jade from the Indian. He did not know how much Angelita knew of her own story. The amulet might have occasioned some wonder, but surely also an additional grief, considering how the story had ended. A rascal, that *inglés*, beyond a doubt, but also brave.

La Niña—would he, Antonio, having won her trust, desert her now? Would he abandon her to the mercies of a crazed grandmother and a devoted but failing servant? How could he do that? So, if he, Antonio Gil Ibarbo, went off to English America, he must take with him his mother, his wife, his son, his good friends —and how many others? *Dios!* Even Don Quixote of La Mancha would have paled at the prospect of such a pilgrimage.

Pilgrimage. The word struck back with savage recoil, bringing him to his feet in a state of shock. This then was the answer—to everything. It had been the solution all along, the only one. He had said so in his original petition. He had said it in pleading before Ripperdá, the Viceroy, the grave-faced judges of the *audiencia*. Send these people home. And, when all, in one way or another, had said no, he had thought that the end of argument. He had been wrong. Everybody had been wrong; but he had been the worst, because he had known what was right. Well, then, the only true course now was to turn back and right the wrong.

Turn back? It would be an act of revolt. Yes, surely; but sedition, it would seem, was in the wind that blew over America these years. It would be dangerous, but no more dangerous than to rot and die in mistaken obedience to a tyrannical ruling that made no sense. "Do not be deceived into making a bargain with Ibarbo. Do not let that man, with or without followers, return to within one hundred leagues of Natchitoches." *Dios!* He, Antonio Ibarbo, now would have a speech to deliver to the citizens of Bucareli. They would have to listen.

Well, the brave, at least, would listen. If these were only a few, still he would make this move. Perhaps, after all, there were more brave and desperate ones than he could count at this distance. He would return to Bucareli. At once.

In a sweat now, he sat down on Turbelino's saddle to make his plans. His head no longer simmered. For the first time in nearly six years he was thinking in clear, orderly progression. Tomorrow he would pick up his guard at their camp. Could he do better than that? A light wind rose, rattling the trees. It wrapped itself around his ribs; and, shivering suddenly, he reached for his blanket. He studied the moon. Could he make a start tonight, under that moon? It was a cold moon, he thought, but very bright. The moon of April. When the earth everywhere, even far to the north, came to life. When animals left their winter burrows, and Indians stirred themselves and made ready for the hunt—or war. The Indians had a name for this moon—or was it the settlers? "Comanche moon."

Comanches—Mother of God, six months had passed since he had said, "There is no danger at present." He stood up and the blanket slipped from his shoulders to the sand. Turbelino whinnied and came nearer. He put his hand on the gray's shoulder and looked down the coast toward the other fire. If he could only ride over the water! But he must go by land, through dense woods where the moonlight could not penetrate and anything could hide. And, however he went or when, he must go safely, surely now. To-morrow, then. He spoke comfortingly to the horse.

"Rest, my brave one, rest. The march will be long, with few halts." That would be the worst, the hours when he and Turbelino must rest. Especially Turbelino. As for himself, he would roll himself in his blanket now to give the appearance of resting, but there would be little sleep for him this night—or in the time ahead.

CHAPTER 6

At Bucareli, that morning late in April was the fairest of the spring. Rain had been overabundant but seemed now to have ceased. At the base of the rise on which the town had been built, the river flowed full and brown, but without the noise and de-vouring suction of floodwater. Driftwood caught in the roots of trees and held, gathering more drift and mud; but the trees re-mained where they stood. In the town and outside, too, garden patches were large and small stretches of mud, with draggled green drooping under a weight of clay; but, with one more day of sun, this would change. New strength would be drawn from the water and mud, and surge up through the stalks, unfolding clean, new growth. The lightest person, barefoot, could not step safely into the fields now, but anyone could see promise there.

Hope, like the expected new growth, was strong in everyone's heart. Angelita Gonzales, preparing for what might be the de-mands of the day in her hospital, was more and more of the opinion that nobody was going to consider himself in need of medicine. Any ailment, from a deep cut to the flux, would natu-rally be better now that the sun shone. Only let the sufferer put himself in the way of that sun. From deep inside the adobe walls, she could hear that many must be doing that. Finally, she, too, put aside her work—a tray of snakeroot which a Bidai squaw had brought her and she had dried over winter. The root was strange to her. The squaw, too, had been a stranger; but Fray Josef had said to dry the bits of root and label them and keep them for a time of need. If someone should be bitten by a venomous serpent and would, if unaided, die of the bite, anyhow, it would be proper to try the medicine. Now it was spring, when snakes were most poisonous. Still, she looked at the dried root with mistrust and was glad, at a burst of laughter in the square, to push it away and go to the door to see what made the merry one so gleeful.

Madre mía, what a blessing it was that the sun shone and the winter was now over! The long, long winter. At least, it had seemed so to her; and she must believe others had thought of it in the same way. Otherwise the houses would not have emptied themselves so completely this morning, everyone with his face upturned to drink in the promise of the sun. Women leaned on the brooms they had brought out to sweep the drying mud from doorsteps and called greetings and questions one to another. Children rolled in the dirt like puppies and, separating, revealed the puppies that rolled with them. Men gathered by twos and threes and talked. Work waited on everyone, but nobody seemed inclined to spend the time that way. Tomorrow, perhaps. Not today. Even the carpenter sat contentedly on his box of tools, which was too heavy for him to carry, but which he would let no other carry for him.

Angelita's heart was big with affection. Her people—so good, so kind, so patient! Let them sit in idleness one day, then, and laugh and talk together. The burst of laughter which had drawn her to the door came again. It was from beyond the plaza. The groups of men she could see broke up and disappeared in that direction. Finally only the carpenter remained, sitting on his toolbox. Pity touched her. Poor Andorro! Each year he found it harder to move about.

She looked away from him, from the women on their doorsteps. She looked now where, perhaps, she had wanted to look when she had first stepped to her door—at the wall of the stockade opposite her hospital, the good stout wall of cedar posts which Rojas and the others had repaired early in the winter, while the authority of command was on them. It was whole now, as whole as anything a man built could be. The gaps under it, where the earth had fallen away, were filled with heavy stone. Even the spring rains had not washed them away. It was reassuring to consider that wall and the gate with its tower, where, since winter had turned to spring, a guard sat day and night beside the old, cracked cannon from Los Adaes.

The gate—Mother of God, if only whoever watched there now should leap down and open that gate, and Don Antonio come riding through! This would be, then, truly a miracle day. He was only one man, he had said. He was not God. He alone could not save these people. They must save themselves. And that was true— with God's help. Then let God, who had turned Don Antonio's heart toward his friends in their deep trouble, bring him back now. Surely he would return. Surely!

The whirl of thoughts stopped. Her hand was over her mouth to keep blasphemy from being spoken. Prayers were blasphemy when they reminded God of his obligations and were not said in faith and trust. They were blasphemy, too, when selfish desire or fear or longing made up the petition. She knew that. If she had not known before, the truth must have been made plain to her by the appearance of a rusty old woman coming up the street now beside the plaza where the women gossiped. It was Constanzia, who, once having settled the poor grandmother in her chair for the morning, would always steal a little time to say a prayer in the church. Angelita wished she would not, knowing from what Constanzia had once in sobbing anguish revealed. She prayed daily that not God but the Devil should come in a ball of fire and claim his own, the wicked woman, her mistress. Consume her with flames and scatter the ashes on this foul, strange land.

Poor Constanzia. Tía Rosario said, forgive her. She still did what was right, did she not? Though under the strain she was likely to become as crazed in her head as the Señora had been now for a long, long time. Poor Constanzia! Fray Josef said the same in his way, his great hand resting lightly on Angelita's head.

"Forgive her, Niña. Do not remonstrate even. Forgive her. God surely will, knowing that her burden is more than she can bear. Forgive her. Keep thou thy faith, child. All will be made right some day."

Poor Constanzia! Just the same, Angelita turned back into the shelter of her clean, dark, empty little house, before Constanzia could see her. She tried to follow Garza's instruction, but it was hard to be sure of God's ability to hear only the old servant's cry of distress and not her appeal to the Devil.

A mestizo trader on his way to his own *ranchería* from San Antonio de Bexar brought the story of an Indian council at the capital. He stopped at Bucareli to rest his mule and dry his packs, at least the outside wrapping, and slake his thirst at the *cantina* of a kinsman. That act accomplished, while he scraped drying mud off his leggings and the mule cracked off what he could by rolling, the trader told how the chiefs of the Comanches had met at Bexar with Governor Ripperdá, *Comandante* Oconor, and the noble French renegade, Capitán de Mezières. They had parleyed for four hours in the main plaza, protestations of friendship passing both ways, also gifts of money and medals on the one hand and furs and buffalo robes on the other. Then the chieftains had gathered their plunder and ridden away; and only when they were a cloud of dust in the distance had it been discovered that the young men who had accompanied them to the council had in the meantime driven off one hundred cattle belonging to the garrison. Why had nobody seen this happen? Everybody was watching the council. So many Comanches had never before been present in one body, and no one had wished to miss the show.

As the trader told it, the tale seemed very funny. How comical the politeness of the Spanish officials, so duped by savages! Whose idea was it in the first place to parley with Comanches? Nobody could say. Every Spaniard in authority in Texas had a different scheme for blunting the weapons of hostile Indians, when only extermination would rid the province of them. Don Hugo Oconor might have asked for the meeting! There was a one! Who could forget that hair and beard? The Comanches had watched him warily as he spoke. If the Comanches, he had been known to say, could be held to a treaty of peace, he would be free to finish his scourging of the Apaches. Or the idea could have come from the Frenchman. He had ideas of all sorts about Indians, but was he to be trusted really any more than the Comanches? It was not, the trader thought, Ripperdá. What man responsible for the safety of a town would invite Comanches in numbers to visit it?

Anyhow, that was how it had happened; and at the time of telling it seemed very funny. Young bucks like Pedro Coronal and Manuel Piedra rolled like the trader's mule, kicking their heels high and shouting with merriment. But two of those present did not laugh. The face of Pablo Rojas, stonemason and commander of the militia, was as still as any rock he had ever chiseled. Luis Ramón's face, too, lengthened as he listened. When the story was done, while men who should have known better laughed as hard as the light-minded young, these two walked off together.

Soberly, by unspoken understanding, they made the round of the stockade. At the first bastion supporting a cannon, they halted.

"Powder?" Luis asked. "Have we a good supply?"

"Yes, thank God," Rojas answered. "And under cover in a dry place. Perhaps this is the time to make sure of a dry charge in the cannon. Is that your thought?"

"Yes," Luis said, "since we have the powder."

In consequence, that afternoon, when the militia drilled, the practice was in loading firearms, including six cannon of varying antiquity. Volunteers were also called for to fire the cannon. There was some hesitation over this; but, when Pedro Coronal and Manuel Piedra had stepped forward and asked for the honor of firing the cannon over the gate, and Pedro had been chosen after he proved that he could climb the tower faster than Manuel and leap much farther when he left it, volunteers for the other guns had been more than enough. Only Manuel Piedra was disappointed in not being awarded the cracked cannon.

"Little Brother," he said, his mouth twisting, to Pedro, who was now half a head taller than he was, "I bid you farewell and a safe journey to Paradise."

"As to that," Luis said quickly, "it is possible for you to take the same route. You may have your choice of the remaining cannon." A look flashed between the two as Manuel made his choice. It was the post nearest the church.

The remainder of the drill passed without other argument, but with a certain increase of excitement. At the end each man in the town knew where he must take his stand and what he must do at the first sign of danger from the outside. Luis Ramón would command the arming of the wall. Pablo Rojas would issue guns and balls and powder and give general orders as needed. Women and children were to remain inside the houses until danger was past. Garza would be in the church, because such treasure as the town had was there. Any wounded would be carried to the hospital, where Angelita Gonzales, helped by Rosario Coronal, would care for them.

All this because half a hundred Comanche chiefs had held council with the Governor and his associates at San Antonio de Bexar and had laughed behind their leather hand shields as they accepted tribute while their young men stole the Spaniards' cattle. There was no connection, to be sure, between that happening and the situation at Bucareli. Three rivers of consequence and many leagues of travel separated the two towns. It was just that any mention of Comanches had that effect on those responsible for Bucareli's safety. Pablo Rojas and Luis Ramón were serious-minded men by nature.

Nevertheless, on dismissal, the militia broke up more slowly than usual, the men stopping to talk among themselves or put questions to Rojas or Luis before seeking out their families. There was little laughing with the talk, and that in the way of personal joking—over someone's clumsiness in the drill. It was suggested that it might have been well for all to practice running and jumping. Some tried it then, to show the need. Finally all scattered, agreeing that there was no more danger now than at any other time except that the skies were clear and it was the season of the full moon; but it was as well, since that was so, to hold serious practice.

They scattered. The plaza was all but empty when a party of Bidais came to the gate, asking that it be opened to them so that they could talk to Garza. Their chief was sick, they said, his body burning with a fire that, so far, no charms of their medicine men could put out. Would the priest, who knew the spells of the white man's God, come and see what he could do now? Garza went away with them at once, stopping only to get a little powdered aconite from La Niña. He would be back before sunset, he said.

Nobody attached any importance to his going. It happened too often. He always came back safely, even when the sickness was a pestilence. Let it not be that, they prayed, those who knew of his going.

Nobody bothered to look closely at the party of Bidais. Nobody counted its number.

The sun set in a sky without clouds. Garza was still away. The journey must have been longer than those who summoned him had said.

Darkness came, full dark except for a pale light beginning to show in the east, forerunning moonrise. Was Garza back now? Nobody had seen him. Pablo Rojas went to the stockade gate to speak to the guard in the tower. At a dozen paces away he stopped and cupped his hands over his mouth to make his hail carry better.

"*Hola!* You in the tower. Have you . . ."

That was all. Something struck him in the back, stopping his wind. He could only gasp for air, and then not even that. A kind of paralysis numbed his chest, his throat, his arms. His legs crumpled under him and he sat down in a heap.

As he did so, a dark form rushed past him and laid hold of the gate. Pablo knew what was happening. He knew the dark form was an Indian. And there he sat. Time, then, was measured in seconds. From the plaza came the crack of musket fire, and the dark one at the gate loosed his hold on the bars and went down. There was a second shot. Wasted. That man trying to open the gate was already dead. Now . . . God be thanked . . . God . . . numbly Pablo Rojas sank closer to the ground, and for a while knew no more.

The two shots brought men running down every street.

"To your posts!" Luis Ramón shouted, a new charge of powder already settled in his gun and rammed home, the bullet in its patch waiting to be nested there. "To your posts!" and then, as he remembered, "Who fired that second shot?"

"I did," the guard called from the gate tower. "I saw a shadow move outside. It was not Fray Josef. It was a man naked, with horns on his head. I hailed him—like this 'Psst!' He stopped. Then

I heard a shot inside the stockade and I fired at the shadow. It does not move now."

There was a great silence.

"That will be two gone," Luis said then. "Take up the one inside and throw him over the fence to join his brother. No need to look at him. Only a Comanche has such aim with an arrow. He got Pablo in the back. Somebody . . . why are so many of you standing here? To your posts, I said. One will be enough to help me raise Pablo. Ah, Tomás! Good. Let us lift him a little. Gently. Poor Pablo! It will be well if he does not waken right now. We must draw the arrow. Best call . . ." he hesitated, "Rosario. There will be blood."

If he had more to say, nobody, except possibly Tomás, heard him. He could never say whether it took two or ten men to elevate the dead Indian inside the gate to the top of the stockade and drop him on the far side. His hands still supporting Pablo, he felt rather than saw the haste with which those who handled the Indian fell back to the ground. A scuffling followed outside, and then a maniacal scream. The Comanches, arriving now in number, had found their dead.

The first screams; but, after that, there was hardly any time when the screaming and the echo of screaming did not add to the terror of the night. If there had not been something for everybody to do, some might have gone mad listening to the sound. It was enough to make the strongest shiver and wish he could be anywhere except inside that ring of flimsy posts; but, when some were so brave, how could others show cowardice?

While the screaming was still a new horror, a wraith in a full blue skirt, almost covered by a white apron and a white blouse, with a blue scarf tying back her hair so that only her fair face showed, came down the moonlit path from the plaza, accompanied on one side by Manuel Piedra, carrying a pail of water and a lighted lantern, and on the other by Pedro Coronal, laden with a wash basin and the basket in which La Niña habitually carried bandage strips and sponges and such medicines as were most in demand. It could have been bright morning and everything at peace from the way they walked, except that they stepped a little faster than usual, acknowledging a need for haste, but refusing to pay attention to any other aspect of the situation. They went up to where Luis still supported the fainting Rojas. Luis looked up, saw them, and frowned blackly.

"Go away," he said. "This is man's business."

"No," La Niña said, "it is mine, Luis. It is what I can do. That is why I am here. If you will take just the one arm now and Papa Coronal the other . . . Set down the pail, Manuel, and hold the lantern so that I may see."

"Ah!" she said of the arrow, and of Rojas, "*El pobre!*"

Then she squatted in the dirt and felt around the shaft.

"He had on his jacket," she said in comment. Pablo never went out to give commands in just his shirt. "That is good. The arrow might have gone deeper but for that. But now the coat must come off. The shirt, too. Mama Rojas won't like this. I must cut both the coat and the shirt in two. Luis, if you will, when I say so, remove the one side and Papa Tomás—that's right. *Gracias.* Mm, I must make a big hole here. The blood has dried, but that, too, is good. The bleeding has not been too much—so far."

To watch her hands wield the scissors! They hardly seemed to touch that stiff, dark pad of cloth glued to the shaft of the arrow. When the pad was all that remained of what had been a good shirt and coat, she told the men how to hold Pablo, while others straightened his legs so that he could be laid on his stomach, his face pillowed on half of his jacket.

"Sometimes, "she said simply, "it is hard to draw out an arrow." It was not easy this time.

"A little water in the basin, Pedro?" she said. "Thank you." She softened the patch of cloth.

"Now!" she said, when she was ready.

Luis drew out the shaft while the others held Pablo.

"*Mamacita!*" Pablo cried out—just the once. Then it was over.

Except for the blood. It welled up like a fountain, soaking the patch of cloth that La Niña held over the hole. Time after time, she took a fresh, cool pack and threw a blood-soaked one away. Finally it began to come more slowly.

"Balsam, Pedro, if you please. Then a dry sponge."

The delicate pungency of the balsam rose from the spot of lantern light, where the white hands moved swiftly and surely.

292

Minutes later, a bandage was all around Pablo, holding a soft pack in place over his wound; and he was awake to the screaming outside the stockade. He struggled to right himself.

"No! Please, no!" La Niña scolded. "You must not. Please, you can sit up—only if you are careful. Don't you remember?" Afterwards Luis was able to describe to Antonio every movement of her hands, so delicately shaped, so sure.

Pablo remembered then that something had hit him in the back, but he still did not know what it was. When Manuel showed him the arrow, he was ready to die a second time, but a burst of yells changed that idea. Presently he was sitting on a stump, shaking his head to clear it, now and then remembering to groan; but, since he could not be heard, there seemed no point in that. Luis went away to see about issuing guns, after which he promised to patrol the stockade. Pedro Coronal fidgeted near the gate, where he could both watch Rojas and wait for the order to fire the cannon.

"Not now," Luis said. "We will say when. It may not be needed."

Manuel went back with La Niña to the hospital, carrying the pail full of bloody bandages, which must be saved with washing, but not until daylight. Daylight?

"There is blood on your apron, Niña."

"Only one little spot. It happens sometimes."

"I do not like even a small spot on you."

"I will change to a clean apron then, to please you. But I do not have too many. How dark the church looks in the moonlight! Shall we go there first, to see if Fray Josef has returned?"

"I will look when I leave you," Manuel promised, "but I think no one is there. The padre would have helped with Rojas if he had been here."

They took six steps in silence—silence except for a chain of long howls.

"If he should come now," Angelita said with a new fear, "he could not come inside to us."

"He will see that in time," Manuel assured her. "Fray Josef knows how to take care of himself. Now, as for you. It is dark in this place for you alone, and the lantern must be covered so that no light shows. You know?"

"Yes, and that I must stay here unless called out. That is the rule for all. We may not even gather in the church. Why?"

"It is best not to be all in one place if . . . It is best. I will set this stinking pail outside behind the house."

He walked on tiptoe through the hospital, as if someone might hear him. How was that possible? A very loud yelling made even him stop before he opened the back door. Angelita covered her ears with her hands and stood that way in front of the house until he came back and took them down, holding both in his stronger ones.

"It is quieter now," he said. "Go inside before it comes again. It does not seem so loud in there."

"More Indians came just now?"

"It is possible."

"There must be a hundred of them at least." She sighed.

"Not that many, I think. That is why they yell—to sound like a host."

A host of hosts, truly.

"My poor grandmother . . . I know. She will not be forgotten. Poor everyone. The poor animals—outside the fence. What of them?"

"Luis opened the corral gates a long time ago," Manuel told her, "to let them run. It will be hard to find them tomorrow; but more would be lost if we did not set them free."

"Brave Luis!" she said. "It was like him to think of the animals. Manuel, where will you be now?"

"At my corner of the wall with my gun. Very near. I can see the church and the hospital from my post. I will keep an eye on you here."

"Brave Manuel. What will happen if the Indians come in too great number?"

"Nothing. Unless they try to climb the wall. Then we will shoot them down."

She shivered, as another burst of yelling came.

"But if there are still too many?" she insisted.

"We will fire the cannon—one, then another—all six. That will kill so many that the others will run faster than the animals set free, I'll bet you."

He looked pale and grim in the moonlight.

"Manuel," she said in wonder, "for the first time I see something about you. Just now you looked like Luis."

He scowled and looked more like Luis than before.

"I am not Luis," he said. "I am Manuel."

"I know. Manuel. Go, then, to your gun. I will wait here—and pray for you."

"Then nothing can hurt me," he said, and lifted one of her hands, then the other, kissing each; and, when that was not enough to ease his bursting heart, "Niña, forgive," he said, and, stooping, brushed her cheek with his lips, awkward, clumsy, even shy in sudden rapture. Then he freed her hands and ran. From the doorstep, Angelita through tears saw him lose himself in the shadow of the church. So young, she thought. Manuel of the merry heart, the impish mischief. Only a little while ago a boy, a child.

That was a night five times the length of any other. Everyone said so. With each hour the fiendish yelling mounted. Fires were lighted outside the wall. Around them naked Indians with buffalo horns danced and harangued and chanted, whipping themselves to a frenzy. Dark forms broke away and brandished spears and guns threateningly toward the stockade. Finally it happened. The dark ones made a rush against the wall. They climbed one another like ladders. Gunfire met them and threw them back to the earth, shrieking a new note. Howling, they dragged off their wounded and dead, then dropped them as fresh gunfire caught them in the open, killing more.

But one repulse did not stop them. The screeching around the fires was louder than ever. A second rush was made, two groups of Indians attacking different points—then three. Three groups were almost too many. In this rush three Indians came over the top of the stockade. Good shooting brought down two. The third fell or jumped to the ground inside, and Tomás Coronal killed him with the butt of his smoking gun.

"The first man I ever killed," Tomás said. "I clubbed him as if he had been a wolf or a mad dog."

He was something of both. He was a Comanche.

There was rest then for a little, a very little, while. Time to allow the fiends to think up a new kind of attack. The fires burned bright and brighter. A long, snaky line began to form, with torches in hand. They meant to set fire to the stockade.

It was possible to kill some of those carrying firebrands, but not all. If the posts caught . . . some surely would. It was time to fire the cannon. The volunteer gunners were called down to light their slow matches. When the wicks were burning steadily, each hurried back to his station with match in hand. Pablo Rojas counted off the time it would take for them to be beside their guns, then gave an order to Luis Ramón, standing by. Luis raised his ranch horn to his lips, filled his lungs and blew. Once, twice . . . six times in all. It was the signal. All six cannon were to be fired at once—and now!

The sound of the trumpet was followed by the first complete silence in hours. The bravest Indian, even one with firebrand ready to apply to a pile of brush against a shadowed corner of the stockade, must stop to ask himself what that horn meant. Courage, frenzy which could sweep aside familiar obstacles, wavered before the unknown. So there was this still minute of waiting. Before it broke, pinpoints of light showed at all the gun emplacements. Good men! Steady now, and jump fast!

Pedro Coronal in the gate tower was as ready as anyone. All through the moonlit and moon-shadowed dark he had kept watch there, calling down to Rojas what was happening outside. His throat was raw from shouting above the noise; but now, when the time came to do what he was there to do, he began to shake. It was excitement, not fear. But he shook until he could hardly make his hands direct the wooden handle holding the lighted wick. He might have been blown to bits where he stood, he was so clumsy.

Boom! The first cannon went off across the town just as the fuse on the quick match in the powder chamber of his cannon began to sputter. *Boom!* Four others fired almost as one, and Pedro remembered to leap. Still, his big one was silent. Striking the ground, he forgot to run. He turned to see what could be wrong. Then, either some warning shudder of movement in the tower or the hoarse command of those who had helped Rojas to a safer place awoke him and he turned again. The gun exploded. Iron fragments, flaming wood filled the air; and the tower, the gate, all that section of the stockade fell apart.

The roar Pedro could have heard, but there was no time to see what others saw. He could and probably did feel briefly the blow that felled him but, blessedly, did not know the weight of the cedar posts that crushed him to the earth.

It took time to recover from that final shattering roar. There was the agony then of seeing the stockade in ruins, the width of the breach, the pieces of wood still blazing. If the Indians should come now . . .

The Indians would not come again that night. With the first boom of the cannon they had taken to their heels and their horses. They were gone, but nobody knew it at first. While the turmoil and dismay still prevailed in the now defenseless town, Manuel Piedra came running from his post.

"Pedro!" he shouted. "Pedro, *amigo*, hero of heroes, where are you hiding? All hell exploded with your cannon. Pedro . . ."

He hushed. He thought he would never shout again in this world. How could he, seeing that hand reaching out from under the fallen posts, that hand clutching at—nothing?

"Go away," he said to those who would have told him what had happened if they could have stopped him. "Do not come here. Do not look!"

And he threw himself like a child into the supporting embrace of Luis Ramón—Luis, whom he had thought he hated.

Pedro was gone. Little Pedro. Young Pedro. So sweet! So impulsive! And finally so brave! Pedro, who could leap like a deer and run even faster. Tomás, his father, wept in the arms of his Rosario, and she shed tears upon him. Both had loved Pedro. They kept telling each other how much.

But there were the others. All together now, and in one place, sad as any suffering of their own could not have made them. What of them? The moon rode high in the sky. The night must be half gone. Could they wait for daylight where they were?

Could they repair the broken stockade? Did they want to do that? Would anyone want to be penned inside it another night like this one?

"Now, then," Luis Ramón said to his young-man nephew. "Now then. That is enough, eh? We can do nothing about what has happened. We must think what to do next . . . for those who still live, don't you think? Surely. There! Shake yourself hard. Good! And come with me. There is something I want to see down at the river."

Near the crossing, where the flat stones made it possible to walk from shore to shore in low water, a skiff with oars and a raft of logs were kept in a willow thicket by those who insisted on planting corn over the river. They were in their shelter unharmed when Luis and Manuel went to look for them. Luis wasted little time in explanation of what he had in mind.

"We can move everybody over before day breaks," he said. "There is a cover of trees not too far away. We must camp there and send for help. I do not think the Comanches will come in pursuit of us. There was something they wanted in the town, I think. Let's go."

It only seemed that the crossing was slow. Everyone moved as fast as possible and some much faster than anyone would have supposed they could. All went willingly. "Only let us get away from that place." Even Señora Gonzales made no fuss. She clutched her shawl and glared at and scolded the men who carried her down to the river and through the cornfield to the woods, but that was the extent of her bad behavior, which for her was good. Since so many crossings had to be made before all were rescued, there was time even for Rosario and Magdalena and others like them to collect blankets and cooking utensils and a supply of food. They knew from experience what they would need. In camp, younger women like Teresa Andorro quieted the excited, fretful children. The Andorros were among the first to cross, Luis Ramón taking them himself in the skiff. Honoring Cecilio, his friend, he was always like that with Cecilio's family.

Finally all were across and under the trees, not comfortable but safe. All were sure that they were better off than they had been before, even with the stockade whole. It was Tomás Coronal, then, who suggested that, just to be sure, they make a count. Because of what had happened to Pedro, he would never sleep again without counting his household.

So they discovered that La Niña was missing. Who had seen her last? Who remembered? A boy spoke up, one of those who waken when others sleep, who always see what others do not notice.

"Señorita Angelita did not cross with us," he said. "She was on the raft, but she got off again. She went to look for something."

Every man was on his feet, but Manuel Piedra was already halfway across the cornfield, running for the skiff.

"Let him go," Luis said, wanting beyond telling to be the one to go, but sending the fleeter Manuel instead. "He will find her. They will be back soon."

When the waiting seemed too long, there was a distraction. From downstream came, faintly at first, then more strongly, a shout:

"*Olé!*" and again, "*Olé!*"

From down the river?

"*Olé!*"

Luis filled his lungs and answered:

"*Olé-e-e!*"

How she had come to forget her medicines, Angelita could not think; but surely she must go back after them. If she ran all the way, she could be down at the river again before the last raft was pushed off the shore. She ran as fast as she could. The road under the moon was white with light; and, when she reached the hospital, the lantern still burned. She had forgotten that, too? What did she remember? The lantern would be useful in the dark camp. She bade her left hand remember the lantern, as with her right she reached for the low shelf where she kept her collection of medicines.

As she did so, she smelled Indian. Wild Indian. Once a person's nose had taken in that smell, it never forgot. Sweat, dirt, animal. That strange boy-man, the Comanche princeling, silent, watchful, schooled to endurance but to nothing else, who had been healed of his injuries here, had smelled like that when he came, then, as time went on, not so much, but still some. After Don Antonio had ordered him and his mother away, it had taken days and many pails of water and two coats of whitewash to cleanse the house of that odor.

Don Antonio! Luis! Manuel! Help me . . .

She did not cry out. Not then. The smell was there. It was alive. It had come into the house after her, or she would have been warned of it as she stepped through the doorway. At first she did not move. She could not. Neither did that other presence. Then, with her heart choking her, she put out one arm cautiously. As she did so, a dark, strong arm reached for her and caught her skirt. She did scream then, but not loudly enough. Not nearly enough. A great evil hand closed over her mouth with the force of a blow.

Fainting, she thought she heard someone call her name: "Niña?" But that cry, too, was stifled. The savage smell was everywhere. Her senses left her.

CHAPTER 7

Never had a journey, with the exception of the pilgrimage from Los Adaes to Bexar, seemed to Antonio so long as his ride westward along the coast to Bahía, then the doubling back to the Trinity, the stop at Orcoquisac, and finally the ride north to Bucareli. If only, as he had ridden westward, he had turned at the Trinity; but, no, he thought he must go to Bahía. To finish his report. To leave everything in order.

At Bahía he had been met by the priest of the mission with strange welcome.

"God be praised, Señor Ibarbo, you have come! Finally. A stranger is here, waiting. A man near death from having made his way alone—from Bexar on foot—to our house to find you. He lives only to tell you something. He will not talk to us. His raving is confusion, mostly about Indians. Will you see him at once? I am afraid . . ."

He was afraid?

The stranger was, of all the people in the world, Hernando Calles.

"Thou omen of misfortune!" Antonio could have cried out as he saw him, except that never had Hernando looked so pitiable. He was as near death as his bones were near to bursting through his skin. And he raved without ceasing.

"There is a woman," the priest said. "Her name is . . ."

"Natividad," Antonio said. "She—excuse me, Padre. I will see if I can make sense out of his ravings."

As it happened, however, all he had to do was to speak the poor fool's name.

"Well, Hernando?"

The bunch of bones on the bed stopped jerking. The raving stopped. Antonio looked at the priest, who nodded, meaning, "Go on, please!"

"Hernando," Antonio said, "it is I, Ibarbo. You have something to tell me?"

Eyes hot with fever, deep in their hollows, opened, closed, and opened again, freed of some of their torment. The death mask composed itself. The wretch tried to smile; but, as consciousness brought its own pain of recollection, the death mask again drew into wrinkles and folds. The twitching resumed.

"Come, Hernando!"

The wrinkles smoothed out once more. The mouth opened. Words came, but in scraps and patches.

"Indians. A plot. Comanches, Apaches. Men—*Isleños*—the villa. Three men. One took Natividad. Three men. A plot. Comanches first—stealing, burning, killing. A plot . . . B-b . . ."

A clawlike hand reached out, the whole arm shaking. Antonio, repelled, took the hand between his own hands.

"There!" he said. "I understand. The *Isleños* have a plot with the Comanches and Apaches. There will be an attack on Bexar . . . no? Bucareli? I thought so. You are a brave man, Hernando. Rest now. I am here, with Turbelino. You remember? We will ride

301

north and give the alarm. But you rest. Eat and grow strong. I will see you again."

But perhaps not.

"You believe what he said in fever?" the priest asked as Calles slept, twitching only a little now. "You believe?"

"If you knew the rogues in the villa of San Fernando as I know them," Antonio said, "you would believe any evil of them. They have dealt with the Apaches before this. I do not dare disbelieve, Father. I will wait here only until my horse has rested and been fed. Then I must go on. You will care for this one?"

"Assuredly, Señor."

"My thanks, Father. Feed him if he will eat. If he recovers, you will be shocked at how much he can eat. Then . . ."

Then? Memory achieved coherence. The report. Riding back along the coast, when he had rested but could not sleep, Antonio had scratched out on paper what he had seen, what he had heard, and what he believed of that possible invasion by the English, which Spain feared in every quarter. The writing was, because of the conditions of composition—often his desk was a flat rock—almost as fragmentary as Hernando's babbling.

"I have papers with me," he said to the priest. "They belong with my report on my exploration of the coast. If I can have a table, I will try to put them in order. With your permission I will then leave them with you, rather than carry them where I am going. They are, I think, important. When Hernando recovers, give him paper and pens and ink, and he will copy them expertly."

"The Brothers of St. Francis," the priest said, "are fair copyists."

"I know," Antonio acknowledged. "There are no better; but let this sad one do the work when he is able. He will surprise you with his skill. He knows, besides, the official forms. Give him the copying to do, and he will be well almost at once. Later I . . . no, you may send the reports, all of them, on to the City of Mexico for me. I will write a word of explanation."

Two hours later, having signed his name with a flourish to a statement about the copying of the report by his good friend Hernando Calles, clerk, so that the document would be recognized as authentic, and having taken another look at Hernando, who still twitched and occasionally cried out, mostly now for Natividad, but slept on, Antonio rode away from the mission at Bahía del Espíritu Santo. The last thing he saw was the friar in his brown robe, his right hand raised in blessing.

I have put something behind me, he thought. He could not say what he had abandoned any more than he could say what lay ahead. There was merely that feeling of separation. He felt free. Of what? Not his sack of stones. He was riding as fast as he dared, meaning to pick up that burden once more and carry it for the rest of time. Still, he felt free. So did Turbelino, it would seem. In spite of Antonio's command or other restraint, he stretched out his neck and pushed on.

"You smell home, you think?" Antonio chided. "What do you call home after six years, my beautiful, mad one? No! No more now. Here we stop again and rest, because we must."

Each day they traveled more hours than they rested. Doubling back to the Trinity now, cursing himself for not having delivered his soldiers and his papers at the small post of Orcoquisac near the mouth of that river instead of being punctilious about returning to Bahía, he heard how the Comanches had driven off cattle from Bexar while their chiefs met with the Governor and Oconor and De Mezières, also how a day later the savages had made a show of surrendering those who, they said, had done the stealing. Let the Great Chief of the Spaniards do what he would to those who had robbed him, they said loudly, then waited to see if he would dare execute their young men. Oconor said death was the thing. It might make the Comanches more hostile, but they would have increased respect for the anger of Spain. However, Ripperdá and De Mezières had thought otherwise, and they were two against one; so the Comanche had gone free.

"And that is all the news? Nothing about the town of Bucareli?"

No. Why should the Comanches attack Bucareli? What was there that they wanted? Antonio did not argue the point. A taste of blood, perhaps. A successful attack to whet the appetite for greater sacking and burning. He could not make of these suppositions a valid reason for asking Orcoquisac to send soldiers with him as he rode northward. The post was small and remote from its base at Bexar, almost as far from Bahía.

But now the point of a spear was really against his back. With

303

only part of a day remaining, he left Orcoquisac, rode until dark, then, after moonrise, a couple of hours more. Finally he picketed Turbelino, slept until dawn, and awoke, not only to daylight, but to the smell of smoke and meat roasting over coals, then to the sight of an Indian squatting beside the fire. Fear clutched him, but subsided quickly. Turbelino with great indifference munched grass near by in companionship with a spotted pony, and the Indian was not Apache, Comanche, or Alibama. Nevertheless, it was with gun in hand that Antonio picked himself up from his blanket. The Indian heard him and turned, showing the broad, homely face of Lope. Lope, whom Antonio had sent home when the new town had taken on the first aspect of fact. Lope, filled out now to the proportions of manhood, but still . . . Lope.

"Hola!" Antonio cried, and laid aside his gun. "Tejas! *Amigo!*"

Lope. From the gladness in his heart Antonio knew how much he had missed his young friend. Still, there were questions. Why had he come?

"My father sent me. It is long since we have word of you."

Antonio took in all of it—the Indian, the smoke, the roasting rabbit.

"How did you know where to find me?"

"Señor *Amigo*, I do not know. I am a long time learning."

"Did you go to the new town?"

"No. There was no need. Before I do that, I know that you are away."

Yes. Over winter that would have become known—to friend and enemy.

"I am told you are at the sea. At the town on the crooked river I learn that." San Antonio de Bexar, that would be. "But nobody can say where you are at the sea. I ride that way."

"Alone?" Antonio said in alarm, though here Lope was, unharmed. "The Indians of the coast are not friendly. You know that."

"Yes, Señor, I know. That made it hard. I could only ride a little way here and there. I am afraid even to go to Bahía. I try Orcoquisac. One, two times. Nobody knows. They have no word. I look some more where the trails lead. I meet the Frenchman from the Great River."

"Nicolas de la Mathe? But he knew nothing of all this."

"He knows more than I know, Señor. He says, let us go once more to Orcoquisac. We go. We arrive at dark—the same day you have been there and gone. So, then I know. I follow." He smiled broadly. "You are very tired. You sleep like a dead man. You do not hear me when I come."

That certainly was true. So was the fact of Lope's presence. But the urgency which had pushed and pulled Antonio before was only stronger for that presence, though Lope, when questioned again, repeated that his reason for being there was the desire of his father for direct news of Antonio. Lope had no report on the town of Bucareli, which was good so far as it went. Nor did he have anything to say about possible Indian hostilities. At the mere mention of Comanches, his face froze and he stopped talking. That was comprehensible. The friendly tribes of eastern Texas, brave as they had proved themselves against other enemies—the Natchez, the Osage, even the Pani-Maha—had both a deadly fear and a hate for Comanches. Trade with those they left willingly to their kinsmen beyond the Trinity.

That had been one reason for Antonio's sending Lope back to his own people. Certain of the strange Tejas Lope had tolerated, but he had shown a sullen, unexplained dislike for the Bidai, who lived nearest the new town site. This, Antonio and Lope did not discuss anew as they rode together. There were many other subjects they left for another time.

"I have a certain anxiety now about Bucareli," Antonio said merely. "I am on my way there. Will you go with me?"

"Yes, Señor *Amigo*, I will go with you to your town."

And that, Antonio could not help thinking, was why he had come. So, driven harder than before by the spearpoint at his back, he rode on with the Indian through the morning, rested through the heat of noon, and pushed on again through twilight and moonlight to the end of the journey, meaning not to stop until he had arrived.

So it was that, shortly before midnight, they were near enough to hear the firing and final explosion of the cannon. Not near enough, however, to hear a lesser sound or to make themselves heard. It was all of an hour later that Antonio shouted and heard,

305

finally, Luis's reply. Not too long after that, they rode up to the shadowed camp, and learned the story of the night up to that point.

Antonio crossed the river with Luis and Lope, to search the abandoned town. They found the door of the hospital hanging open and the lantern still burning where Angelita had set it on the earthen floor.

"Comanches," Lope said, holding his nose. "Comanches here. One, maybe two."

Two, Antonio thought. Two Comanches had been sent back to pick up some dead warrior or to scout the town—or could it have been the girl they had wanted all along? Seeing the church still standing, creeping cautiously forward in its shadow, they had spied Angelita running along the road in her white apron. Later, then, there had been Manuel. Luis Ramón, outside the little hospital, leaned his head against the door frame and wept. Not for Angelita Gonzales. He turned hot with rage and cold with fear for her; but, as to his nephew . . .

"Manuelito!" he sobbed. "I did not mean . . ."

Then he stood away from the door, his face pale under the moon, and hard with resolution.

"Where Manuel is, there she is," he said. "I must find them, if I go alone."

"Hold!" Antonio said. "You will not go alone. Lope, how much of the night remains?"

Lope hesitated between the count of three or four hours. Whichever it was, it had to be time enough.

"Señor *Amigo*," Lope said, "I will track the Comanches for you. It will not be too far—if we go tonight—now."

It would be this night and at once; but, as for Lope leading the pursuit . . .

"Señor *Amigo*, for you and the Señorita I will go—anywhere. Will I be able to show my face to my father otherwise?"

Antonio wasted no more time on useless opposition. Lope, he knew, would, even at night, pick up the trail of the fleeing Comanches. He turned to Luis.

306

"Summon help," he said. "Not too many. Twenty will be enough if they are willing to follow the Comanches and do what needs to be done when we find them. Go quickly. Time is passing —though I am not in despair about our lost ones. Garza is with them, I feel sure. He must have been taken captive first of all— outside, this afternoon. Those who came for him came just for that. But . . . go!"

Afterwards, Antonio could not have said who made up the twenty men who on moccasined feet moved out in single file and in silence down the trail behind Lope and Luis Ramón, with Antonio bringing up the rear of the march with Turbelino and Lope's pony. Luis had chosen the men for strength and youth and daring out of twice as many as would have gone. Mostly it was the older men who remained to guard the camp, and some had other reasons—Pablo Rojas and Esteban Andorro because of disability, Tomás Coronal because in the first daylight he meant to cross the river and with help raise the posts from the body of his son and prepare him for burial.

Twenty strong and able men, their hearts beating faster than usual, walked cat-footed over spongy ground that further muffled any sound of footsteps. Each man had a gun, with extra powder and balls, also a knife. Lope, cat-eyed as well as cat-footed, had found the trail before the file assembled. He led them off then at almost a trot. Occasionally, when some question arose in his mind, he halted, and the column with him, breathing hard but noiselessly. On those halts, Lope would stand still for a minute, all his senses stretched to attention. Finally, under some inner command, the tension would break and he would move on, sometimes changing the direction a little; but the stops were neither long nor frequent.

How long they marched this way it was impossible to say exactly. It could have been an hour, judging by what remained of darkness afterwards. Abruptly then, the fast advance was over. This time, when Lope stopped, it was to argue something out with Luis. Finally the difference was settled. Luis placed himself, arms outstretched for a barrier, across the path; and the Indian vanished. Minutes later, Luis stepped aside and Lope was back.

Then, at a pace that was hardly more than creeping, the march was resumed.

Everyone's senses were at their sharpest now. Nobody failed presently to hear, faintly at first, then increasing in volume, the sound of wailing, and to see, also faintly, a light ahead that was not the moon but might be a fire burning low. They were nearing the Indian camp. The ground seemed softer now, or was it that their feet had a caution of their own? Whatever the reason, the column moved more and more slowly. Now, along with the wailing, was a sound some of the twenty had never heard before—the singsong, flat tonelessness of Indian harangue. The firelight showed red through the brush, which helped in a way. They were at the edge of a swamp. Fallen trees lay everywhere. The Comanches had bivouacked at the brink of a bog.

It was necessary then to pick one's steps with extreme care. Antonio had the feeling of lifting each of Turbelino's four legs over every log. It was not so bad as that, because Turbelino had had some practice lately in such places. The Indian pony seemed to have had more. He gave no trouble; so Antonio let him choose his own footing. All this occupied Antonio to such an extent that he was taken by surprise when a dark hand reached out and took the reins of both horses from him, but with no violent intent. It was Lope, now in battle array—naked except for breech cloth and moccasins—but in high spirits. He had done what he had said he could do. He had led the way to the Comanche camp. More than that, he had found the missing ones. A sign of the cross and one finger meant Garza. Two fingers and emphatic nods meant the other captives.

Happily Lope gave his news, then, keeping his hold on the horses, motioned Antonio forward. He, Lope, would now mind the horses. All that Antonio had to do then was to lift his own leaden feet and take his proper place up front. That came sooner than he had reckoned on. When he was able to look up, the line had shortened to half a dozen men, with Luis standing with his back to the Indian camp. Silently, as each man approached, Luis gave him his orders. He was dividing the file, one man to the right, the next to the left. His left hand, spread to show all five fingers, meant five paces beyond the last man in place. His right hand to his mouth and a shake of the head meant no talking, no sound until he gave the command.

Everyone seemed to understand. Silently the men obeyed his directions. Twenty, placed so, made a longer line for watching and for the attack, when the time came. With a last touch on the gun each man carried and a final warning shake of his head, Luis sent all twenty to their stations. Then, as he and Antonio faced each other, Antonio saw what others might have missed. Luis, for all that his eyes glittered and his mouth was stern, was still badly shaken by what had happened. When Antonio put out his hand to grip the younger man's shoulder, he felt the flesh quiver. Wordlessly then he slipped his hand down and put his arm through Luis's, and turned him about, so that it was together they took their first look at the Indian camp.

The scene, in their anxiety all confusion at first, assumed slowly a pattern of light blending into dark—the light the dull red of fire reflected on the painted faces and naked bodies of a rough half-circle of Comanche warriors seated about the fire, looking not at the flames, but beyond them, at the stark trunk of a still-standing dead tree.

There was movement both in the circle and in the dark behind it. That in the dark was a shifting and stirring of lumpish forms. It was from there that the wailing arose. It sounded like the wailing of women, except that it seemed unlikely that women should have accompanied a war party. Whether made by women or wounded or medicine men, the sound was desolate.

But where were the Indians' horses? A Comanche never traveled far on foot. There was no movement, however, of animals anywhere near. They must be beyond the bog.

There was also the question about the captives. Had they, too, been taken farther away—to what might be a larger camp? A convulsive movement by Luis ended speculation, brief as it had been, the thoughts flashing and passing. At the jerk Antonio tightened his hold on Luis's arm, and it was well he did so. All of Luis's attention had been centered on the savages facing the fire and the dead tree. A breath of wind now brought a brighter glow to the embers, and the area of light widened. The captives had not been carried farther. At least two of them were here. A man was tied to the tree. It was possible now to see the thongs that bound him and the outline of an arm. The arm was that of a young man, white. The man was Manuel.

Again Antonio tightened his hold. Sickened himself at what he saw, he knew that a rash movement now would not save Manuel and would endanger everyone who had come to his rescue. In a minute Luis saw that for himself. Helplessly he had been brandishing his gun and trying to pull free of Antonio's grip. Now he dropped the gun to his side, and violence went out of him. Antonio's hold was then a support. Antonio steadied Luis, then with his free hand motioned toward the tree, meaning to point out something he had had time to see and Luis might have missed.

One reason they had not been instantly aware of the bound captive was that between the tree and the fire a bulkier object had turned aside the light. That object now changed its position. It was Garza. His sculptured gray head had never seemed so handsome, rising above the great cowl of his robe. He stood, straight and strong and solid, between the captive and the Indians. His arms were bent, suggesting that his hands rested on some object he held, possibly his knotted rope girdle. The Comanches must slay him before they could torture Manuel further.

Luis saw, too. His eyes, when he turned to look at Antonio, still glittered and his face was desperate, but he could wait now. How long? The moon had begun its western descent, but two hours might remain of darkness. How could twenty men—twenty plus two—wait in silence that long, gun in hand? All except Antonio. Turbelino had carried his gun on the march and had it still in its holder on the saddle. Antonio had only a loaded pistol in his belt and a hunting knife. Well! It was too late to go for the gun, even if he had known the direction. Pistol and knife and his wits must take care of him when the time came for fighting. But his hands felt empty.

His hands were empty, and his head, without warning, swam a little. That was fatigue. He had pushed himself hard coming up from Orcoquisac. The night and its weird tableau swam dizzily, steadied, swam again, then was sharply alive as one of the crouching warriors got to his feet and resumed the harangue which they had heard faintly in the distance as they approached. The flat singsong tonelessness was the same, but was now broken periodically by some word that came out in a startling scream. Each such yell was wilder than the one before. Gesticulation accompanied the oratory. The Indian moved up and down before the circle. He pointed to the fire, to the captive, to the moon. What he said only Satan could know—Satan and the Comanche's own tribesmen. The harangue was having its effect on them. Their eyes rolled. They moved more and more restlessly, until at last one of them, snatching a spear, leaped to his feet, crouched and leaped again, the spear ready for a thrust. A leap carried him past the fire, straight toward the tree and the helpless prisoner. Just as abruptly then he halted, and stood like a figure cast in bronze, powerless to throw or thrust, as Garza stepped toward him, holding up his crucifix.

That a savage could be stopped by such a symbol, in which he had no belief! The fact remained that he did stop. If the Comanches in seizing Garza had thought to steal strength from Bucareli, they had that strength to deal with now.

The glow of the fire shone on the cross, as Garza began his singsong—one of his Latin chants. Slowly the spear came down, and the Indian shrank back, only to rouse a new fiendishness among his fellows. As he fell back, another arose, pointed at him with a howl of scorn, then at the fire. He must have been a chief of influence. Immediately two others sprang up. One snatched a bundle of fagots that had been gathered to feed the fire and piled them at the base of the dead tree. The other lighted a firebrand in the embers.

"Let me go!" Luis said hoarsely, unheard because of the savage yelling and Garza's mounting chant. "Let me go. He doesn't see . . ."

Ah, but Garza had seen. Still raptly intoning, holding out his cross, he knew all that was taking place. He waited only until the fire was lighted; then, before anyone watching could realize his intent, he gave a single strong kick to his skirts, and fell back, sitting down squarely on the blazing fagots.

The movement stunned both the savages and those who looked on from the outer darkness. Before anyone could recover from stupefaction, somewhere, high in a tree but very close, an owl hooted. This was a natural occurrence and, under other circumstances, not to be noticed; but now, with the priest sitting there, smothering the blaze, holding the cross in hands that showed no tremor, a man so armored by the secret magic of faith that fire could not consume him, though the smell of scorching wool was strong, a man whom probably no spear or arrow or bullet could slay . . . The same thought must have come to either savage or white man looking on. It is not a bird. It is a sign.

The sound was repeated. Close at hand, but in a different direction. It came again. Surely it was a sign. But what did it mean? To the savage it could have been the spirit world coming to the aid of the priest. Or it could have been Spanish scouts signaling to soldier reinforcements. Soldiers sometimes did turn up in force where they were needed, all with fleet horses and active guns. In the dark of a night now surely drawing to its close, they dared do nothing but fall back and wait.

They fell back, muttering. The watchfire burned to ash. Darkness came down over everything, and silence, broken only by the well-spaced cries of night birds hunting. An hour remained before day broke. It was a long hour. In the first relief from anxiety over Manuel, Luis Ramón dropped his head to his chest and gave a deep sigh. Antonio released his arm and patted his shoulder. For further distraction, he showed Luis his arsenal of weapons, the pistol and knife. When Luis stared in unbelief, he shrugged off question and answer, bared the knife, and pointed to the dead tree, indicating that he would like to be the one to cut Manuel's thongs when the time came. Again Luis stared, but finally nodded consent. After all, he could not do everything; and everything must be done at once—presently.

An hour. How many slept at their posts nobody knew. There was no movement now on the part of the Indians, as the moon continued to slide downhill in its arch, and darkness deepened. Two, Antonio would have said, did no sleeping. They would be Luis, going over and over what he must do when daylight came, and Garza, still sitting on his scorched robe. God grant that the fire had not burned through to his flesh, making it hard for him to rise and walk when he must rise. Manuel, uncomfortably

bound to the dead tree, but in no imminent danger, might merci-
fully have slept some. Care must be exercised when the time came
to set him free. He would be numb. Numb . . . numb . . . Antonio
nodded, caught himself, found a small, living tree, balanced himself against the support, and closed his eyes.

Movement aroused him. Day was here at last, pale, new, but
day. In the Indian camp a lone squaw rolled over and stood up.
She looked familiar to Antonio, but any squaw her age would
have looked the same. She rubbed her eyes, then hurried to the
fire and began blowing on its embers. Garza was on his feet,
speaking to Manuel. The first Comanche warrior appeared, giving a command to the squaw.

"Now!" Luis hissed. "Ready! *Olé!*"

All the tension of the night was in his cry of rally. As he spoke,
he raised his gun and shot the Comanche brave through the heart.

Everything then was screaming confusion. The Comanches
were bold raiders, but they were not schooled to stand and give
battle. They had been caught sleeping, and the twenty Spaniards
from Bucareli seemed three times that number. Almost at once
the Indians were in flight. Some headed directly into the bog and
were shot as they floundered there. It was a madness of yelling
and killing; but to most of it Antonio was not a witness. At Luis's
shout he kicked himself wide awake and broke through the brush
to free Manuel.

"Hold him, Padre," he warned, as he cut the first thong.

In another minute he and Garza were both rubbing circula-
tion back into Manuel's arms and legs; and Manuel was in one
breath cursing those who had left him not so much as a breech
cloth and asking for Angelita.

"Over there," Garza said, indicating the place where the squaw
had slept. "She was insensible but unharmed, the last I saw. Leave
this one to me now, Antonio, and go to her."

She was still insensible when Antonio found her, lying on the
ground, with only light clothing between her and the dampness.
There had been no attempt to rob her of her simple garments—
the blue skirt, the white apron and blouse, the blue head scarf.
Poor Niña! This was your reward for kindness to a wounded
Comanche. His people came to steal the Woman in Blue, to

make a prisoner of her magic. Apron, skirt, and blouse were torn. She had been handled roughly, but she was alive.

"Niña!" Antonio said again, in pity, and froze. Through a bush he saw a gun barrel pointing.

But he had his pistol now in his hand. He had only to raise that hand a little to fire into the bush. The Indian's gun went off a second after the pistol shot, but harmlessly; and a broken yell said one more Comanche would not live to create others of his kind.

Antonio wasted no more time on emotion. He put his gun away; but before he could touch Angelita, who had remained unconscious through the uproar, Luis was there. He had heard the crack of Antonio's pistol and the louder explosion of the Indian's gun, and had come running, fearful of what he might find.

"Thank God!" he said, seeing Antonio unharmed. Then he saw La Niña and was still.

"She lives," Antonio said quickly. "Her sleep is heavy, but she is all right. Can we go now?"

"Yes," Luis said tensely. "Manuel and Fray Josef are already on the way. The others are coming back. The fighting is over. Will you . . ."

"No. You carry her," Antonio said. "You are stronger."

No stronger actually, but equal in strength; and once Luis had the helpless girl in his arms, and knew for himself that she lived, he would walk like a giant, beyond any tiring. He stooped now as Antonio spoke and lifted La Niña from the ground as lightly as if she had been a broken doll.

"Lead on," he said, shifting the weight a little, for her greater comfort, and walked away without waiting. Antonio had difficulty in passing him, to find the path and establish the right direction for escape.

What he chose to follow finally was hardly a path, merely a break in the brush beyond the ashes of the Indians' fire and the dead tree to which Manuel had been bound. Leaving that break, Antonio charted a course more prayerfully than hopefully through the drowned forest, guided by what seemed to him signs of fresh trampling of the ground and newly snapped off branches

of trees. Presently he heard behind him—but at some distance—
the voices and the crashing through obstacles of the twenty
chosen militiamen returning victorious from battle. Fatigue, however, fettered their feet now; and the distance grew no less.
Afterwards, they said they had been able to see Luis and that he
was carrying someone, so knew that all was well and thought
then that they could take their time.

A little later, Antonio saw ahead the brown robe of Garza
making a slow advance through the forest. Before him Manuel
stumbled, clothed now in a ragged shirt, his own probably, torn
from him by the Indians and abandoned later as they fled before
the surprise attack, and in nothing much in the way of trousers.

A horse nickered then, not too far away; and a cuckoo called.
That would be Turbelino and Lope, who could also hoot like
an owl. Thank God, Antonio thought, for a good horse, for a
faithful Indian friend, for Garza. Thank God . . . The ghostly
woods broke away, and there stood Lope holding the horses.

From Turbelino's back Antonio reached out now to take La
Niña from Luis. Turbelino would receive a double load more
patiently if Antonio made up most of it, though even the horse
was in a mood of acceptance now. Around the mounting, twenty
grimy and tattered citizen-soldiers stood in awe, silenced by the
white face of the unconscious girl.

"She is so still," Luis said fearfully as Antonio took her. "Once
I thought she was about to speak, but it was nothing."

"She breathes," Antonio reminded him. "She will waken in
good time. Now go and mount Manuel on Lope's horse. Say it is
my command that he ride the rest of this march. He is a sick
man—just for today. Tell him that tomorrow he can look for a
double share of marching if he wants it. Now, say no more. Go!"

Garza continued on foot—of necessity. A good breadth of
cloth had been burned away from the rear of his robe and his
flesh was so seared that it would be a long time before he could
ride a mule again or even sit on a chair in comfort. When he
rested, he must lie on his face.

"But I learned early in my novitiate," he growled, "to prostrate myself before the Lord."

The rest of the march went more rapidly then. The way was

cleared by daylight. The sun had been up a good hour when in silence they rounded the breached stockade. Then there was the river to cross; and a short way beyond that they hailed the camp.

CHAPTER 8

After all, there was no need for Antonio to make a speech to his friends encamped a short distance east of the Trinity.

In mid-afternoon of the day following the Comanche raid, he sat with Pablo Rojas on the trunk of a fallen tree near the makeshift camp. Helpless against great weariness, he had slept away the morning; but now every sense was alert and reaching. It had been necessary to give this day to rest, to recovery of the townspeople from the terror of the night just past, and to the recovery of the twenty stalwart warriors from their supreme exertion. In advance Antonio would have said that few of the twenty could or would have endured what all finally had endured; so now let them rest. A few still were sleeping, but most of the men of the town and the older boys, attended by some women, were now over the river, helping, under the direction of Tomás Coronal, to dig two graves.

One was for Pedro Coronal.

"Bury the boy where he has lived," Antonio had said to Tomás before sleep had claimed him. "You cannot in any case take your son with you, except as the memory of him will live with you and all who knew him wherever we go."

He had his arm about the shoulders of his friend as he spoke; and he was so tired at the time that Tomás, he thought, gave him more support than he gave Tomás. And Tomás was just as worn and weary.

"We are going away—somewhere?" he asked vaguely.

"Yes," Antonio said. "I will talk to you about that later. This evening, perhaps."

So, now almost all the strong and able were over the river, preparing a place of burial for Pedro and also for Señora Gonzales. When the Señora had learned in the camp that Angelita was missing, it was, people said, as if a sword had been run through her heart. She had died with a cry for mercy unfinished, perhaps unheard, except by those around her. When Garza reached the camp, he had silenced Constanzia's blasphemy, then ordered her to bed. So, she had no part now in the burying.

Nor had Pablo Rojas. He did very well today, but only when he was quiet. If he moved about or talked too much, he had a rending sensation in his back. This, Rosario said, was because there had been more bleeding and the bandages had now stuck fast. That was what made the pulling when he moved, but it was best that he should not be too active. Mama Rojas agreed, and was of the opinion that, when the time was right, the bloody rags would drop away naturally.

"What do you think?" the strong one asked Antonio.

He was so beset now with awe of his wound that Antonio had to laugh.

"If you will rest today as ordered," he said, "by evening we can perhaps use a little water to free the bandages. Now, now! You expect to wash your back sometime, do you not? Old friend, you were brave last night, I am told, when you were in pain. You are in no pain at present? See, then. Move over to that tree behind you and rest against it. You have lost blood and are weakened. That is all. Tomorrow you can mount a mule, or even walk as well as anybody. No one will be driving us with whips on this march. We can take the time needed."

Rojas, who had cautiously placed one shoulder and his head against the supporting tree, sat up strongly.

"What is this about a mule and marching?" he demanded. "Where are we going—without haste? Bexar? I will wish that Comanche had finished me with his arrow."

"And I would wish it for you, my friend. Do you think you are the only one who feels that way? My thought led in another direction. What do you say? Shall we go home now?"

Rojas did not believe his ears.

"Home?" he repeated. "You mean Los Adaes?"

317

"It does not need to be just there," Antonio suggested. "Since we make a new beginning, build from the foundations, we can choose. There may be some place that way just as fair, with no bitter memories cursing it. I remember . . ."

Rojas stopped him. The blood was coursing through him now visibly, bringing color to his broad face.

"I never thought of going home," he said. "I never thought . . . There was one place early in the march . . ."

"Hold it," Antonio said. "We are only two out of many. The choice of place can come later."

"I can talk to *mamacita?*" Rojas asked.

"Assuredly. I will call her now to sit with you. Then I must see how La Niña is doing, and be off to the burying. I promised Tomás and Rosario."

"La Niña," Rojas said. "How will it be with her now?"

"She will recover," Antonio said stoutly, though he was by no means sure. "She takes a little food and will take more. Otherwise, sleep is probably best for her now. *Adiós, amigo.* Be of good heart. I go now for Mama Rojas."

That was why he did not need to make a speech that evening, stating his intentions and recommendations. Pablo told Mama Rojas. Tomás Coronal asked Rosario what she thought Antonio had in mind when he had spoken that morning about going away. By evening everybody knew what was in the wind.

They buried Pedro Coronal late that afternoon in the garden behind La Niña's hospital, where the roses bloomed which he had watered.

"I can see now," his father said, "that he was not meant to grow old."

Later, when Luis, knowing then something of Antonio's plan for turning home, asked about the roses, Antonio said:

"Leave them where they are. We will plant new ones in the new town. Everything there will be new."

Later still, he thought of the small Madonna with the opal-studded crown; but, when he went into the church to look for it, it was gone. He said nothing to anyone about it at the time. If the Comanches had stolen it, it was gone forever. If, on the other hand, it was Luis . . . Antonio certainly would raise no fuss. Not now.

But that followed the burying of Señora Gonzales—in the churchyard, where in the past they had laid Gil Flores and others of the town. Garza gave permission, but would not accept, in payment for prayers, the money she had hoarded. God would make that judgment, he said, without man's meddling. Then Constanzia had wanted the money buried with her mistress, but Antonio had spoken against that. If the sum were put to a fair use, he suggested, the curse on it might be lifted. At that Constanzia's face had lighted up as if his word had opened gates of glory for her and her poor, stricken young mistress. She had thrown herself at Antonio's feet in thankfulness, not knowing then what he had in mind for her, for La Niña, for all.

By evening everyone knew. On Antonio's return to camp, men and women swarmed about him before he was off Turbelino's back. Was it true that they were going back now? All the way?

"As far as you like," Antonio said. And, "It is as true as you will make it."

That seemed to them foolish talk. When would they start? Tonight? Why not tonight? A little something in hand to eat and they would be ready.

"We will not go like that," Antonio said. "There is no need. This is not a flight."

What was it, then? Never mind that. It was not flight, because no one pursued. Bexar was twice as far away as the Sabine River. Nobody in Bexar knew even that the Comanches had come to Bucareli. It might be weeks before the news flew that way. Then, with a change of governors, and the problem of other Comanche raids . . .

"There is time," he insisted, "to do everything in good order. To make some preparation. No, I do not mean delay. Only time to take powder and balls, for example, from the magazine across the river—for the hunters' guns. We shall need to kill for meat as we go. And you will think between now and tomorrow of what you left behind last night in your houses. Things you can use now and later. Blankets, clothing, salt for meat, all that you have of that. There will be no stores of anything along the road and none when the journey ends. The journey will be hard, as before; and toil waits when it is over."

Still they murmured. The march could not be that hard when each day they would go to meet the rising sun.

"You have no mules or horses as yet," Antonio reminded them. Except a few that Luis had caught after the burying. "Tomorrow Luis will take what horses he has and men to help him and bring our beasts in as he can find them. That, while others take what is wanted from the town and the rest get things together here."

Again they murmured. Tomorrow, no later, they would be on their way.

"We will see how tomorrow goes," Antonio said. "Rest now, and sleep. We want nobody sick this time, nobody tired or hungry."

"You hear?" Rojas called out, his voice back in sudden full power. "Do as Don Antonio says. Who is our friend, if he is not? Who has been our friend? Who will save us now?"

"Don Antonio—Antonio—Ibarbo!" they shouted.

"Then do as he says. To bed when you have eaten. To bed, everybody!"

When they had eaten. . . . Was there food even now? Miraculously, it seemed that there was—a little for each one. Fires were extinguished soon; and quiet—a murmuring quiet—descended. Not far away a cuckoo bird called:

"All's well! All's well!"

The next day went better than anyone could have expected. Dawn was shattered by Luis's horn. Fifteen minutes later he and Manuel, with half a dozen volunteer *vaqueros*, were splashing through the river, on their way to round up horses, mules, and cattle. A shepherd, without permission, had gone across the evening before, with a dog, to gather the sheep.

Shortly after that, Antonio led the other men back to the town, to direct the packing of the powder and to gather tools and hardware that could be useful. A party of women followed, Magdalena and Mama Rojas among them, to see about food and blankets and clothes. Pablo, his bandage softened and removed from a wound already healing, and Tomás remained in camp. Later Tomás would cross the river with Rosario when she could get away—Rosario to gather her and La Niña's medicines, Tomás to collect shuttles and spools and such material as he had on hand for weaving, but not the clumsy loom. He could build another and better one at the new place, he was sure—he who was now an expert at the manufacture of looms.

Early that morning Rosario would not leave La Niña, who moved restlessly in her sleep now and seemed to try to speak. If this should mean fever, Constanzia, frightened into near insensibility herself, would be no good as a nurse.

It was not a fever, only the first signs of senses returning. By mid-morning La Niña was again sleeping quietly, Teresa Andorro watching her and Constanzia, and Rosario was in the town, with three grown girls to help her or anyone else who needed help.

By noon everybody was back at camp. The *caballard*, with only a small shrinkage, was under control; the *vaqueros*, now *arrieros*, had the mules ready for their packs; and kettles simmered and steamed. Everyone was admittedly hungry; but as for siesta, no!

"*Vamos, amigos!* Home!"

Antonio, on Turbelino, led the way at first, stopping frequently to wait for his followers. Turbelino was as ready as any other to run, but there must be no running. Presently Antonio planned to turn the lead over to a responsible man on foot. Rojas was the natural choice, but Antonio would not summon him until the first cross beside the road had been met and passed. If the thirty crosses east of the Trinity still stood. Some did. He dismounted at the first of them; and, as he did so, Rojas appeared.

"The walking goes well," Rojas said, "thanks be to God."

He had not seen the cross. When he did, he halted and a second later drew another in the air with his big right hand.

"Even they," he mumbled softly, "are here, to show us the way."

Antonio could go back then along the line, to look at the other marchers. A shorter line, but long enough. Some of the people panted a little. Here and there a child fretted. Burdens were on almost every back, but smiles met Antonio and Turbelino. Now God give him what was needed to justify such trust! Luis appeared then, leading his horse with three little ones in the saddle. Constanzia and Zapatero were the next to receive special greeting. They rode the patient mules between which swung La Niña's litter. Garza, his stride shortened, his robe patched with a piece of blanket, his face as immobile as ever, followed.

It was much like the other marchings, but also very unlike them. Four hours of steady, forward plodding; and a grove of trees appeared with a sentinel waiting. An Indian on a spotted pony.

"Good shelter and water," Lope said when Antonio rode up to him. "The next place is too far."

"This is just right," Antonio said. "They are more tired than they know. I give you thanks in their name, my friend."

Then he on one side of the road and Lope on the other motioned the pilgrims into the grove of trees.

"Forward! We camp here." He said it, Antonio thought, more than a hundred times. Some, hearing him, smiled. Some protested.

"So soon? No farther today? It is not enough."

Then from among the trees came a shout, enough to make Turbelino rear:

"A pine tree! A pine tree! Look! A pine tree!"

They advanced day by patient day, east and north now. Pine trees ceased to be occasions for shouting jubilation, but as they increased in frequency, were more and more a blessing. Seen from a distance, a stand of pines promised cool, dense shade if the day was warm, and shelter if rain came down. Each night children climbed them, to roost in the branches like wild turkeys. Tomás Coronal would watch such ascent, his eyes filling; and Antonio, standing by, could not comfort him, for sorrow filling his own throat.

"The boy seems so far away, so alone back there," Tomás mourned one day, as they moved along. "Sometimes I think I cannot go any farther."

322

"March on," Garza said, appearing unexpectedly alongside. "Pedro is not there, nor is he here, but he is somewhere. You will know that some day."

Tomás turned then to Pablo Rojas.

"Is the loss easier to bear as time goes on?" he asked. "Does one forget?"

"No," Pablo said, "one never forgets. One accepts finally, I should say. What else can we do? As Fray Josef says, you will not find Pedro by going back. You know that. So, forward, for better or worse, with the rest of us. I think it will be better. So do you, except for this special injury, which heals more slowly than the hole in my back. *Mamacita* says it is a very small spot now. It was a hole big enough to put your fist in at first—or so it felt to me. I could not see it, of course. So put on a good face, even if a sad one comes more naturally at present. Out of regard for Antonio, if for no other reason. Now, truly, he has thrown caution overboard for our sake. Not that he shows any regret. I never knew him to be in better spirits. Here he comes now. Let's hail him. *Olé*, Antonio, you on that fiery charger. Have you time to talk to two old friends a while?"

Always, when the friends were these.

"I was just saying to Tomás," Pablo said, "I think you like having your head in a noose. It comes over me more every day that, in leading us this way now, you are tossing aside, as of no worth, all the favor you have won in high places."

"That is as it may be," Antonio said, dismounting, to match his pace with that of the others. "I never had a stronger sense of doing right than I have now. Look! Surely you remember this part of the march six years ago. It was here that the sickness overtook us. Is anyone ailing now—except the blessed Niña? No. Strength and courage grow continually. I marvel at these people, who go to bed every night exhausted, and rise every morning new with hope and eager to weary themselves all over again. Why? Because they are going in the right direction. And they are. You will see. I have plans."

He had, but dared not speak of them just yet. Presently, he said; and suddenly the time was just ahead, though there had been many a day when he thought this journey, too, would never end. Contemplating a solution leaped over distances which walking people covered slowly. This left so much time between contemplation and accomplishment that disaster, failure seemed possible still. Some days he felt he must give Turbelino his head and gallop away, to set things going while these slow ones plodded and plodded along.

Really they covered ground more rapidly than he had ever calculated they might. The morning marches went especially well. Afternoons were slower. Still, they advanced. Time, which seemed to drag, was necessary. Other scars than sorrow or an arrow's stab needed healing. Time allowed people to grow together again. Some unity had been lost in the bitter years.

La Niña in her swaying litter helped to bring unity back. The outrage of her being carried off had been a common hurt. Then that men had sprung up on all sides to join in rescuing her was a common pride. And now that, sick as she was, she should be returning to the Sabine country with them was a symbol of hope —as she herself had always been in the time of bitter sorrow. Hardly a person let a day go by without managing to approach the litter, to look at her, lying there so pale and still, but alive and growing better every day, Rosario insisted. She knew Rosario now, Rosario was sure, also Garza and Antonio—and, perhaps one or two others. She still did not speak, but her eyes said that she knew them.

It had better be so, Antonio thought—for the sake of all, for the sake of one. Each morning it was Luis Ramón who hitched her litter between the mules and carried her to it. At noon he carried her to a resting place, without motion for a change, under a tree. At evening he carried her to her bed.

One day he said fiercely to Antonio that if she should not recover, if she should lie like that always, he wanted to be the one to care for her through life.

"For me," he said, "there will never be any other."

"She will recover or she will die," Antonio told him, speaking sharply because of his dismay.

"I know," Luis said. "I am prepared for anything. Still, that is how it is with me. If she should go, I mean to speak to Fray Josef about entering his order."

"Luis, no!" Antonio cried, only because, seeing Luis striding along so strong and alone, he could also see him wrapped in a friar's robe.

Then La Niña began to show improvement, but Luis still was determined on some sort of renunciation. Now it was:

"If possibly her happiness should depend on someone like Manuel . . ."

"It is not Manuel and will not be," Antonio scolded. "Manuel knows."

"How can you be sure what he knows?" Luis asked. "Have you talked with him?"

"No, he has talked to me."

"It is Luis," Manuel had said. "It has never been any other. He was the only one who could not see. And I thought . . . surely it did no harm to worship at the same shrine."

No harm. It might even do good, if one did not cherish false hope. Manuel had no hope, he said. He had never been that serious. He was not Luis. No, he was not Luis. He would find another angel somewhere some day to fill that part of his life. And he would sing a merry note again, but not now. Not just now.

Just now, as Luis talked with Antonio, it being early in the afternoon marching, they rode ahead of the mules with the litter, and, as was their way while near, they looked back from time to time to see that all was well behind them. Now, as they looked back, La Niña's eyes were open and fixed on them.

"*Dios!*" Luis said. "Could she hear what we have been saying?"

No harm, Antonio thought, if it was so, but he thought it was not so.

"She hears voices probably," he said, "no more. All is a dream with her these days, even when she is awake."

A dream. She was not staring vacantly. She saw, she heard; but thought remained out of reach. It was that way with speech. The power of speaking was there, Rosario claimed. She murmured without meaning while asleep, but weakness blocked both will and thought when she drew near the border of consciousness.

Antonio's eyes met those of Luis with grave, immediate question. What would the real awakening be like? Without answering, both looked back again, and La Niña's eyes were closed.

"I have the small Madonna," Luis said softly then. "Would it help to place it beside her?"

Antonio thought not. Not yet. Presently let it be where she could see it when she opened her eyes, but not now.

Presently. A day came when Antonio knew, and Lope said, that they were nearing the Neches River, the last great river before the Sabine. They were now in rich forest land. Beyond the Neches almost all would be forest. They would cross a second, smaller river a day or so later; and not far beyond that they would come to a valley, bright with flowers and deep in grass, cut through by a sparkling, still smaller stream—a spring branch.

"Señor," Lope explained as Antonio described the scene, "that is the place. You remember all of it. It is the first home of my people. There is the Mission of the Nacogdoches—Our Lady of Nacogdoches. The church still stands."

"How much of it stands?" Antonio asked.

"All, Señor. Four walls complete and part of the roof—that part near the tower, where the bells used to be. And the priest's house—that is whole."

"Good!" Antonio said, suppressing doubt. "Walls without too much roof might be better for these wanderers at first—except when it rains. Would they, would we be welcomed by your people if we should want to settle in the valley—on your land?"

"Our land is your land," Lope said. "It would make us very happy."

"Well, we will see," Antonio said, and wanted at once to hunt out Rojas and others, to discover whether they might be thinking of this same spot. It was a long march west of old Los Adaes; but it was, if possible, even fairer country and had other advantages; but here he was, galloping ahead of himself again. The same was true of Lope.

"Señor, the way is now clear. The distance is short. I would like to carry word to my father."

"How many days remain?" Antonio asked.

"Two—three—not more."

326

"Tomorrow, then. Now come with me. Have you seen La Niña close by?"

"Not since the dark night, Señor. I want, but I say no. I am Indian. If she should be afraid . . ."

This had been Antonio's thought, too. When La Niña came fully awake—and that, like the bright valley—seemed near now —what memories would waken with her? Could she be fortified sufficiently by loving friends around her to forget horror and fear? Or would the horror always stand between her and true understanding? There was this matter of Indians. A few days and they would be all about her—friendly Indians; but would she see in them only savages?

He wished now that he had taken Lope near her earlier than this, while all she saw was a dream and fleeting; but then he could not have explained that this was a Tejas, a friend, not an enemy. Now it was his belief that each day La Niña came nearer to comprehension of what went on about her. Well, he would be taking a risk to show her an Indian now; but again, nobody else would dare.

"Come," he said to Lope. "If you are with me, she will understand better. Say nothing unless she takes fright. Then speak— you know."

Lope still held back, but Antonio insisted. La Niña was awake. She was awake much of the time now, thinking, he believed, as far as she dared. She saw Antonio first. Recognition was in her eyes. Her still face was less still.

"Niña," Antonio said. "I have brought a friend. Friend—do you hear? You know Lope, my Tejas partner."

She saw Lope then. Her face contorted alarmingly.

"Friend," Antonio said stoutly. And again, "Tejas. The Tejas are our friends, *muchachita*. You know."

The mules had now halted. Zapatero and Constanzia watched breathlessly.

"Tejas, *amigo*," poor Lope said, and went down on his knees in the dust.

"Tejas, *amigo*," Antonio said after him.

La Niña's face smoothed, but her eyes still were wide with fear.

"Those others," Antonio soothed, "are gone now. Far away. We have only friends here—Tejas, friends."

Her lips moved. He thought she tried for the words. She looked again at the kneeling Indian. A light shudder passed over her, but there was no other expression of terror.

"Go now," Antonio said to Lope. "It is enough for today."

"Tejas, *amigo*," the Indian entreated, rising to his feet and backing away. "Tejas, *amigo*."

And he was gone. La Niña's eyes searched Antonio's face.

"There is my brave one," he said gently. "Sleep now without fear. Now and always."

They crossed the Neches that afternoon. On the morning of the second day after that they crossed the Angelina River and, just before sunset, came out of the forest into the bright valley.

Nobody needed to say that this was the end of journeying. All knew it. Some laughed, some cried. Then, one at a time, the reverent—those who remembered—dropped to their knees. That was after Garza, breaking through the hysterical ones, set the example. As long as he lived, Antonio remembered Fray Josef that day. He strode through the groups of people, turned his face to the empty, staring church on the hill, and knelt to pray. One minute only, and he was up again, walking off toward the hill. He walked a hundred yards, perhaps, and knelt again. Then he went on a little farther and again stopped to pray. He went all the way up the hill that way; and when he stood at last before the ruin of the church, he prostrated himself as he knew how.

"Up!" Antonio shouted to the kneeling people—in loud, ringing tones, so that they should not look at his red eyes. "Up! Night is coming. Tomorrow is another day. Up . . . please!"

CHAPTER 9

Some there were who, after deep sleep, were afraid to open their eyes when morning came, thinking that the good fortune of the evening would have vanished overnight, that it could not be real or lasting. Others, standing up at once at the first bird song, rubbing sleep from their eyes, opening them bravely to find enchantment still present and even more real than at the first encounter, shouted a greeting to the morning and ran through wet grass to plunge into the creek, ragged clothes and all. . . . They yelled then at the shock of the cold water, but went under the next minute and came up, wet as otters, then danced themselves dry in the sunshine.

Before the early ones were dry, the sleepy, the timid, had joined in the fun. Then, with a clearing of the senses, came reason. There was work to be done. Chickens must be let out of their crates to scratch as soon as pens could be devised. Goats and cows must be milked. Fires must be kindled. There was no corn and little salt. Never mind, there was milk, and a little meat from yesterday to be crisped over the fires. Later in the day fish could be caught and the hunters would go out. Meantime, the water was delicious, was it not? They could wait.

However, before any duties could be undertaken, Luis Ramón's ranch horn sounded from up the hill. There, beside him, stood Fray Josef. The summons was for matins. Today, with so much to be done? Today, surely, with so much gratitude to be given and so much favor still to be asked for. With their hands the eager people smoothed their wet hair. They shook out their damp clothing. The big ones picked up little ones, and everybody went up the hill to the church. Garza received them with arms spread out in blessing. His rugged face, turned to the morning sky, had a radiance they had never seen on it before.

Dios! Those were matins to remember always. As the last stragglers neared the church, the Indians came. They came singing. It was a mass they sang—in Latin. They could not know what the words meant. And the words might not be right; but who would know except Fray Josef, who must have taught them the chant? The sound was magnificent. Even the birds hushed to listen. Many of the Indians carried burdens, bulky ones, covered with deerhide. They set the burdens down outside the church and went in after Garza, who now led the singing.

Indian, Spaniard, and mestizo all crowded into the church, where Fray Josef celebrated a mass of thanksgiving. With the blue sky, like heaven, smiling through where there was no roof. Then all went outside again and Garza blessed the Indians' burdens, which were shawls, blankets, and, most of all, food—corn, some salt, and kettles of a pudding made from ground meal and water, set thickly with nut meats. It was strange to the taste, but a little of it was very satisfying. Indians, Spaniards, and mestizos, they made the morning meal together.

While they did so, Don Antonio could be seen standing a little apart, talking to the young Tejas, Lope, and to an older Indian, who was probably Lope's father. There was an exchange of small presents before the Chief called his people together and led them away. By then everyone knew that at least one problem had been solved. They knew that they would not be hungry now. Perhaps never again.

Reason once more admonished them. Don Antonio had bargained with the Indians for food. Right now, immediately, it had to be that way, but not always. As soon as they could, they must provide for themselves. Some of the Indian corn must be used as seed. Corn should grow fast here, but other things even faster. Had anyone thought to bring seed from Bucareli? A few had—squash, beans, melons. Time must pass before that harvest, too; but meanwhile there would be wild greens and fruit.

Rojas and others like him went among the people, saying how they should proceed. A cornfield surely would be marked off and cleared and planted—a common field for all this year. Next year each family would have its own field, but that took planning. Now, as with the militia, the people would be divided into groups, each with its own leader to direct the planting and say where the chickens could scratch and so on. Let there be some kind of order to everything, please! If a group leader did not know the answer to a problem, he would go to Rojas. If Rojas did not know, he would consult Don Antonio. One thing was certain. There was work for all. This was their town, or would be. All must work hard at its building.

Work? Who minded that now?

It was a day of wonders. La Niña came out of troubled dreaming at last, to live again like other people. More like other people, finally, than ever in her life before this; but it went slowly at first. Only she could say how it came about that she awakened on that day instead of another, and she herself was not too sure.

A number of things, she thought, had called to her that morning, had taken her by the hand, and touched her heart, saying, "Come! You have slept much too long now. Rise. Stir yourself."

Hot sunshine on pine branches was part of it. She had been aware of this before, but today the strong, medicinal odor, balm to weak breathing, was more potent than usual. She awoke to that and then to a sharp, clear comprehension of her surroundings. She was in a kind of tent. Really it was only the stout canvas that had made the carrying litter, now stretched between two trees for a roof. The cot on which she slept was directly under the canvas, but she could see the trees outside and the blue sky through their branches. There had been talk, Rosario told her later, of placing her in the priest's house overnight, but the air in that closed house was damp and musty and it had been so sweet and soft outside that they could not bear to shut her up there, even with the door open.

"*Gracias!*" she said, when she heard this. She might have smothered in the musty house.

So, it was the rude tent and the trees and the sky she saw first. Then she heard birds singing—and, sweeter than the singing, chattering around their nests. Finally she heard Luis's horn, then voices, many voices—and, suddenly, the Indian chorus.

At once Rosario was beside the bed, and Constanzia at the foot of it.

"Tejas," Rosario said. "Tejas, *amigos*, Niña."

She knew. How? She could not say, but she knew.

"Tejas, *amigos*," she repeated to Rosario.

Aloud, with no effort, her first words in weeks. Rosario bent over the bed, breathing hard, her face flushed. And Constanzia stood with her hands upraised, calling heaven to witness the miracle.

"Niña," Rosario said then, when she could speak. "You are awake and so strong? Even without eating . . . Will you take a little something now?"

"Yes, please," she said, but reached for Rosario, got hold of something, and pulled herself up to a sitting position. Immediately Rosario had a strong arm at her back, holding her.

"Niña, Niña, Nina," she said in sobbing thankfulness.

So it was Constanzia who brought a bowl of milk and a spoon; and Niña put the spoon aside and took the bowl into her own hands and drank. Although she spilled some, it tasted good that way. Rosario told her afterwards that she had asked for bread, of which there was none, and they were desolate. But sleep returned then, and she didn't know.

The next time she awoke, a shelf had been affixed to one of the trees that held the canvas, and there on the shelf stood her Madonna. Never had the silver crown with the jewels looked so bright or the painted face so fair. But then her attention was distracted. A man knelt before the shrine—a strong young man with a straight back and sleek black hair. She knew him at once. She almost spoke his name, then did not, because she wanted to see him just that way, to remember. When he moved, she closed her eyes to hold the picture, but lost it in more sleep. Yet it was a different sleeping. Rosario said; and Rosario must have been right. The next time La Niña awoke, Constanzia knelt in that corner and La Niña laughed softly, finding the change amusing. Constanzia heard the sound and came to the bed at once to investigate.

"It is nothing," La Niña said, still smiling, "dear Constanzia. Dear, good Constanzia. Tell me now about the Madonna."

Now Don Antonio had said, when he heard how La Niña was coming awake, that if she should ask questions about anything, she should have true answers—sparingly, if the truth was sorrowful, but the truth, nevertheless. Constanzia was glad to talk about the Madonna if it did not lead to something harder. Señor Luis, she said, had brought the small statue from Bucareli. He also had put the shelf on the tree.

"Surely," La Niña said. "But before that—tell me."

But she knew how the Madonna had come to be, Constanzia said—how Señor Andorro had made it and Don Antonio had ordered the silver crown.

"With opals," La Niña said. "Tell me about the opals."

She had forgotten that? Don Antonio had bought them in Mexico with money belonging to young Señor Luis, who had asked him to buy a present for La Niña. Don Antonio—Luis, too—had thought of silk for a fine dress; but then Don Antonio had seen the opals and bought them. For Señor Luis. Didn't she know?

"Señor Luis," La Niña said, merely.

"He is a man," Constanzia declared. "Next to Don Antonio, he is the best."

"Surely," La Niña agreed, and went back to sleep, still smiling.

The next day Angelita Gonzales was reborn. This, to her at least, meant someone other than La Niña. She asked to be released from the cocoon in which Rosario encased her while in bed and to wear a dress again—on the chance of a visitor. Also she thought she would like to sit up now, outside preferably, if she had something to sit on there.

The day after that there was a chair and Luis carried her to it.

"*Gracias*, Luis," she said. "It is not the first time, I think."

In his confusion he almost dropped her. He remembered the first time well enough, but how could she?

"You have not walked in a month," he said evasively.

"Poor Luis," she said. "I can walk now a little." Two slow steps today.

She could remember, Luis thought. She remembered more and more. On his return to the camp he hunted out Antonio and said he thought La Niña now should be told everything before some clumsy person spoke in a way to hurt her.

"Again I am chosen?" Antonio said. "Well, since you are afraid, I will try. Tomorrow? We will go together."

So, with Luis and Rosario and Garza standing by, Antonio held Angelita's hands in his and went back with her to the night when the Indians came to Bucareli. She listened gravely. She remembered all of it really, she said, and told how dark it was in the hospital when she went to it that last time, except where the lantern stood; but when the Comanche seized her, that was the end of remembering until now.

"Manuel was there," she said, turning to Luis. "Where is Manuel? Why doesn't he come to see how I am now?"

"He has turned shy for some reason," Luis said. "He was there that night. He wanted to save you, but the Indians carried him off, too."

"Manuel?" she said.

"Also Fray Josef," Antonio said quickly, then told how he and Luis with twenty men from the town and Lope to guide them had come to the Comanche camp in time to save all three captives. He spared her the details, but she recalled one.

"Luis carried me from there," she said suddenly.

"Now, *muchachita*, how could you know that?"

"I know," she said.

But she remembered nothing of the withdrawal from Bucareli. She did not know that her grandmother was dead. She had not once asked about her, Constanzia said afterwards. It would be good if she never remembered. She cried a little when Antonio said merely that the grandmother had been too old and feeble to bear the shocks of that black night, and now she was gone.

"Poor grandmother," Angelita said. "It is so sad."

She cried more for her grandfather when she learned that this beautiful place was where he had died. The grave, Garza said then, was as they had left it. He would show her some day.

"*Gracias*, Padre," she said through the tears. "I remember my fine grandfather very well. Some day, then, when I am stronger; but now," she turned back to Antonio, "what I want most is to be down by the little brook with the others. It is beautiful up here on the hill, but it seems so apart."

"It is noisy down there," Antonio warned. "Pounding and sawing and chopping down trees and shouting."

"I know. I hear them. I want to be where it is noisy like that. It is a wonderful sound. It is wonderful to be alive again. I don't want to miss anything now."

A picture of her sitting in deep grass, in the sun, and garlanded

334

with flowers gathered by happy, laughing children went with Antonio a week later as he rode off to Lobanillo. To Lobanillo at last, then on business almost as urgent—it could be even more so—on to Natchitoches.

But Angelita was not the only one to send him away with cheers and a prayer for his early return. Just as indelibly printed on his memory was a ring of earnest men faces about a campfire his last evening. They were the leaders of the groups into which the people had been divided. He had talked with them every day since their coming to this valley, but the meeting this evening was the last for a month, perhaps. And he had a final word to say.

"You are busy, you are tired, you are happy. Good! I am happy for you. You have worked hard for a week and it shows. It is good to work, and necessary—to plant again, to organize your possessions, such as they are, to provide shelter for your families, and food. For this summer it is enough to accomplish just that, but it will not be enough always. Again we are beginning a town. This time it must succeed. We must prosper. We must give this town a reason for being. Have you thought of that?"

"How can we fail?" This was Juan Piedra, of all people—jolly, easygoing idler, now proving himself a giant with an axe in his hand.

"I know, I know," Antonio said. "The land is good. Water is plentiful. There is stone and wood for building. We can exist. But what can we do to make our town important enough to last? I have spoken to many of you of *importance* long before this—when Los Adaes received the order for its extinction. Well, here we are now—most fortunately at a time when our governing officials have so many other troubles to deal with that we may have two or even three years in which to justify our flight to this place and our settling here. But in the end we must justify the building of the town. Well, have you something to say about that?"

"The trees?" Piedra said. "We have lived where they have no such trees, and we have them here to spare. They stand closer than needed in the forests. If we could sell the trees, the boards they would make . . ."

"My felicitations to you, Juan Piedra," Antonio cried. "It has been my thought all the time. We can sell them, I am sure."

"But how can we sell the trees or their wood to far places?" Rojas asked.

"Those who want the wood will send for it. They will send wagons and oxen. A road will be made just for that if the wood is ready and waiting. And there are other ways."

He told then of the traders from the English colonies on the western rivers, who made barges out of the wood from their forests and, after a voyage down the Mississippi on them, loaded with goods, sold the wood at a profit in New Orleans, and made their way back home over land.

"There is a way," he said. "Perhaps the Neches to the Gulf, but I will ask. From Lobanillo I will go on to Nakatosh. The Lieutenant-Governor there is a man of bold ideas, and a friend."

Athanase de Mezières, whom he had once labeled renegade. He had not thought until now of communicating with him. It would be a risk, but it was absurd at this point to consider risks. In any case, De Mezières would be among the first to hear about the settlement at the Mission of the Nacogdoches.

"And there is my business agent and partner at Punta Cortada on the lower Mississippi. He has always advice to give. I will talk to both these wizards."

The faces around him were graver when he had finished than when he began, but they were not bewildered or alarmed. Great difficulties lay ahead, but none at this moment that a man by patient, well-directed effort could not eventually overcome. His people had, as Antonio had once foretold to Ripperdá, hope. That made all the difference.

The next morning, young and old massed behind him mounted on Turbelino, calling last-minute messages to him, cheering him on his way.

"Bravo, Ibarbo! Good luck attend you."

Finally, as he rode off, it was:

"Come back, Don Antonio. Do not forget. Come back . . . soon!"

The cry rang in his ears for most of an hour as he rode; and, when it died away, loneliness beset him. No goat on a string, no mewing cat in his *morral*, no tired child to pick up. Except for the dim echo of the outcry, and a number of messages he was to carry in his head until they were delivered, he was alone. The messages—he would forget half of them, he was sure. It might be well to go over them now, to see how many he could recall.

As he did so, attaching each message to a person, one by one, people walked beside him—an aged shoemaker who had forsworn his status as a "King's man" to share at the end of his life in an act of rebellion; a crippled carpenter calling himself blessed after a life of sorrow; Magdalena, who begged him to assure Paco and Esperanza that she had not forgotten them; women he knew only as Rosa, Tina, Felicidad, with children in their arms and hanging to their skirts; a strong young man, once a ranch foreman, now a hewer of wood and builder of houses, his face bright with hope; a young woman radiant with returning health and the promise of abundant life and love—all walked with him a little way.

Necessarily, he traveled slowly. He did not wish, he told himself, to weary Turbelino. He camped that evening on the far bank of the Sabine River, in the exact place, he was certain, where the weary exiles had made camp six years before. Remembering was like squeezing the sound box of a concertina, a collapsing of time. He kindled a small fire and ate the cold food that Magdalena had packed for him, stretched out on his blanket—and thought instead of sleeping.

"It is a bad thing, Padre, to have a mind that simmers continually."

The simmering had not been noticeable recently, but here it was again. What is it now, he wondered. Finally the night wind sang a song in the pine branches, and sleep came.

In the morning, after a quick dip in the river and a cautious scraping of whiskers, wearing a fresh and spotless shirt that Magdalena had also packed for him, he felt more equal to what might lie in wait for him, though that was hardly cause for mental simmering.

"I am going home," he reminded himself. "Home at last. So, let this dawdling cease!"

Over more and more familiar ground, with Turbelino also in a mood for a brisker gait, he came closer by the minute to his journey's end. However, swiftly as he went, another, traveling in the same direction, went more swiftly. In mid-morning, a man alone, on a dark horse, one who by all the signs knew the country well, galloped over an unmarked course in the hills above the *Camino Real*. He flashed into view and disappeared.

A courier, and in great haste, Antonio thought, then put the thought aside. A government courier, for safety, followed the *Camino Real* wherever there was one. No other idea came as to the galloping rider's identity. He was a man on a fine horse and rode superbly. That was all.

Shortly before noon Antonio turned Turbelino into the ranch road. Nothing had changed. Nothing. It could have been yesterday that he had gone away. The little hill with the red-roofed house and the high-walled garden. The blooded mares in their private pasture, the wilder, wooded general pasture, the stable—ho, enlarged now?—Lobanillo Creek, the pueblo. Light smoke rose from the pueblo chimneys, also from the kitchen of the main house. Naturally, at this hour.

Again he sat on a horse before the gate with fretted ironwork, his eyes burning, but not from smoke. All of it just as he remembered, even to there being no one present to open the gate. He dismounted. As he did so, a brown face, familiar, though he had not a name for it, looked through iron lacework, then in haste lifted the bar and threw the gate open.

"Master!" the man said in welcome, and Antonio knew him.

"Juanito!" he said. "You are here. You have been here all the time."

Juanito, the boy Flores had lost, older now, but as quick as ever to take fright. He began to be frightened now.

"Almost always, Señor. I hid two days and then I came."

"And I never knew," Antonio said, "because I never asked, I suppose. Do not be afraid. I am not scolding. The *Señor Alcalde* spoke of you often, wondering. Now he is dead, not knowing."

"Señor, you told in a letter that the *Señor Alcalde* had died in that faraway town. My Señora here—Doña María—communicated then with Señora Flores in Nakatosh and obtained permission for me to remain here. I have charge of the flowers."

The flowers—they were everywhere. Flowers in tubs. Flowers in raised beds, bordered with bricks and sea shells. Flowers climbed the walls. A gaudy sheet of bloom covered the kitchen opposite him. Was it the flowers of this vine that smelled so sweetly? Probably not. Probably some small flower putting all its vitality into fragrance. That was fancy. He knew nothing about flowers, really. Not even names, except roses. Roses . . .

"Señor," Juanito said, "you were not expected today, I think. Shall I announce . . ."

"No," Antonio said. "I will announce myself in a minute. You may take this one to the stable, if you will. Can you lead a horse? He is tired now and will give you no trouble, I think. Well?"

"Señor, I will lead him to the stable. Nobody here is considered of any use if he cannot lead a horse. Olivaro will be at the stable, or one of his sons."

Boys, as Antonio remembered them. Men now, he corrected. He gave Turbelino to Juanito.

"Is the family at home?" he asked. The reply was like an echo.

"Oh, yes, Señor. Both the Señoras and the young Master. The young Master . . ."

"Never mind," Antonio said. "Go on to the stable."

He stepped through the gate, closing it carefully after him. The fragrance of the flowers was almost overpowering. It included— no, that came from the kitchen. But the kitchen was too quiet. Someone, not Esperanza, was in charge there. Well, that could wait. He turned to the house, mounted the steps, and stopped with his hand on the door latch. The family, indeed, was at home, and, in addition, he thought, entertaining a visitor—a man, a stranger, who talked rapidly, in a fever of excitement. He thought of the one who had galloped over the hills, distancing him, down on the road. But why had Juanito not mentioned the visitor? A second later he knew why.

"But I saw with my own eyes, mother mine—grandmother. Lope told me how it was, but I would not believe until I saw. We hid the horses in the forest, and crept forward, in the way of Indians, scouting, until we came to a place where we could look down into the valley without being seen ourselves; and there it was—all as Lope said. It is only a week since they came, but already houses are going up at the edge of the forest. Fields have been cleared and planted. It was late afternoon, but every-body was still working busily, the women at the edge of the creek, or around the cooking fires, the men among the trees. It will be a town, Lope says, in another moon. It is a settlement now. And he did it all, my father, Don Antonio Gil Ibarbo. Nobody ordered him to do this. Nobody gave him leave. After the Comanches came, he said what should be done. What a man he is!"

The one who spoke was another. He rode a horse too hard for its own good, but, *Dios*, how he rode! My son, Antonio thought, his heart near to bursting. My son! And then Doña María spoke. No other could put such feeling into simple words.

"So near," she said, "and still he does not come."

Antonio opened the door.

His family, his own! It seemed to him that he embraced them all at once in the first rush of welcome. Then he held them separately, one after another.

"My mother," he said gently, feeling the tremulousness of Doña Isabella's happiness.

Anastacio. It was like seeing himself in a mirror twenty years ago. No. Anastacio was handsomer than he had ever been. Equally dark, now that the pallor of too much poring over books had departed, and a young beard showed; but with a blackness, a refinement of feature that came from his mother, and a proud way of holding himself—from the same source. Thin—no, lean and hard, as a young man finding his strength should be. A little shy now of the father he admired so fiercely, but that would pass with better acquaintance.

And Doña María, his lady. Six years older, and fair as she had never been before. A new dignity, a new grace. She wore the black dress of a matron, but of a softer silk than Doña Isabella chose. Her beautiful hair was dressed high and held by a shell comb. She meant not to tremble, but her chin betrayed her.

"Six years," she said, her eyes dark and deep as he remembered. "Six years."

"*Querida*," he begged, "let us forget now. It is over. I am here."

As if six years of time, however spent, could be forgotten. As

340

if one could take up the old life just where it had been when the ties of nearness were broken, as if the break could be mended so that it could not be seen! For two days Antonio tried. In that time he came to know his Doña María as he had never known her before. After the one murmur about the length of his absence, she had no more reproaches. His happiness was her happiness. She, with dear ones close and living in the home she loved, had been as lonely for Antonio as he had been for her, more lonely, she believed; but that he would not accept.

With Olivaro riding on one side of him and Anastacio on the other, he visited every corner of Rancho Lobanillo. He talked with the shepherd about the sheep, with Olivaro's two *vaquero* sons about the cattle, with Olivaro and Anastacio about the horses.

"It looks good—prosperous," he said. "You have done well."

"Any praise belongs to Anastacio," Olivaro said. "He has full charge now."

"Without Olivaro," Anastacio declared, "I could never have learned what I needed to know."

Without Olivaro—Olivaro in that case, Antonio thought, must remain at Lobanillo, but there were his sons. Strong, lively young men, born *vaqueros*, and trained to a sense of responsibility. One of them might be spared. That question now, when he had been home only two days? He put it away for future considering.

At the stables, he fondled Fatima, running his fingers through her silken mane, speaking the old words of endearment into her twitching ears. Six years older, she was still the most beautiful horse in the world, and his treasure. He put her saddle upon her and the bridle with the silver bells, and rode her a short way and back again. He thought she tossed her head with a special flourish, ringing the bells.

The dark horse that was Anastacio's favorite mount was Fatima's son, a yearling colt when Antonio had left the ranch. She had foaled again in Antonio's absence, then no more. This one was a filly, also dark, with a beautiful dapple showing in strong sunlight—a princess.

Eastward from the settlement now building near the Mission of the Nacogdoches, a river, deeper and flowing more swiftly than the stream that bordered the settlement, ran southward to join the Neches. The Attoyac, the Indians called it, both above and below where the lesser stream joined it. The waters were cold and so clear that the scoured stones that made its bottom could be seen through the depth of a fathom or more. Little creeks ran through the pine woods to join it. The forest was heavier in trees than that at Lobanillo, but a ranch could be cleared and developed on the Attoyac that might even surpass Rancho Lobanillo. It would be near the new settlement and yet apart. If he should care to establish such a ranch, he would want Fatima stabled there and her daughter. It would be understood, naturally, that later, when the filly became a mare, old enough for breeding, Lobanillo would have first choice of her offspring.

"It is a bad thing, Padre, to have a head that simmers continually."

He put that thought, also, away, but knew it would visit him again.

It was now evening of that second day. The stars shone brightly in a soft summer sky; but their light on Rancho Lobanillo was dimmed by the red glow of many fires. Lobanillo was holding a fiesta in honor of the return of Don Antonio. Such a celebration would have been held in any case—if not that day, then the next—but other visitors had come, of a sort that demanded much roast meat; so, why not the grand fiesta now, at once?

Coming home from his long morning ride with Domingo Olivaro and Anastacio, Antonio had found Sancho, the aging Great Chief of the Nacogdoches, encamped with twice his usual retinue between the house and the ranch pueblo. Antonio gave his horse to Olivaro and went forward with both hands extended in welcome.

"Sancho, my friend!" he said; and the old chieftain's eyes were bright as jet in his many-wrinkled face.

The greeting over, Antonio then turned to his son.

"Have we food for these visitors who honor us with their presence?"

"It shall be made ready at once," Anastacio said, and went

342

with Olivaro to the pueblo to see what could be provided.

Food then was brought to satisfy the Indians immediately; but roast pig and sheep and beef called for more time. Fires were started in the roasting pits, also in outdoor bake ovens. From mid-afternoon on, a savor of smoke and succulence hung on the air which could be counted on to make the best-fed person in the world hungry, to say nothing of those who habitually ate meagerly.

This promise of feasting would have shortened the ceremonial speeches between Antonio and the Indians, if anything could have done so; but nothing could. With proper flourishes Antonio presented Sancho with a hat trimmed with silver braid, to match his own. This was an expression of gratitude for the aid Sancho had given him in the loan of such a son as Lope. He said the prosperity of the new settlement near the old mission would depend greatly on such continued friendship of the Nacogdoches. The memory of that friendship had made the people unhappy in the cities to the west and had given them a great longing to return to the homes they had left in sorrow. Now they had returned; and he, Antonio Ibarbo, hoped that their presence in the land of the Nacogdoches was welcome, that friendship would be even warmer and that trade between the Indian and the Spaniard would flourish as never before.

"Your people," Sancho replied at even greater length, "are welcome. It will make the hearts of my people happy to hear the bells ring once more from the house of the Spaniard's Great Spirit. It is well also to exchange goods with our friends. Our hearts beat fast with joy over their return. They leap in our breasts with greater joy over your return, O Ibarbo. Where you dwell, there the sun shines brightest for the Nacogdoches Tejas."

It went that way back and forth until the feast was ready. Antonio remained a while longer with the Indians, then drew away, saying he must visit the other fires. He did so, with Doña María on one arm and Doña Isabella on the other, until Doña Isabella's strength gave out and she begged to have a chair placed where she could watch the dancing and the fun, now at its height.

Then, with Doña María only, Antonio sought out each family

343

for which he had a message. A dozen times he stopped, and, wherever he did, the people gathered around to hear what he had to tell, no matter if they had heard it all before. They listened with sorrow to his tale of how life had been in San Antonio de Bexar, then brightened at his report on the Governor and his lady and their house, also the wonders of Mexico City, the cathedral, the mint where gold and silver became money, the noble Viceroy and the long-faced judges, the earthquakes, and My Lord Fiscal, who interpreted the King's law for the people and also understood horses.

Or there would be someone who remembered La Niña, and all the pueblo must hear about her—clear to the end of the story. They shivered with horror over the Comanches. But why had they carried away La Niña rather than some other maiden?

"Because they thought there was magic in her healing," Antonio said, then quickly, before anyone could mention the Woman in Blue, about whom he never wished to hear again, he changed the subject.

Finally he had to repeat all of it to Tío Paco and Esperanza, seated with honor near Doña Isabella. They listened to his tales of wonders, which they must hear so that they could say to others, "I know. I heard all that." But their main interest, naturally, was for his report on Luis, on Magdalena, even Juan Piedra, then Manuel, and, one by one, all the other children and grandchildren. They were proud to bursting over the good report. Antonio shared this pride. It was possible that he even gilded pieces of his story to feed that pride. If he did, it was not only to please Paco and Esperanza. From a background of night shadow two hundred attending spirits hung on his every word. They were the people he had left in the new settlement. Friends who could not share in this feasting, who in reality probably slept soundly in utter weariness at this very time; still, they were present. When he spoke of one by name, that one stepped forward—respectfully but insistently.

Now, without warning, Esperanza's face crumpled.

"It is still too far," she wailed. "I will never see a one of them again."

Complaints like that Antonio had heard from others and had

turned protest aside with the same answer that he now gave to Esperanza.

"It is not so far. The road is plain and direct and not hard to follow. It will be easier as visitors travel back and forth over it between here and there."

"Visitors?" Esperanza said. "I am too old to make visits. I will not see the town of the Nacogdoches."

"Then the town will visit you," Antonio said.

As she pondered this, her eyes became dangerously bright. He should have taken warning.

"And you, Master Antonio—how do you come back to us? Are you the master or also a visitor?"

"I a visitor at Lobanillo?"

"Where do you live—which end of that road?" she insisted.

"Look!" he said, with heat. "I must be at the new town much of the time, in the beginning, at least. It is my responsibility, but Lobanillo is my home."

He looked around defiantly, but Doña María's eyes met his softly. Excuse the foolish old woman, they begged. Doña Isabella, however, wiped away a tear. He saw her. At the same time from the shadows came a cry:

"*Come back, Don Antonio. Do not forget . . . come back soon!*"

"What a way," he said, "to spend even a little part of this gay evening! I, for one, am hoarse with talking. I am hungry again and thirsty, and I want to dance. Who is with me?"

Not the ghosts that waited in the shadows:

"*Come back, Don Antonio. Come back . . . soon.*"

They were with him in the dancing, in his sleep that night; and in the morning they waited for their turn while he went over the ranch accounts with Doña María and Anastacio. The accounts were in beautiful order, everything written down in its place, and the credits well in excess over the debits. There was money in the Lobanillo strongbox. There was credit at Natchitoches, at Punta Cortada, at New Orleans. After satisfying all possible tax claims, he could still buy whatever he might need at Natchitoches.

"Excellent," he said with pleasure. "Everything is as clear as if

345

I had seen it happen. You had a good teacher, my son."

"Monsieur de la Mathe," Anastacio said, "is wonderful."

"I agree," Antonio said. "He is a wizard. You should see him in his den at Punta Cortada. You have never been there? But you should go, then on to New Orleans. You have reached the place where you should be present when an important venture is at stake."

"I should like that," Anastacio admitted. "I thought of it, but now . . ."

"Now? But now is the time. You are your own man. You are not bound to this one place because it belongs to you. I went away frequently when I had charge. Lobanillo was always here when I returned. As it is now."

"I don't know what to say." Anastacio stammered a little. Still shy of his father. "I . . . I am glad if you are pleased."

"I am extremely pleased. You may go now and tell Olivaro how pleased I am. He is counting yesterday's losses, no doubt; and you can help him. Go. Your mother and I will pursue this pleasant exchange a while longer."

Anastacio went away, whistling like a wild bird in the mating season.

"Antonio, my husband, you are really pleased, I think," Doña María said softly.

"I could not be more so," Antonio said. "Lobanillo never appeared more beautiful than it does this morning—even with the smell of wet ashes. *Dios*, if a sudden rain cloud had not come, we would still be dancing, which God forbid. I have done too little of that lately."

"Beautiful," Doña María agreed, "but that is not enough for you now."

"Oh, yes. It is enough, and more, for any man; but . . . how can I say it?"

I must speak truly, he thought, to her more than anyone.

"For me, it is a thing that has been done, something finished. I am not needed here any more. I am needed at the new settlement."

"Those people," she said. "You are still not free of them."

"*Querida*, I will never be free. I know that now."

346

"You do not want to be free," she said. "Freedom, if it means being bound to no one, is not worth having. I knew how it would be when you went away."

"*Querida*, I did not want to go."

"No," she said. "You felt that you must. That was all."

"Yes. It was as I told the *audiencia* in Mexico. Someone had to speak for them, and I was there. But again and again I wished I had not felt that compulsion. I said to Nicolas de la Mathe in Bexar that these people were a sack of stones about my neck which some day would drown me. However, by then they had become a charge and I could not lay the burden down. As late as last year I wanted to be free of it. Then I said no, finish what you have begun, Ibarbo. That, perhaps, will free you. Now . . ."

"Now you do not ask or want to be free, my husband. They are your life from now on. Is that not true? Can you talk to me of your plans?"

Could he talk to her? With those deep, sympathetic, understanding eyes fixed upon him, the words ran like any little river flowing downhill. He told her of the bright valley and the joy of the people, of their trust in him. He told her of the prospect of marketing the wood from the trees.

"I must go to Nakatosh tomorrow to talk to De Mezières. I must not delay. God grant that he will be in residence there, to hear me."

"You are sure he is your friend, my husband?"

"He must be," Antonio said. "And I must write a letter to De la Mathe today, and carry it with me to dispatch from Nakatosh."

"And you, Antonio?" Doña María asked.

He groaned, and he laughed.

"I will be *Justicia Mayor* again," he said. "And it may go very well this time. On the other hand, I could be thrown into a dungeon for my presumption. However it is, this time as *Justicia Mayor*, I think I will live a little apart from the town."

He described then the ranch site on the Attoyac.

"But who will work with you there?" Doña María asked, "if Luis remains in town to manage the business of the trees?"

"Whether Luis lives in town or on land of his own," Antonio answered, "he will be his own man now. I could have Manuel, perhaps, in his place. Manuel is not Luis. He himself says so. But he would be a good manager finally."

Then he mentioned Carlos Olivaro, Domingo's older son. He would not want to take away from Lobanillo for his new ranch, but he could use a skilled *vaquero*. Also he would want to begin to stock the land with animals from Lobanillo. He spoke af Fatima and her daughter.

"You have it all planned," Doña María said.

"No. I am moving forward in my mind very cautiously. One important condition must still be met. You have not said you would like to live in the new place."

"You want that?" she said breathlessly. "You are sure?"

"Am I sure? For six years that has been my great privation. The ranch on the Attoyac becomes real only if you are there. Look! Anastacio will marry one of these days. Until then Doña Isabella will manage this house. . . ."

"Antonio, my husband, you do not need to arrange everything for me. You do not need to persuade me. I would have wanted to die if you had not asked me to go with you."

"*Querida!*"

Now surely he must not wait to see his friend in Natchitoches. He must write his letter. He must draw up a paper giving Lobanillo to his son. He must hurry back to the settlement. Even so, it might be some time before he could send for Doña María.

"I will not wait to be sent for. I will go with you now."

"But there is no house."

"With all that wood, can you not build a shed?"

But as yet there was no shed. Would she wait that long? No? Had she, he demanded, ever slept in a pine tree?

"No," she said, "but I could. I will not wait. I will not let you go without me."

"*Querida!*"

AUTHOR'S NOTE

When I was in Texas in the spring of 1958, in connection with the publication of *Destiny in Dallas*, a charming resident of that city, who prefers to remain anonymous, thinking I might like to write another Texas story some day, spoke to me of the episode which is the basis of fact in *By the King's Command*. At the time so much was going on around me that I am afraid I gave the lady not half the attention that her good will merited. I am sure she thought I would forget all about the story, and I thought so, too.

It didn't work out that way. Some time later, after my return home, I was in the library of the Missouri Historical Society of St. Louis one day, supposedly concentrating on other research. For diversion, because research sometimes builds up a paralysis of tension, I opened a copy of *Texas, a Guide to the Lone Star State*. There, in a write-up of Nacogdoches, was the story as it had been given to me. A paragraph. A bit of drift on the tide of history, but provocative. Drama was there—one man against the power of Spain. Tragedy, but with a happy outcome. The hero was identified and named. The time of the story, 1773–1779, fell within the period of our American Revolution. Four of the journalist's five *W's—Who, What, When,* and *Where*—were answered. Only the last—*Why*—needed study. Within minutes I was at the catalog, shuffling the cards on Texas.

That was how it began. That is usually how it begins. My plan of research is simple. I open a book. To open that book means opening six others. First thing I know, I am up to my ears. That day I read enough only to answer the question Why, and went back to the task in hand, which was the writing of *Look to the Rose*, then well under way. All the time I knew that the story of the Texas–Louisiana border under Spanish rule would be next. Now here it is—*By the King's Command*.

The major events of the story are fact. To give the book body, reality, and continuity, they have been enlarged upon and minor incidents have been invented. Information was by turns superabundant and maddeningly nonexistent. I read a long list of contemporary letters, journals, and reports in translation, some scholarly treatises, one priceless, detailed exposition of the exact powers of a viceroy, and much fine print in crumbling old volumes. At one point in the writing I needed to know how to explode a cannon. I had absolutely no knowledge of eighteenth-century artillery. It is astonishing how such a small but vital bit of information can be neglected by an authority. Finally after some guessing on my part in collaboration with certain military gentlemen of my acquaintance, Elizabeth Tyndall, reference librarian at the Missouri Historical Society, dug up an ancient encyclopedia which yielded an illustrated exposition of portfires, slow matches and quick matches, touchholes—all of it.

The scenes of the story are as close to reality and the period as the reading of crumbling old accounts can make them. In these days of superhighways and overpowering industrialization it is almost impossible to reconstruct a picture two centuries old. I had to rely on the descriptions of those who were there at the time. The best of these authorities was a Franciscan friar who was compelled, against his will, to travel from one end of Texas to the other, accompanying a royal inspector, and to set down his version of all that he saw. Except for certain natural wonders, his reports are not flattering. I think he probably spoke the truth. If I am wrong, who alive today can be sure?

The place names are as they were and, mostly, still are. The settlement, the founding of which closes the story, was the beginning of the thriving modern city of Nacogdoches, which owed its early growth to its position atop the lumber industry in the "pineries" of east Texas. The name is that of a tribe of Tejas Indians, and is pronounced as spelled, with the "g" silent. It is not to be confused, but sometimes is, with the French city on the Red River called Natchitoches, which usage simplified to Nakatosh. The latter name was used so universally that it even appeared on many documents.

The capital of Texas at this period was San Antonio de Bexar, which we now call San Antonio. In the story the name has either been given in full or shortened to Bexar. At the time everything in that locality was San Antonio de Something. The mission in the story, for example, was called San Antonio de Valero. It is interesting to know that the church of that mission was the building that later became famous as the Alamo.

Another place name about which something should be said is the Colorado River. In this case, of course, we mean the Colorado River of Texas, completely within the boundaries of that province. There is no connection between it and the Colorado River of the Far West, the one that dug the Grand Canyon.

There is then the matter of distance. The Spanish seemed always to have measured it in leagues. A league is an indefinite unit, averaging close to three miles. I do not recall any use of "miles" in the Spanish writings of that day. So, I had to follow the custom.

The principal characters are also real. *Ibarbo* is an accepted spelling of the hero's name, though *Ybarbo* is the more usual Spanish way. For general use, *Ibarbo* looks easier to pronounce. His character, of course, is my own interpretation from the evidence at hand. To his enemies—Don Hugo Oconor, the Red Devil of the Apaches, in particular—he was capable of any sort of villainy. But his friends, of whom he had a number, have only the highest praise for him. His accomplishments were as given in the story. After his "act of rebellion," he was not punished, but rather appointed Lieutenant-Governor, civil and military captain, and judge of contraband over the entire area about Nacogdoches. This was the result of circumstance. After the death of the Governor of Texas, who was his friend, another friend, the Lieutenant-Governor at Natchitoches, Louisiana, was made interim Governor of

Texas. Ibarbo already stood high with other powerful officials; so he came off very well.

Afterwards, he did establish a new ranch on the Attoyac River—Rancho Lucana. He lived there the remainder of his life, except for a short period when new charges against him made it convenient for him to claim residence in Louisiana. However, when that squall blew over, he went back to Rancho Lucana, where he died in 1809.

The Franciscan friar—Fray Josef Francisco Mariano de la Garza—was real enough, and a staunch friend of Ibarbo; but he was actually the mission priest in only the latter part of the story. I thought I might be pardoned the slight deviation if I gave him that role throughout. Other real characters were Nicolas de la Mathe, Ibarbo's partner and agent at Pointe Coupée on the lower Mississippi; the Viceroy of Mexico; and the Viceroy's friend and adviser, Mexico's Fiscal, Señor Areche. (The title corresponding most closely to "fiscal" in our government is attorney-general.) Bucareli, the Viceroy, was the same man whose support made it possible for Junipero Serra to establish the famous Franciscan missions in California. Much of his character I learned from reading a biography of Junipero Serra. Bucareli died of the pleurisy mentioned in the last part of the book. Ripperdá, Governor of Texas, died on a visit to Mexico and never went on to Honduras.

Finally, the development of the story as a story, and all the minor characters, are my own fiction, not purely imaginary, because they, and the roles they played, were all possible. The whole thing, to paraphrase Mark Twain when he embroidered a legend, may have happened as I told it or may not; but it could have happened so. And that is what can come of a bit of conversation and a short paragraph in a guidebook.